Praise for #1 *New York Times* bestselling author Sherryl Woods

"Sherryl Woods writes emotionally satisfying novels about family, friendship and home. Truly feel-great reads!"

—#1 *New York Times* bestselling author Debbie Macomber

"Woods…is noted for appealing character-driven stories that are often infused with the flavor and fragrance of the South."

—*Library Journal*

"Woods is a master heartstring puller."

—*Publishers Weekly* on *Seaview Inn*

Praise for Lee Tobin McClain

"*Low Country Hero* has everything I look for in a book—it's emotional, tender, and an all-around wonderful story."

—RaeAnne Thayne,
New York Times bestselling author

"Fans of Debbie Macomber will appreciate this start to a new series by McClain that blends sweet, small-town romance with such serious issues as domestic abuse.… Readers craving a feel-good romance with a bit of suspense will be satisfied."

—*Booklist* on *Low Country Hero*

With her roots firmly planted in the South, #1 *New York Times* bestselling author **Sherryl Woods** has written many of her more than one hundred books in that distinctive setting, whether it's her home state of Virginia, her adopted state, Florida, or her much-adored South Carolina. Now she's added North Carolina's Outer Banks to her list of favorite spots. And she remains partial to small towns, wherever they may be. Her Chesapeake Shores books have become a highly rated series success on Hallmark Channel and her Sweet Magnolias books are in development for a ten-episode series coming soon to Netflix.

Sherryl divides her time between her childhood summer home overlooking the Potomac River in Colonial Beach, Virginia, and her oceanfront home with its lighthouse view in Key Biscayne, Florida. "Wherever I am, if there's no water in sight, I get a little antsy," she says.

Sherryl loves to hear from readers. You can visit her on her website at sherrylwoods.com, link to her Facebook fan page from there or contact her directly at Sherryl703@gmail.com.

Publishers Weekly bestselling author **Lee Tobin McClain** read *Gone with the Wind* in the third grade and has been an incurable romantic ever since. When she's not writing angst-filled love stories with happy endings, she's probably cheering on her daughter at a gymnastics meet, mediating battles between her goofy golden-doodle puppy and her rescue cat or teaching aspiring writers in Seton Hill University's MFA program. She is probably not cleaning her house. For more about Lee, visit her website at www.leetobinmcclain.com.

#1 *New York Times* **Bestselling Author**

SHERRYL WOODS

NEXT TIME...FOREVER

 HARLEQUIN®BESTSELLING AUTHOR COLLECTION

ISBN-13: 978-1-335-46999-1

Next Time…Forever

First published in 1990. This edition published in 2019.

Copyright © 1990 by Sherryl Woods

Secret Christmas Twins
First published in 2017. This edition published in 2019.
Copyright © 2017 by Lee Tobin McClain

PLEASE RECYCLE • THIS PRODUCT IS RECYCLABLE

Recycling programs for this product may not exist in your area.

This edition published by arrangement with Harlequin Books S.A.

For questions and comments about the quality of this book, please contact us at CustomerService@Harlequin.com.

H HARLEQUIN®
™ www.Harlequin.com

Printed in U.S.A.

CONTENTS

NEXT TIME...FOREVER

Sherryl Woods

Prologue

May 16

Bold streaks of pink and gold banded the twilight sky and shimmered across the calm surface of the Savannah River. It was a dazzling, postcard-splashy sunset, but the lazy, mournful wail of a ship's horn more accurately reflected Catherine Devlin's mood as she watched the huge freighter inch through the narrow channel.

Sipping a glass of overly-sweet white zinfandel wine, she tried to remember the precise moment when her once storybook-perfect life had gone so terribly wrong. What had been the turning point? When had Matthew fallen out of love with her and turned to other women? Even more disturbing, how had she ever allowed her own dreams to become so over-shadowed by her need to please her husband? Everyone thought Mrs. Matthew Devlin was so strong, so clever, but no one really knew *Catherine* Devlin. She didn't even recognize herself anymore.

"More coffee?"

Lost in her private desolation, she waved the waiter away without glancing up. "No, thanks."

"Are you sure?" he said. There was an oddly plaintive note in his deep, rumbly voice that brought her head up. Dark brown eyes that glinted with the devil's own laughter watched her closely.

"It's fresh," he promised, passing the pot temptingly beneath her nose so she could savor the rich aroma.

She found herself breathing deeply, then smiling apologetically into those irresistible, teasing eyes. She pointed to the clean, empty cup beside her plate. "Sorry. I'm not drinking coffee, just wine."

"Oh." He sounded incredibly disappointed and looked as though he couldn't quite make up his mind what to do next.

Catherine found his apparent uncertainty endearing, but oddly out of character. "Are you new?" she asked kindly. Though she'd asked merely to put him at ease, she realized as she was waiting for his reply that she was clinging to the interruption. She was tired of being alone with nothing but her gloomy thoughts for company. Those eyes, so filled with life and humor, were the perfect antidote to her unexpected loneliness.

"You could say that," he agreed, instantly looking more hopeful and twice as appealing. "You're the first person I've waited on."

"Ever?" she said skeptically. Another close examination aroused more puzzling contradictions. He appeared to be in his mid-thirties, too old to be waiting tables for the first time unless he was down on his luck. Yet she found herself dismissing that possibility immediately. There was an undefinable look of success, an aura of confident masculinity about him that seemed just as out of place as his vulnerable demeanor. It was as though she was watching a badly miscast actor struggling to play against type. The incongruities intrigued her.

"My first customer ever," he confirmed. "Are you absolutely sure you wouldn't like some coffee?"

She decided to play the game—if that's what it was—and find out where it led. "Are you trying to see if you can pour without spilling?"

A roguish dimple formed in one cheek. "Actually, I'm trying to find a way to keep talking to you."

The direct, boldly flirtatious response was the last thing she'd expected. Waiters in Atlanta's elite establishments did not make passes at the customers. But then again, she'd rarely dined there alone. Maybe women by themselves were considered fair game.

"Why?" she asked cautiously.

"You're a beautiful woman. You're apparently alone. And you looked so sad that I thought someone ought to cheer you up."

Her gaze narrowed slightly. "You figure you'll get a bigger tip for doing that?"

He shook his head. There was just the tiniest suggestion of guilt in his expression. "No tip." He leaned closer. "If you promise not to tell, I'll confess something."

Increasingly bemused by the entire conversation, Catherine was nonetheless fascinated. She found herself promising. Solemnly. Crossing her heart, in fact. She hadn't done that since she was ten. It felt good to feel young again and to be sharing secrets, especially with a man as devilishly handsome as this one.

He grinned in apparent satisfaction. "I knew I could

count on you. Actually," he confided, "I'm not even a waiter. I grabbed the coffeepot on my way past the service station." He pointed toward a strategically placed counter filled with pots of coffee, decaf and hot water, plus an assortment of silverware, napkins and extra salt and pepper shakers.

Falling prey to his teasing tone, she said lightly, "Let me guess. You're a busboy and you're hoping for a promotion."

He laughed. "Wrong. I don't even work here."

Catherine glanced at the coffeepot in his hand, then more closely at his attire. The perfect fit of his charcoal slacks hinted of custom tailoring. The fabric was definitely not polyester. His shirt cuffs were monogrammed, the material some sort of expensive silk and cotton blend. She glanced down. His shoes looked exactly like the last pair she'd bought for Matthew. They'd cost in the neighborhood of two hundred dollars. It was definitely a pricey neighborhood for a busboy or a waiter, even taking into account generous tips.

"Okay, then," she said sternly, wishing she could keep her lips from curving into an all-too-easily-forgiving smile. "It's confession time. What's the real story?"

He feigned a sheepish expression. At least she assumed it was feigned. Now that she'd taken a closer look, he didn't appear to be the type to make explanations for himself.

"I was eating over there all by myself," he confessed, "when I saw you." He gestured toward a table where the remnants of a meal had yet to be cleared away. A matching charcoal jacket had been slung across the back of a chair and a tie draped over that. "I watched you come in and knew I had to meet you. You didn't look like the kind of lady who'd like being picked up in a restaurant, so voilà! The coffee."

"Definitely enterprising," she commended him, surprised to discover that she was enjoying the unexpected flirtation. It had been a very long time since anyone had dared to come on to her, unless they'd been drinking so heavily that the prospect of Matthew's possessive wrath no longer fazed them. This man appeared to be stone-cold sober and openly fascinated. In her present mood, it was a difficult combination to resist.

Catherine propped her chin in her hand and met his gaze evenly. "What kind of lady do I appear to be?" She was honestly curious. The divorce papers still folded in her purse said quite plainly that she was no longer a wife. Without that role, she wasn't so sure what she actually was anymore. Maybe this stranger could give her a clue as to what Catherine Devlin had become.

"Classy," he said at once, pleasing her. "Self-contained. Maybe a little lost."

"Interesting."

"Why? Am I that far off the mark?"

"No. Closer than you could ever know, at least about the latter," she said with a regretful sigh.

He frowned. "Want to talk about it?"

"To you?"

"Why not? I'm here. I even have an entire pot of coffee we could share. It's a lot cheaper than a shrink."

She laughed at that. Suddenly feeling more daring than she had in years, she nodded. "Sure. Why not?"

He retrieved his jacket and tie, grabbed a cup from a neighboring table, poured them each a cup of coffee, then sat.

"So," he said, looking straight at her in a way that

the two-timing Matthew hadn't dared for months. She liked that, liked the fact that this man didn't evade, liked that he was relaxed and unhurried, liked even more that he actually seemed interested in what she had to say. "Tell me why a beautiful woman like you is feeling lost. First though, tell me your name."

"Catherine," she said, feeling almost giddy with a shyness she hadn't experienced in a long time. After-noon teas and charity balls had made her adept at small talk with strangers. Female strangers. Something about the man across from her suggested that inside where it counted he was no longer a stranger, that he was in-tuitively in tune with her, that he wanted to know her well. Best of all, he apparently saw her as a desirable woman and not as the eminent Dr. Matthew Devlin's cast-off wife.

"And the rest," he encouraged. "Who are you, Cath-erine, and why are you sitting here all alone?"

"I suppose if you wanted to drag out a cliché you could say that today is the first day of the rest of my life."

"You're getting a divorce."

She gave him a startled look.

He chuckled. "I'm not omniscient. You're tugging on your wedding band as though you can't quite make up your mind whether to take it off or leave it on. It's a dead giveaway."

She held out her hand and tried to examine the spec-tacular two-carat diamond and its simple wide gold set-ting with a certain amount of objectivity. She couldn't. She sighed as she admitted, "I hate what it represents, but I love the damn ring." She glanced at him ruefully. "Isn't it ridiculous to be so attached to a piece of jewelry?"

Instead of laughing tolerantly as Matthew would have, he took the question seriously. "It depends on why."

"Because we had it made to order from a stone that belonged to my great-grandmother. Nana Devereaux was a wonderful old lady. She was eighty-seven when she died. That was ten years ago and I still miss her."

"I think I understand, but don't you think it was a bad sign that your husband didn't buy you a new diamond?"

The criticism wasn't without merit, but Catherine found herself defending Matthew's choice. "Not at the time. I liked this one. It has sentimental value. Besides, he was just finishing a long surgical residency. I was barely twenty-one and just out of college. We were lucky he could afford the setting."

"Ah, the doctor syndrome. You nurtured him all through the lean years and then he ups and runs off with his nurse the minute the practice starts paying off."

"It was not his nurse," she retorted, just to remind this amazingly astute stranger that he didn't know *everything*.

"Oh?"

"It was a pediatrics resident."

He nodded and with obvious effort struggled to keep his impudent, know-it-all grin in check. "I'd forgotten about women's lib. What did she have that you don't have? I can't imagine anything."

"A career."

"And he found that attractive?"

"He found that convenient. Similar interests. Similar hours. And, I suppose, frequent opportunities to make it in the linen closets."

"And you're bitter."

"No," she admitted with mild astonishment. "I'm past bitter. I'm even past numb. Now I'm just frightened." The candor surprised her. She was not in the habit of revealing herself to anyone. Matthew had been a stickler for privacy, which had limited her friendships to mostly superficial ones. She found now that she'd missed the days of college confidences and shared intimacy. The man watching her so compassionately encouraged them, promised with gentle brown eyes to keep them private.

"I don't know where to go from here," she said. "What does a thirty-two-year-old woman do when she's on her own for the first time?"

"What have you been doing?"

"Raising money for a new pediatrics wing for the hospital." She couldn't keep the irony out of her tone.

"Hmm," he said with a solemnity that was mocked by the laughter in his eyes. "I can see why that might no longer appeal."

"I thought you might," she said wryly.

"Have you ever worked?"

"Try organizing a few luncheons for five hundred people and talking people out of a few thousand dollars. Believe me, that's work."

"But not the stuff of which résumés are built."

"Exactly," she said without the usual trace of defensiveness. "I have no idea what you do, but if you had a company, would you hire me?"

Apparently taking the question seriously, he looked

her over very slowly. Catherine felt heat flooding her cheeks at the intense thoroughness of his survey. It was not entirely the cool, professional examination of a prospective employer. Her blood pulsed to a long-forgotten beat. "Maybe," he said finally.

She couldn't decide whether to be piqued by his caution or encouraged by his willingness to consider the possibility. "As what?"

"A model."

She burst out laughing. "Really, now. A man who can use a coffeepot to wrangle an introduction can surely come up with something more original than that."

"Don't laugh. You have nice bone structure, great skin and sexy, mysterious eyes. The camera would definitely love those eyes."

"Next thing I know you'll tell me you could make me a star."

"I probably could," he retorted so matter-of-factly that it gave her pause. "At least in commercials or print ads. I run an advertising agency in New York. I have a lot of accounts that could benefit from a spokeswoman with your obvious class." He glanced pointedly at the ring. "The diamond trade, for instance."

She turned her hand until the diamond glinted in the candlelight. "See. I told you it would come in handy. Why are you in Savannah? Are you scouting locations? This is a beautiful city."

"It is, but I'm just here to pursue a new account. We finished our meetings early, so I should have flown back. The last few months have been hell, though, so I decided to stay over a night." His gaze collided with hers, lingered. Her pulse raced wildly as he added in a seductive tone that promised unimaginable delights, "I'm glad I did."

"Me, too," she admitted quietly, shocking herself with the depth of her sincerity. After so many years of holding herself aloof, she found she was thriving on the unexpected intimacy, the sympathetic ear, the unthreatening banter with its faint hint of sensuality.

"Have you finished your dinner, Catherine?"

She stared down at the shrimp she'd barely touched and nodded. "I wasn't very hungry."

"Then let's get out of here and go for a walk along the river. Afterward, I'll buy you a nightcap."

The obligatory warnings screeched through her head. She peered deep into the stranger's eyes and saw nothing but honesty and compassion and the tiniest flame of desire. All drew her. All—even that carefully restrained suggestion of masculine interest—made the warnings seem unwarranted.

"If you can find my real waiter, so I can take care of my check, I'd love to join you for a walk," she said with an uncommonly bold sense of daring.

"I'll take care of it."

"No, really," she protested, thinking of her inbred sense of propriety.

"I won't take no for an answer. Someday you can return the favor when you see someone who looks lost and alone."

When the check had been paid, he guided her out of the crowded restaurant and across the cobbled street to the riverwalk. A soft, sultry breeze stirred the muggy air. A handful of glittering stars had been tossed across the velvet sky. The silence as they strolled was every bit as companionable as their conversation had been.

With every step, though, the air of expectancy built. It pulsed and teased like the beat of a tango.

Unable to bear the mounting tension a moment longer, Catherine forced an innocent question. "You're not from here originally, are you?"

He glanced at her knowingly, obviously recognizing the query for what it was: a coward's step back from an unfamiliar closeness. "What was your first clue?" he taunted with a light acceptance of the diversion.

She laughed. "No drawl, for one thing."

"Any others?"

"You were eating dinner alone."

"Maybe I enjoy my own company."

"Maybe so, but I rather think a man like you could have the company of any number of women if you were on your home turf. A wife, for example?"

"Is that a leading question?"

She tilted her head up and smiled flirtatiously, even as she said, "It would only be a leading question if I were interested in you. Since we're just strangers passing in the night, it's simply a point of information."

"Ah, a fine distinction. As a man who knows the value of precise wording, I approve."

"You still haven't answered the question."

"Perhaps because, like you, thinking of my personal life is too painful."

"You're divorced?"

"In the process. My wife couldn't handle the amount of traveling I have to do, the impossible number of hours I have to put in."

"So she gave you an ultimatum?"

"Nope, no ultimatum. Just my walking papers. Apparently she didn't feel there was much point in discussing the obvious."

"The obvious being that you would choose work over her?"

"As she saw it."

"Was she right?"

His steps slowed and it was a long time before he answered. She had the feeling he was honestly soul-searching. "I wish I could say no," he said finally. "But I honestly don't know. I loved her and I miss our kids. That's the hardest part of all—knowing that I won't see them grow up, at least not the way I would living in the same house."

"Shouldn't you fight to get her back, then?"

"Would it be fair to do that if I couldn't keep the promise to change?"

"But you don't know that," she argued. "You haven't tried."

He sighed deeply. "No, I haven't tried. Maybe that says it all. When push came to shove, I didn't love her enough to try. She deserves much more than that. She's a terrific lady."

In the soft glow of the streetlight, Catherine saw the profound sadness and regret in his eyes. She wanted to reach out, to touch his cheek, but she held back. "At least you don't sound proud of walking away," she said.

"I'm not. If I could go back ten or fifteen years, maybe I'd do it all differently, but this is where I am today. I have to live with that."

"Isn't the trick to recognize where you are, decide if you like it and, if not, then make changes? That's what I'm trying to do. That's what brought me to Savannah. I'm looking for a new direction."

"Why here?"

"There's a school. It offers the kind of courses I once wanted very badly to take. They weren't really available when I was in college. In fact there's only one place in the country even now that offers a degree in historic preservation and it's here in Savannah."

"And?"

"I went by there today. Now I'm not so sure. Everyone seemed so young."

He opened his mouth, but she laughed and warned him, "Don't you dare tell me that age is only a state of mind."

"Ah, but it is, Catherine."

"Maybe so, but there's a season for everything and I think it's past time for me to be starting all over again as a college student."

"Don't give up so easily. Think how much knowledge and experience you'd take into a classroom. You'd be way ahead of your fellow students."

"I'd never thought of it quite like that. Thank you."

He stopped and turned her to face him. "Let's make a pact, you and I."

"Okay," she said, her serious tone matching his expression.

"Repeat after me, I do solemnly swear…"

"I do solemnly swear…"

"That I will spend the next year…"

"That I will spend the next year…"

"Discovering who I am and what I want out of life. No half measures, no rushing into things because of outside pressures."

Catherine felt a sigh building deep inside as she repeated the vow.

Her gaze met his. His eyes were filled with longing and regret as he lowered his head slowly until their lips barely met. His were soft as velvet as they brushed across her mouth. Then his arms slid around her waist, strong and possessive and loving. The kiss turned hungry and urgent, as feelings far too complicated swept through her, fulfilling earlier promises and altering forever the memory of their encounter. The innocence of it fled and in its place came a startling awareness, a powerful yearning to discover more of the taste and feel of him.

He finally pulled away, his hands lingering at her waist, his gaze searching her face. A faintly rueful smile tugged at his lips. "Ah, Catherine...if only things were different."

"If only... Two of the saddest words in all the language. Is that the way two people should live their lives?"

"Perhaps not. Shall we make another vow before I put you in a cab and send you off to your hotel?"

"Why not?" she said, fighting the sense of loss that was already stealing over her at the thought of their parting. A second loss—today of all days—was almost more than she could bear. Still, she managed a wavering smile.

"Do you remember the play about the couple who met just once a year and through the years came to know more about each other's lives than those who lived with them most intimately?"

"Same Time, Next Year," she said at once. "I loved that play."

"Then let's make a promise to meet right here next year and see how our lives have changed."

"I'd like that," she said, entering into the fantasy of a time far in the future when things might be less complicated, when emotions might be less in turmoil. So much could happen in a year, so much could change. Just look at the past few months: her safe, predictable life had been turned topsy-turvy. She met his intense gaze and felt a slow heat begin to build deep inside. "I'd like that very much."

"Then I'll be waiting for you," he promised. "Coffeepot in hand." He stole one more kiss before whistling for a cab, tucking her inside and then walking away.

It wasn't until he was almost out of earshot that Catherine realized she didn't even know his name. With a sudden sense of urgency, she told the driver to stop, threw open the door and ran after him. At the sound of her footsteps on the cobblestones, he turned around. She halted in midstride, feeling suddenly foolish for wanting more, for needing that one link with someone she'd most likely never meet again, despite vows and best intentions.

"I don't even know your name," she explained with a helpless shrug. "I'd like to."

"Dillon," he replied, his voice so low she had to strain to catch the response.

"Dillon," she repeated. It fit somehow. Unique, thoroughly charming Dillon, an Irish rogue if ever she'd met one. She smiled with a serenity she hadn't felt in weeks and waved again as she got back into the taxi.

"Until next year," she whispered to herself as he disappeared from sight. It seemed as close as tomorrow.

And as far away as forever.

1

May 16—one year later

"Catherine Devlin, what do you mean you're not going?" Beth Markham asked, her wide-eyed expression reflecting her amazement. "For the past twelve months all I've heard about is Dillon this and Dillon that."

"You're exaggerating. I haven't mentioned the man in ages." Catherine turned away to hide her embarrassment. With forced concentration she began piling the latest donations to St. Christopher's thrift shop onto the counter in front of her. She eyed the clothing critically, set the price and tagged each piece, hoping that Beth would go away or at least change the subject. Talking about Dillon made her nervous. So did, for that matter, remembering him. For a man she'd only talked with for a short time an entire year ago, a man she'd kissed just twice, he'd made an incredibly lasting impression.

"Last night," Beth said, sneaking up on her.

Catherine's black felt tip pen skittered wildly across

the tag. Her heart hammered. "What?" she said as she ripped the ruined tag off and attached another one.

"You mentioned Dillon again last night."

"I did not." The denial was halfhearted. Though she hated admitting it, she suspected Beth knew exactly what she was talking about. She usually did. When it came to romance, Beth had the finely honed instincts of a successful matchmaker. Catherine was one of her few failures. Sensing that another meeting with Dillon could turn that around, Beth wasn't about to let Catherine off the hook.

"We were sitting at your kitchen table," Beth began, her amusement apparent. "I remember exactly how it happened. You started to take off your wedding ring. It's about time you did that, by the way. Anyway, then you said—and I quote—'Dillon said I could always be a model for the diamond trade.' And then you sighed."

"I did not," she repeated, only barely resisting the urge to sigh, thereby confirming Beth's smug statement.

"You did," Beth contradicted anyway. "You sigh every time you mention his name."

Catherine stopped tagging the clothes and turned slowly toward the woman who'd become her best friend over the last months when she'd been getting her feet back on the ground after the divorce. Beth was a delightful scatterbrain with a heart big enough to embrace the whole world. Though they'd been neighbors for years, it was only after Matthew had left that Catherine had gotten to know and appreciate her rare combination of wisdom, humor and blunt honestly.

"I do?" she said, dismayed by the sappy, love-struck

picture of her that Beth was presenting. "I actually sigh?"

Beth nodded, grinning victoriously. "And you get this mysterious, faraway look in your eyes. You're smitten, Catherine Devlin, and I for one don't intend to listen to you going on and on about the man for the rest of your life. Today's the day you are supposed to meet him in Savannah. Now get out of here. It's a long drive and you'd better get started now if you intend to be there by dinnertime."

"I am not driving all the way to Savannah to meet a total stranger," she protested weakly.

"He's not exactly a stranger. Heck, I feel as if I know him by now."

Catherine glared at her. "I haven't been that bad."

"You have been, but don't worry. I think it's wonderfully romantic."

"You would." She shook her head. "No. It's ridiculous. It was a once-in-a-lifetime meeting. It's not the sort of thing you try to prolong." Despite the protest, the temptation to go, to take a risk for once, was gaining momentum.

Beth must have sensed her weakening. She pulled out her most powerful argument. "You made a vow, a solemn oath, didn't you? Are you going to go back on your word? Whatever would your mother say?" she drawled, deliberately mimicking the honey-thick Southern accent of Catherine's very proper mother.

"Don't drag her into this. If my mother knew I was even considering running off to Savannah to meet a man—a Northerner—I hardly know, she'd say plenty and it would blister your ears. I'd never hear the last of her disapproval. She barely tolerated Matthew because he'd only lived in Atlanta for a few years when we met."

"In the case of your ex-husband, she was right to be disapproving. The man was a self-righteous bore."

"He was not," she defended automatically, then realized that essentially she'd come to agree with Beth. Matthew had been a little stuffy, which had made that fling with the pediatrics resident all the more shocking. Maybe that had changed him, but the old Matthew would never in a million years have sanctioned exchanging polite chitchat with a total stranger, much less traipsing off to Savannah to meet a man she'd only known for a few hours. Still…

"Maybe…"

Beth seized on the hesitation with enthusiasm. "I knew it! You're going, aren't you? Now hurry up. You don't want to miss him."

"It's the middle of the week. The man does work, you know. He probably won't even be there."

"If he's not," Beth said practically, "you can go by the Savannah College of Art and Design again and check out the classes. It won't be a wasted trip."

"Don't start that again. I'm thirty-three. It's too late for me to take up a whole new career. I realized that when I was there last time."

"Fiddle-faddle! It's only too late when you're dead. Think about it, Cat. You're wasting yourself working in here. Not that I don't love having your help. I've actually had time off since you started volunteering, but you could do so much more."

"I'm happy now," she argued. "I have enough money to live on from the investments I made with the divorce settlement and with the trust fund from my father. What's wrong with just trying to make myself useful, giving something back to the community?"

"Nothing if it makes you happy, but it doesn't. I don't care what you say. You're going through the motions, filling up hours. Your year of mourning is up, sweetie. It's time to take some chances."

"Going to meet Dillon is about as much of a chance as I can cope with today."

"Then you'll go by the school tomorrow," Beth said with the persistence that had made her one of the best fund-raisers the church had ever had.

Catherine laughed. "Okay. You win. I promise I'll think about it."

She should have anticipated that wouldn't be quite good enough for Beth. "I'm going to ask to see catalogs and class schedules when you get back," Beth warned.

Catherine groaned. "No wonder your kids like to hide out at my house. You're a nag."

"If your house was littered with potato chips and socks, you'd nag, too."

"Maybe so," Catherine said, unable to keep a hint of unexpected wistfulness from her voice. At one time she'd wanted so badly to have children, but Matthew had been adamantly opposed. He liked to travel. He liked having her at his beck and call. And, though she could have defied him, she'd known that an "accidental" pregnancy was no answer. It would have created a horrible environment in which to bring up a child. The irony, of course, was that practically fifteen minutes after their divorce was final, Matthew had remarried because the pediatrics resident with whom he'd been having the affair was pregnant. Catherine figured it served him right.

"Maybe so," she said again, this time with more bitterness than she usually permitted herself.

Beth sobered at once, obviously reading the direction of her thoughts with her usual uncanny accuracy. "Don't look back, Cat. You can't change the past. Go out now and grab the future."

Catherine felt her heart begin to beat a little faster as the image of Dillon reappeared in her mind as it had so often over the past year. She recalled the way he'd listened to her, really listened, and the way he'd looked at her with such warmth and affection, as if they'd known each other forever.

"What the hell," she murmured finally. "You only live once."

All the way to Savannah, Catherine told herself she was a fool. Dillon wouldn't show up. Why would he? He was an attractive man in a profession that threw him into contact with women far more beautiful, successful and sophisticated than she was. It had been an entire year. Just because she hadn't been able to get him out of her mind didn't mean he would remember their few hours together or the promise they'd made.

No matter how determinedly she tried to balance her excitement with a healthy dose of reality, though, the anticipation was winning. She'd had a lot of dates during the past year, but none had filled her with this pins-and-needles expectancy. In fact, she only dimly remembered feeling this way with Matthew during the first heady days of their courtship fifteen years earlier, when she'd just started college and he'd been in medical school. Recalling that reminded her how fleeting such emotions could be.

But even that sobering reminder wasn't able to dampen her sense of adventure six hours later as she dressed in a simple red dress that flattered her dark coloring. She added gold jewelry and a subtle touch of her favorite perfume, a French floral scent that Matthew had hated, probably because she'd paid a hundred dollars an ounce for it. Sliding her feet into a pair of very high black heels that made her look sinfully wicked, she left for the restaurant, which was only a few blocks away on the waterfront.

It was a balmy night with only the faintest breeze stirring off the river. As she walked, she recalled that slight flaring of desire she'd seen in Dillon's eyes before he'd kissed her and said goodbye. Her pulse throbbed at the thought of his lips on hers again—warm, sensuous, demanding. An aching heaviness low in her abdomen told her once more just how captivated she'd been, how much she wanted him to be waiting for her tonight.

At the restaurant door, she hesitated, stricken with a sudden shyness, a sudden onset of sanity. Was she crazy for coming? Was she taking an incredible risk? The news was filled with such horrible stories.... The memory of Dillon's gentle kindness allayed her fears. She caught her reflection in the restaurant window and saw the slow curve of her mouth. "Don't back out now, Cat," she murmured and slipped inside before she could change her mind.

She quickly scanned the dimly lit room. It was early yet and there were only a few customers. There was no sign of a familiar man in a designer suit, looking as if he'd just stepped out of the pages of some elite men's magazine. Her gaze slid to the table where she'd been sitting when they met. It was available. She asked the hostess if she could be seated there.

Once she was sitting down, she realized that her hands were trembling. She hadn't been this nervous on her very first date. She'd never been this afraid of being stood up. She ordered a glass of white wine and the shrimp, the same meal she'd had a year earlier. For luck, she told herself.

"More coffee?" The seductive masculine voice sent a jolt of pure electricity sizzling down her spine.

"I'm not drinking coffee," she said in a voice that went breathless in midsentence. She looked up into serious brown eyes that studied her with relentless intensity.

"You came," she said softly, fighting to hide the sigh of relief that whispered through her.

Dillon's smile seemed to hold a similar measure of satisfaction. "So did you."

"I didn't think you'd remember," they said together, then laughed. The laughter broke the tension and made Catherine delightfully aware that she'd never wanted to be anyplace more than where she was right now with this handsome, kind man regarding her with such obvious warmth.

"You look wonderful," he said as he sat down, his appreciation evident in eyes that caressed, paying loving attention to every detail from head to toe. Catherine's skin burned under the intense scrutiny. "I'm sorry I'm late."

"You're not. I mean we really didn't set a time exactly. I wasn't even sure if you'd bother to come all this way for a dinner. Or did you get that account down

here? Do you come often now?" She had to bite her
tongue to stop the nervous rattling off of questions.

"Yes, I got the account and I do come down oc-
casionally. I made it a point to be here tonight. I was
hoping that you'd remember, that you'd want to see me
again. I can't tell you how many times in the last year
I've regretted not getting your last name, not being able
to call you to see how you were doing."

She regarded him curiously. "I've felt the same
way," she admitted with unfamiliar boldness. "Why
didn't you ask for the phone number?"

His expression turned thoughtful. "I suppose it was
because we were both at a low point in our lives that
night. We were both reaching out for something that,
amazingly enough, we each had to offer, but that's a
dangerous time to start something. For once in my
life I listened to my conscience, instead of rushing
into something. I knew in my gut that we needed time
to sort out our lives. I took a risk and turned things
over to fate."

This once, then, the Fates had proved kind. Generous, in fact. She propped her chin in her hand and
asked, "And did you sort out your life?"

"As best I could. The divorce is final. I'm working on building a better relationship with my children.
Ironically, I seem to spend more time with them now
than I did when I was married, maybe because I make
the time. I've stopped taking them for granted."

"Ah, yes, one of life's greatest sins, taking those we
love for granted."

"What about you? Have you sorted things out?"

"I've survived. I'm learning to rely on myself. I'm
building an identity that's separate from being Dr. Mat-

thew Devlin's wife. I don't have it entirely together yet, but I'm trying."

"Is there a man helping you to find your way?" he asked. Catherine thought she heard a note of caution in his voice, an unexpected tentativeness.

"No," she said adamantly, drawing a broad smile. "This time I thought it wise to find my own way, to discover who I really am and then see if a man fits into that picture, instead of the other way around."

"See," he teased, "it is possible to learn from our mistakes."

Catherine found herself smiling back at him. She was slowly relaxing, falling under the magical spell of his interest all over again, wanting to share things with him that she'd never shared with anyone, not even Beth. "It seems to me we've both paid quite a price to learn that lesson."

"Ah, but we're much better people now. Think how good we'll be to each other."

The low, seductive taunt set off a fire in her belly. She wanted to look away, but his gaze held her, demanded that she acknowledge the desire that was building so quickly between them, a longing so intense that it made her weak. He took her hand in his, rubbing her knuckles with the pad of his thumb.

"I can't believe how I've missed you," he said softly. "How is it possible that two people could connect so easily after one brief meeting?"

"Are you certain it's not just wishful thinking?" she asked shakily, clinging to reality even as it seemed to be falling away, leaving her senses raw and vulnerable.

"I'm not certain of anything, but I do know that if you hadn't been here tonight, I would have moved heaven and earth to find you. I would have come after you sooner, but I forced myself to keep my word, to wait a year. Even so, there wasn't a trip to Savannah that I didn't stop by here hoping to catch a glimpse of you again, not a moment that I didn't look at every tall, dark beauty to see if she might be you. There were so many things I wanted to talk over with you, so many times I've wondered what you'd think about an ad campaign I was creating or a play I was seeing or a book I was reading."

"But why?" she asked, bemused by the passionate declaration. "Why would you want the opinion of someone you barely knew?"

He shrugged ruefully. "I wish I understood that. I know all about the psychology of advertising, all about titillating the public, but I don't understand what's going on between us. There was just something about that night, an overwhelming intuition. I knew at once that you and I were on the same wavelength, that what we had was too special to lose. You must have felt it, too, or you wouldn't be here now."

Catherine was shaken by how closely his feelings matched hers. "I suppose I did," she admitted finally. "Beth—she's a neighbor I've grown close to this last year—says I'm still quoting you after all this time." She flushed. "I probably shouldn't tell you that."

"Why not? I just told you how I felt."

"But women are supposed to be coy. Don't you know that in the South at least it's something we're trained to do from the cradle on? My mother would be horrified if she knew I was giving away my feelings like this. Frankly, I'm a little surprised at myself."

"Why?"

"Because I've always been so cool and reserved, not just coy, mind you, but private. For some reason I open up with you."

"Because you know I'd never hurt you."

She stared at him and thought about his statement. It could have been nothing more than glib charm, but she believed it was true. She knew in her heart that Dillon would do anything in his power to keep from hurting her, that he was a gentle, compassionate man. And she was responding to that knowledge like a flower opening to sunshine.

That didn't mean the feelings didn't confuse her. "How do I know that?" she wondered.

"You have superb instincts," he suggested lightly.

"I chose Matthew," she reminded him.

"Maybe it's my honest face, then."

"You have the face of a heartbreaker."

"Then maybe it's magic."

"Or illusion."

"Cynic."

"Realist," she countered, laughing at his crestfallen expression.

"We are going to have a wonderful time finding out, though, aren't we, Catherine?"

"Yes," she said quietly, folding her fingers around his. "Yes, I think we are."

For the first time in years, something other than work was on Dillon's mind the instant he woke up. Catherine! The memory of the trusting way she'd looked at him last night, the delight that had come over her fragile features when he'd appeared at her table, the yearning he'd recognized when he'd left her at the door of her hotel room at 1:00 a.m. with one sweet, lingering kiss. He'd wanted so much more, but he'd sworn to move slowly with her, to take the time to treasure these rare new feelings that were bursting within him. Restraint was far from a habit for him and he was just now discovering it was the pits. His whole body ached from the effort.

Though his actions had been restrained, he hadn't minced words. He'd told her the absolute truth. Not a day had gone by in the past year, when she hadn't crossed his mind, when he hadn't recalled her combination of sophisticated looks and gentle vulnerability. He'd wanted to explore her quick intelligence just as much as he'd wanted to savor her incredible body. The fact that he'd given her mind precedence over her sensuality told him exactly how far-gone he was. From the very first, he'd known that she was going to be someone important in his life, someone to respect and cherish, not use and discard. Thank heavens for once he'd listened to his conscience.

Right now, though, he was damning it. He was lying in bed, aching with the need to touch her. Aching was the operative word, too. It was not the first time that thoughts of Catherine had driven him into an icy shower. This morning though, he would be seeing her again, albeit far too briefly. He had a noon flight back to New York to make a three o'clock meeting that couldn't be postponed. He'd had to rearrange half a dozen appointments to get here at all, but it would have taken a collapse of the airline industry and the force of a hurricane to keep him away from Savannah last night. He'd spent three hundred and sixty-five days dreaming of holding her in his arms again.

He reached over, picked up the phone and dialed her room. "Wake up, sleepyhead," he said cheerfully.

"It's early," she murmured in a whispery voice that set his blood on fire all over again.

"We only have a few hours. Let's not waste them. Breakfast in twenty minutes. I'll pick you up."

"An hour," she bargained.

"Thirty minutes and not a second more." He hung up on her protest.

She met him at the door of her room, still barefooted and with her long, dark hair curling damply about her perfect, just-scrubbed face. If anything, she was even more beautiful without makeup. She smelled of soap and lavender. If he'd recognized the product he would have offered to write an entire ad campaign for free. The scent was heady, deliciously provocative, yet innocent of artifice.

"You're early," she accused.

"I'm right on time."

"I'm not ready."

"You look beautiful."

"I look wet."

He brushed a damp tendril back from her face and watched the heat flare in her blue eyes. "Beautiful," he said huskily, claiming her lips. They were morning soft and mint-scented moist. He wanted to taste them for hours, to discover the shape and texture at every stage of arousal. He let her go on a ragged moan. It took all of his strength to resist the urge to demand more, to release her when he felt her body molding itself to his.

"You're dangerous, lady."

Surprised pleasure registered on her face. "Me?"

"Yes, you. Have you no idea how tempting you are?"

"No."

The honest admission made his heart flip over. What a glorious feeling it would be to show this woman exactly how desirable she was, to tap her passions in a way he suspected her ex-husband had ignored. *Not now,* he warned himself. As badly as he wanted her, as convinced as he was that she wanted him, he wasn't going to rush her and scare her to death. She might enjoy their passion, she might come to life under his touches, but she wouldn't thank him for it. She reminded him of an orchid, hothouse sultry, but fragile.

"Hurry," he said, sending her off to dry her hair. "I'm a hungry man."

A short time later, Catherine picked daintily at her breakfast of dry toast and half a grapefruit, while he wolfed down eggs, bacon, grits and toast, then wondered about the blueberry muffins.

"Surely not," she said, her eyes widening incredulously.

"Just one. You can share it with me."

He placed the order and when the huge muffin came, he broke off bits, buttered them and fed them to her. He talked of his meeting in New York, keeping her attention diverted from the food she was accepting. She'd finished the whole muffin before she realized that he hadn't had a single bite. "You tricked me," she said.

"How did I do that?" he asked innocently.

"You didn't want that muffin at all."

"But you obviously did."

She studied him with apparent astonishment. "How did you know?"

His expression sobered as he took her hand, slowly licking the last crumbs of muffin from her fingertips.

The pulse that beat in her neck leaped at his touch. "I know everything about you."

"Oh?"

"Well, maybe not everything, but what I don't know now, I will soon."

"Soon?"

"I've been thinking."

"Why do I think that's a dangerous precedent?"

He scowled at her. "Memorial Day is coming up. Could you get away and meet me here again? We'd have the whole weekend then to explore the area, to get to know each other."

She hesitated and his heart seemed to stand still. "Maybe we're trying to turn this into something it isn't," she responded cautiously.

"And maybe we're not. How will we know unless we explore the possibilities? Are you willing to walk away again without trying?"

"No," she said finally, then lifted her gaze to collide with his. Her chin rose almost imperceptibly. "No, I'm not."

Dillon grinned. "One week from tomorrow then. Same time. Same place."

She nodded slowly. "Same time. Same place."

2

Memorial Day Weekend

Dillon's plane was late. An impatient man under the best of circumstances, today he was infuriated by the delay. He paced. He cursed the airline. He cursed the cluttered skies over New York. He cursed himself for having sold his private jet. And while he was at it, he cursed Catherine for so quickly becoming an obsession. From that very first meeting he'd known that she was capable of driving him mad with longing. Still, he hadn't been able to resist her.

In fact, had it not been for Catherine, he'd never have made the rash decision to take the Savannah account in the first place. Every finely honed business instinct had told him to turn it down. White Stone Electronics was a small company and though the potential was great, it could be years before the account became really profitable for him. Yet, during those brief hours he'd spent with Catherine, he'd known he was going to accept, known he was going to grab the excuse to return to the city where they'd met, to cling to the one link between them.

Oddly, the small account had become the most satisfying he'd handled in years. Most of the *Fortune 500* firms with which he worked didn't really need his help. They wanted catchy ads to maintain an already high profile or a public service program to enhance an already established image. This company had no national reputation, except among a few discerning clients. It needed everything, and the results, the sudden spurts of growth that had followed the first ads had been gratifying in ways he'd almost forgotten.

Even so, even though he'd proven that his faith in the company was justified, no one in the New York headquarters of his agency could understand his continued involvement, much less the all-too-frequent trips to Savannah. After the first few years in business, his role had been to land the most illustrious new accounts, set the direction of campaigns and keep the major clients happy. As a result, it had been years since he'd experienced the satisfaction of seeing one of his own creations move from conception to television screens or the pages of a slick magazine. In the past few months he'd found himself reliving the gut-level kick of hearing people on the subway or in the supermarket talk about one of his commercials.

For the past few months, he'd found himself increasingly anxious to get back to Savannah where his creative juices flowed more freely than ever before. Today, though, his impatience was caused by something else entirely.

Catherine.

Since he'd left her this last time, he hadn't been able

to get her out of his mind. If the memories had tantalized him during that long year apart, the past week or so had been sheer torture. She was in his blood, heating it in a way that no woman had in years. With her pale-as-cream complexion, those huge vulnerable blue eyes and that regal aura of self-containment that taunted a man, she was a delightful challenge. He'd said it all when he'd told her she had class. To a kid from his poor background, a man who'd struggled for every single success that had dragged him from a lousy neighborhood to the Upper East Side, she represented the unattainable, the sort of woman to be put on a pedestal. She was a dream for him, but she was also flesh-and-blood real.

A dozen times he'd picked up the phone to call, but held back. Sensing her skittishness, he hadn't wanted to pressure her. Or maybe he'd simply panicked, fearing the rapid deepening of his own involvement. Suddenly, after discovering that her hold over his senses hadn't diminished, maybe he was running scared, maybe that—not sheer lust—explained the way his pulse quickened at the thought of her. However strong the fear though, he hadn't been even remotely tempted not to fly down to meet her tonight. If the plane didn't take off in the next ten minutes, he was going to change airlines, charter a jet, whatever it took to get him there.

Two hours later, when he finally walked off the plane and saw her waiting for him, his heart caught, then hammered. Hanging back for just an instant, he saw her anxious eyes scanning the arriving passengers. As the exodus dwindled down, her high brow furrowed in a slight frown. Unable to hide in the shadows a moment longer, Dillon began striding toward her. When she caught sight of him, the worried frown vanished, replaced by a dazzling, heart-stopping smile of welcome. The warmth in her eyes, the childlike spark of anticipation set his blood on fire all over again. He was hooked all right. No man could inspire a look like that without feeling a fierce swell of possessiveness, a sudden yearning for the sort of passion that was all-too-elusive in life. Matthew Devlin must have been a first-class fool to let her get away.

Dillon reached out and took her hands. Hungry for a kiss, for the feel of her lips crushed beneath his, he satisfied himself with the amazingly shy, trusting clasp of her fingers around his.

"Sorry I'm late."

She tilted her head inquiringly, revealing a flash of the finest gold on her delicately shaped ears. "Were you flying the plane?"

Grinning at the teasing question, he shook his head.

"Then there's no reason to apologize, is there? Besides, do you have any idea how fascinating an airport can be?"

"Frankly, no."

"Interested in a tour? There's a lovely newsstand and the coffee shop has a waitress who must have come from New York. She'd make you homesick, she's so rude. It reminded me of a deli I went into once in midtown Manhattan. The nastiest waitresses seemed to get the biggest tips. Why is that? You all not only put up with it, you actually encourage it."

"Maybe because their regulars know they can count on them to be there day in and day out, never changing. Constancy is something to be treasured, especially in a city as quick to change as New York."

She looked doubtful.

"Okay," he said. "You don't buy that. Maybe it's just because it gives us somebody we can justify yelling back at before we've had our morning coffee. If we snap at a waitress, she'll punish us with cold coffee. If we snap at our wives, they'll divorce us and take us to the cleaners in the process."

"That sounds more like it. What about you? Are you a morning person?"

"Actually, I am. I never snapped at Paula over breakfast. I'd usually left the house long before she even got up. And I never growl at waitresses. Do you really want to stand here talking about my temper in the morning?"

"Actually, yes," she said.

Puzzled, he glanced into her too-serious eyes. "Why?"

Her aristocratic chin lifted with the faintest suggestion of defiance. Once again he spotted that astounding vulnerability and the stubborn determination to overcome it. "Because a part of me is terrified of what comes next," she admitted.

"Nothing that you don't want," he promised, touched by her determined honesty and awed by the suggestion of innocence in a woman who should have been filled with self-assurance. He recognized once more that such personal revelations were rare for her, something to be treasured and encouraged.

"Even if I have to spend the entire weekend in an icy shower," he added wryly.

"Maybe my mother would overlook your Northern beginnings after all," she said thoughtfully, a teasing glint lighting her blue eyes. "You have definitely captured the spirit of a Southern gentleman."

The praise was a mixed blessing. "Let's just hope my weak flesh can live up to my willing spirit," he said.

"I have every confidence in you," she said, linking her arm through his and playing havoc with his honorable intentions.

"I know," he said, barely containing a sigh of pure pleasure at her touch. "That's what makes it so damned difficult. If I ever succumbed to a moment of intense passion, I'd feel guilty about it for the rest of my life. Now let's stop talking about this. Have you decided where you'd like to go for dinner?"

"The same place. I feel as though it's lucky for us."

"You're superstitious?"

"Just hedging my bets. Do you mind?"

"Not at all, as long as you don't expect me to serve the coffee. Last time the people at the next table complained because I didn't pour for them."

Catherine's lilting laughter, suddenly carefree and unrestrained, filled the air. Dillon felt as though she'd bestowed a precious gift on him.

The restaurant was packed to capacity with holiday weekend visitors to Savannah, but the hostess took one look at Dillon and promised to do what she could. They were seated within minutes. The dinner was the best yet. Catherine actually tasted the shrimp for the first time and savored the spicy seasonings.

"This is terrific," she said with unconcealed astonishment.

"It's the third time you've had it," Dillon pointed out.

"But it's the first time I was paying any attention." She regarded him intently. "You actually remember what I had over a year ago on the night we met?"

"I remember everything about that night," he said and her heart thumped unsteadily. He placed his hand on the table, palm up, and after only the tiniest hesitation she linked her fingers through his. The contact sent shivers racing along her spine. His hot, hungry gaze melted her resolve to move ahead slowly, to keep him at arm's distance until she really knew him.

"Dillon, you promised," she accused in a breathless voice.

He stared back innocently. "I'm not doing a thing."

"You are," she insisted, drawing back her hand. Even without his touch, though, her pulse didn't quiet and her flesh didn't cool. She folded her hands tightly together in her lap and sat up straighter. "Tell me about your week."

His low chuckle washed over her, teasing at her senses and making mincemeat of her attempt to regain control over her rampaging hormones. "I made a few bucks. How about you?"

She ignored the flip reply. She'd pursue the details about his week later. "I worked at the shop and went to three tedious luncheons for very good causes," she said just as glibly. "I'd rather have sent them the money."

"Why didn't you?"

"Because they tell me that listing my name on the committee helps to raise more money. What it really means is I feel guilty unless I get on the phone and insist that my friends turn out. Then I have to do the same for their charities. Pretty soon I'm up to my eyeballs in chicken salad and fresh raspberries."

"You said something about calling the College of Art and Design this week to make an appointment. Did you? I'd like to go by and take a look at the place.

I've heard a lot more about it since I've been coming down here regularly."

Despite Dillon's apparent interest, Catherine immediately felt defensive. "You sound like Beth," she grumbled lightly. "Please, don't you turn into a nag, too. I'll get to it one of these days."

"It's not too soon to check out fall classes," he persisted with the determination of a man not used to wasting time. "If you were living in Savannah, we could see even more of each other."

He held out the possibility of more time together like a delightful temptation, but it came with strings. She wasn't prepared to make a change so drastic in her life-style, not for any man, especially when she wasn't ready to do it for herself.

"Can't we table this conversation?" she pleaded.

He seemed genuinely confused by her hesitation. She envied his self-assurance, his quick decision-making skill. Dillon was obviously a man who always grabbed for the brass ring, relishing the success, but willing to risk the defeats. She wasn't nearly so brave. Yet, she amended. She was getting stronger by the day.

"Why don't you want to discuss it?" he asked.

She took a deep breath and admitted, "Because every time one of you brings it up, I start to feel like a failure."

Dillon looked stunned at her heartfelt candor. "A failure? This isn't about failing, Catherine. I thought working in historic preservation was something you wanted. I'm just trying to encourage you."

"I mentioned it a couple of times. What you and Beth are doing feels more like pressure than encouragement."

"Because you're scared," he said with another of those uncanny flashes of intuition. "Is that it?"

"Damn right, I'm scared," she retorted. "I'm leading a safe, secure life right now. Why should I turn it upside down on some whim?"

"If that's all it is, then you're right." He studied her intently. "Is it just a whim?"

Catherine sighed. "I don't know anymore. Every time I walk through this town and see how much has been accomplished, I get excited all over again. Then I go home and fall back into a familiar routine and I don't see the point. There are plenty of other people to tackle preservation projects. The school's reputation is growing. The work is exciting. It's new. The country is finally beginning to see the importance of preserving history, instead of knocking it down and replacing it with another high rise. Savannah's been a leader in that fight."

"Things may be changing here. People in Savannah do have a genuine commitment, but there aren't that many leaders for the fight yet in other cities. How many historic buildings in Atlanta fell so they could build the new downtown stadium? That's right in your own backyard."

Catherine cringed at the accuracy of the charge. She'd spoken out, but she hadn't actually led a crusade. She hadn't been in there pitching alternatives. Maybe she was just one of those people who was committed to a cause only as long as it was easy, only as long as the main requirements were cash and time, not the risk of controversy.

"You're right," she said miserably. "I walked away from a fight. Maybe that's the worst carryover from my marriage. I've forgotten how to stand up for myself and what I believe in. I spent too many years focused totally on Matthew's goals and one of his primary objectives in life was to avoid controversy."

"It doesn't have to be that way, you know. You're too intelligent and caring to take the easy way out forever."

She grabbed at the praise like a lifeline. "What makes you so confident of that?"

"I see the spirit in your eyes, the flashes of temper. You bank them before they get out of hand, but they're there. Yelling back just takes a little practice."

Suddenly she realized just how often she did bite her tongue to avoid making a scene, how often she kept her opinions to herself in the name of diplomacy. Matthew had prized her tact and her even temper almost more highly than her knack for choosing the best wine and creating the most extravagant entrées. "Be careful," she warned Dillon. "You may be creating a monster. The next thing you know you won't be able to utter a word without me challenging you."

He grinned. "I'm a born street fighter, sweetheart. I'll take my chances. Now finish that wine and let's get out of here. There's someplace I think we should go."

"Where?"

"You'll see," he said mysteriously. No matter how hard she prodded, he wouldn't reveal his plans.

It was just as well. When they left the restaurant, the waterfront was alive with holiday weekend activity. There was a concert in progress and the crowds from each of the restaurants and clubs spilled out onto the riverwalk. Some paused to listen to the music. Others strolled at a leisurely pace, pursued by the sultry strains of jazz.

"Stay or go?" Dillon asked, watching her face.

The beat of the music came alive inside her, tugging at her heart. "Stay," she said at once as flute and trumpet soared with impossible beauty and clarity.

Dillon found a spot to stand, where they could hear the music and see the shadowy forms on the river. Leaning back against the low wall, he pulled her back against him, his arms linked around her midriff. The heat of his body surrounded her, the press of his hard, muscled thighs tempted. Every fiber of her being from head to toe was vibrantly aware of him, filled with the musky, masculine scent of him. Her breasts ached from the longing to be touched. She folded her arms around her middle, her hands atop Dillon's. It took every ounce of restraint she possessed to keep from lifting those strong fingers just inches higher to caress and tease. His warm breath whispered past her ear and Catherine felt a sigh shudder through her.

"Look up," he said in a hushed, awestruck voice. "Quickly."

She glanced at the sky.

"A falling star," he said, pointing. "Make a wish."

Savoring the unexpectedly powerful feeling of contentment that being in his arms brought, she told him honestly, "I don't think I could wish for anything more than this."

Catherine awoke to the sound of impatient knocking and Dillon's voice.

"Rise and shine, my long-stemmed beauty!"

Laughing, she drew on her robe and opened the door. "Long-stemmed beauty?"

"Isn't there some poem about a love that's like a

red rose? That's how I think of you. You're as elegant and petal-soft as an American Beauty rose. For a bit I thought you were more like an orchid, but last night I began to detect the strength, the thorns."

"Thanks…I think. Do you always go on so poetically at—" she glanced at her bedside clock "—barely 9:00 a.m.?"

"I rarely have the inspiration," he admitted. "Do you want your breakfast on the table over there or in bed?"

"That depends," she said cautiously. "Are you sharing it with me?"

"Absolutely."

"Then you'd better put it on the table."

He sighed dramatically. "I was afraid you were going to say that."

"What did you bring?" she asked, realizing that she was starved. Maybe Dillon wasn't going to be good for her after all. Now that she had her appetite back in his presence, she had a feeling she could puff up like a pastry in no time if she didn't watch herself.

As if he could read her mind, he taunted, "No dieting allowed this weekend. You'll eat everything on your plate."

"Now you sound just like the family housekeeper. My mother's grapefruit breakfasts and my half-grapefruit and dry toast made her crazy. When my father had to give up eggs, Maisie almost retired. She said there wasn't any point to knowing how to cook if nobody in the house was going to eat a blasted thing. She threatened to put out bowls of birdseed and be done with it."

"Did she do it?"

"Of course not. Maisie would die if she didn't have my parents to boss around. Her biggest regret is that she only gets to bully me at Sunday dinners now. I can't bear the look on her face when I turn down dessert. Are you ever going to open those bags or am I going to have to steal them from you?"

"That could be interesting," Dillon said, lifting the two huge white sacks just beyond her reach. She stood on tiptoe and stretched. His laughing gaze locked with hers, then drifted slowly down, turning hot and leaving fire and breathless anticipation in its wake. As his burning gaze lingered on her chest, Catherine realized that her robe was coming loose, leaving only the faintest scrap of lace to cover her breasts from Dillon's intent examination.

"Catherine..." he began, his voice suddenly hoarse.

Her own breath had lodged in her throat and her heart hammered in her chest. "Yes," she whispered.

"I..." He cleared his throat, then shook his head as if coming out of a trance. "I think we'd better eat."

She nodded weakly and sat down hurriedly, tugging her robe more tightly around her and belting it securely.

Opening the bag with fingers that trembled, Dillon removed croissants that were still warm from the oven, containers of homemade jam, cups of fresh chilled melon, real silverware borrowed from the inn's dining room and huge cups of steaming coffee. Reaching back in the bag one more time, he extracted a thick pamphlet and placed it in front of Catherine. She recognized the logo of the College of Art and Design and suddenly her appetite vanished.

"Dillon, you're pressing."

"It wouldn't hurt to look it over, would it? I thought we could stop by later and talk to someone over there about fall enrollment."

Catherine began to feel as if she was battling a steamroller. And losing. "Why is it so important to you that I do this?"

"It's not important to me that you do this. It's important for you."

"How can you say that? You don't even know me. You latched onto one little thing I said and you're turning it into a cause."

"Hardly that," he said, calmly putting jam on his croissant. Catherine felt like shaking him for being so disgustingly in control. Despite her fierce scowl, he kept on. "You did tell me this was something you'd once wanted badly. You keep saying you're bored with all those luncheons. As far as I can tell the only thing keeping you from enrolling in this program is the age thing. I just want you to see how silly that is. Now do you still think I don't know you?"

"Okay, superficially, maybe," she admitted grudgingly, not willing to concede any more than that. "That doesn't give you the right to interfere in my life, to take the decision out of my hands."

"Is it interfering to want what's best for you?"

"Not if I get to choose what's best."

"Then choose, Catherine. Make a choice. Any choice. I'll back you up."

There was an odd note of censure in his tone that infuriated her. He had no right, none at all, to suggest that what she was doing with her life now wasn't enough. She threw down her napkin and stood up. "Maybe this is a mistake, Dillon. Maybe we should have left well enough alone."

He seemed to go perfectly still. "Meaning?" he said very quietly.

She began to pace, glaring at him for ruining what had seemed so perfect only twenty-four hours earlier. "That some fantasies don't hold up all that well under closer scrutiny. You're every bit as domineering in your way as Matthew was in his. I won't let another man run my life. I don't want to be molded into your version of the ideal woman."

"Hey, slow down. I don't want to run your life. I want you to do it. There's a big difference."

"I am running my life."

"Are you really? I don't see it."

"That's because you're obsessed with your career. You think everyone who isn't a workaholic is bored."

"I don't give a good damn whether or not you have a career," he retorted with obvious impatience. "Can you honestly tell me you were totally happy being a housewife? Did that satisfy you? Were you content with running a house and doing good deeds?"

The harsh words hammered at her. "No, dammit," she exploded finally, shocked by the anger that was racing through her like a heady wine. She was shaking with years of pent-up fury. "I hated it. I deplored the sameness of it, but it was expected of me and I was good at it."

Surprisingly, Dillon heaved a sigh of relief at the explosion. "I'm sure you were," he said more gently and Catherine felt the anger begin to ebb. "I think you'd be good at whatever you did."

She turned tear-filled eyes to meet his as he added, "This time, though, make it something that means something to you, something important, something your very soul needs to feel fulfilled."

Suddenly it dawned on her what he'd done. She

wasn't sure which irritated her more, that he'd tried it or that it had worked. "You made me fight with you on purpose, didn't you?" she said suspiciously.

"Maybe."

"Don't try to manipulate me again, Dillon," she said seriously. A new strength seemed to fill her. She probably should thank him for that, but she didn't. She warned instead, "You might win the battle, but I guarantee you'll lose the war."

Rather than looking one bit intimidated, he looked pleased. "Deal," he said.

Unconvinced by the sudden reversal of tactics, she stared into brown eyes that never once wavered. Finally, she nodded and sank back into her chair. She took a long, grateful sip of coffee. Her voice calmer, she asked, "Is that the way advertising is for you? Would you feel empty without it?"

"Sometimes," he said with surprising caution.

"I thought you loved it. Every time you talk about White Stone Electronics you get this spark in your eye, like you can't wait to get back to it. I was envious of that. I want something I care about that much."

"White Stone has made me see how much I've lost by becoming a success."

"Isn't that a contradiction?"

"I don't think so. Not if being a success takes you away from the part of the job you love the most. It's like a teacher who adores working with students suddenly being tapped to be principal. That's success. He's still an educator. But he's no longer in the classroom."

"What does that mean for you?"

"I'm not sure yet. Maybe, like you, I'll find the answers here in Savannah. Are you game?"

With a deeply indrawn breath, she finally nodded. "Where do we start?"

"Let's visit that school. We'll take the rest one step at a time." At her doubtful look, he emphasized, "Both of us."

"Sure," she said at last. "What have I got to lose? A job in a thrift shop that doesn't pay, has no fringe benefits and could be done by any able-bodied adult with a speck of sense. Almost anything would be better than that, right?"

"That's the right attitude," he said approvingly.

"Spunky?" she said with apparent distaste.

Dillon chuckled. "Definitely spunky." He picked up her hand and kissed the palm. "Sexy, too."

The lightest touch of his lips generated the force of an earthquake. Catherine felt the tremor clear down to her toes. Maybe spunky was going to turn out to be all right, after all, she thought as she met Dillon's bold, heated gaze. He winked slowly and her pulse quickened.

Then again, she decided with equal parts regret and anticipation, it was probably just going to get her into trouble.

3

Fourth of July

"What's this?" Beth asked with feigned innocence as she picked up the sheer negligee tossed on Catherine's bed.

Catherine snatched it back. "What does it look like?"

"Pure seduction." Beth settled herself on the bed and turned a curious gaze on Catherine. "Tell me again about this weekend. What does Dillon have in mind?"

"He's rented a cottage at Hilton Head."

"Well, well," she said with gloating approval. "I take it things are working out."

Catherine glared at her friend. "He's a nice man," she declared defensively.

"Did I suggest otherwise? Even if I had, you certainly don't have to justify yourself to me."

"That's right." Noting Beth's increasingly amused expression, Catherine sighed and sank down on the edge of the bed beside her, twisting the sheer negligee fabric into knots. "I sound so self-confident. Why do

I feel as though I'm still a teenager sneaking around behind my parents' backs?"

"Because you haven't mentioned Dillon to your mother," Beth said at once. "Why does that bother you so much? You're way past the age when you should have to account to anyone other than yourself for your actions."

"I know that, but mother is hurt that I won't be spending the holiday with the whole family while they're in North Carolina. She's also convinced that I'm going to sit around here by myself moping. You know how she feels about that sort of self-indulgence."

"Then tell her the truth. Tell her moping is the last thing on your mind these days."

"Beth!"

"Well, it's the truth, isn't it? You're the happiest I've seen you. Maybe it would be good for her to know that there's a new man in your life. She'd stop worrying so much."

"You've got to be kidding. My mother has turned worrying into a full-time profession. No, if I tell her, she'll just ruin it for me. You've seen her in action. She'll have Dad investigating Dillon's credit rating. Then she'll call him herself and invite him to Atlanta for a full-dress inspection. I'm not ready to face all that. I doubt Dillon is, either. He's not the kind of man who'll enjoy being trotted out for a stamp of approval like a hunk of meat."

"Don't you think he'll measure up? From everything you said this man could pass a government security check and the judging for hunk-of-the-month."

"Mother's standards are higher. Even so, Dillon could meet them."

"Then maybe the real issue is that you're afraid to

have him meet your family. The Devereaux clan can be a bit intimidating."

"I doubt that the Ayatollah could have intimidated Dillon. It's just that the timing is all wrong. The whole relationship is still too new. It may not even be anything important. Why subject it to all this outside scrutiny?"

"You don't believe for a single minute that it's unimportant," Beth said with feeling. Catherine stared at her in surprise.

"You sound so sure, far more confident than I do. How come?"

Beth rescued the filmy negligee from Catherine's nervous grasp and waved it in the air. "This. You're far too proper and cautious to be taking along something this provocative if you're not already head over heels in love with the guy."

Beth's observation made her heart thump erratically. "I'm intrigued. I'm hardly in love," she contradicted, ignoring the thumping.

"Intrigued doesn't call for silk and lace. Mad, passionate love calls for silk and lace. Are you trying to convince me you don't have the hots for Dillon?"

Catherine recalled the tender seduction of his lips, the provocative caresses. Heat flooded through her. "I'd say that's a pretty apt description," she admitted ruefully. She gazed at her neighbor beseechingly. "Beth, what am I going to do? I am not the sort of woman to have weekend flings. It goes against everything I was brought up to believe in."

"We're not talking casual sex here. You and Dillon are beginning to care for one another. And there's absolutely nothing wrong with a weekend fling," Beth said staunchly, "especially if it's the natural progression of a meaningful relationship."

Catherine regarded her skeptically. "What pop psychology book was that in?"

"No book. That's from a romantic bill of rights. It's about time you studied them. The next one is don't be late. Finish packing and get out of here. Have yourself a wonderful time. If Dillon can put those sparks in your eyes, then he has to have something pretty special going for him."

From the envious gleam in Beth's eyes, Catherine could tell exactly what her friend thought that something was. And while sex appeal was a very strong part of the attraction, Dillon's kindness and strength were equally important. She could feel herself blossoming under his interest. She'd never felt brighter or more enchanting. She'd never felt more like a woman.

If only their lives weren't so very different. If only they lived in the same place, so the relationship could evolve more naturally. As it was, all this chasing around the country to be together added an unrealistic edge of adventure to the relationship. How well would it hold up under the light of everyday living? Since there was absolutely no way to know that yet, she finally decided to give up making herself crazy over it.

"Thanks, Beth," she said, giving her a hug.

"For what? Just go and have the time of your life. Thinking about your madcap weekend will keep me occupied while I'm folding the stacks of laundry."

Catherine was halfway to the car, when she heard the phone ringing. She tried to justify ignoring it, but she didn't have it in her. She kept imagining a friend in desperate need of someone to talk to, her father being carted off to the hospital, her mother trying one last time to persuade her to come to North Carolina for the long holiday weekend. The last almost kept her right where she was, but the next thing she knew she was fumbling for her house key and running up the front steps.

"It's probably one of those computerized calls for a carpet service," she grumbled under her breath as she yanked up the receiver. "Yes, hello."

"Catherine?"

"Dillon? Is everything okay?"

"Maybe I should be asking you that. You sound breathless."

"I was almost in the car when I heard the phone ringing. My conscience wouldn't let me ignore it."

"For once I owe something to your conscience then."

Her spirits plummeted at his dire tone. "Something is wrong."

"Yes. I'm sorry. I can't get to South Carolina after all."

Catherine tried to swallow her disappointment. "A problem at work?"

"Yes. A client in Los Angeles is thinking of switching firms. The account executive has tried everything short of giving him the next ad campaign free. I tried to find a way around it, but I can't. I have to fly out there."

"Of course you do," she said automatically. "I'll miss seeing you, though. I was looking forward to those walks on the beach you promised."

"So was I," he said, in a voice so thick with emotion that Catherine went still. "We don't have to be apart, though. Come with me to Los Angeles instead. I have a friend who's loaning me his place at Malibu. We can still have those long walks on the beach."

To her amazement, she was actually tempted. Changing plans on a whim had never been one of her strengths. Maybe she'd inherited her rigidity from her mother. Whatever the case, her marriage had only solidified her desire for an orderly existence. For a doctor, Matthew had been amazingly adept at maintaining a schedule. Or perhaps it had only seemed that way because he'd blocked such a huge percentage of his time for work in the first place. Personal plans rarely had to be shifted if they weren't made.

"Do I sense reservations?" Dillon asked.

"Yes."

"Why? We were going to be together. The only thing changing is the location."

"How would I explain that I'm traipsing off to Los Angeles?" She ignored the fact that she hadn't even had the nerve to explain that she was traipsing off to Hilton Head.

"You're thirty-three years old. To whom do you owe an explanation?" he began impatiently, then obviously caught himself. Lightening his tone, he said, "Or is there a jealous lover you haven't mentioned?"

Surprised, Catherine noted the edge of anxiety beneath the banter. "No lovers, Dillon, just a family that is not used to my gallivanting off on my own at the drop of a hat."

"Sounds like a pitiful excuse to me," he said, determinedly maintaining his light tone. She could hear the strain of his effort in his voice. "Maybe it isn't L.A. you're really worried about."

"What's that supposed to mean?" she asked.

"Were you having second thoughts about seeing me again? You sounded fine when we talked the other day."

She couldn't bring herself to admit that he'd hit the nail on the head. She was scared witless at the prospect of a long, romantic weekend alone with him. Though a part of her longed to take Beth's advice and plunge ahead, another part kept shouting caution. "I just told you that I was already out at the car when you called," she responded far too defensively.

"You could have been going out for groceries."

"I was about to drive to Hilton Head. Maybe I still should," she declared stiffly, fully aware that she was trying to pick a fight, but unable to stop herself.

Dillon sighed heavily and backed away from the argument. "No. I'm sorry. I just don't understand why you're so reluctant to do this."

Catherine forced a laugh. "Frankly, neither do I. Habit, I suppose."

"Maybe it's time to break it," he suggested with more gentleness. "Catherine, I really want to spend this weekend with you and I think you want to be with me. Don't let old fears hold you back from taking a step into the future."

Basking in his warmth and his effort to understand, Catherine felt her anxieties begin to fade. Finally, her pulse racing expectantly, she whispered, "Maybe it is time."

Dillon pounced with the acute sensitivity of one who always recognizes subtle shifts in mood. He obviously knew exactly when to press an advantage. No wonder he was one of the top advertising executives in the country. "Then let's do it," he said briskly. "I'll call my travel agent and she'll have a ticket waiting for you at the airport. You can help me seduce this guy into keeping his advertising account right where it is."

"Dillon, I don't know anything about advertising."

"But you do know all about seduction," he teased. "You've had my head spinning ever since we met. Believe me, the techniques are essentially the same."

Despite herself, Catherine felt flattered. "Could be interesting. What do I do if this guy starts suggesting weekend meetings halfway across the country?" she queried innocently, enjoying Dillon's quick growl of displeasure.

"Turn him down," he snapped with what she suspected was only slightly feigned ferocity.

"Maybe he's the type who won't take no for an answer. I hear there are men like that."

She heard his deeply indrawn breath, then, "Wait by the phone. I'll have my travel agent call you about the arrangements, Catherine. We'll discuss this further when I see you."

"Yes, Dillon," she said meekly, but for the first time in years she wasn't feeling meek. She was filled with the satisfaction of knowing that she was able to turn the tables on a man, that her quick-witted responses could taunt and tempt. She felt, finally, like the Southern belle her mother'd been waiting all her life for Catherine to turn into.

The beach at sunset was a sight to behold—vibrant orange and the hottest pink splitting a sky of purest blue. There was no suggestion of the infamous smog to mute the colors.

"Beautiful, isn't it?" Dillon said, putting his arms

around her from behind as she watched the waves wash over the wide stretch of beach.

"Glorious."

"Glad you came?"

She nodded.

"Me, too. I only wish we didn't have to go to this dinner. I'd much rather spend the evening out here with you, listening to the tide roll in and drinking champagne."

"Nice thought, but champagne makes me sneeze," she said. "The first time it happened, my parents were horrified. They wouldn't believe that a daughter of theirs had no tolerance for one of the finer things in life. They made my wedding hell because they insisted on serving champagne. I could have avoided it, I suppose, but everyone kept offering toasts and Matthew kept handing me a glass. By the end of the reception my nose was red and my eyes were watering." She giggled at the memory. "I figure it served him right that in all the pictures the bride looked as if she was just recovering from the flu."

"I'll bet you didn't laugh about it then," Dillon said.

She glanced up over her shoulder. "What makes you say that?"

"I'm sure you counted on everything being perfect to please your parents and your husband. Causing them even such a tiny embarrassment probably spoiled the whole day for you."

She turned in his arms and rested her hands on his shoulders. Her eyes were almost even with his. She felt as if he could see though to her soul. "You're amazing."

"I know," he said immodestly, his lips tilting in amusement.

"Stop it. I mean it. No one else saw how I felt."

"Probably because they were too worried about appearances and their own feelings."

"I'm painting an awful picture of my family, aren't I? They're really not like that. They just want what's best for me. The Devereaux have always maintained a certain life-style and my mother's family was doubly concerned with tradition. You can imagine what sort of monster a merger of the two families created."

Dillon shook his head and pressed his lips to her forehead. "No, sweetheart. That's not what I see at all. They created you, didn't they? For that I owe them my undying gratitude."

Catherine melted at the sweet sincerity of Dillon's words and the genuine appreciation in his eyes. "No one has ever said anything so beautiful to me before," she said, blinking back tears. One escaped and Dillon brushed it away with the tip of his finger.

"I will never grow tired of saying things like that to you," he promised. "I mean it, Catherine. You're just beginning to discover how much you have to offer. I hope when you fully realize your worth, you'll still want me in your life."

"I think I will always want you in my life," she said slowly, her heart suddenly filled to overflowing with tenderness and gratitude and something far deeper, an emotion so overwhelming she was awed by its intensity.

Dillon's mouth covered hers, capturing her breath, sharing his. In that passionate mingling a commitment was born, a commitment that she wasn't at all sure she was ready to make, but one that was undeniably real.

When her knees were weak and her body ablaze, he finally pulled away.

"If we keep this up, we'll never get to dinner and I will lose that account," he said, his breath coming in harsh, ragged bursts. Brown eyes devoured her, the look every bit as hot and uncompromising as the kiss had been. "It would almost be worth it."

"This must be a very big account," Catherine said shakily, trying to insert a note of teasing into the throbbing sensuality that had caught them both in its grasp.

"The biggest. An entire film studio."

She stepped back. "We're having dinner with some movie mogul?"

"The hottest studio head in L.A. He's a little rough around the edges, but he's had three blockbusters in a row. We've been working on polishing up his image."

Despite the headiness of Dillon's kiss, she couldn't ignore the edge of excitement spawned by his announcement. "Let's go then," she said at once.

"Wait a minute," he said. "You're throwing me over for some Hollywood type?"

"I'm not throwing you over. I'm just trying to help you with business," she said primly.

"Right. And I suppose the first actor you spot, you'll swoon."

"It is a southern tradition for the ladies to faint when their senses are overwrought."

"Lady, I will be the only man playing havoc with your senses tonight."

She grinned at him. "Promises, promises," she said daringly. The look in Dillon's eyes was headier than any champagne…and it definitely didn't make her feel like sneezing.

* * *

Dillon thoroughly enjoyed watching Catherine's reaction to Ruben Prunelli. The studio chief was short
and at least thirty pounds overweight. Wisps of un-
tamed gray hair stood out in every direction. Not even a
top Hollywood stylist and a container of mousse could
have tamed it. He talked in short, blunt bursts, punctu-
ated by gestures with his smelly cigar. Dillon had always admired the man's straightforward no-nonsense
style, his refusal to compromise. Catherine seemed
taken aback by the lack of polish, which was exactly
the problem Prunelli had come to him to correct. She
clearly hated the cigar. Every time it passed over his
dinner plate, she winced. Dillon recognized the precise moment when she decided not to take it anymore.

"Excuse me, Mr. Prunelli," she said briskly, taking
the cigar with a dainty, but determined move. He appeared too startled to object. "You don't really want
to spoil your dinner with this, do you?"

A waiter was at her elbow to take the offending
cigar at once. Dillon chuckled at Ruben's expression
of bemusement as his expensive cigar vanished in a
cloud of smoke.

"I'm sure your veal will taste much better now," she
said, smiling demurely at him.

"Veal was just fine as it was," Ruben grumbled.

Catherine's smile remained fixed in place. "Mine
wasn't."

"Never thought about that," Ruben said, turning to
Dillon. "Why didn't you speak up, man? You know
I don't pay attention to the social niceties. Too busy
to pay attention. It's up to you to fix my image. Can't

make any money producing those damned family films, if the public thinks I'm a low-class lout."

"You're absolutely right, Mr. Prunelli," Catherine said smoothly, before Dillon could even begin to gather his composure. He had to keep swallowing back his laughter.

"But you're obviously a very smart man," she said. "If you really put yourself into Dillon's hands, instead of just paying lip service to his advice, I'm sure he could turn around your image in no time. You might start by not referring to your movies as those *damned family films*. They're really quite good. I've taken my nieces and nephews to all of them."

Dillon finally found his voice. "She's right, Ruben. If you don't respect your product, why should anyone else?"

Prunelli appeared stunned by the barrage of criticism. Catherine was right, though. He was a smart man. Dillon could see the information being quickly absorbed. "Send me a plan," he barked. "By next Friday. If I like it, we'll keep you."

He pulled another cigar out of his pocket. Catherine's nose wrinkled in disgust and Prunelli chuckled. "Don't worry. I'm not going to light up 'til I get out of here."

She looked aghast. "But Mr. Prunelli, you've barely touched your meal. I hope you're not upset."

"Never finish," he said. "I'm taking three more meetings tonight. Can't eat four whole meals in one night. You two stay. Enjoy your dinner. It's on me."

He pumped Dillon's hand vigorously. "Keep her, Ryan. She's a breath of fresh air. Too damn many fakes out here."

When he was gone, Dillon turned his amused gaze on Catherine. She was looking miserable. Absolutely mortified. He'd never been prouder.

"I can't believe how rude I was," she said with a moan. "I just yanked that man's cigar out of his hand."

"He loved it. He's surrounded by sycophants. He meant what he said. Your honesty is refreshing. You kept the account for us. He knows the advertising was producing results, but the press was having a field day with him personally. You pointed out why."

"But I could have blown it. I didn't think. I just acted."

"Like a lady. Besides, it would have been worth it to see that look on his face. Now, let's stop talking about Ruben Prunelli and his smelly cigars. I have plans for the two of us for tonight...and tomorrow... and Sunday."

At the quick flaring of heat in Catherine's eyes, he felt a throbbing tension begin in his own abdomen. If he hadn't known it before, he did now: she was a woman who belonged by his side. Together they could accomplish anything. With her in his arms, he could reach heaven.

He held out his hand. "Shall we go?"

"No dessert for you, either?" she said, her voice suddenly tremulous.

"At home," he responded. "We'll share dessert at home."

Catherine's pulse raced as nervous anticipation sped through her. The drive to the beachfront cottage seemed interminable.

And far too short.

By the time they walked through the front door, she thought she'd die if Dillon didn't kiss her. Instead, he simply took her hand.

"Let's go for that walk on the beach. We've already delayed it far too long," he said.

The velvet night wrapped itself around them as they walked hand in hand along the cooling sand. Waves battered the shore, echoing the pounding of Catherine's heart. She shivered and Dillon stopped, pulling her into his arms.

"Cold?"

The shudders abated and she sighed. "Not with you holding me like this."

"Then I won't let you go," he whispered huskily. Catherine lifted her gaze to meet his and what she saw in his eyes made her go weak with longing. Such obvious masculine appreciation. So much love.

"Catherine…" he began, then abandoned the thought. His lips molded themselves over hers—gentle, persuasive lips that robbed her of breath and filled her with joy. A fierce hunger began to build inside her, a need so primal, so intense that she swayed against him, seeking his warmth, aching for the feel of his bare skin next to hers. The desire was so all consuming, she was shaken by its force. Never had her body burned so. Never had she been so captivated by a touch.

Dillon's fingers traced the arch of her back, the curve of her hip. She moaned in response, alive as she'd never been before.

"Let's go inside," Dillon said.

"No," she whispered, her lips pressed to his neck. The skin was on fire, every bit as hot as her own. "Here, Dillon. Make love to me here. Now."

He opened his mouth to object, but she sealed off the argument with an urgent, demanding kiss that left them both trembling. Her fingers fumbled with the buttons of his shirt, then tugged it free of his pants. He groaned as she caressed the bare flesh of his chest. For one instant, she was startled by her own abandon, terrified by it, but then she was lost to the feelings, awash in sensation.

"You should have satin sheets and candlelight," Dillon murmured apologetically as he freed her breasts from the lacy bra.

"Starlight is better." In starlight, he wouldn't see her fear. Under the night sky, he wouldn't know the power of his touches. With the crash of the waves as background, perhaps he wouldn't hear the whimpers of pleasure that even now were building and building inside her. Matthew had never made her feel like this, never made her forget that she was a lady. In Dillon's arms she was discovering that she was a wanton, that there was a sensuality buried deep inside her that pulsed and burned and cried out for fulfillment. The hunger terrified her...and drew her inevitably.

Responding to her bold touches, Dillon stripped away the last of her clothes. For one awestruck moment, he stared at her and in his eyes she saw herself as a complete woman. She held out her arms and the last of Dillon's gentleness fled. His caresses became more intimate, his lips more possessive, his skin more beaded with sweat. His muscles quivered beneath her deep strokes until at last he sank to the sand, pulling her down on top of him.

She saw the flaring of passion in his dark-as-midnight eyes as he moved deep inside her. Once. Then again. Slowly and tantalizingly. Until there was nothing but the roar of the ocean and Dillon and the hot, urgent feelings that consumed and swelled and finally shattered inside her.

In that moment, Catherine knew she was lost. She knew that for however long it lasted, she would treasure what she had found with Dillon. It promised to be one hell of a ride.

4

Labor Day Weekend

Catherine felt as though she were under siege. Dillon and her mother—two of the most unreasonable people she'd ever met—were coming at her from opposite directions. Her mother was emphatic about Catherine joining the whole family in North Carolina for the holiday weekend. Dillon was being just as pigheaded about finally getting away for that long-postponed weekend at Hilton Head. He sounded more tense and short-tempered than she'd ever heard him.

"What would you think about changing our plans for this weekend?" she asked cautiously.

"You can't be serious. I haven't seen you since July. As it is, I'm shuffling appointments right and left to make this work. I've made the reservations in Hilton Head and I have the plane ticket. I'm leaving New York in a few hours. Now's a hell of a time to talk about changing."

Catherine glanced anxiously toward the living room, then finally rolled her eyes. "You're right. I've been looking forward to it, too. Let's leave things the way we planned them."

There was a long pause before he finally said, "Are you sure? You aren't running scared on me, are you?"

She heard the concern, the quick shift to put her needs first. "No," she reassured him. "It's nothing like that. I'm as anxious to see you again as I ever was."

"Then we're all set. You have my flight number. Be sure to check on it so you don't end up waiting around at the airport in Savannah half the day."

"I'll check," she promised.

"Gotta run. I'll see you tonight, sweetheart. I can't wait."

"Bye, Dillon."

Catherine replaced the receiver and stood where she was for several minutes, before gathering the strength to face her mother again. She took a deep breath, then went back into the parlor where Lucinda Devereaux was just finishing her morning coffee.

"I'm sorry," she told her. "My plans can't be changed, after all."

Blue eyes sparkled with maternal indignation. "Now, dear, don't be stubborn. Nothing is that important. I'm sure you could make other arrangements for whatever it is that you have planned."

"I don't want to make other arrangements, Mother. I'm looking forward to going to Hilton Head." That was quite possibly the most incredible understatement of her life. After being in Dillon's arms at last, she could hardly wait to have them around her again. The past few weeks without him had been incredibly empty. How could a city she'd lived in all her life suddenly be so lonely? Long-distance phone calls, no matter how frequent, didn't take the place of his touches or those darkly passionate looks that made her melt inside.

"What on earth is in Hilton Head, of all places?" her mother demanded in a tone suggesting that, despite its long-running popularity with the rich, the resort was still far too new to be considered an appropriate destination. Moreover, Lucinda Devereaux was not used to being crossed, especially by her eldest daughter. Catherine had always been docile and accommodating. Obviously it was a habit she'd taken far too long to break.

"A man," she blurted before she could think of the consequences. "I'm going there to meet a man."

Shock registered on her mother's still lovely, aristocratic features. "What man? Catherine, what on earth has come over you?"

"Nothing has *come over* me, Mother. I met someone. I've been seeing him for a while now. We're going to spend the holiday in Hilton Head and that's that." She was very proud of the firm tone of defiance, though she didn't hold out much hope that her mother would simply roll over and play dead.

"Do we know this man?"

"No. He's not from Atlanta."

As expected, her mother appeared scandalized by that news. "Then how did you meet him?"

"We met when I went to Savannah last year."

"Then he lives in Savannah," she said, looking relieved. "I know some lovely families in Savannah. Perhaps I know him, after all."

"No, Mother. He was just there on business. He lives in New York."

"Dear heavens!" Her mother sank back against the sofa and waved a handkerchief in front of her face.

Catherine didn't buy the convenient attack of the vapors for a second. Sure enough, when she failed to respond, her mother sat up straighter and said with the force of a regal decree, "You must bring this man to North Carolina, then. That's all there is to it. I won't have you racing about to keep some sordid rendezvous with a stranger."

Catherine drew herself up with quiet dignity, proving that she was every inch her mother's daughter. "He is not a stranger to me and there is nothing sordid about it," she retorted. "No matter what you think, though, I absolutely refuse to spend what little time we have together parading him out for review."

Her mother's gaze was penetrating. A month ago or even a week ago, Catherine would have cringed under that look. Not now. Since knowing Dillon, she had grown stronger, more confident in her own decisions. "Are you ashamed of him?" her mother demanded. "Is he not suitable for a Devereaux?"

"His suitability is not the issue! He's a fine man."

"Then it must be us."

Catherine groaned. "Don't be ridiculous. I am not ashamed of anyone. If my relationship with Dillon appears to be turning into something permanent, then I assure you I will bring him home so that you can cross-examine him to your heart's content. Until then, I will handle this in my own way. Have a lovely holiday, Mother. Give everyone my love."

She dutifully kissed her mother's cheek, then spun around and left the room before her stunned mother could react. Catherine wasn't sure she could have withstood a full-fledged assault. Her mother was a master at instilling guilt and Catherine was still far too new at resisting. Only the prospect of having Dillon all to herself on a secluded beach had kept her strong. She wondered what it was going to take to brace her for the moment when she told her mother she was planning to start spending weekdays in Savannah going back to college...and seeing Dillon every chance he got to fly down.

She had finally gone through the Savannah College of Art and Design catalog after she'd gotten back from Los Angeles. In those first few days after her return, she'd felt as though she could conquer the world. A second college degree—this time in a subject of her own choosing—had seemed like a snap. She'd driven to Savannah on a Thursday, planning to meet Dillon for one night, only to discover on her arrival that he'd had to fly to Chicago instead. Though she'd been bitterly disappointed, she'd used the time to go by the school and enroll.

Then, as if to prove her commitment, she'd immediately searched for and found a small apartment in a carriage house. She'd been enchanted by the light that flooded in the high windows, the promising, but untended rooms and the old furniture that had been cast aside with such neglect. She had planned to tell Dillon about her decision when they'd talked later that night, but instead she'd held the secret as a surprise.

Catherine decided that she would tell him when they arrived in Hilton Head. Maybe they would even drive back into Savannah one day so he could see the apartment. Just in case, she dropped off a bottle of his favorite wine and stocked the refrigerator with food before going to pick him up.

At the airport in Savannah, she found herself pacing impatiently. The arrival board said his flight was on time, but she was so eager to be in his arms again, the minutes seemed to crawl by.

When he arrived at last, she was shocked by his appearance. He looked utterly exhausted. His rugged features were haggard, his eyes dull and lifeless until they came to rest on her. Then they brightened ever so slightly and his lips curved into a beguiling, tender smile.

"You are definitely a sight for sore eyes," he said, dropping his suitcase and pulling her into his arms. Catherine nestled against his chest and hugged him tightly.

"You, on the other hand, look like hell," she said bluntly, studying him with concern. "Bad week?"

"Lousy weeks," he said, emphasizing the plural.

She was astounded and admittedly a little hurt that he hadn't shared his problems with her. "But you didn't let on when we talked."

"The last thing I wanted to discuss on the phone was business," he murmured. "God, it feels good to hold you again."

Catherine was struck by a sudden brainstorm. It was late. Dillon was beat. Why should they drive all the way to Hilton Head when she had this wonderful apartment right here? "Let's get out of here and go someplace where you can hold me properly," she suggested.

"Improperly was more what I had in mind."

She grinned at him. "Me, too," she said with heartfelt enthusiasm.

In the car, Dillon's eyes drifted closed at once. Glancing over at him, she watched his struggle to keep them open. He stared out the window, then frowned.

"This isn't the way," he protested when she turned onto the highway into downtown Savannah.

"I know," she said, her eyes directed straight ahead.

The silence that greeted her response was so long, she finally glanced in his direction. He was wide-awake and regarding her curiously. "What do you have in mind, Catherine Devlin?"

"You'll see," she said, thoroughly enjoying the unexpected chance to be mysterious.

When she pulled up in front of a stately old house facing one of Savannah's many squares, Dillon's curiosity turned to obvious dismay. "Catherine, please. I'm too tired to go visiting."

"We're not going visiting."

"What is this, then? One of those bed-and-breakfast places? I hate that. There's not enough privacy."

"Have a little faith, mister. Grab your bag and follow me."

After a lengthy pause in which he seemed to be considering her rare display of bossy teasing, he gave a resigned shrug and took his suitcase out of the back seat. Catherine led the way through a yard filled with the heavy scent of roses in full bloom. A side path, lit by old-fashioned gas lamps, wound around to the back, where the old brick carriage house sat at the end of an overgrown cobbled drive.

"Who lives here?" Dillon asked, regarding the building with a critical eye.

"Do you like it?"

"It has a lot of charm. Whose is it?"

"Mine," she said, watching his eyes. They widened in surprise as they met hers.

"Ours," she said hesitantly. "That is, if you want it

to be. I mean for whenever we can meet here. What do you think? Dillon, say something."

A slow smile began to play about his lips. "You bought this place?"

She shook her head. "I rented it. It was cheap. It's been fixed up some, but there's still work to be done. They agreed to keep the rent down, if I'd do some of the restoration. The college sent me over."

Suddenly his arms were around her again and he was swinging her in the air. "You enrolled!"

Laughing, she nodded. For the first time the decision seemed real. For the first time she allowed her excitement to show. Once she began telling him, the words spilled out. "I start classes this fall. I'll probably only stay here during the week. I'll need to get back to Atlanta on the weekends to make sure the house there is kept up and to do all the family things. I've cut back on my committees, but there were a few I was committed to helping. I can catch up on all that on weekends, too. What do you think?"

"I think you're wonderful. I am so proud of you."

The expression in his eyes wiped away the last traces of doubt. She lifted her hand and touched the tired lines on his face, lines that had almost, but not quite vanished in his enthusiasm for her decision. "Want to stay here with me this weekend?" she whispered. "There's food in the house. We wouldn't have that long drive. It would be like really living together, even if it is just for a few days. This will be the first place that will be ours together."

"You haven't stayed here?"

"Not yet. I was waiting for you. I wanted to share my first night here with you."

His eyes darkened with some emotion she couldn't identify. Pleasure. Passion. A vague hint of laughter. "You weren't planning to go to Hilton Head at all, were you?"

"Of course I was," she insisted indignantly, then wondered herself if that was the truth. "I just thought maybe we could stop here on the way back. I didn't get the idea for staying until I saw how exhausted you looked. What do you think?"

"I think we never will get that weekend in Hilton Head." He took her hand. "Let's go inside, so I can greet you properly."

She shook her head as she clasped his hand more tightly. "You promised me improper. I'm going to hold you to it."

Catherine was finally in her element. Dillon could tell as he watched her at work in the tiny kitchen. Wonderful aromas were emanating from the oven. She was humming under her breath. Though the apartment was furnished haphazardly, every piece of furniture in it gleamed. A bowl filled with roses sat in the middle of the tiny dining room table. Awed by her knack at creating a homey ambiance so quickly, he wondered briefly if he'd been wrong to push her to return to school. Still, she seemed happy about her decision. For the moment, he'd have to take her enthusiasm at face value.

He came up behind her and slid his arms around her waist.

"I'd rather have you than dinner," he said, nibbling on her ear. She smelled of lavender, a scent far more subtle than what she usually wore and twice as enchanting.

She squirmed against him in a half-hearted attempt to get away. The movement was maddeningly provocative.

"When was the last time you ate a proper dinner?"

"About as long ago as the last time I had you in my arms."

"Food first," she said staunchly, though he could tell from the shiver that ran through her that she was just as hungry as he was to experience that rare joy they had found together in Los Angeles.

When dinner was on the table, she watched every bite he put in his mouth. The close attention began to nag at him.

"More green beans?" she offered.

"No."

"How about more chicken?"

He shook his head. "If I eat any more chicken, I'll start clucking." He reached over and took her hand. "Sweetheart, you don't need to fuss over me. I'm all grown up."

Though his reproach had been mild, she looked as if he'd slapped her. Dillon felt like a heel. That quick flash of hurt in her eyes wiped away his impatience. "Catherine, I didn't mean that I don't appreciate what you've done. The dinner was wonderful."

"What's so wrong about my wanting to fix you a nice meal for a change?" she said stiffly.

"Nothing. I'm just not used to anyone worrying about me. And I'm definitely cranky. Everyone at work is ready to quit if I don't come back in a better mood. Don't you turn tail and run out on me, too."

She sighed and that awful look in her eyes began to fade away. "I'm not about to run out on you," she said finally. "But, Dillon, the last thing I want to do is smother you."

"You're not smothering me. I really am sorry if I sounded as if you were. Now come around here. I've eaten my vegetables and I'd very much like dessert."

"I baked an apple pie."

"It'll keep. I have something much healthier in mind."

Catherine came around to sit in his lap. Though her arms were around his shoulders, she was holding herself so rigidly that Dillon knew at once that she was still hurting from his unthinking criticism. He'd waited weeks for this moment, weeks longer than he'd anticipated and he ached from the loneliness of it. Though he'd worked harder than ever during their separation, for once his career hadn't blocked all other thoughts from his mind. Always there had been the memory of Catherine taunting him. Now he'd spoiled their reunion by taking his lousy mood out on her.

"Forgive me," he whispered in her ear. A sigh shuddered through her. She nodded finally and her arms tightened around him.

"Then show me," he pleaded. "I've missed you so much. I haven't been able to concentrate on anything. And at night, after we'd talk, I'd lie awake for hours wishing you were there with me, so I could touch you. Here." His fingers stroked the fullness of her lips. "And here." He circled the tip of her breast, thrilling as it responded to his touch. "You've missed me, too?"

"I thought I'd die from loneliness," she admitted, her fingers already at work on the buttons of his shirt. Her lips found the hard-throbbing pulse at the base of his neck, lingering, teasing his flesh with her tongue, then leaving it to cool it the sultry air.

Dillon's arousal was swift and urgent. His breath snagged as her hands began to stroke and caress his shoulders, then his back and finally his bared stomach. "Catherine, sweetheart," he began, then moaned with pleasure. "Catherine!"

"Hmm?"

"Do you suppose, just this once, we could actually get as far as the bedroom?"

"How utterly boring," she taunted, her blue eyes smoky with passion. "But if you insist...."

He lifted her into his arms. "I'm afraid I do. If we make love on the dining room floor, that is where I'm very likely to spend the night. Tomorrow I'll have aches and pains in muscles I'd forgotten existed."

"I'd be happy to massage them for you," she said generously.

"I'm tempted," he admitted, noting the wicked gleam in her eyes. "But all things considered, I'm opting for bed. I promise to try very hard to keep it from being boring for you...."

"Where did you learn that?" she asked a few minutes later, gasping for breath.

Dillon grinned. "Unless you've been married to a man for forty years, I'm not sure it's a good idea to ask him where he learned how to make love. Unless, of course, you're really angling to discover his past sexual history. Did you want references for this?" he inquired as he stroked and teased in a way that left her writhing beneath him.

"No," she whispered raggedly. "Just don't stop."

"Not even for this?" he taunted. "Or this?"

Catherine gasped again, then arched into his touch. Whispering his name, her eyes wide with surprise, she trembled beneath him. His own body aching for release, he watched as hers slowly began to relax again.

A tear slid down her cheek as she touched his face. "Why?" she asked.

"A gift," he said. "I wanted you to know how much I love you."

A second tear clung to her dark lashes, then rolled down her cheek. "Oh, Dillon," she whispered, her hands tangling in the hairs on his chest. "I love you, too. You've already given me so much. You've given me back my self-confidence. I'll never forget that."

She moved until her long, shapely leg was draped over his thigh and they were laying hip to hip. Her heat was as alluring as any flame and he found himself seeking it, reaching for the hottest center. There was little finesse to her movements, just an instinctive sharing, an overwhelming desire to enhance his excitement. She asked with anxious eyes and then she gave, urging him higher than he'd ever been before, crying out with him when they reached the top. It was a cry of exultation, of joy and of love.

When Catherine finally woke up in the morning, Dillon's place in bed was cold and empty. She glanced at the bedside clock. It was barely seven-thirty. For a moment, she panicked, wondering if he'd left, wondering if she hadn't been forgiven for last night's tension after all. Then she smelled the aroma of coffee brewing and heard the pop-up sound of the toaster. After several minutes, when there was still no sign of Dillon, she got up and pulled on her robe before padding barefooted into the kitchen.

She found Dillon seated at the kitchen table, papers spread all over, a cup of coffee and a plate of partially eaten toast beside him. He was wearing jeans, but no shirt or shoes. He looked impossibly sexy and every bit as tired as he had the previous night. She wanted to yell at him, to tell him he was killing himself, but had learned a bitter lesson the night before. He wouldn't appreciate it. She bit her tongue and simply dropped a kiss on his forehead as she passed by on her way to the coffeepot.

"Good morning," he murmured distractedly. "You're up early."

"I missed you. What time did you get up?"

"About six, I guess. My mind started turning over all this work I have to do, so I figured I might as well get started."

"I thought this was a holiday."

"It is. I'm not in the office."

"That's a lousy definition of a holiday," she said, struggling to keep her tone bantering. "Want some breakfast?"

"I had coffee and toast."

"No eggs? Bacon? Maybe French toast?"

"Nothing, really. I won't be able to relax until I get this done." His smile was apologetic, but his eyes were distracted.

Catherine nodded finally. "I'll leave you to it, then."

"Thanks," he murmured, but he was already absorbed again by what he was doing.

Catherine took a shower, then dressed in shorts and a T-shirt. She stood in the doorway of the kitchen and announced, "I'm going for a walk. Can I bring you anything?"

He glanced up, his gaze lingering appreciatively on her bare legs. "I wish I were going with you."

"Then come. It might relax you. You'll get even more done when you get back."

For an instant, he looked tempted, but then that familiar determined look came into his eyes and he shook his head. "Sorry, sweetheart. Not now. Maybe after dinner."

"Fine," she said, once again choking off her concern. How long could he continue with this sort of demanding pace? She had been able to delude herself on their past meetings that though Dillon was a self-avowed workaholic, he did permit himself some moments of release. Now she wondered. Had their previous meetings really been all that carefree? For the most part they'd been hurried. Only in Los Angeles had he seemed to relax once their meeting with Ruben Prunelli was over. Was her ability to distract him fading already or was it simply that Dillon was so compulsive about his work that no woman could ever compete for long? Certainly it had cost him his marriage. He'd already admitted that much.

Feeling every bit as lonely as she had during the weeks when Dillon had been in New York, Catherine walked until well past lunchtime. Only when she was practically starving did she return to the apartment. Dillon's papers were still strewn over the table, but he was on the sofa, a dictating machine in his hand, a thick report on his stomach. He was sound asleep, snoring softly, the tired lines in his face finally relaxed.

Catherine bent over him and smoothed his brow.

"Oh, Dillon, how is this ever going to work? We're not even together when we're in the same room."

He sighed at the sound of her voice and stirred slightly, then settled more comfortably on the sofa. Catherine left him to sleep, while she ate her lunch. Then she began fixing dinner. She chose one of her favorite recipes, a complicated one which required endless chopping and mincing and stirring. It kept her hands busy, but unfortunately not her mind. The thoughts that tumbled about like colors in a kaleidoscope weren't nearly so pretty.

By the time Dillon awoke she knew that they were going to have to talk about the way he was working himself to death and, just as important, the way he was shutting her out. When he came into the kitchen, though, sleepy-eyed and contrite and loving, her doubts and criticisms slid away.

It became the pattern for the rest of the weekend: enchanting evenings, tumultuous lovemaking and then long empty hours of mental, if not physical, separation. It was their final morning together before she found the courage to confront him.

"Dillon, how do you feel about this weekend?"

He regarded her blankly. "It was wonderful. I loved being here with you."

"That's just it. You weren't with me. For all the time we really spent together, you might just as well have been in your office in New York."

"But I wasn't. I was here, even though it probably would have made more sense for me to stay up there. I came because I missed you, because I wanted to be with you. Why are you just bringing this up now? We've had the whole weekend and you haven't complained once. I thought you understood. Now, just when I'm ready to leave for the airport, you tell me that you've been miserable."

"I know. I should have said something sooner. I was trying to understand, but the truth of the matter is that I don't. Or maybe I do. Maybe you're more like Matthew than I thought. Maybe you like having a woman around for convenience, but don't want to make the effort necessary to keep the relationship alive."

His jaw tightened at the reference to Matthew. "I am not your ex-husband and I do not regard you as a convenience. I love you," he said angrily, yanking up the phone.

"What are you doing?"

"Calling a cab."

"I'll take you to the airport."

"I think not. I think it would be better if you stayed here and thought about what a real relationship is like."

"And you?" she countered furiously. "What are you going to be thinking about? Work?"

"Yes, dammit. I'm going to think about work. It gives me enough money to go where I want and to be with a woman I love, a woman I thought was starting to love me." He stomped through the front door, leaving Catherine to stare after him, openmouthed and trembling.

It was only after her fury had died down, after the loneliness had set in worse than ever, that she began to think about what he'd said. Never once all weekend had she asked him what he was working on. Never once had she wondered if there was some serious problem that demanded all of his energy. She'd been far too concerned with her own sense of loss, her own conviction that once again she was involved with a man with whom she'd come second.

It was going to be three or four endless hours before she could call Dillon in New York, an eternity before she could try to talk this out without anger and recriminations. She turned on the news which featured several holiday features. Labor Day. She lifted her glass of wine in a solemn toast to the occasion.

The phone rang as she was contemplating the irony. Her heart skipped a beat. Only Dillon had this number.

"Yes," she answered shakily.

"It's Dillon."

"Where are you?"

"Someplace over Virginia, I think. There's a phone on the plane. I called to say I'm sorry."

"No, I'm the one who's sorry. I shouldn't have added to your stress."

"And I shouldn't have shut you out. Want to try this again in a couple of weeks and see if we can get it right?"

Catherine felt a wave of relief sigh through her. The familiar pins-and-needles excitement began again. "Absolutely."

"I'm glad. I'll call you again when I get home."

"I'll be waiting."

Forever, she thought as she hung up. If that's what it took for them to make a life together, she would wait forever.

5

Oktoberfest

It was nearly midnight by the time Dillon finally called Catherine back. She was still sitting up in bed, half-asleep, trying not to worry and already beset by loneliness.

"Sorry to call so late," he murmured in the familiar low tone that sent her pulse racing. "Were you asleep?"

"Almost." She curled up and held the phone tighter, as if that would bring him closer. "What happened? There wasn't a problem with the plane, was there?"

"No, nothing like that. I stopped by the office. My assistant was there trying to resolve a crisis. Before I knew it the night was shot."

Catherine felt a chill creep through her at his words. So much for good intentions. She sat up just a little straighter. "Are you home now?"

"Yes. I just got here. I wish I were still there with you, though. I miss you already. I wish I'd had one last kiss to think about, instead of all those harsh words."

"Me, too," she said in a voice thick with regret. "Any idea when you can come back?"

"Actually, I did have one idea. I was reading an article in the in-flight magazine about Oktoberfest in Savannah. It's one of those first Saturday things they do down on the waterfront. We could drink beer and eat sausages and maybe dance a polka or two. How about it?"

She could tell he was trying to make amends, trying to prove to her that the next visit would be different, that they would have more time together. No matter how many doubts she had that he could change, she owed the relationship that chance. "Oktoberfest in Savannah, huh? It may not be Munich, but it sounds like fun. I'm up for it, if you are."

"I wish I could get back there sooner, but the way my calendar looks, it's not likely." His voice dropped seductively. "Will you keep my spot warm?"

"Absolutely," she said, rubbing her hand across the pillow that was still fragrant with the scent of him.

"Good night, sweetheart. I'll dream about you."

"I'll dream about you, too," she said softly. And count the days until Oktoberfest, she thought as she finally turned out the light and pulled his pillow into her arms.

As it turned out, the days flew by for once. Her classes began and were far more demanding and twice as exciting as she'd anticipated. She spent long hours after class talking with her fellow students and her professors. Dillon had been right. They did tend to look at her as a natural leader because of her experience. She basked in the mental stimulation. It was like being exposed to sunshine after a long, dreary winter.

She had to force herself to go back to Atlanta on the weekends and face her mother's frowning disapproval. Her father made the trips bearable. Though he seemed somewhat bemused by her decision, he quietly gave her his support.

"You finish that program and we'll start looking around Atlanta for a worthwhile project," he said, ignoring his wife's scowl. "Maybe it's time I gave something back to this city by saving one of those fancy old buildings."

Pleased, Catherine threw her arms around him. "Dad, thank you for understanding."

"It's good to see you find your own purpose in life," he said, amazing her with his perceptiveness. "What about that young man your mother tells me you've been hiding from us? How does he feel about this?"

"He's the one who urged me to go back to school. I think he's really happy for me. We talk every day and he's coming down from New York next weekend."

Her mother looked up at that and her frown of displeasure grew. "We'll finally meet him, then?"

Catherine winced at having opened up an all-too-familiar can of worms. "Not really. He's coming to Savannah. We thought we'd go to Oktoberfest."

"Catherine!"

"What?" she said, her expression deliberately blank, though she knew exactly why her mother had reacted the way she had.

"That's so common."

"Mother, really," she said, unable to prevent a laugh. "It should be fun. Maybe you and Dad should drive down."

Her mother looked horrified, but there was a glint

of amusement in her father's eyes as he said, "What about it, Lucinda? As I recall, there was a time when we could do a pretty mean polka."

Her mother flushed prettily. "If you think I'm going to swill beer and dance in the streets at my age, you have another think coming, Rawley Devereaux. Besides, we have theater tickets next weekend. We couldn't possibly go to Savannah."

Catherine sighed. "Maybe next time then. I really do want you to come down and see my apartment."

"It is hardly *your* apartment," her mother objected. "It belongs to some landlord. I really don't see why you insist on living like some transient."

"Would you rather I had bought a house in Savannah?"

"Of course not. You have a perfectly good house here in Atlanta."

"I can hardly commute from Atlanta to Savannah on a daily basis."

"You don't need to commute at all."

Catherine turned to her father and gave a helpless shrug.

"Don't mind her," her father said. "She hates having her chicks leave the nest."

Catherine regarded him and then her mother in astonishment. "But I left the nest when I married Matthew."

Her father grinned and patted her mother's hand consolingly. "Ah, but she thought you might come back after the divorce."

"I did not," her mother denied hotly, but the pink tint in her cheeks said otherwise. "I know perfectly well that Catherine is a grown woman now and has every right to make her own decisions. If she wants to live in somebody's garage, I suppose that's her business."

"I'll remind you of that, Mother."

To her amazement, there was a twinkle in her mother's eyes as she said mildly, "Yes, dear. I'm sure you will."

At the airport on Friday, Catherine studied Dillon's expression and determined that he looked decidedly guilty. She regarded his luggage suspiciously, then poked at his briefcase. "How much work is hidden in there?"

"Hardly anything," he vowed, though he didn't quite meet her gaze.

She gestured toward the carry-on suitcase. "And in there?"

"Nothing."

"Then why do I get the feeling that this weekend is going to be very much like the last one we spent here together?"

"Because, unfortunately, you are a very intuitive woman."

"Oh, Dillon."

"It's not so much the paperwork this time," he said, his attitude so determinedly cheerful that Catherine's fears mounted.

"What then?"

"Ruben."

Her stomach plummeted. "Pruneface?"

"Prunelli. He has a big public appearance coming up and he needs my assistance to prepare himself for it. He's getting an award for his contribution to the trend bringing back family pictures."

"Who on earth's giving it to him?"

"Catherine, he has made a contribution. There were three pictures in a row that no one else would take a chance on. Everyone thought the market for G-rated pictures was too soft. He turned them into box-office blockbusters."

"Okay, I won't try to take that away from him, but what about *Ninja Chaos* or whatever it is that came out last week? Now there is a really high-class piece of filmmaking. At least fourteen people had been killed or maimed before the opening credits finished rolling."

She almost laughed at the expression of horror that crossed Dillon's face. "What on earth do you know about that? You didn't see it, did you?"

"I can understand your astonishment. Actually, I did. Some of the kids from school were going. They invited me along."

Dillon started chuckling, which only made her more indignant. "I would have given almost anything to be there," he said. "How much of the movie did you actually see?"

"Not much," she admitted. "After the first ten minutes, I concentrated very hard on eating my popcorn one kernel at a time. I do not want the producer of that awful movie in my house."

"He won't be. He's taking us to dinner."

"Pruneface? Here? Why isn't he out in L.A., where they apparently think he's a genius and he can take four meetings in a night?"

"Because he needs my advice right now and because I insisted that the meeting would have to take place in Savannah or not at all. Remember when you're looking down your nose at him that you're the one who saved the contract for me."

"My mistake," she said with a moan. Then she regarded Dillon closely. "You actually told him he had to fly here if he wanted to meet with you, and he agreed?"

He nodded. "Actually, I think he's anxious to see you again."

"Heaven help me then. I will try to be polite, Dillon, but do not expect me to keep my mouth shut if the subject of that Ninja thing comes up."

"Just be yourself. Even though you're impossibly bossy, he seems to like you. I, however, have far more passionate leanings where you're concerned. Do you suppose we could go home?"

"Home?" she repeated, suddenly smiling. To demonstrate her goodwill, she even picked up his briefcase, then linked her arm through his. "I like the sound of that."

"So do I, sweetheart. So do I."

Catherine's goodwill almost lasted through the entire evening. Dillon knew the precise moment when she lost patience with Prunelli. He was amazed it had taken so long. She had tolerated the cigar, primarily because the producer had refrained from lighting it until after dinner. She had even ignored Prunelli's overindulgence in the wine and his enthusiastic consumption of beer when they'd taken a stroll along the busy waterfront. He had plunged into the spirit of Oktoberfest with gusto. Catherine had looked pained, but had kept silent.

Then the man who was being honored for his family pictures had spotted a trio of women half his age.

He'd set out to woo them. When he pinched one and delivered a sloppy kiss to the cheek of a second, the last of Catherine's patience fled.

"Mr. Prunelli," she snapped, pointedly ignoring Dillon's eyes. "For a man who is about to receive an award for the family values imparted by his films, you are behaving like a juvenile delinquent. If the press ever got wind that you'd been pawing and grabbing at women young enough to be your daughters they'd have a field day. Your production company would become a laughingstock, if that manipulative Ninja thing hasn't already made it one."

Prunelli blinked several times as he tried to focus on the woman who was facing him, hands on hips, eyes flashing with indignation. "Come on, Katydid," he said, his words slurring. "Don't be mad. Just having a good time. Nothing else to do in this town." He peered around for Dillon. "How do you stand it, Ryan? Never mind. You have Katydid. Hell of a woman, Katydid. Hell of a woman. Not scared of me. Like that. Too bad she's yours."

Dillon leaned over and whispered, "I told you he liked you."

Catherine struggled against a smile, but lost. She supposed the man did have certain endearing qualities. "Mr. Prunelli, maybe we should just take you back to your hotel, so you can get some sleep."

"Sleep?" he repeated, as though the word were alien. "Never sleep more than a couple hours. Lighten up, Katydid. Let's have fun. Come dance with me."

He took her hand and hauled her to her feet. Dillon started to intercede, but Catherine waved him back. "It'll be okay. Maybe a brisk polka will wear him out."

Instead, though, the dance seemed to revive him. It was two in the morning before they were finally able to drop him at his hotel room and go home themselves.

When they finally got back to the apartment, Catherine kicked off her shoes at the door and collapsed on the sofa. "Are all your business meetings this strenuous?"

"Strenuous? I'm fresh as a daisy."

She regarded him malevolently. "Sure. You weren't waltzing with the Hindenburg."

Dillon moved to stand behind her. His fingers began to work at the tight muscles in her shoulders, massaging until she moaned with pleasure, her head thrown back. The pale column of her neck, exposed and vulnerable, drew him. He leaned down and pressed his lips to the satiny flesh. That exotic floral scent she loved was every bit as alluring as a field of scented wildflowers. He wanted to bury his head between her breasts, to be surrounded by her heat, to be captured by her quick responsiveness.

He needed very much to love her. He had watched her tonight as he might a stranger. He had seen new facets in her personality that intrigued him. He had witnessed for the first time the strength she had attained since that night more than a year ago, when she had been lost and alone and vulnerable. He had a feeling that keeping pace with this new Catherine was going to require a man not easily intimidated, a man not threatened by a woman's dawning self-confidence. This was what he had wanted for her; this was the power he'd suspected was just waiting to be tapped. For a few brief moments, he'd been taken aback by it, but now he knew how right he'd been to encourage her to stretch and grow. Catherine Devlin was definitely becoming a woman to be reckoned with. If he didn't want her so badly as his wife, he might very well have offered her a job as his partner. Anyone who could tame Ruben Prunelli with a glance could take on Manhattan.

"Dillon," she murmured sleepily. With her dark hair spilling loose and her lips pouty from his kiss, she looked more seductress than power broker. The fact that she was quickly becoming both took Dillon's breath away. He couldn't imagine what his life would have become if he hadn't met her.

"Yes, love."

She lifted her arms to him in a gesture that was at once innocent and powerfully provocative. "Take me to bed," she whispered.

With his blood pounding through his veins, Dillon scooped her up. "Gladly, sweetheart. Gladly."

Catherine slid out of bed while Dillon was still sleeping. She was delighted that he finally seemed to be getting some rest. After a quick shower and her usual half grapefruit, she settled herself on the couch to study for a Monday exam. She was still reading and making notes, when Dillon finally wandered out two hours later.

"What's all this?" he said, indicating the papers.

"Homework."

He grinned. "My lady the student. I like the glasses. I've never seen you wear them before."

She pulled them down and peered over the rim. "I just wear them for reading. You want some breakfast?"

"It's closer to lunchtime. Why don't we go up to one of the inns for lunch? Has Ruben called?"

"Nope. He's either sleeping in or he's found his one true love and is chasing her around one of the squares in town."

"If he's found his true love, Mrs. Prunelli is going to be slightly put out."

Catherine's head came up so quickly, her glasses almost slid off. "Some woman is actually married to that man?"

"Very happily, from what I understand."

"Since when? Last week? No one could take him longer than that."

"Twenty-five or thirty years. Actually, they're one of Hollywood's real marital success stories. Don't you ever look at all those supermarket tabloids?"

Catherine didn't deign to acknowledge that. She regarded Dillon suspiciously. "You're putting me on. Was she some Vegas showgirl or something?"

"High school sweetheart, actually."

"Dillon Ryan, I don't believe you. I don't believe that man went to high school."

"Your bias is showing." He actually seemed delighted about it.

"You bet it is. You're making it up."

"It is in the press releases. I put it there myself."

"That doesn't necessarily reassure me. I know all about Hollywood press releases. The accuracy bends like a willow."

His expression turning grim, Dillon advanced on her and bent down. He placed one hand on either side of her hips. "Are you accusing me of lying?"

She supposed he meant to sound menacing. Instead, he was terribly seductive. She wanted those clever lips of his to come another inch or two closer until she could taste them again. "I am," she murmured.

He levered himself between her thighs. "Then I guess you'll just have to be punished."

"Sounds intriguing."

His lips quivered, but he managed to hold back the laugh that clearly threatened. "You're becoming a terrible wanton, Mrs. Devlin."

She grinned and shoved aside her books. "I know. Isn't it wonderful?"

Then her arms were around him, his weight was satisfyingly heavy on top of her and his mouth found hers with unerring accuracy. The contact released an inferno and as the fire raged between them, she whispered raggedly, "Dillon, I need you so much."

"I know, sweetheart. I know." Clothes were stripped away or pushed aside until finally they were united again. "You have me," he promised. "Always."

Always only lasted an hour. They showered together, made love again, then Catherine finally sighed ruefully. "I really do have to study."

Dillon pulled her back into his arms. She buried her face against his still-hot flesh. Her tongue savored the salty taste of him, but this time the thought of all the work she had to complete before Monday wouldn't vanish in the haze of sweet sensations that had held them captive.

"I'm sorry, Dillon. I really do have to get back to work," she said.

"Couldn't you study after I leave tomorrow night?"

"There's too much to read. I'd be up the whole night.

I may be anyway, even if I get through this one text today."

"Are you going to stay with it all day?"

"Just another hour or two. I promise."

His brows lifted. "I suppose if I objected you'd say something about turnabout being fair play."

"I would never hold up your own behavior as an excuse," she said with exaggerated piety. She grinned. "But if the shoe fits..."

"Go. Study. I can sneak in some time on my own paperwork now without feeling guilty."

"I suppose you can," she said. She went back to her place on the sofa and Dillon spread his papers over the dining room table. They took turns refilling the coffee cups. As she poured what she'd vowed would be one last cup, Dillon snagged her arm.

"See how companionable this can be."

She compared the long nights of studying alone to the past few hours. She supposed he did have a point. "We are together."

"Exactly."

"Maybe the problem last time was that I had no real interests of my own to pursue," she admitted.

"Maybe so."

She regarded him with an arch expression. "What happens when I get to be even busier than you?"

"Then I'll be the one grumbling about being abandoned." He smacked her on the bottom. "Until then we'll be content with what we have. Won't we?" he said pointedly.

Catherine realized suddenly that she truly was content. She went back to Dillon and slid her arms around his neck from behind, resting her head atop his. "We're very lucky, you know that?"

"I think I do."

"Do you think it'll get better than this?"

She felt his shoulders grow stiff. "Better how?" he asked cautiously.

"I don't know. We can't spend the rest of our lives running back and forth between cities."

"Right now that's the only choice we have," Dillon said.

"I know," she lamented.

She could tell from his tone of voice and his almost imperceptible withdrawal that it was not a topic to be pursued now. Though her remark had been made without thought, now that the seed had been planted she couldn't get it out of her mind. It sprouted and thrived like a deadly weed, choking off all the good thoughts. Contentment fled in the blink of an eye.

How long could they go on like this? It was unrealistic to expect that a commuter arrangement could work indefinitely.

How long, she wondered time and again. Those two words, hanging like a shadow over the future, threatened to take away every bit of pleasure she had felt in the wonderful present she and Dillon were sharing.

6

Halloween

"**W**here would you like to meet for Halloween?" Dillon asked in a low seductive murmur. Since he'd returned to New York this last time, the calls had grown more frequent than ever. He woke Catherine up each morning and was on the phone again to whisper goodnight. Since his day often didn't end until midnight, it was wearing her out. Dillon seemed capable of surviving on four or five hours of sleep a night. She could not. She was turning into a walking zombie.

"I can hardly wait to see you in a costume," he said. "What would you choose, I wonder?"

"A witch," Catherine murmured sleepily. "Dillon, it's almost one o'clock. Can't we talk about this in the morning?"

"I love talking to you when you're all muddleheaded," he argued. "I get my best responses then."

"You mean I give in more easily then, which is exactly my point. I'm hanging up so I can get some sleep.

If I don't, you're liable to talk me into wearing harem garb and going trick-or-treating."

"An interesting possibility. You'd be fascinating in all that billowing, see-through stuff. Now all we have to decide is where to go. Halloween is only a couple of weeks away."

She yawned and tried to think coherently. Halloween was not a national holiday. Apparently, though, Dillon was ready to use any excuse to see her again. At any other hour of the day that realization might have pleased her. "People do not get a day off for Halloween," she informed him. "Don't go getting some crazy idea about a long, wild-and-crazy-weekend. I have classes."

"Couldn't you play hooky for a day? People who've just won a potential six-figure account for a candy company practically swoon at the thought of Halloween, official holiday or not."

That jolted her up. "Six figures for candy corn?" she said incredulously.

"Well, not candy corn," he admitted. "Something slightly more upscale."

"You must live in a ritzier neighborhood than I do. Not even my parents give out Belgian chocolates to trick-or-treaters."

"Maybe not this year, but by the time I finish with this ad campaign, they will next year."

That piqued her curiosity. "You're representing some Belgian chocolate manufacturer?"

"Not exactly. Actually, I took on that candy company on the waterfront in Savannah. It'll give me a third reason to come down there more regularly."

"Third reason?"

"White Stone, you and now the candy company."

"I'm glad I rank higher than nuts and chocolates. Is this the place where we spent a fortune the last time you were here?"

"Where you spent a fortune," he corrected with ungentlemanly accuracy. "Yes, that's the one."

"Dillon, I thought you said this account was going to be profitable. That's a tiny little operation."

"With huge mail-order potential."

At first she'd thought his decision entirely capricious, but she was beginning to see the sense of it. The candy was delicious. "So that's what you were talking to the owner about while I was overdosing on pralines."

"That's right. Even chocophobics won't be able to resist, once I get finished with touting the virtues of their pecan fudge and pralines."

"And that gives you satisfaction?"

"That gives me the time and money to meet you someplace over Halloween and, yes, it brings me tremendous satisfaction to watch some small local company go big-time because of my work."

"Remember that the next time you want to spend an entire weekend wooing a jerk like Ruben Pruneface. He doesn't need you."

"That's not what you were saying when you ripped apart his image. As big as he is, he definitely needs a make-over. I think this firm can do it for him."

"At heart, though, he'll still be an arrogant, egotistical boor."

"A *rich* egotistical boor. And I thought you liked him. Once you robbed him of his cigar in L.A. and discovered he could polka, you seemed to get along famously."

"I wouldn't go that far. But you're missing my point."

"Which is?"

"If you applied the same high standards to your clients that you do to your ads, you would not deal with the Ruben Prunellis of the world."

When Dillon stayed silent for several seconds, Catherine wondered if she'd gone too far. Just because she hadn't liked the studio executive didn't mean Dillon shouldn't work with the man. She had no place meddling in his business decisions. Handling Prunelli's studio probably did bring Dillon a certain amount of prestige, despite the man's personal obnoxiousness.

"Maybe you're right," he said finally, cutting off the apology she was ready to offer. "I never thought of it that way. You are judged by the company you keep. I tell my clients that all the time. Maybe it's time I started practicing what I preach. Of course, Prunelli did take me on to change his image, along with selling his movies. Doesn't that show that his heart's in the right place?"

"Or his pocketbook. Let's drop it. When you get right down to it, I had no right…"

"Of course, you have a right to your opinion. That's one of the things I love about you. You're honest to a fault once you finally get the courage to open your mouth. Poor Prunelli didn't know what hit him, when you told him you thought his last blockbuster success was a manipulative piece of trash."

Catherine groaned. "I might have hated that Ninja garbage, but I could have been a little more diplomatic for your sake."

"Absolutely not. Even I enjoyed watching the way his eyes bulged and his mouth kept opening and closing like a fish. I doubt he'd ever been rendered speechless before. Unfortunately, in no time he probably forgot all about it."

"Certainly by the time he'd finished the second bottle of wine."

"Tell me the truth. You enjoyed telling him what you thought, didn't you?"

She thought it over. To be honest, it had felt good. "I have to admit, I did. Does that make me a terrible person? I actually liked seeing that sleazy man squirm."

"That just makes you human, sweetheart. You spent too many years reining in your opinions. I'm glad you're learning that the walls won't collapse if you say what's on your mind."

"The walls may not collapse, but I could cost you millions."

"In my business, knowing when to be blunt is an art. I think you're a natural at knowing the best timing. Prunelli asks about you every time we talk. You've definitely made a lasting impression."

"He's probably trying to make sure I'm not in the vicinity," she said, unable to control another yawn. "Dillon, I have to get some sleep. People are beginning to ask about the circles under my eyes. They seem to think I'm suddenly leading a life of nonstop debauchery."

"If only that were true," he said with a heartfelt sigh. "Go to sleep, my beauty. We'll settle this Halloween thing in the morning."

True to his word, Dillon was back on the phone before 7:00 a.m. He sounded wide-awake and disgustingly cheerful.

"I've made a decision," he announced.

"Good for you," she grumbled, wondering just how guilty she'd feel if she skipped her nine o'clock class and slept until noon.

"Don't you want to hear it?"

"Tell me," she said. Maybe then he'd go away and let her dream about the nicer, gentler Dillon who only kept her awake to do wonderful, exciting things to her body.

"I'll fly in on Friday and then first thing Saturday we'll drive over to Hilton Head for the weekend. The weather's still nice. Most of the tourists have probably headed home. We should have the whole beach practically to ourselves. We can sleep late Sunday morning, have breakfast in bed."

Sleep late? Breakfast in bed? Now the man was talking her language. "Make the reservations," she said, then hung up and pulled the pillow back over her head.

The trip to the beach turned out to be just what they needed. They arrived by midday on Saturday, checked into their hotel, then for lunch, found a place with a view of the water. They lingered for hours over the seafood and wine, talking and catching up on all the little details of their lives that they never seemed to find time to discuss in their hurried phone conversations.

With sweaters wrapped around their shoulders and their pant legs rolled up, they walked the beach hand in hand until the sun finally began to fade and the pine- and salt-scented air grew uncomfortably chilly.

As they walked back to the hotel, Dillon slowed and turned her to face him. Catherine reached up and smoothed the lines of his face. "You look more relaxed than I've ever seen you."

"And you look even more beautiful."

A sigh of pure pleasure caught in her throat. There was something almost bittersweet about the rare quiet moment. Deep inside, where her heart called the shots, she had this weepy, desperate feeling that they were reaching a terrible turning point, a make-or-break time in their lives.

Over the past couple of weeks whenever she'd allowed herself, she'd thought about where the two of them were headed with their lives. No matter how romantically she viewed their love, she couldn't avoid the reality. What they had wasn't the stuff of happily-ever-after. Oh, she loved Dillon and deep in her heart she believed that he loved her, but what they were building together was a make-believe existence.

That night, as she slept in his arms, she felt as though it was all slipping away and there was nothing she could do to change it. Tears clung to her lashes, then spilled onto his chest. He stirred restlessly, but fell into an even deeper sleep when she brushed his face soothingly with her fingertips. She traced his wide brow, his nose, the tiny scar at the corner of his mouth. When she stopped to think about what she was doing, she realized she was trying to memorize Dillon, to learn the scent and texture and shape of him for the empty nights she feared were ahead.

In the bright, clear light of morning, she tried to tell herself to stay silent, to hold on to what they had for however long it lasted. Their love was special. There was no reason to ask for more, but then she realized that was exactly the problem. As good as it was, she did want so much more.

At breakfast she toyed with her food. Dillon watched

her closely, but apparently her odd mood had communicated itself to him because he was far more subdued than usual. There were no teasing remarks, no provocative looks.

"It's warm outside," he said finally. "Why don't we take a blanket and spend a couple of hours on the beach? Maybe the fresh air will make you feel better."

"I feel fine."

"Then why so glum?"

She stared at him helplessly. "I don't know if I can explain it."

He held out his hand. "Let's go outside. We'll talk when you're ready." His patience in the face of her inability to communicate her worry made her feel like weeping.

A few minutes later, they had changed their clothes. Dillon's gaze traveled over her appreciatively. "I like the duds. Or maybe I should say the lack of them. That's a helluva bathing suit for a former debutante."

She'd thought the bright blue suit was a modest one-piece until she'd seen the look of masculine approval in Dillon's eyes. Maybe the neckline did reveal a little more than she'd realized of her full breasts. Maybe the high French-cut styling showed off a little too much leg. She reached for a long T-shirt, but Dillon touched her hand.

"I like it," he reassured her. "Any woman would kill to have a figure like yours. And every man on the beach is going to envy me."

She blinked back unexpected tears. "How do you always know the right thing to say?"

Dillon appeared startled by her intensity and by the

sudden tears. He reached for her and held her close. "Sweetheart, what's wrong?"

Once again, she took the coward's way out and merely shook her head. "Let's go outside."

When they found a secluded cove, Dillon spread out the blanket, then stretched out beside her. Her gaze drank in the sight of his well-muscled legs, the flat stomach and broad shoulders. Without a word, he handed her the suntan lotion. She applied it with fingers that trembled. As if each touch might be her last, she caressed and lingered until she could tell by the look in his eyes and the set of his jaw that he was losing the struggle not to respond.

"Your turn," he said finally, his words hoarse.

His hands were gentle as he massaged in the cool lotion. She gave herself up to the pure sensual delight as he stroked her back. He followed the line of her suit as it dipped to just above the swell of her buttocks. Then he coated each leg, slowly, provocatively, lingering at the erogenous spot behind her knee, the sensitive curve of her calf. He even applied the lotion to her feet, his hands sure and confident as they followed the curve of each instep and tenderly stroked each toe. Her whole body was aflame by the time he was done, the heat spreading from a point low in her abdomen until even her cheeks felt flushed.

Forcing herself to turn over and sit up, she caught the expression on Dillon's face. It was a painful mixture of desire and hurt, of longing and confusion. Troubled brown eyes met hers and in a voice that barely held steady, he asked, "Catherine, what's wrong? Have you met someone else?"

She reached out and took his hand, holding it tight against her cheek. "No. No, nothing like that. I swear it."

A sigh shuddered through him. "Then tell me, please. I think I could take anything but that."

She drew in a deep breath, tried to find the right words, then said simply, "I think we're getting to a turning point and I'm afraid."

His eyes filled with puzzlement. "What sort of turning point?"

"This isn't enough for me anymore. I don't want to live from month to month, waiting for the weekends you can get away, praying that some business crisis won't interfere with our plans." Avoiding his gaze, she lamented, "What we're doing isn't real."

Waiting for him to reply, she dug her toes into the warm sand with sensual appreciation. She could feel Dillon's eyes on her. He reached out and trailed a finger the length of her thigh. The touch raised goose bumps.

"Deny the reality of that," he challenged in a low voice that sent yet another shiver of pure delight running through her.

"Oh, Dillon, that's very real. I can't deny all the physical attraction. You've brought me alive again. I feel things with you that I'd never imagined possible. It's the one thing that's never been a problem with us."

"Then nothing else matters."

"Of course it does. We can't spend our lives running away from home for these idyllic interludes. We're romanticizing the relationship. We live in a constant state of anticipation. We're so anxious not to spoil what little time we have that we ignore the petty little frustrations. We avoid dealing with anything that isn't pleasant until it's almost too late."

"Then marry me. Will that be real enough for you? Will that give you enough time to talk about the frustrations?"

She closed her eyes against the anger that was building in his expression. "I'm not challenging you to a duel, Dillon. I'm not looking for drastic solutions. I just want us to face what's happening realistically."

"Meaning what? What do you really want, Catherine? Do you want to move to New York and live with me and see how it goes? Do you want to set a schedule, to take turns commuting weekends? Your place one weekend, mine the next?"

"At least that would make more sense than what we're doing now. Do you realize you've never met my family or friends, that I've never seen your apartment or met your children?"

"You may not know the color of my wallpaper or the size of my bed, but you know everything that's important about me."

"Do I really? I don't think the picture can possibly be complete without knowing the little details of day-to-day living, without getting to see how you interact with your kids, with the people who work for you. They're an integral part of who you are, Dillon."

"Then come to New York. Come for Thanksgiving. Stay for a week, longer if you can. You can send me out the door to work in the morning and have dinner on the table at night. You can see whether or not my closets are neat. You can check out my office and listen to my kids grumble about whatever you fix for dinner. Will that be real enough for you?"

"It would be a start," she said solemnly, ignoring the sarcastic tone that had crept into his voice.

He shrugged, feigning a display of disinterest. "Then let's do it."

"Don't make it sound like the beginning of the end, Dillon. If we're not heading toward a life together, then maybe we're wasting our time."

"Is marriage the only kind of relationship you want to have with a man? Is it impossible for an Atlanta debutante to simply fall in love, to take one day at a time?"

Cathcrine couldn't think of how to answer that. There had been a time only a few short months ago when she'd been convinced that she never wanted to be married again, when one day at a time might have been enough. Knowing Dillon had changed that. She'd begun yearning again. Not just for a husband, but for a family, for the closeness that two people have when they live together, when they commit to happily ever after.

"A piece of paper doesn't guarantee happiness, Catherine," he said as if he'd read her mind. "You and I both know that."

"No. But if we're not willing to work at what we have now, how in the hell will we ever dare to consider more?"

"Will you be satisfied with less?" he asked in a hushed tone.

She felt as if the sun had gone behind a cloud. She shivered in the suddenly icy atmosphere. "Is that all you're offering?" she asked slowly.

He uttered a harsh curse, then ran his fingers through his hair. "I don't know what I'm offering. Until a few minutes ago, I could have sworn that all I wanted was to spend the rest of my life with you, married or not. As soon as the subject of the future came up, though, I felt like a fighter pilot who's trained all his life for a mission and suddenly discovers he's terrified to fly into combat. I guess I have more battle scars than I'd realized."

Catherine laughed despite herself, though there was a certain bittersweet edge to the humor. "I'm not sure I'm crazy about the analogy, but I know what you mean. What's happening between us scares me, too, but I don't want to let my fears stand in the way of what we might have."

"Brave words," he said, his gaze intent.

She dared then to touch his cheek. "I don't feel very brave," she admitted softly.

He captured her hand and held it tight, kissing her fingers. "Neither do I, but if you're ready to move forward, then so am I. Thanksgiving week, okay?"

Catherine didn't think she could squeeze even a simple yes past the raw emotion that clogged her throat, so she nodded. Tears stung her eyes as they had earlier, but when the first one began to roll down her cheek, Dillon was there again to wipe it away. Patient. Enduring. Tender.

She had insisted on this daring, risky new course. Now she could only pray that he would always be there, because for the hundredth time that day alone she acknowledged how very much she loved him and how much she feared that she was wrong to want so much more than what they had right then.

7

Thanksgiving

"What do you mean you won't be home for Thanksgiving?" Catherine's mother demanded, setting her silver teapot down with a thud that rattled the ancestral English bone china. "We have the entire family coming for dinner. Whatever will I tell them?"

"Tell them the truth, Mother. Tell them I'm in New York with Dillon."

"That man," Mrs. Devereaux huffed. "I don't know why you can't find some nice man right here in Atlanta. George Banes, for instance. He's always been partial to you."

"George Banes is sixty-five years old."

"He's rich and quite respectable."

"He's Southern. Isn't that what you really care about?"

"I do not have such a parochial view of the world, young lady. I just don't want you running off to live in New York. You're the only daughter I have left here in

Atlanta now that your sisters have married and moved away."

It was the closest her mother had ever come to admitting out loud that she loved her. Catherine clung to the words, but she couldn't let them sway her. She leaned down and kissed the still-smooth ivory cheek. "I'm not going to run away anywhere. I'm just going for a long holiday weekend."

"And what about Christmas? Will you abandon your own family then, too?"

"We haven't talked about Christmas. We're trying to take this relationship one day at a time right now. This trip to New York is a big step for us. We've both made mistakes in the past by jumping into a relationship too quickly."

"Will you be staying with his family?"

"No. They live in Queens. We'll be in Manhattan."

"Catherine!"

"Mother, don't look so shocked. You know perfectly well what sort of relationship Dillon and I have."

"That doesn't mean I want the whole world to know it. In all these years haven't I taught you anything about maintaining appearances? Couldn't you stay at the Plaza or perhaps the Waldorf? It would look so much better."

"To whom? You and Dad already know where I'll be. Who else will care? You're just looking for anything to make me feel guilty and stay here."

Her mother sighed and lapsed into her thickest drawl. She'd perfected the role of martyr years ago, but she also knew when to quit. Not, however, without one final sniper shot. "I suppose I might's well save my breath. No one ever pays a bit of attention to me anyway."

Catherine had to fight to keep from smiling at her mother's resigned air. "You and Dad could come to New York, too, you know. Think how much fun we could have shopping. We could go to the parade. It would be wonderful."

"I have no desire to go someplace where I'm likely to be mugged."

"You're just as likely to be mugged here in Atlanta. I know perfectly well you've seen the statistics. You read every inch of type in the newspaper just to make sure that none of your social set has run amuck."

"Okay, I'm just too set in my ways to go running off over a big holiday. I'm getting old. I like having the whole family around me."

"If you start talking about your declining years, I'm going to get up and walk out. Don't try playing on my sympathies. You have more energy than I do. I will be here for Christmas, though. I promise."

She appeared partially pacified. "That man, too?"

"I'm sure Dillon will do his best to be here, too."

Her mother nodded, her expression suspiciously satisfied. "Well, then, I suppose that will just have to do." She picked up the teapot. "More tea, dear?"

Catherine noted that suddenly too-innocent expression with suspicion. She had the oddest feeling she'd just been maneuvered. "Nope," she said emphatically, before she could find herself unexpectedly agreeing to move back home, where her old room still had ruffled pink curtains on the windows and an extravagant doll collection on the bookshelves amid the leather-bound children's classics. "I have to run. I'll call from New

York on Thanksgiving Day so I can say hello to everyone."

Her mother squeezed her hand tightly as Catherine leaned down to kiss her. "Have a wonderful time, dear," she said with unexpected gentleness. "It's about time you had some fun out of life."

Catherine stared at her in amazement. Even more improbably, her mother actually winked. "Why, you old devil," Catherine said.

"Remember that," her mother chided. "I'm not half as stuffy as you and your sisters think I am."

Catherine was still shaking her head in astonishment as she left to fly to New York the following afternoon. That momentary relaxing of her mother's reserve gave her a whole new perspective. She had a feeling when she got back from the holiday she ought to begin spending a bit more time with her mother to discover exactly what sort of a woman she really was. Maybe she'd spent too many years thinking of her only as a restrictive mother and not nearly enough time recognizing that there were far more facets to her personality.

When her plane landed at La Guardia, Catherine called Dillon's office. Helene Mason, with whom she was on increasingly friendly terms because of the number of phone calls she and Dillon made to each other, began apologizing the moment she heard Catherine's voice.

"I know he was supposed to be at the airport, Mrs. Devlin, but he was called into a meeting downtown. He called from the car phone not five minutes ago to say that the traffic is impossible because of the rain and everyone's trying to get out of town for the weekend. He'll never get there. He wants you to take a cab and meet him at his apartment."

Catherine felt her high spirits begin to sag ever-so-slightly. It was a small thing, but she'd really wanted Dillon to meet her at the airport. She sighed. "If you talk to him again, tell him I'm on my way."

"You shouldn't have any problem coming in. You should be at his place in twenty minutes or so. He'll wait for you downstairs with an umbrella. This rain is coming down in buckets. They say it'll turn to sleet or snow by tonight."

Terrific, Catherine thought with a groan. "Thanks, Helene. I hope I get to meet you before I go back."

Catherine made a valiant attempt to recapture her enthusiasm in the midst of the airport chaos. The baggage area was filled with tired, irritable travelers and tons of luggage that all seemed to look exactly alike as it circled past on the conveyor. By the time she found her two pieces and lugged them to the taxi line, she was exhausted.

The trip into Manhattan across the 59th Street Bridge went as quickly as Helene had predicted, but in town the traffic came to a rush-hour halt. "So this is gridlock," she muttered, sinking back against the seat as horns blared impatiently. At least it gave her some sense of appreciation for Dillon's inability to get to the airport.

He was, however, waiting at the curb for her. Dressed in a topcoat, his hair windblown and wet, his complexion ruddy from the cold, he didn't seem like the man she'd come to know over the last few months at all. There was a new tension about him, a vibrancy that excited her, even as it made her unaccountably afraid.

He reached over and practically lifted her from the car. "You're here at last," he murmured, pulling her close and kissing her. "Sorry about the airport, but it couldn't be helped. You've seen the traffic. It's a bear. Let's get inside before you get soaked." He hurried her through the lobby and into a glass-lined elevator, which rose quickly and smoothly the twenty-two floors to his apartment.

Inside, when their coats were hung to drip in the guest bathroom, she said, "I didn't know you had a meeting this afternoon."

"I didn't know about it when I called you this morning. It came up at the last minute. It's a big Wall Street account and when they want to talk, I have to go listen. Come on, let's get your things unpacked and then I want to take you out to dinner. We've been invited to join the Farrells for a drink at six. I've told you about them, haven't I? He's my top creative man. I've been thinking lately about making him a full partner. Maybe you can help me decide if that's the right way to go."

Catherine was so taken aback by the busy schedule Dillon had planned for their first night that his request for her decision-making assistance barely registered. She glanced at her watch and protested, "Dillon, it's already five-thirty. I need to change."

"No, you don't. You look beautiful. They're going to love you. And I can't wait for you to meet the O'Haras. They want us to stop by for a nightcap. Tomorrow we're having Thanksgiving dinner at the Plaza with the Petersons. It's an annual bash."

"A bash?" she repeated weakly. "How big?"

"I think they had fifty or so last year, mostly clients."

"But I thought we'd be having Thanksgiving dinner with your family."

"I told them we'd try to get by at some point over the weekend. We'll fit it in somehow. The Petersons are an important account for me."

"What about your kids? Maybe we could just get a turkey and invite them."

"They're going to spend the day with Paula's family. Then they'll come into the city Sunday. I told them we'd go skating at Rockefeller Plaza."

"Ice skating?"

"Sure. You skate, don't you?"

"No."

"We'll fix that. I'll have you skimming over the ice like an Olympic champion in no time."

"On my feet or on my bottom?"

"On your feet, I promise."

Catherine felt another attack of trepidation. She'd known what sort of life Dillon led in New York. She knew he was a high-powered executive. In fact, she had known from the beginning that was what had broken up his marriage. She was just beginning to understand why. There was a dynamic, full-speed-ahead side to his personality that matched the frenzied pace of New York. In Savannah it had been muted. She'd fallen in love with the charm and energy, but she wasn't quite prepared for the full force of Dillon in high gear.

As she went into the bathroom to freshen her makeup at least before they left for the evening, Dillon followed her, perching on the side of an extraordinarily lavish tub big enough for two. That tub aroused some intriguing ideas, but Dillon appeared oblivious to its proximity or its promise. He continued to run through his plans for the holiday.

"Dillon, if we cram all that in, when will we breathe?" *When will we make love?* She left that question at least unspoken. Maybe he didn't want her as much anymore. Maybe in this environment, he'd already recognized that she was out of place.

He dismissed her plaintive question with a wave of his hand. "I just want to make sure you have a good time. I talk about you so much that everyone wants to meet you. And that's what this weekend is all about, isn't it? You wanted to see how I live."

Catherine supposed she should feel flattered that he was so anxious to open his life to her. Instead, she felt overwhelmed. He was right. This was what she'd wanted. She didn't dare attempt to throw a damper on his enthusiasm. "Let the games begin," she muttered mostly to herself.

"What?"

She plastered on her very best smile, the one she'd used to effect at a hundred charity balls and boring dinners with Matthew's medical associates. "Nothing," she said, linking her arm through his. "Let's go. I can't wait to meet your friends."

She hated them. She had been with Evan and Shirley Farrell for precisely fifteen minutes and already her nerves were screaming for release. There was nothing really wrong with them. They were polite. They were delighted to meet her. They adored Dillon. But Evan laughed too loudly, drank too much and had the personality of a bulldozer in overdrive. Shirley, by comparison, was a timid gray mouse, totally overshadowed by her exuberant husband.

"Shirley, do you have children?" Catherine asked, hoping to find some topic that would animate the woman's dull demeanor.

"Two, a boy and a girl."

"How nice. How old are they?" she asked, genuinely interested.

"Seven and eleven. Evan thought that four years was the best spacing. They're friends, without being quite such rivals."

Catherine cringed inwardly. "I see. Are they involved in a lot of school activities? I know my friends seem to spend half their lives carpooling their kids. My neighbor Beth says she hasn't had control of her life since the kids were old enough to talk."

"Actually, I don't have to worry about that. They're in boarding school. They came home for Thanksgiving, of course, but they'll be going back on Sunday."

Then, why are you here, Catherine wanted to demand. Instead, she merely said, "You must miss them, or do you have a career that keeps you busy?"

"No. The house is large, though, and Evan likes to entertain. That takes all my time. We've tried several housekeepers and none of them can seem to get the work done to his satisfaction."

Catherine thought at once about how many times she'd made similar statements to Matthew's friends, always feeling a little ashamed that she wasn't doing more with her life. She felt sorry for Shirley and wondered if she'd been the object of similar pity for all those years she'd been content to bask in her husband's shadow.

Before she could try to instill some sense of renewed purpose in Shirley, Dillon was on his feet, explaining that they had dinner reservations. Five minutes later they were back in his car.

"Thanks for keeping Shirley occupied," he said. "You're terrific. I knew you'd get along with her."

"She's pathetic."

Clearly offended, Dillon turned to stare at her. "What's that supposed to mean?"

"She has no life of her own, no personality. She is exactly the way I was up until the divorce. I feel terrible for her."

"Don't. She's happy."

"Do you honestly believe that or have you never really talked to her?"

Dillon stopped for a red light and studied her curiously. "You're really upset about this, aren't you?"

She realized that he was genuinely worried. "I'm sorry. She just got to me because she sounded so much like I once did. It brought back a bad time in my life. I don't want to begin falling into that old pattern again."

"And you thought that's what was happening tonight?"

"It felt uncomfortably familiar. The men sitting around talking business, while the womenfolk chatted about inconsequential things."

"That's just part of business entertaining."

"I suppose so. Right now, though, it seems more like a dangerous trap."

The whirlwind of activity never slowed long enough for Catherine to take stock of it again. By Sunday morning she was exhausted and more frightened than ever. While she'd been increasingly aware that she was falling into a trap she'd sworn to avoid, Dillon had been in his glory. Every bit of entertaining had a purpose. There was not a single dinner or a single party that was held for the sheer pleasure of being with close friends. They had almost no time alone, except for the hours they spent in bed. Even their lovemaking seemed to adapt to the New York pace—more hurried and less satisfying.

Reluctantly she got out of bed, pulled on her robe and went into the dining room, where she knew she'd find him already engrossed in the morning paper, even though it was not yet seven o'clock. He looked up and smiled.

"I thought maybe you'd sleep late. I'm afraid I've worn you out."

"We need to talk," she said determinedly, sitting down opposite him and pouring herself a cup of coffee from the pot that always seemed to be at hand.

"You look so serious."

"That's the way I'm feeling. Dillon, don't you ever slow down?"

"Sure I do. I've taken this whole weekend off to be with you."

"Really? How many deals have you finalized since Friday night?"

He seemed bemused by the question. "Two, maybe three. I don't know. Why?"

"Isn't that work?"

"I suppose. What are you getting at?"

"That you haven't done one single thing just for fun since I've been here."

"Have you been bored? Is that it?"

"No, I haven't been bored. Not exactly. I just expected that this weekend would be different."

"How?"

"For one thing, I thought I'd get to meet your family."

"The kids will be here about nine."

"And your parents?"

He seemed uncomfortable. "I guess that's not going to work out this trip after all, but you'll be back. There will be plenty of opportunities for you to meet them."

Catherine sighed and gave up. He just didn't get it. Maybe he never would, even after losing Paula and the kids. He was happy filling his hours with nonstop work. Though he'd invited Catherine to be a part of that, he would probably have been just as content if she hadn't been there. Was there really any place in his life for the sort of relationship she'd dreamed of them having?

She was feeling more depressed than she had in those first weeks after her divorce, when the front door burst open and two miniature versions of Dillon came racing in. The two boys skidded to a stop at the sight of her.

"Hello there," she said, holding out her hand to the taller of the two. "I'm Catherine. You must be Jonathan."

He took her hand and pumped it energetically. "Yes, ma'am. This here is Kevin. He's only four. His hands are probably dirty, so you may not want to shake with him."

Catherine grinned. "Oh, I don't think a little dirt is going to hurt me." She took Kevin's grimy hand very solemnly. "I'm glad to meet you, too."

Jonathan giggled at that. Tossing his coat on the floor, he went tearing straight toward the den, where Dillon was on the phone with Evan Farrell about a deal that had nearly been lost the previous day. "Hey, Dad, did you get the doughnuts like you promised? I want the jelly kind."

Laughing, Catherine followed the children into the den. She could hardly wait to see Dillon's response to all this unbridled exuberance. Kevin was already scrambling onto his father's knee, while Jonathan waited impatiently for him to hang up the phone.

"Evan, I have to go," Dillon said, hugging Kevin to him. "I've been invaded by small Martians demanding food. Yes, I know doughnuts are not good for them. That's why they're a special treat." He glanced up at Catherine when he said it, his expression as guilty as if he'd admitted to income tax evasion.

When he'd hung up the phone, she teased, "Don't look at me. I'm not going to reveal your awful secret. Assuming, of course, that I get my share."

"Yeah! Come on, Dad. We're starving."

"I'm sure," Dillon said dryly. "How long has it been since breakfast?"

"Hours and hours. Besides, all we had was yucky oatmeal."

"Yucky," Kevin confirmed.

"I agree, guys. But it is good for you. Promise to keep eating it or no doughnuts."

The two boys exchanged serious glances, then nodded. "We promise."

"Good. Now who wants jelly and who wants cream-filled?"

Apparently this was a familiar game, because Dillon had just the right number of each. To her amazement, he even insisted on orange juice and milk to go with them.

"Hey, Catherine," Jonathan said, obviously accepting her presence without questions. "You gonna go skating with us?"

"I'm going to try," she said, her delight in Dillon's boys overriding for now her concerns about the future. The expression on his face as he watched them was almost painful to see. There was a yearning there she would never have suspected. Maybe he did realize how much he'd sacrificed, after all.

"She's never skated before, guys," he said. "We're going to have to teach her."

"It'll be okay," Jonathan reassured her. "Girls can learn how pretty easy. Mom did, huh, Dad?" His expression sobered slightly. "She doesn't like to come into the city anymore, though."

"But you do?" Catherine asked.

"You bet. We do neat stuff when we come to see Dad. He takes us to museums and movies and we even went to a play once. I liked it, but Kevin fell asleep."

"Did not."

"You did, too, you little dweeb."

Dillon scowled at him. "What did I tell you about calling your brother names?"

"Sorry, Dad. Can we go now? They have this really neat place right next to the ice rink. Dad always gets us hot chocolate there."

"One thing for certain," Catherine teased, her amused gaze meeting Dillon's. "These children will never starve to death."

"They're bottomless pits," he confirmed. "Now you

see why I have to work so hard. I have to keep them supplied with doughnuts and hot chocolate."

"And pizza," Jonathan said.

"Hot dogs," Kevin countered. "We had pizza before."

"Guys, you've just finished breakfast. How about we take this one meal at a time? Now go bundle up."

They obediently scooted out of the kitchen, but not before dumping their dishes into the sink.

"They're good kids," Catherine said as Dillon stared after them. "I really like them."

He turned back to her and smiled. "They're what keeps me going. I was a little worried right after the divorce. Kevin cried a lot and Jonathan was angry, but I think they're finally adjusting. I think they're going to be okay."

"Because they can tell you still love them."

He pulled her into his arms and kissed her quickly. "Thank you for saying that. Sometimes I worry that I'm bungling things."

"Not that I can tell."

"Hey, Dad, aren't you two ever gonna get ready?" Jonathan demanded.

"They were kissing," Kevin observed, bringing a blush to Catherine's cheeks.

"Can't put anything past you two," Dillon said easily, taking her hand. "Let's go, everybody. I can't wait to get this lady on the ice."

After the first half hour, Catherine decided that only a masochist would ever go ice-skating. Her ankles bent in unnatural directions. Her bottom was sore and cold. Dillon patiently picked her up again and again. Even the boys tried to help by offering suggestions.

"Let us show her," Jonathan finally said, clasping one hand. "Kevin, you get on her other side."

He tugged her gently forward. Kevin hung on tightly with his tiny, mitten-covered hand. Taking smaller steps, she began to get her balance. Finally she tried to glide. She made it halfway around the rink before she realized that they'd let her go. She caught sight of Dillon. "I'm skating," she shouted. He lifted his hands and applauded. Jonathan's face was split by a broad, dimpled smile. She was almost back to them before her feet shot out from under her again. This time Dillon caught her before she hit the ice. She fell against his chest.

"Enough," she said breathlessly. "I demand hot chocolate and warmth. You all can stay out here and freeze to death, if you want to, but I'm taking a break."

"Me, too," Jonathan said loyally.

"I don't want to spoil your fun. You three can stay out here. I'll watch from inside."

"We'll all go in," Dillon decided. "Then we'll take another few turns around the rink before we go to lunch."

After hot chocolate, more skating and a pizza with everything on it, even the two pint-size bundles of energy admitted exhaustion.

"By the time we get back home, it'll be time for your mom to come by and get you anyway," Dillon said.

"Maybe we could stay over tonight," Jonathan said hopefully.

"I'm afraid not. You guys have school tomorrow and I have work."

"Mom says that's all you ever do."

Dillon watched Catherine as he admitted, "She may be right, Jonathan."

When they'd left amid hugs and promises from Catherine to come back again, Dillon led her into the living room, turned on the stereo and poured them each a glass of wine. She was stretched out on the sofa, when he came and sat beside her, pulling her across his lap. "Tired?"

She nodded. "But it's a nice tired. You're like a different person when you're with them, Dillon. The way you were today, that's the Dillon I first met in Savannah. That's the man I fell in love with."

When she looked up, his eyes were closed. His fingers idly smoothed her hair. He opened his eyes finally and met her gaze. "I want to be that man all the time, sweetheart. I really do. I'm just not sure it's possible."

She sat up and took his face in her hands. "Anything is possible, Dillon. All you have to do is want it enough."

When her lips met his, the kiss began as a gentle reassurance. Dillon turned it into a tender promise. There was so much desire, so much longing in that kiss that it shattered her fears and left her filled with hope again.

8

Christmas

It was barely eight o'clock on Christmas Eve, Dillon had been at her parents' house for less than an hour, her sisters and their families had yet to arrive and Catherine was already a nervous wreck. At this rate by the end of the holiday weekend, they'd have to commit her to one of those discreet sanitariums for a lengthy rest cure.

Wincing as her mother launched yet another enthusiastic anecdote about Matthew, Catherine took a deep breath and interrupted. "Mother, I'm sure Dillon isn't interested in how skillfully my ex-husband carved the turkey. He's a surgeon, for heaven sakes. What did you expect?"

"Catherine, don't speak to your mother in that tone," her father said, then resumed puffing on his pipe. His mild words didn't fool her. His quiet commands were always deadly serious. She cast a pleading look in his direction, then sighed in resignation and sat back.

"I was just trying to make a point," her mother said. "More canapés, Mr. Ryan?"

"Thank you. What point was that, Mrs. Devereaux?" Dillon said with apparent interest. Catherine felt like smacking him for encouraging the recitation. This was not going at all the way she'd hoped. She'd wanted Dillon to experience what a real family holiday was all about. Instead, he seemed to be undergoing one of her mother's finest trials by fire.

"That Matthew will be missed on holidays," her mother concluded with a triumphant gleam in her eyes. She was observing Dillon's reaction and missed Catherine's moan entirely.

"Not by me," Catherine muttered under her breath, then said aloud, "Dillon, wouldn't you like to take a walk? I'll show you the garden." She couldn't keep an edge of desperation out of her voice. Her mother ignored it.

"You'll catch your death of cold out there," her mother objected.

"Let them go, Lucinda. Can't you tell they'd like their privacy?" her father said indulgently.

"But the rest of the girls will be here any minute now."

"We aren't going clear to Macon, Mother. When everyone else arrives, have Maisie call us." She grabbed Dillon's hand and tugged him from the room.

"I wish I thought you were as anxious to be alone with me as your father thought," he said when they were shivering outdoors.

"I am." She circled his waist with her arms and rested her head on his chest. She felt better at once. "Why does coming here reduce me to adolescence all over again? I was a lousy teenager. I'm no better at it now. Thank you for agreeing to put up with this. I couldn't think of any way around spending Christmas here without causing World War III."

"You survived the tortures of New York with me. It's the least I can do. Besides, it gives me a chance to see how you managed to turn out to be such a sexy, dynamic woman," he murmured, brushing his lips across hers.

"Oh, I wish... I'm afraid you won't see much evidence of those qualities around here, if all I do for the next forty-eight hours is apologize."

"Then stop apologizing," he said, gently stroking her cheek with the back of his fingers. "Your mother's behavior is not your responsibility. Are you afraid I'm going to be put off because your mother keeps dragging Matthew out as an example of the highest masculine virtues?"

Catherine rolled her eyes. "What man wants to hear that his predecessor was the Rolls-Royce of husbands?"

He tilted her chin up. When she dared to meet his gaze, she caught the sparks of laughter. "Do you believe that Matthew Devlin was exemplary?" he asked.

"Hardly."

"Then it doesn't really matter what your mother thinks. Let her have her illusions."

"Believe me, she had no illusions where Matthew is concerned. She was just as rotten to him as she's being to you," she admitted ruefully. "You seem to be taking it better than he did, though. Matthew wanted very badly to impress her. He thought it would help him up the Atlanta social ladder. She saw straight through him. You probably impressed her by not running for your life."

His arms tightened around her. "Catherine, do you suppose we could stop talking about Matthew and your mother?"

"What did you have in mind?"

"I thought maybe we could do something to generate a little heat. It's cold out here."

"Good thinking."

"No thinking, Catherine. Just feel." With his mouth slanted across hers, with his hips hard and decidedly masculine against hers, and his hands splayed over her buttocks, it was all too easy to comply. The temperature rose by several degrees in no time at all. The prospect of facing her mother again seemed far less important than the solid strength of the man holding her tightly to him. And the memory of the very real problems they'd had in New York seemed very far behind. Maybe the magic of Christmas would make everything all right, after all.

The gleaming cherry wood table stretched a good eight feet down the length of a dining room that was larger than many New York apartments Dillon had visited. A centerpiece of pine and berry-laden holly added a festive note of color to the stark white damask placemats and napkins. Heavy crystal goblets and wineglasses sparkled in the candlelight from a huge old-fashioned chandelier. Unless he missed his guess, the gold-edged china and ornate sterling were family heirlooms, probably from some ancestor who'd crossed on the *Mayflower*.

Old money and staid ideas. Mrs. Devereaux had let

him know practically in her first breath that she was a member of the Daughters of the American Revolution and proud of it. Catherine had already warned him that she was also staunchly Southern and had little tolerance for "damn Yankees." Not counting her insistence on bringing up Matthew Devlin every ten seconds, she'd been polite to Dillon despite his Northern roots. He had no illusions. It wasn't that he'd charmed her. Catherine and a sense of duty probably demanded she treat him reasonably well, at least in front of the rest of the family.

Besides he and Catherine, there were fourteen other adults seated around the table; the children had been banished to an equally lavish spread in the parlor. As far as he could tell, the grown-ups had little in common besides family ties, and it seemed to him that most of them weren't any more fond of each other than a sense of obligation required. All things considered, it was the oddest Christmas gathering Dillon had ever been part of, a Gothic ritual with undercurrents of hostility that fit every stereotypical idea he'd held of the starched Devereaux clan. It was so far from his own humble beginnings, he had absolutely no basis for comparison. His parents hadn't even been able to put a turkey on the table most years, but they'd managed to create a holiday atmosphere of warmth and laughter.

Here, only the free-flowing French wine kept the occasion from being deadly dull. In fact, as tongues began to loosen, Dillon anticipated fireworks. He was just getting interested in the ebb and flow of the tense conversation around him, when the elderly, blue-haired belle beside him put a gnarled, but perfectly manicured hand on his and drawled in a sweetly seductive tone that belied her age, "Why, Mr. Ryan, where ever has Catherine been keeping you?"

"In a closet," he whispered confidentially and enjoyed the confusion that flickered for only an instant in the depths of her quick, intelligent eyes.

"A closet?" she repeated skeptically, amusement playing about her pursed lips.

"Why, certainly. Isn't that where all the best-kept secrets are hidden?"

After another slight hesitation, she reproached him lightly, "Oh, Mr. Ryan, you are teasing me, aren't you?"

Dillon grinned and decided he liked this slightly dotty, aging coquette. "Yes, ma'am. I believe I am."

Her laughter was pure as a bell. "You young devil. I'm so glad Catherine found you. You're not at all like that stuffy ex-husband of hers."

"Matthew was stuffy?" According to Mrs. Devereaux's earlier recitation, Matthew had been the next best thing to a saint. Though he understood why she'd trotted out the memory of her ex-son-in-law, he was anxious for another view from a more impartial observer.

"Dull as dishwater," she confirmed. "But don't you dare say I told you so. Catherine's a very private woman. She wouldn't like me spreading gossip about her marriage. Still and all, a woman like Catherine should have a family, don't you think so?"

"A family?"

"Children, Mr. Ryan, a whole houseful of them. You look as though you could do the job," she said bluntly. "You do want children, don't you?"

He'd never really given the question any serious thought. He already had Jonathan and Kevin. He found himself glancing across the table at Catherine and trying to imagine a tiny version of that dark beauty. The image took his breath away. "Yes," he said softly. "I think you're right, Mrs. Brandon."

She nodded in apparent satisfaction. "You call me Aunt Mildred, young man. I suspect it won't be long before you're family, if you have any say about it."

"Not long at all," he confirmed impulsively before the older man on his left claimed his attention with a brusque opinion on the disgraceful state of banking.

"You're just as well off hiding your money under the mattress as putting it into one of those savings and loan places," George Franklin declared, waving a shaky finger at Dillon. Like Aunt Mildred, he seemed to be well into his seventies, but also like her, age hadn't dimmed his wit one little bit. He leaned closer and peered into Dillon's eyes. "Well, what do you have to say about that?"

"I think it's a matter of choosing the investment program that's best for you," Dillon said diplomatically.

"Bah! That's a wishy-washy answer, young man. What do you really think?"

"I think you're trying to get me into trouble, sir. I know perfectly well that you are president of one of the largest savings and loan institutions in the state of Georgia."

The old man threw back his head and hooted at the reply. "Done your homework, boy. I like that." He banged his fork against his water goblet to get the attention of the rest of the people at the table. "I'd like to propose a toast," he declared. "To Catherine and Dillon. May your love prosper along with your bank account."

At the foot of the table Mrs. Devereaux looked as if

she'd been forced to swallow vinegar. A deep blush colored Catherine's cheeks as Dillon's gaze caught hers. Her sophisticated, cool veneer slipped away and she became once more the vulnerable, sensual woman with whom he'd fallen in love on that sultry, long ago night in Savannah. He grinned with unabashed enjoyment at the transition.

"Later," she mouthed, attempting to look stern.

"Indeed," Dillon replied, lifting his glass in a more private toast.

He had not counted on Mrs. Devereaux when he'd uttered that seductive taunt at the dinner table. Either the old lady was a mind reader or she'd long ago decided to do everything in her power to keep Catherine and Dillon apart. She sent the men off to the living room for cigars and brandy. The suggestion, which carried the weight of a matriarchal order, clearly startled several of the younger women, who were already on their feet.

"Sit down, Catherine, Melanie. We'll have our tea in here."

"But, Mother," Catherine protested mildly, only to be silenced by a look that would have withered the heartiest weed in the vast Devereaux gardens.

Grinning at Mrs. Devereaux's obvious ploy and Catherine's apparent frustration, Dillon bent over to whisper in her ear as he passed. "Try to bear up, darlin'. We menfolk will come to rescue you soon."

"Go to blazes," she whispered back just as sweetly as Mrs. Devereaux looked on disapprovingly.

Not bothering to hide his amusement, he winked boldly. "That's the spirit, sweetheart." It reassured him that she no longer seemed one bit intimidated by her mother's repressive actions. Only when he was casting one last lingering look back did he notice the glint of mischief in Lucinda Devereaux's eyes.

"I can't imagine what got into Mother," Catherine said later, when she and Dillon had finally managed to escape to the sun porch that swept across the southern side of the huge old house. Christmas lights twinkled in the yards of distant neighboring houses. If it hadn't been for her mother's attitude, it would have been a magical evening. She'd liked watching Dillon hold his own with Aunt Mildred and Uncle George. This was the way she'd imagined things would be in New York. Instead, they'd spent all their time with business associates. Despite the quirky nature of her family, she loved them. She just didn't understand them all the time. "Why do you suppose she insisted on such an old-fashioned tradition? She never has before."

"She's protecting her chick from Northern invaders," Dillon suggested.

"I suppose that could be it," Catherine agreed.

"You aren't planning to let her intimidate you, are you?"

Catherine met his fierce gaze with a look that was pure southern belle. She wondered if he had any idea how manipulative her mother was capable of being, of the influence her mother tried to wield, not just over her, but the entire family. "I'm not the one she's trying to intimidate."

"You're wrong, my beauty. She read my intentions the first time she looked into my eyes. She's been preparing her battle plan ever since."

"Don't worry. It's been a long time since Mother has successfully run my life."

"But not so long since she's tried."

"It's in her blood," Catherine confirmed with an easy laugh that bore surprisingly little resentment. Over the past months she actually had come to terms with that. Maybe she was getting stronger and more independent after all.

"She would have made a wonderful queen, don't you think?" she said thoughtfully. "She loves waving her hand and watching everyone scatter to do her bidding. If she'd had her way, my father would have arranged marriages for all of us while we sat demurely in the garden and awaited word of our fate."

"If that had happened, would you have gone along with it?"

Catherine thought it over, realizing that in many ways that was exactly how she'd come to choose Matthew—through the subtle prodding and encouragement of her parents. Her mother might not have been crazy about him, but she had found him suitable. "I think perhaps I did," she admitted.

"And now?"

"Now I'll make my own choices."

"Are you going to choose me, Catherine? Even if I don't fit in with your mother's idea of a respectable husband?"

"Who wants respectable?" she taunted, refusing to be led into a serious conversation on the subject of marriage. Though the thought entered her mind with increasing regularity, she had yet to think of a way to make it work. At her age, she was just beginning to realize marriage often took more than love. Dillon's obsession with work was not something to be so easily overcome. And tonight was not a night for discussing anything that serious.

"I'm after your body," she said in an attempt to distract him.

She felt Dillon stiffen. His fingers caught her chin and tilted her head up until she was forced to meet his gaze. His eyes condemned the flip remark. "Why would you say something like that? It sounds like a line from some silly romantic comedy."

She kissed his cheek. "I was teasing, Dillon. You're always telling me to lighten up."

"Not when the subject is as serious as marriage."

"We were not talking about marriage."

"Weren't we?"

"Dillon, we've been over this and over this. We can't even think about marriage until we can figure out how to keep this relationship afloat. Your life is in New York. I can't imagine myself even visiting there more than a couple of times a year, much less living there."

"So much for whither thou goest."

"Exactly. Unless I miss my guess you feel exactly the same way about Atlanta."

"I have nothing at all against Atlanta, but my business is in New York."

"And my life is here or will be as soon as I finish school in Savannah. That's another reason why I can't very well pack my bags and go traipsing off to New York. You pushed until I enrolled. I'm happier than I've ever been. Do you expect me to walk away before I graduate?"

Dillon sighed. "No," he admitted with obvious reluctance. "I'm glad you're taking the classes. You're obviously more focused now, more self-confident. But what happens when you do graduate? Will you be willing to work in New York then?"

"That's too far down the line even to contemplate."

"So you want us to put our life on hold until then?"

"Isn't there room for compromise?"

"Offer me one," he said reasonably.

But as hard as she tried, Catherine couldn't think of a solution that was any more workable than what Dillon was asking. Finally, though, she was forced to admit that they'd simply been dancing around the real issue, at least as she saw it. "Dillon, it's more than simply choosing a city to live in. I don't like the way you are in New York, the way we are," she finally said wearily. "We were at each other's throats the first night. We had no time alone. You barely take the time to be with your children. You plan your entire life around business functions with people you barely know and don't even seem to like very much."

"That's the nature of the work I do. Are you saying you want me to give that up?"

"Of course not. But couldn't you modify it just a bit, separate your work and your personal life a little more?"

He refused to meet her gaze as he paced around the room. "I don't know. I honestly don't know. But I do know that I love you. That I want this to work more than I've ever wanted anything. Come back with me now, Catherine. Let's try it again until classes start after the first of the year. If we can talk about what's not working, we can handle this. Please, sweetheart. Give it another chance. The kids are dying to see you again. New York is especially beautiful this time of year. We can spend New Year's Eve in Times Square."

The very idea made her shudder. "Not in this lifetime," she vowed fervently.

He grinned at that. "Okay, a quiet dinner just for the two of us at the fanciest restaurant in the city. We can dance 'til dawn. No business." He touched his lips lightly to hers, sparking a fire deep inside her. "Please," he urged, his tongue caressing the curve of her mouth. A delicious shiver raced through her. There was no place on earth she would rather start the new year than in Dillon's embrace. If she was going to have to brave the gray gloom and idiotically fast pace of New York to be in his arms, then brave it she would.

This time.

"When do we go?" she asked as he pulled her willingly against him.

"We could sneak out tonight, but I'm trying to win points with your mother. I suspect that's not the way to do it."

"Good guess."

"Then we'll leave in the morning after dutifully paying homage to the queen and opening our gifts."

"Don't let her hear you call her that. She doesn't know that's how my sisters and I think of her."

"Coming from me, though, she'll just think it's her due," he said dryly.

"Oh, Dillon," Catherine said as a low chuckle escaped. "I do love you so."

"I love you, too. And we're going to make this work. I promise you that."

9

New Year's Eve

For a while Dillon thought it was going to be all right. When they first got back in the city, they played tourist. They saw a play, an off-Broadway production that Catherine loved and he hated. They argued about it for hours over cappuccino and cannoli in a Little Italy bakery. They went to an exhibit at the Museum of Modern Art that she found offensive and he found fascinating. Without wasting her breath, she dragged him into a taxi, asked to be taken to the Metropolitan and tugged him into one of the galleries, waving at the paintings by the Old Masters.

"That's art," she told him.

"But if artists only painted portraits and landscapes in that style, they'd stagnate. Art is a creative medium. It's supposed to change and evolve. That's what you said about that play that didn't make any sense."

Cheeks pink and eyes flashing, she stared back at him. "Well…"

"Come on, Catherine. Admit it. I'm right. Experimentation is important."

"I never said it wasn't," she said huffily.

"Didn't you?"

"No. I just said I didn't like *that* experimentation. Now take me to lunch. All this debating is making me hungry."

"Where would you like to go? The Russian Tea Room, maybe?"

She shook her head. "That deli in your neighborhood. I have a craving for pickles."

Dillon stopped in his tracks, bemusement settling on his face. "A craving for pickles?"

Catherine nodded. "What's so odd about that?"

"A craving for pickles?"

She regarded him blankly, then finally her eyes widened in understanding. "Oh, for heaven sakes, Dillon. I'm not pregnant."

"Are you sure?" he said, his throat clogged with sudden emotion. He remembered the way he'd felt on Christmas Eve when Aunt Mildred had suggested that Catherine ought to have a houseful of babies. "It would be okay. In fact, it would be wonderful."

"Dillon, it would not be wonderful. Call me traditional, but I do believe couples ought to be married before they become parents."

"No problem. We could be married by tonight. I can't think of a better way to spend New Year's Eve."

There was an odd expression on her face, just the tiniest hint of longing, but she was quick to tell him, "Silence those bells, Romeo. The only aisle you and I are walking down in the immediate future is in Bloomingdale's. I want that dress I saw in their holiday catalog."

"We'll just see about that," Dillon vowed.

"The dress?" she inquired.

"The wedding."

"Don't try to turn this into a contest of wills, Dillon. The only way you'll ever change my mind is by showing me that we can make it work."

"And how am I supposed to do that?"

"Time."

"We've known each other for nearly two years."

"Yes, but we've only actually been together about a month if you add up all our visits."

"Be sure to tally in the time we spend on the phone," he suggested with an edge of sarcasm. "What the hell does time have to do with anything? Some people meet and get married practically overnight."

"That's very romantic. Then they discover all the problems."

"And they work them out."

"Or they get divorced. I'd rather resolve the big ones before I make any vows, thank you very much. One divorce in a lifetime is about all I can handle."

Dillon finally retreated. If he'd learned nothing else about Catherine, it was that once she'd made up her mind, only gentle persuasion, not bulldozer tactics were effective. Maybe if he thought of this as an advertising campaign, he'd be more successful. He was the product. Catherine was the target audience. All he had to do was convince her that her life wouldn't be complete without one Dillon Ryan in the house. For a man with his collection of advertising awards, it should be a snap.

As it turned out, it wasn't. The campaign was sabotaged before it could even get into high gear. He made the mistake of calling his office from a pay phone at the deli. It was a compulsive habit. He did it without thinking of the consequences. Naturally there was a crisis. There was always a crisis.

"I'll get back to you in twenty minutes," he promised his secretary. "See if you can arrange a meeting for this afternoon."

By the time he returned to the table, his mind was already at work. He dragged out a leather-bound pocket notepad and began jotting down ideas.

"You called the office," Catherine accused.

Dillon regarded her guiltily. "Yes."

"You're on vacation."

"That doesn't mean I don't continue to have responsibilities."

"I thought you left Evan in charge."

"I did, but…"

"Dillon, how do you expect him to become a partner, if you don't let him handle the day-to-day work?"

"I am letting him handle it. I'm just giving him a little input," he said defensively.

She sat back in the booth. "What time's the meeting?"

"Who said anything about a meeting?"

"I know the way your mind works. Input equals meeting. What time?"

Dillon didn't want to give her the satisfaction of admitting she was right. Unfortunately there was no alternative. "I'm not sure," he said. "Helene is setting it up."

"And what about our New Year's Eve plans with the kids? They're going to be at your apartment at three o'clock expecting to spend the night with us. We promised them video games, movies and pizza."

"Damn, I forgot about that," he muttered. "It's okay,

though. You'll be there and I won't be at the office more than an hour. Two tops. I may even get back before they arrive." He took her hand. "I'm sorry, sweetheart. I know this isn't fair to you. I'll keep the meeting short, so you won't be stuck with the boys alone for too long."

"Jonathan and Kevin are not the issue. We'll have a wonderful time together. I'm looking forward to seeing them. They, however, are counting on seeing you."

Guilt increased his defensiveness. Since the divorce, he'd made an honest effort not to disappoint the boys. "Catherine, it's not as though I'm cancelling anything. What's the big deal?"

She sighed and shook her head. "You honestly don't see it, do you?"

"And apparently you can't accept that this is the way I am. I will always live up to my obligations."

"Your business obligations," she corrected. "Family obligations seem to take a back seat."

Thoroughly frustrated by her refusal to understand, he slid out of the booth and threw some money on the table. "I'm going to the office. I'll be home when I can get there."

At the door of the deli, he turned back for just an instant. Catherine was sitting ramrod straight in the booth, angrily tearing napkins into shreds. As if she'd suddenly realized he was watching, she looked up and the expression in her eyes almost broke his heart. She looked like a woman who'd just lost everything important in her life.

Dillon knew exactly how she felt.

Catherine let herself into Dillon's apartment with the key he'd given her when they'd arrived from Atlanta. In the hour before the boys were due to arrive, she took a long, hot bath and questioned every angry word she'd uttered at Dillon. Was she being so unreasonable to expect him to balance work and his life with her and his sons? Was she a harridan for being concerned that his compulsive, type-A personality was a danger to his health?

Maybe the truth of the matter was that he was too much like Matthew and not nearly enough like her father. Rawley Devereaux had been born into family wealth. Though he worked every day of his life to maintain the family's financial position, he'd never had to scramble. Catherine had led a secure, moneyed life. Her father had made it seem easily attainable. Matthew hadn't had to claw his way to the top of the medical profession. He'd been naturally talented. He'd been to good schools. Everything had fallen into place for him, except the social position he'd wanted badly enough to marry her to get. Once he'd had money and a place in Atlanta society, he'd been free to indulge in the one thing he really loved: surgery. He'd spent all but the few hours he needed for sleep in the operating room.

Still debating about the best way to handle this afternoon's argument, she dressed in a hip-length red cashmere sweater and black wool slacks. She deliberately brushed her hair back in a smooth style that Dillon hated. He called it her country club look and said it made him nervous. Good, she thought, as she fastened it back with a black velvet clip. He ought to be nervous. He ought to be shaking in his boots. Guilty as sin. He ought to be...

Before she could think up any worse fates, the doorbell rang, followed by the noisy arrival of Jonathan and Kevin.

"Hey, Dad, we're here. You in the den?" Jonathan called.

Catherine met them in the hall.

"Hey, you two. Happy New Year!"

"Yeah," Kevin said, running to throw his arms around her. "We get to stay up 'til midnight? Are you gonna stay up, too?"

"I don't know," she teased, kneeling down to help him get off his boots. "That's pretty late for me. What about you, Jonathan? You think you'll be up that late?"

"Sure," he said, standing just a little straighter. "I'm nine now. I stay up late all the time."

"You're nine, huh? I thought you were eight just last month. That must mean you had a birthday."

"Yeah," he said. "I got some really neat stuff. You wanna see? I kept some of it here." He peered into the den. "Hey, where's Dad?"

"He had to stop by the office for a little while. He should be back shortly."

Kevin's eyes widened to big round circles. "Uh-oh, Mom's gonna be mad. We're not supposed to be here if Dad's not here."

"I'm sure it'll be okay, since I'm here," Catherine said, wondering if that were really true. The boys were being supervised by an adult, but Paula didn't know her. She very well might be furious. "Maybe I should call her. What do you think?"

"I'll call Dad," Jonathan said. "Maybe he can call her."

Catherine nodded. It was his responsibility, after all. "Okay, you call your father. Kevin, why don't you show me how to make some popcorn?"

"Don't you know?"

"I've done it before, but you're probably much better at it than I am."

"Okay," he said solemnly. "I'll help."

"You get started then wait for me to remove the bag from the oven," Catherine added. He ran off to the kitchen, while she lingered as Jonathan placed his call to Dillon's office.

"Hi, Aunt Helene. It's Jonathan. Is my dad there?"

His expression grew increasingly troubled. "Okay. Uh-huh. Okay. Bye."

"Everything okay?" Catherine asked.

"She said Dad's in a meeting."

Catherine felt her blood begin to race furiously. "You didn't talk to your father at all?"

"She asked me if I was here and said she'd have him call me the minute he got out of the meeting."

"Damn!" she muttered without thinking. She felt a small hand patting her arm.

"It's okay, Catherine. Mom won't mind that you're baby-sitting us."

"What if it had been an emergency?" she said, helpless in the face of his nine-year-old aplomb.

"I would have told her, that's all. Dad told me to be sure and tell her if it was really, really important and he would always take the call. I figured this wasn't an emergency. We're just fine here with you."

She reached out and hugged him. "Yes, Jonathan. You are just fine with me. Now let's see how Kevin's coming with the popcorn."

When Dillon still wasn't back by seven, Catherine called out for the pizza. They'd finished it and played three different video games by the time he finally walked through the door. She had to steel herself not to react to the exhaustion she could see in his eyes. She had to be equally adept to hide her fury.

Jonathan and Kevin greeted him exuberantly, apparently unbothered by his failure to get home sooner. He scooped Kevin into his arms and ruffled Jonathan's dark curls.

"We've been having a great time, Dad," Jonathan said. "Catherine's real good at video games."

He stared at her over Kevin's head. "I'll bet she is. Did you guys leave me any pizza?"

"It's in the oven," she said. "I'll get it."

"Thanks, babe."

When she returned to the den, he was on the floor helping Kevin compete with Jonathan in yet another video game. Though the tired lines around his eyes were more pronounced than ever, he had one arm around Kevin. His attention was completely focused on the game. It was yet another indication that Dillon was a compulsive competitor, no matter the forum. Even a children's game required his total energy. He lifted his head and turned the full force of his smile on her as he accepted the pizza.

"Wine?" she asked.

"I think I'd better have something with caffeine in it, if I'm going to stay awake 'til midnight."

"Coffee or a soda?"

"A soda."

When she returned with the soft drink, she tried to stay aloof, but it was no time before Jonathan had drawn her into the game on his side, declaring that

Kevin had an unfair advantage. "You've got to help, Catherine. Dad's vicious."

"So I see," she murmured. "Let's see what we can do about that."

A half hour later, when she and Jonathan emerged victorious, Dillon laughed. "Tamed at last," he said.

"Hardly tamed, I'm afraid."

"Boys, why don't you go get those horns and things I bought for New Year's? They're in your room." When they were gone, he leaned over and kissed her. "I'm sorry about earlier."

Catherine sighed and ran her fingertips over the lines on his face. "You look exhausted."

"I am."

"Dillon, why..."

"We'll talk about it later," he promised. "I'll try to explain. I owe you that much at least."

"Then you are aware of what you're doing to yourself?"

He nodded, then managed a bright smile as his sons returned and engaged him in more rambunctious horseplay. If it weren't for the serious talk hanging over them, Catherine would have been thoroughly content. This was the family she'd always wanted. The boys had welcomed her into their lives as naturally and easily as any woman could ever hope. If she accepted Dillon's oft-repeated proposal, she would be with the man she loved, with his children, maybe even with a child of their own. That was so much; more than many women ever had. Why was she clinging so stubbornly to the one flaw in the arrangement?

Because it wasn't some tiny, incidental character trait. It wasn't that Dillon left his socks on the floor or his whiskers in the sink. Socks were easily picked up. Whiskers could be washed away. A husband who was never around, who put his job above his marriage was something else entirely.

"Catherine, look," Kevin said excitedly. "It's almost midnight. That big ball is starting to move."

The television announcers and the mob in Times Square rang in the new year. Kevin and Jonathan blew their horns. Dillon drew her into his arms. "Happy New Year, sweetheart!"

"Happy New Year," she said, tears streaming down her cheeks. If only they could capture this moment, maybe it would indeed be a happy new year.

When the boys were in bed at last, Dillon pulled her down on the sofa beside him.

"Dillon, maybe this should wait until tomorrow. It's nearly 1:00 a.m."

"No. You'd better catch me while I'm feeling mellow. This isn't something I normally talk about."

Catherine's heart filled with dread. He looked so sad. "What, Dillon? Don't you know there's nothing you can't tell me?"

"I know that. I know you want to understand what makes me the way I am about business. It all started thirty years ago."

"But you were just a boy then."

"That's right. Just about Jonathan's age. Very impressionable. My father lost his job. It happens to a lot of men, right? The company was badly managed. It went into bankruptcy and my father was out on the streets. At first he and Mom tried to hide that there was anything wrong. He left the house every day looking for a new job. But he was older. His skills were becoming obsolete. He was willing to take job skills training, but there weren't so many programs for that then. He took odd jobs. My mother took in laundry and cleaned houses. We survived, but my father was never okay after that. We never stopped loving him, but he lost respect for himself. A man can't survive that."

It wasn't so much Dillon's words that moved Catherine as the haunted expression in his eyes, the sadness of his memories. "It must have been terrible for all of you."

"Just a lesson. I swore I would never be dependent on another human being for an income, that whatever business I was in, I would own it."

"You've done that, darling. You're successful. Your business is flourishing."

"I have to see that it stays there, not just for myself, Catherine. Not even for the boys. I have employees. Over a hundred of them now, here and in Los Angeles. I have a responsibility to them, too, and to their families."

It was too much, Catherine thought, far too much burden for one man to shoulder alone. But she understood at last; she could feel his need to stay on top, to provide for those who'd been loyal to him.

"Dillon, couldn't you share some of that responsibility?"

"It's mine, Catherine. I accepted that the day I opened the doors of the business."

"And what if you ruin your health? What if you drive yourself so hard that you have a heart attack and die?" she said angrily. "Who will be responsible for all those people then, Dillon? Who will see that they're provided for? Are you so sure that you're not being selfish? You're everyone's hero. You're sacrificing your life to see that all those people have food on their tables. It must make you feel wonderful. If you had to share that, it would lessen your role as hero, wouldn't it? But I ask you again, what if you kill yourself in the process? Who'll be the hero then? And what in God's name will your sons and I do without you?"

10

Valentine's Day

"Have you heard from Dillon today?" Beth Markham asked as Catherine paced up and down the jammed aisles of St. Christopher's tiny thrift shop idly picking up merchandise and putting it back again. "Cat, some of that stuff is practically threadbare as it is. If you keep fiddling with it, it will fall apart. Why don't you just sit down and tell me what's on your mind?"

"I can't sit down," she said. She continued pacing, but she kept her hands to herself. Beth waited patiently, until finally Catherine admitted, "I think I've made a terrible mistake."

"What mistake?"

"I told Dillon he was killing himself and that I'd never marry him unless he stopped it."

"Okay," Beth said slowly, as she obviously struggled to absorb the implications of the blunt pronouncement. "I think I get it. What's so terrible about that?"

"What if he can't? It's a long story, but all his life

Dillon's had this terrible need in him to succeed. What if he can't ever put it into perspective?"

"Have you talked to him about this?"

"I haven't talked to him at all, not since I left New York after New Year's. He hasn't called once."

"I see. Tell me something, Cat. If you had it to do all over again, would you still fall in love with Dillon?"

Catherine grinned. "I wasn't aware that we got to choose the people we fall in love with."

"Now you sound like me," Beth chastised. "You know what I mean. When you first met Dillon, you didn't even know his last name. He didn't know how to find you. You could have left it like that. It would have been some lovely romantic memory. Knowing what you know now, would you have done anything differently? Would you have ended it right then?"

She thought about that, remembered how much stronger and more self-confident she was for knowing Dillon, how much love she'd felt in his arms. "No."

"Why? What was it about the man you met that night that drew you?"

"He was warm and supportive and attentive. He made me feel incredibly special in a way I had never felt before."

"Do you still have times like that?"

"Some," she said, beginning to understand the point Beth was trying to make. "Mostly in Savannah."

"Then it seems to me that the answer is obvious."

"I don't think I can talk Dillon into moving to Savannah. Not in a million years. The one time I even broached the possibility of his leaving New York, he threw a fit."

"What if he opened up a branch office down there?

He already has a couple of accounts in Savannah, doesn't he? It would be a natural step. I don't know all that much about advertising, but wouldn't it give him a presence in the southeast?"

"It makes sense to me, but he really seems adamant about staying in New York. I'm not sure he'd even listen to the idea."

"Maybe he would if you present it properly, say with a little wine and candlelight. It seems to me like Valentine's Day would be a good time to try."

"What would I do without you?" Catherine said as the idea took hold and began to blossom. She hugged Beth in an unusual display of affection. "Thank you. You're wonderful."

"Just trying to keep my rating as the best matchmaker in town."

"You didn't introduce me to Dillon," she reminded her. "You don't even know him."

"But who sent you back to Savannah to see him again? Who pushed you to move down there so you could see him more often?"

"Okay, okay," she said, laughing. "If it works out, you get the credit."

"I don't want credit, just an invitation to the wedding."

"You've got it. Keep your fingers crossed for me, will you?"

"I always do. Something tells me that this time you don't need it."

"I hope you're right. I really do."

Catherine packed her bag without the slightest regard for neatness. She tossed it into the back of the car, then ran back inside to call Dillon's office.

"Mrs. Devlin," Helene said, clearly surprised to be hearing from her. "How are you?"

"I'm just fine, Helene. Is Mr. Ryan in?"

"No. I'm terribly sorry, but you just missed him. He left on a business trip."

Catherine had to bite back her disappointment. Maybe it was better this way. Maybe it would be more effective if she didn't speak to Dillon directly. If he was furious with her, a message passed through a third party might be more likely to get his attention.

"Can you reach him?"

"Of course."

"Then please tell him that I must see him at once. It's urgent. I'm leaving Atlanta now and I should be back in Savannah by midafternoon. Can you get that message to him?"

"Right away, but…"

Catherine hung up before the secretary could say anything that might dissuade her from her plan. The last thing she needed to hear was that Dillon's trip was also urgent or that he'd flown off to Los Angeles to engage in mortal combat to save Ruben Prunelli's soul.

The tedious drive to Savannah had never taken longer. All during the five-and-a-half-hour trip she went over her arguments, trying to brace herself for the moment when she'd have to use them to convince Dillon that this could work, that they could have a life together without sacrificing his needs or hers.

By the time she'd parked in front of the carriage house, she was sure she could make it work. Two hours later, when Dillon still hadn't called, her faith began to waver. She began to cook. She chopped. She minced. She stirred. Like therapy, she found it soothing. She'd made coq au vin, a salad that could have served all the tourists in town, fresh rolls and three pies. She was considering baking a cake, when she heard the scrape of a key in the lock. She froze. Despite all her pep talks, she wasn't ready to face him.

"Catherine?"

"In the kitchen," she said breathlessly.

When she finally found nerve enough to turn around, he was standing in the doorway. His dark hair was windblown, his tie was askew. He looked very much like a man who'd rushed to get there. He looked wonderful.

"You look wonderful," he said quietly.

"Thank you."

"I've missed you."

"I've missed you too."

"I've been thinking," they said together, then laughed nervously.

"You first," she said.

"Maybe we should have some wine. Do you have a bottle?"

"In the dining room." While he was gone, she clung to the counter and dragged in a deep breath. She was determined to be composed when she faced him again. She was determined he would never see how just the sight of him had shaken her.

"Catherine," he said softly.

She whirled around and found herself nearly in his arms. Their gazes collided and held. She swallowed hard and tried not to back away.

"Your wine." He held out the glass. She took it, careful not to allow their fingers to brush. The temperature in the kitchen had already risen several degrees.

One touch was all it would take to set her blood on fire. One touch would ignite all of the old passions and they would never say the words that had to be spoken.

"To warm thoughts," he said, his eyes never leaving hers.

She pulled her gaze away and sipped desperately at the wine. It only made her hotter, more uncertain. She'd longed to seem cool. She'd wanted desperately to be bold. Instead, she was simply Catherine. For better or worse.

"I've been thinking," he said again. "I've made some decisions."

"Oh."

"The past six weeks have been the most miserable I've ever spent in my life. I finally had to do some serious reevaluating of my goals."

"And? What did you come up with?"

He leaned nonchalantly against the counter. His carefully chosen words belied the casual stance. "It all kept coming back to you. I don't want to lose you."

She bit her lip to keep from crying out. She clung to the wineglass to keep from throwing her arms around him. She waited, tension spreading through her, hope held desperately at bay.

"I've finally sat down and had a long talk with Evan about the company. As a result, he's now a full partner. He's going to run the New York office. He can't handle it all alone yet, but it's a start."

"He must be very happy," she said cautiously.

"I've also decided to open an office here in Savannah. I have two clients here now and prospects seem good for more. I'll still have to travel to New York and

Los Angeles, but I should be able to change my pace quite a bit if everything works out with Evan."

Catherine felt a wave of relief wash through her, followed by one nagging suspicion. The timing of this seemed very odd. Was it possible that Beth had called Dillon and prodded him into making these radical changes today, the same notions that had been planted in her mind by a worried friend?

She cleared her throat. "Um, when did you decide all this?"

"Evan and I started talking about it about two weeks after you left. The pieces finally fell into place today. I took the first plane out to tell you about it."

Catherine had to fight off the desire to laugh hysterically. Today! He'd finalized the plans today. But he'd made the decision on his own, reached the same exact conclusion she had reached.

"Well," he said. "You're not saying anything. What do you think?"

"I think…" She began to grin. She could feel the smile growing wider and wider. "I think this is the most wonderful news I've ever had in my life," she said, no longer fighting her elation.

"Are you sure?" he said, regarding her hesitantly.

"Oh, Dillon, I've never been more certain of anything in my life. We'll be happy here. I know we will. We can go to New York as often as you want to see your sons. We can find a house. The boys can have their own rooms for when they come to visit. I'll sell the one in Atlanta. It's going to be perfect."

He seemed to be struggling with an emotion every bit as powerful as what she was feeling. "I was so afraid," he admitted in a choked voice. He pulled her into his arms and held her. "If I'd lost you, Catherine, I don't know what I would have done."

"But you didn't lose me. There wasn't a single minute that I didn't believe that we would find a way to work it out."

He leaned back and regarded her so skeptically that she finally smiled. "Okay, maybe there were one or two minutes, when I had a few doubts. It didn't last."

"I don't know why it took me so long to see it," he said. "I've liked Savannah more and more each time I've been here. The work I've been doing for White Stone is some of the best I've ever done. Most important, you're happy here. Evan suggested I locate the office in Atlanta, but I like the idea that this will be a fresh start for both of us in the city where we met."

"I agree."

"You won't mind not being in Atlanta?"

"No. My ties there have loosened with every week I've been away. My parents won't be happy, but it's not as if I'll be at the ends of the earth. They'll adjust."

"Your father may, but your mother? I'm not so sure."

"She'll grumble, but if we offer her two new grandsons to spoil, it should make up for my absence."

"Two? You are ambitious."

"I meant Jonathan and Kevin."

"What about their baby sister then?"

"I didn't know you were even pregnant," she teased him.

"Okay, enough. You're happy about Savannah. You'd enjoy working here after you finish school?"

"Absolutely, and best of all there are no ghosts here. Just long, lazy days to build a new life together."

"Lazy?" he said, one brow lifting quizzically.

"Okay, bad choice of words. I won't ask for the impossible."

He touched her lips. "No, sweetheart. Always ask. Together, even the impossible seems within reach."

Epilogue

May 16

"I simply don't understand why you insisted on getting married on May 16," Lucinda Devereaux told Catherine as she rearranged her veil. "It's the middle of the week. No one can take off to come clear down here for a wedding."

"We met on May 16 two years ago," Catherine explained patiently as she put the veil back the way it had been. "And I don't know how you can complain about the guest list. You must have had two hundred acceptances. The owner of the restaurant is ecstatic."

"I should think he would be," her mother said haughtily. "It's probably more business than he usually gets in an entire week."

"Hardly. It's a very popular restaurant."

"It's a seafood place, Catherine. No one holds a wedding reception in a seafood restaurant."

"Maybe no Devereaux does, but the Ryans of New York, Atlanta and Savannah do. It has a sentimental meaning for us."

"I suppose that's where you met."

"It is."

"I just hope they aired it out. I'd hate to have all our guests smelling like catfish."

"Mother, stop fussing. Go talk to Dad or something. I want to find Dillon."

"Dillon? For heaven sakes, Catherine, you can't see him before the wedding."

"Oh, but I can," she said, marching off.

"Catherine!"

She turned back. "Think of it this way, Mother. I'm setting new trends."

"You're playing havoc with traditions."

She found Dillon trying to tie Kevin's bow tie. He was making a real mess of it. "Let me," she said, pushing him aside. "You look very handsome, Kevin. You, too, Jonathan."

"What about me?" Dillon demanded.

"I'm not supposed to look at you."

"You've obviously been talking to your mother again. She is not happy that there's no full orchestra to play the wedding march."

"She'll have to learn to live with the flute and the trumpet."

"How did you ever find those two musicians we heard on our first real date?"

"A desperate woman can accomplish miracles."

"The ad in the paper helped," Beth noted, coming up behind them. "I don't suppose you all would like to get this show on the road?"

"What's the matter?" Catherine teased. "Don't you get full credit for your matchmaking talent until after the ceremony?"

"Matchmaking?" Dillon repeated, his expression confused. "Do I know this woman?"

"No, but you will," Beth promised. "I will remind you until the day you die how much you owe me. Without me, Catherine might never have had the nerve to try and convince you to move to Savannah."

"Beth!" Catherine protested weakly.

The warning came too late. Dillon had already picked up on the remark. Beth looked from one to the other and moaned. "Uh-oh."

"Indeed," Catherine said.

"I think I'd better go check the flowers."

"Good idea."

"What was she talking about?" Dillon demanded.

"You remember Valentine's Day?"

"The day I came down here after you."

"Well, I never did mention that I'd called your office that morning and I guess Helene never mentioned it, either, because you never said anything, right?"

"I'm with you so far."

"Remember I told you that I'd been thinking, but then I told you to go first?"

"I think I remember something like that."

"Well, I had decided that I was going to try and convince you to move to Savannah and open an office. Beth prodded me into at least talking the idea over with you. I told Helene I needed to see you urgently. When you came in, I thought that was why you were here."

Dillon started chuckling when she was halfway through telling him. "I guess my announcement must really have thrown you for a loop."

"You could say that."

"It just proves one thing."

"What's that?"

"Two minds that much in tune belong together. We'll be unbeatable."

"You bet we will," she said softly just as his mouth closed over hers. The kiss was filled with all the tenderness, all the love that Dillon had to offer.

It was definitely the beginning of forever.

* * * * *

Visit the Author Profile page
at Harlequin.com for more titles.

SECRET
CHRISTMAS TWINS

Lee Tobin McClain

To Shana Asaro and Melissa Endlich,
who offered me the opportunity
to work on this special Christmas project,
and to Mark S., with appreciation for the
informal legal counsel and the delicious cider.

1

Detective Jason Stephanidis steered his truck down the narrow, icy road, feeling better than anytime since being placed on administrative leave. He'd checked on several elderly neighbors near Holly Creek Farm and promised to plow them out after the storm ended. Now he was headed back to the farm to spend some much-needed time with his grandfather.

It wasn't that he was feeling the Christmas spirit, not exactly. Being useful was how he tamed the wolves inside him.

Slowly, cautiously, he guided the truck around a bend. Amid the rapidly falling snow, something flashed. Headlights? In the middle of the road?

What was a little passenger car doing out on a night like this? This part of Pennsylvania definitely required all-wheel drive and heavy snow tires in winter.

He swerved right to avoid hitting the small vehicle. Perilously close to the edge of the gulch, he stopped his truck, positioning it to provide a barrier against the other car going over the edge.

There. The car should be able to pass him now, safely on the side away from the ledge.

Rather than slowing down gradually, though, the other driver hit the brakes hard. The little car spun and careened into an icy snowdrift, stopping with a resounding thump.

Jason put on his flashers, leaped from his truck and ran toward the vehicle. He couldn't see through the fogged-up window on the driver's side, so he carefully tried the door. The moment he opened it, he heard a baby's cry.

Oh no.

"The babies. My babies! Are they okay?" The driver clicked open her seat belt and twisted toward the back seat. "Mikey! Teddy!"

There were two of them? "Sit still, ma'am. I'll check on your children." He eased open the back door and saw two car seats. A baby in each. One laughing, one crying, but they both looked uninjured, at least to his inexperienced eye.

Between the front seats, the driver's face appeared. "Oh, my sweet boys, are you okay?" There was an edge of hysteria in her voice.

"They seem fine, ma'am. You need to turn off your vehicle."

She looked at him as if he were speaking Greek, then reached a shaky hand toward the baby who was wailing. "It's okay, Mikey. You're okay." She patted and clucked in that way women seemed to naturally know how to do.

The baby's crying slowed down a little.

"Turn off your vehicle," he repeated.

"What?" She was still rubbing the crying baby's

leg, making soothing sounds. It seemed to work; the baby took one more gasping breath, let it out in a hiccupy sigh and subsided into silence.

She fumbled around, found a pacifier and stuck it in the baby's mouth. Then she cooed at the nearer baby, found his pacifier pinned to his clothes and did the same.

Unhurt, quiet babies. Jason felt his shoulders relax a little. "Turn the car off. For safety. We don't want any engine fires."

"Engine fires?" She gasped, then spun and did as he'd instructed.

He straightened and closed the rear car door to keep the heat inside.

She got out, looked back in at the babies and closed the door. And then she collapsed against it, hands going to her face, breathing rapid.

"Are you all right?" He stepped closer and noticed a flowery scent. It seemed to come from her masses of long red hair.

"Just a little shaky. Delayed reaction." Her voice was surprisingly husky.

"How old are your babies?"

She hesitated just a little bit. "They're twins. Fifteen months."

He focused on her lightweight leather jacket, the nonwaterproof sneakers she wore. *Not* on her long legs nicely showcased by slim-fitting jeans. "Ma'am, you shouldn't be out on a night like this. If I hadn't come along—"

"If you hadn't come along, I wouldn't have gone off the road!"

"Yes, you would've. You can't slam on your brakes in the snow."

"How was I supposed to know that?"

"Ma'am, any teenager would know not to…" He trailed off. No point rubbing in how foolish she'd been.

She bit her lip and held up a hand. "Actually, you're right that I shouldn't be out. I was slipping and sliding all over the place." Walking up to the front end of the car, she studied it, frowning. "Wonder if I can just back out?"

Jason knelt and checked for damage, but fortunately, the car looked okay. Good and stuck, though. "You probably can't, but I can tow you." As he walked around the car to study the rear bumper in preparation for towing, he noticed the Arizona plates.

So that was why she didn't know how to drive in the snow.

He set up some flares, just in case another vehicle came their way, and then made short order of connecting the tow rope and pulling her out of the drift.

He turned off his truck, jumped out and walked over to her. Snow still fell around them, blanketing the forest with quiet.

"Thank you so much." She held out a hand to shake his.

He felt the strangest urge to wrap her cold fingers in his palm, to warm them. To comfort her, which would shock the daylights out of his ex-fiancée, who'd rightly assessed him as cold and heartless. He was bad at relationships and family life, but at least now he knew it. "You should wear gloves," he said sternly instead of holding on to that small, delicate hand.

For just the briefest second he thought she rolled her eyes. "Cold hands are the least of my problems."

Really? "It didn't look like your children are dressed warmly enough, either."

She turned her back to him, opened her car door and grabbed a woven, Southwestern-looking purse. "Can I pay you for your help?"

"*Pay* me? Ma'am, that's not how we do things around here."

She arched an eyebrow. "Look, I'd love to hang out and discuss local customs, but I need to get my boys to shelter. Since, as you've pointed out so helpfully, they're inadequately dressed."

"I'll lead you back to a road that's straighter, cleared off better," he said. "Where were you headed?"

"Holly Creek Farm."

Jason stared at her.

"It's supposed to be just a few miles down this road, I think. I should be fine."

"Are you sure that's the name of the place? There's a lot of Holly-this and Holly-that around here, especially since the closest town is Holly Springs."

"I know where I'm going!" She crossed her arms, tucking her hands close to her sides. "It's a farm owned by the Stephanidis family. The grandparents...er, an older couple lives there." A frown creased her forehead, and she fingered her necklace, a distinctive silver cross embedded with rose quartz and turquoise.

A chill ran down Jason's spine. The necklace was familiar. He leaned closer. "That looks like a cross my sister used to wear." Sadness flooded him as he remembered the older sister who'd once been like a mother to him, warm and loving, protecting him from their parents' whims.

Before she'd gone underground, out of sight.

"A friend gave it to me."

Surely Kimmie hadn't ended up back in Arizona, where they'd spent their early childhood. An odd thrumming started in his head. "Why did you say you were going to the Holly Creek Farm?"

"I didn't say." She cocked her head, looking at him strangely. "The twins…um, my boys and I are going there to live for a while. Our friend Kimmie Stephanidis gave us permission, since it's her family home. What did you say your name is?"

"I didn't say." He echoed her words through a dry throat. "But I'm Jason. Jason Stephanidis."

She gasped and her hand flew to her mouth. She went pale and leaned back against her car.

Jason didn't feel so steady himself. What had this redheaded stranger been to Kimmie? And was she seriously thinking of staying at the farm—with babies—when she obviously knew nothing about managing a country winter? "Look, do you want to bring your kids and come sit in my truck? I have bottled water in there, and it's warm. You're not looking so good."

She ignored the suggestion. "You're Jason Stephanidis? Oh, wow." She didn't sound happy as she glanced at the babies in the back seat of her car.

"And your name is…"

"Erica. Erica Lindholm."

"Well, Erica, we need to talk." He needed to pump her for information and then send her on her way. The farm was no place for her and her boys, not at this time of year. And Jason's grandfather didn't need the stress.

On the other hand, given the rusty appearance of her small car, a model popular at least ten years ago, she probably didn't have a lot of money for a hotel. If she could even get to one at this time of night, in this storm.

She straightened her back and gave him a steady look that suggested she had courage, at least. "If you're Kimmie's brother, we do need to talk. She needs help, if you're willing. But for now, I need to get the boys to shelter. If you could just point me toward the farm—"

He made a snap decision to take her there, at least for tonight. "I'll clear the road and you can follow me there." She'd obviously been close to Kimmie. Maybe a fellow addict who needed a place to stay, dry out.

If he caught one whiff of drug use around those babies, though, he'd have her arrested so fast she wouldn't know what had hit her.

"I don't want to put you out." Her voice sounded tight, shaky. "I'm sure you have somewhere to go."

"It's no trouble to lead you there," he said, "since I live at Holly Creek Farm."

The detective in him couldn't help but notice that his announcement made the pretty redhead very, very uncomfortable.

Erica Lindholm clutched the steering wheel and squinted through the heavily falling snow, her eyes on the red taillights in front of her.

Jason Stephanidis *lived* there. In the place Kimmie had said belonged to her grandparents. What nightmare was this?

How could she take care of the babies here? Kimmie's brother, being a detective, was sure to find out she'd taken them and run with no official guardianship papers. That had to be a crime.

And he might—probably would—attempt to take them away from her.

She couldn't let him—that was all. Which meant she couldn't let him know that the boys were actually Kimmie's sons.

Somewhere on the long road trip, caring for the twins and worrying about them, comforting them and feeding them, she'd come to love them with pure maternal fierceness. She'd protect them with her life.

Including protecting them from Kimmie's rigid, controlling brother, if need be. She'd promised Kimmie that.

In just ten minutes, which somehow felt all too soon, they turned off the main road. The truck ahead slowed down, and a moment later she realized Jason had lowered the plow on the front of his truck and was clearing the small road that curved up a little hill and over a quaint-looking bridge.

A moment later they pulled up to a white farmhouse, its front door light revealing a wraparound front porch, the stuff of a million farm movies.

Behind her, Teddy started to fuss. From the smell of things, one or both of the boys needed a diaper change.

Jason had emerged from the truck and was coming back toward her, and she got out of her car to meet him. He looked as big as a mountain: giant, stubbly and dangerous.

Erica's heart beat faster. "Thank you for all you've done for us tonight," she said. "I understand there's a cabin on the property. We can go directly there, if you'll point the way."

"No, you can't."

"Why not?"

"That cabin hasn't been opened up in a couple of years. The heat's off, water's off, who knows what critters have been living there…" He shook his head. "I don't know what you were thinking, bringing those babies out in this storm."

Guilt surged up in her. He was right.

"For now, you'll have to stay at the farmhouse with me."

Whoa. No *way*. "That's not safe or appropriate. I don't know you from—"

The front door burst open. "There you are! I was ready to call the rescue squad. Who'd you bring with you?"

All she could see of the man in the doorway was a tall blur, backlit by a golden, homey light that looked mercifully warm.

"Open up the guest room, would you, Papa? We've got Kimmie's friend here, and she has babies."

"Babies! Get them inside. I'll put on the soup pot and pull out the crib." The front door closed.

Jason looked at Erica, and for the first time, she saw a trace of humor in his eyes. "My grandfather's house. He'll keep you and the twins safe from me and anything else."

Behind her, through the car's closed windows, she could hear both twins crying. She didn't have another solution, at least not tonight. "All right. Thank you."

Moments later they were inside a large, well-heated farmhouse kitchen. Erica spread a blanket and changed the twins' diapers while Jason's grandfather took a dishrag to an ancient-looking high chair. "There you go," he said, giving the chair's wooden tray a final polish. "One of 'em can sit there. You'll have to hold the other for now." He extended a weathered hand. "Andrew Stephanidis. You can call me Papa Andy."

"Thank you." She shook his hand and then lifted Teddy into the high chair. "This is Teddy, and—" she bent down and picked up Mikey "—this is Mikey, and I'm Erica. Erica Lindholm." *Who might be wanted by the police right about now.* "I'm very grateful to you for taking us in."

"Always room for the little ones. That's what Mama used to say." The old man looked away for a moment, then turned back to face Erica. "Sorry we're not decorated for Christmas. Used to have holly and evergreens and tinsel to the roof, but…seems like I just don't have the heart for it this year."

Jason carried in the last of her boxes and set it on the table. "I put your suitcases up in the guest room, but this box looks like food." He was removing his enormous boots as he spoke. "Sorry about the mess, Papa. I'll clean it up."

The old man waved a hand. "Later. Sit down and have some soup."

Erica's head was spinning. How had Kimmie gotten it so wrong, telling her the mean brother never came to the farm? And it sure seemed like Kimmie's grandmother, the "Mama" Papa Andy had spoken of, had passed on. Obviously, Kimmie had completely lost touch with her own family.

In front of Erica, a steaming bowl of vegetable soup sent up amazing smells, pushing aside her questions. She'd been so focused on feeding and caring for the twins during four long days of travel that she'd barely managed to eat. The occasional drive-through burger and the packets of cheese and crackers in the cheap motels where they'd crashed each night couldn't compare to the deliciousness in front of her.

"Go ahead. Dig in. I'll hold the little one." Papa Andy lifted Mikey from her lap and sat down, bouncing him on his knee with a practiced movement.

Erica held her breath. With the twins' developmental delays came some fussiness, and she wanted to avoid questions she wouldn't know how to answer. Wanted to avoid a tantrum, too.

But Mikey seemed content with Papa Andy's bouncing, while Teddy plucked cereal from the wooden high chair tray and looked around, wide-eyed. The babies cared for, Erica scooped up soup and ate two big pieces of buttered corn bread, matching Jason bite for bite even though he was twice her size.

When her hunger was sated, she studied him from under her eyelashes and tried to quell her own fear. Kimmie had been afraid of her brother's wrath if he discovered that she'd gone back to drugs and gotten pregnant out of wedlock. And she'd feared disappointing her grandparents. That was why she'd become estranged from the family. She hadn't said it outright, but Erica had gotten the feeling that Kimmie might have stolen money from some of them, as well.

None of that was the twins' fault, and if Kimmie's family history were the only barrier, Erica wouldn't hesitate to let Jason and Papa Andy know that the twins were their own relatives. She wasn't foolish enough to think she could raise them herself with no help, and having a caring uncle and great-grandfather and more resources on their side would be only to their benefit.

But Kimmie had said Jason would try to get custody of the twins, and seeing how authoritative he seemed to be, Erica didn't doubt it.

Kimmie hadn't wanted her brother to have them. She'd insisted there were good reasons for it.

Erica wished she could call and ask, but Kimmie wasn't answering her phone. In fact, she'd left a teary message two days ago, saying she was moving into a rehab center. She'd assured Erica that she was getting good care, but might not be reachable by phone.

Now that Erica was sitting still, for the moment not worried about her and the twins' survival, sadness washed over her. For Kimmie, for the twins and for herself. With all her flaws, Kimmie had been a loving friend, and they'd spent almost every moment of the past month together. Like a vivid movie, she remembered when Kimmie—addicted, terminally ill and in trouble with the law—had begged her to take the twins.

"I know it's a lot to ask. You're so young. You'll find a husband and have babies of your own…"

"No, I won't," Erica had responded. "But that's not what's important now."

"You have time. You can get over your past." Kimmie had pulled a lock of hair out of Erica's ponytail. "You could be beautiful if you'd stop hiding it. And you need to realize that there are a few men out there worth trusting."

Remembering Kimmie's attempt at mothering, even at such a horrible moment, brought tears to Erica's eyes even now, in the bright farmhouse kitchen. Erica *wouldn't* get over her past, wouldn't have kids of her own, as Kimmie would have realized if she hadn't been so ill.

But Erica had these babies, and she'd protect them with her life. They were her family now.

The old black wall phone rang, and Papa answered it.

"Yes, he's here." She listened. "No, Heather Marie, he's not coming out again in the storm just because you forgot to buy nail polish or some such crazy thing!" He held the phone away from his ear and indistinguishable, agitated words buzzed out from it. "You saw a *what*? A *dog*?"

Jason took one more bite of corn bread, wiped his mouth and stood. He might have even looked relieved. "It's okay, Papa. I'll talk to her."

Papa narrowed his eyes at him. "You're an enabler."

Jason took the phone and moved into the hall, the long cord stretching to accommodate. Minutes later he came back in. "She thinks she saw a dog out wandering on Bear Creek Road, but she was afraid if she stopped she couldn't get going again. I'm going to run out there and see if I can find it."

"And visit her? Maybe get snowed in? Because that's what she wants."

Jason waved a dismissive hand. "I don't mind helping." Then he turned to Erica. "We have to talk, but I'm sure you're exhausted. We can figure all of this out tomorrow." He left the room, a giant in sock feet. Moments later, a chilly breeze blew through the kitchen, and then the front door slammed shut.

A chill remained in Erica's heart, though. She had the feeling that Kimmie's big brother would have plenty of questions for her when he returned. Questions she didn't dare to answer.

* * *

It was almost midnight by the time Jason arrived back at the house. Exhausted, cold and wet, he went around to the passenger side to get leverage enough to lift the large dog he'd finally found limping through the woods near Bear Creek.

He carried the dog to the house and fumbled with the door, trying to open it without putting down the dog.

Suddenly, it swung open, and there was Erica, her hair glowing like fire in the hallway's golden light. "Oh, wow, what can I do?" She hurried out to hold open the storm door for him, regardless of the cold. "Want me to grab towels? A blanket?"

"Both. Closet at the top of the stairs."

She ran up and came back down and into the front room quickly, her green eyes full of concern. Her soft jeans had holes at the knees, and not the on-purpose kind teenagers wore.

After she'd spread the blankets on the floor in front of the gas fireplace, he carefully set the dog down and studied him. Dirty, yellow fur, a heavy build: probably a Lab-shepherd mix. The dog didn't try to move much but sighed and dropped his head to the floor as if relieved to have found a safe haven.

"Go take off your wet things," Erica ordered Jason. "I'll watch the dog."

"The twins are asleep?"

"Like logs."

Jason shed his jacket, boots and hat, got two bowls of water and a couple of thin dishrags, and came back into the warm room. It hadn't changed much since he was a kid. He half expected his grandmother to come around the corner, bringing cookies and hot chocolate.

But that wasn't happening, ever again.

"Was he in a fight?" Erica asked. She was gently plucking sticks and berries out of the dog's fur. "His leg seems awful tender."

"I'll try to clean it and wrap it. He's friendly, like he's had a good home, though maybe not for a while." He put the cold water down, and the dog lifted his big golden head and drank loud and long, spilling water all over the floor.

"He's skinny under his fur," Erica said. "And a mess. What are all these sticky berries on him?" She plucked a sprig from the dog's back, green with a few white berries.

"It's mistletoe." Made him think of Christmas parties full of music and laughter. Of happy, carefree times.

Erica didn't look at Jason as she pulled more debris from the dog's fur. "Then that's what we'll call him. Mistletoe."

"You're *naming* the dog?"

"We have to call him something," she said reasonably. "You work on him. I'll be right back."

He puzzled over Erica as he carefully examined the dog's leg. She seemed kind and helpful and well-spoken. So how had Kimmie connected with her? Had Kimmie gotten her life together, started running with a better crowd? Was Erica some kind of emissary from his sister?

He breathed in and out and tried to focus on the present moment. This homey room, the quiet, the dog's warm brown eyes. Letting his thoughts run away with him was dangerous, was what had made him okay with administrative leave. The only crime he'd committed was trusting his partner, who'd turned out to be corrupt, taking bribes. With time, Jason knew he'd be exonerated of wrongdoing.

But still, he was all too aware that he'd lost perspective. He'd been working too hard and getting angrier and angrier, partly because of worrying about his sister's situation and wondering where she was. He'd had no life. Coming here, taking a break, was the right thing to do, especially given his grandmother's death earlier this year.

He should have come home more. He'd made so many mistakes as a brother, a son, a grandson. And a fiancé, according to what Renea had screamed as she'd stormed out for the last time. Funny how that was the weakness that bothered him the least.

Erica came back into the room and set a tray down on the end table beside the couch.

A familiar, delicious smell wafted toward him. *Déjà vu.* "You made hot chocolate?"

She looked worried. "Papa Andy showed me where to find everything before he went to bed. I hope it's okay. You just looked so cold."

He took one of the two mugs and sipped, then drank. "Almost as good as Gran's."

Her face broke into a relieved smile, and if she'd been pretty before, her smile made her absolutely gorgeous. Wow.

"How's Mistletoe?" She set down the other mug and knelt by the dog.

He snorted out a laugh at the name. "He let me look at his leg. Whether he'll let me wash it remains to be seen." He put down the hot chocolate and dipped a rag into the warm water.

"Want me to hold his head?"

"No." Was she crazy? "If he bites anybody, it's going to be me, not you."

"I'm not afraid." She scooted over, gently lifted the dog's large head and crossed her legs beneath. "It's okay, boy," she said, stroking his face and ears. "Jason's going to fix it."

Jason parted the dog's fur. "Don't look—it's not pretty."

She ignored his instruction, leaning over to see. "Aw, ouch. Wonder what happened?"

"A fight, or clipped by a car. He's limping pretty bad, so I'm worried the bone is involved." As gently as possible, he squeezed water onto the wound and then wiped away as much dirt as he could. Once, the dog yelped, but Erica soothed him immediately and he relaxed back into her lap.

Smart dog.

Jason ripped strips of towel and wrapped the leg, aiming for gentle compression. "There you go, fella. We'll call the vet in the morning."

"That wasn't so bad, was it?" Erica eased out from under the dog's head, gave him a few more ear scratches and then moved to the couch, picking up her mug on the way. "I love hot chocolate, but in Phoenix, we didn't have much occasion to drink it."

Jason picked up his half-full cup and sat in the adjacent armchair. "How did you know Kimmie?"

The question was abrupt, and he meant it to be. People answered more honestly when they hadn't had a chance to relax and figure out what their interrogator wanted to hear.

She drew in a deep breath and blew it out. "Fair question. I met her at Canyon Lodge." She looked at him, but when he didn't react, she clarified. "It's a drug rehab center."

"You're an addict, too?"

"Noooo." She lifted an eyebrow at his assumption. "My mom was. I met Kimmie, wow, ten years ago, on visits to Mom. When they both got out, we stayed in touch."

And yet she hadn't turned to her mom when she'd needed a place to stay. "How's your mom doing?" he asked.

She looked away. "She didn't make it."

"I'm sorry."

"Thanks." She slid down off the couch to sit beside the dog again, petting him in long, gentle strokes.

"Where's Kimmie now? Is she in Phoenix?"

Erica hesitated.

"Look, we've been out of touch for years. But if she's sober now..." He saw Erica's expression change. "*Is* she sober now?"

Erica looked down at the dog, into the fire, anywhere but at him.

Hope leaked out of him like air from a deflating tire. "She's not."

Finally, she blew out a breath and met his eyes. "I don't know how to answer that."

"What do you mean? She's straight or she's not."

Erica's face went tense, and he realized he'd spoken harshly. Not the way to gain trust and information. "Sorry. Let's start over. Why did she send you to Holly Creek Farm?"

Simple enough question, he'd thought. Apparently not.

"It's complicated," she said.

He ground his teeth to maintain patience. His superiors had been right; he was too much on the edge to be working the streets right now. For a fleeting, fearful moment, he wondered if he could ever do it again.

But interviewing someone about your own kin was different, obviously, than asking questions about a stranger.

"Kimmie isn't...well," she said finally.

Jason jerked to attention at her tone. "What's wrong?"

She opened her mouth to speak, but his cell phone buzzed. Wretched thing. And as a cop, even one on leave, he had to take it.

"It's late for a phone call." Then she waved a hand, looking embarrassed. "Not my business. Sorry."

A feeling of foreboding came over Jason as he looked at the unfamiliar number. "Area code 602. Phoenix, isn't it?"

She gasped, her hand going to her mouth. "Yes."

He clicked to answer. "Jason Stephanidis."

"Mr. Stephanidis." The voice on the other end was male, and there was background noise Jason couldn't identify. "Are you the brother of Kimberly Stephanidis?"

Jason closed his eyes. "Yes."

"Okay. This is Officer John Jiminez. Phoenix PD. You're a cop, too?"

"That's right."

"Good. My information's accurate. Do you know... Have you seen your sister recently?"

"No."

Silence. Then: "Look, I'm sorry to inform you that she's passed away. I've been assigned to locate her next of kin."

A chasm opened in his chest. "Drugs?"

"The coroner listed the cause of death as an overdose. But it also looks like she had advanced lung cancer."

Jason squeezed his eyes closed, tighter, as if that could block out the words he was hearing. What he wanted to do was to shout back: *No. No. No.*

Erica sat on the couch, her arms wrapped around herself. Trying to hold herself together.

Kimmie was gone.

The twins were motherless.

Grief warred with worry and fear, and she jumped up and paced the room.

After Jason had barked out the news, said that a lawyer would call back tomorrow with more information, he'd banged out of the house.

What had happened? Had Kimmie gone peacefully, with good care, or died alone and in pain? Or, given the mention of overdose, had she taken the low road one last time?

Erica sank her head into her hands and offered up wordless prayers. Finally, a little peace came to her as the truth she believed with all her heart sank in: Kimmie had gone home to a forgiving God, happy, all pain gone.

She paced over to the window and looked out. The

snow had stopped, and as she watched, the moon came out from under a cloud, sending a cold, silvery light over the rolling farmland.

Off to the side, Jason shoveled a walkway, fast, furious, robotic.

Wanting air herself, wanting to see that moon better and remind herself that God had a plan, Erica found a heavy jacket in the hall closet and slipped outside.

Sharp cold took her breath away. A wide creek ran alongside the house, a little stone bridge arching over it. Snow blanketed hills and trees and barns.

And the moonlight! It reflected off snow and water, rendering the scene almost as bright as daytime, bright enough that a wooden fence and a line of tall pines cast shadows on the snow.

The only sound was the steady *chink-chink-chink* of Jason's shovel.

The newness, the majesty, the fearfulness of the scene made her tremble. God's creation, beautiful and dangerous. A Sunday school verse flashed through her mind: *"In His hand is the life of every creature and the breath of all mankind."*

The shovel stopped. Heavy boot steps came toward her.

"You should have contacted me!" Jason's voice was loud, angry. "How long were you with her? Didn't you think her family might want to know?"

His accusatory tone stung. "She didn't want me to contact you!"

"You listened to an addict?"

"She said you told her you were through helping her."

"I didn't know she had cancer!" He sank down on

the front step and let his head fall into his hands. "I would have helped." The last word came out choked.

Erica's desire to fight left her. He was Kimmie's brother, and he was hurting.

She sat down beside him. "She wasn't alone, until just a short while ago. I was with her."

He turned his head to face her. "I don't get it. On top of everything else she had to deal with, she took in you and your kids?"

She saw how it looked to him. But what was she supposed to say? Kimmie hadn't wanted her to tell Jason about the twins. She'd spoken of him bitterly. "I was a support to her, not a burden," she said. "You can believe that or not."

He leaned back on his elbows, staring out across the moon-bright countryside. "Tough love," he muttered. "Everyone says to use tough love."

Behind them, there was a scratching sound and then a mournful howl.

Jason stood and opened the door, and Mistletoe limped outside. He lifted his golden head and sniffed the air.

"Guess he got lonely." Jason sat back down.

Mistletoe shoved in between them and rested his head on Jason's lap.

They were silent for a few minutes. Erica was cold, especially where her thin jeans met the stone porch steps. But she felt lonely, too. She didn't want to leave the dog. And strangely enough, she didn't want to leave Jason. Although he was obviously angry, and even blaming her, he was the only person in the world right now, besides her, who was grieving Kimmie's terribly early death.

"I just don't get your story," he burst out. "How'd you help her when you were trying to care for your babies, too? And why'd she send you and your kids here?"

Mistletoe nudged his head under Jason's hand, demanding attention.

"I want some answers, Erica."

Praying for the words to come to her, Erica spoke. "She said this was a good place, a safe place. She knew I…didn't have much."

He lifted a brow like he didn't believe her.

"She'd loved my mom." Which was true. "She was kind of like a big sister to me."

"She was a *real* big sister to me." Suddenly, Jason pounded a fist into his open hand. "I can't believe this. Can't believe she OD'd alone." He paused and drew in a ragged breath, then looked at Erica. "I'm going to find out more about you and what went on out there. I'm going to get some answers."

Erica looked away from his intensity. She didn't want him to see the fear in her eyes.

And she especially didn't want him to find one particular answer: that Kimmie was the biological mother of the twins sleeping upstairs.

2

Sunday morning, just after sunrise, Jason followed the smell of coffee into the farmhouse kitchen. He poured himself a cup and strolled around, looking for his grandfather and listening to the morning sounds of Erica and the twins upstairs.

Yesterday had been rough. He'd called their mother overseas—the easier telling, strangely—and then he'd let Papa know about Kimmie. Papa hadn't cried; he'd just said, "I'm glad Mama wasn't alive to hear of this." Then he'd gone out to the barn all day, coming in only to eat a sandwich and go to bed.

Erica and the twins had stayed mostly in the guest room. Jason had made a trip to the vet to get Mistletoe looked over, and then rattled around the downstairs, alone and miserable, battling his own feelings of guilt and failure.

Tough love hadn't worked. His sister had died alone.

It was sadness times two, especially for his grandfather. And though the old man was healthy, an active farmer at age seventy-eight, Jason still worried about him.

Where was his grandfather now, anyway? Jason looked out the windows and saw a trail broken through newly drifted snow. Papa had gone out to do morning chores without him.

A door opened upstairs, and he heard Erica talking to the twins. Maybe bringing them down for breakfast.

She was too pretty and he didn't trust her. Coward that he was, he poured his coffee into a travel cup and headed out, only stopping to lace his boots and zip his jacket when he'd closed the door behind him.

Jason approached the big red barn and saw Papa moving around inside. After taking a moment to admire the rosy morning sky crisscrossed by tree limbs, he went inside.

Somehow, Papa had pulled the old red sleigh out into the center of the barn and was cleaning off the cobwebs. In the stalls, the two horses they still kept stomped and snorted.

Papa gave him a half smile and nodded toward the horses. "They know what day it is."

"What day?"

"You've really been gone that long? It's Sleigh Bell Sunday."

"You don't plan on..." He trailed off, because Papa obviously did intend to hitch up the horses and drive the sleigh to church. It was tradition. The first Sunday in December, all the farm families that still kept horses came in by sleigh, if there was anything resembling enough snow to do it. There was a makeshift stable at the church and volunteers to tend the horses, and after church, all the town kids got sleigh rides. The church ladies served hot cider and cocoa and home-made doughnuts, and the choir sang carols.

It was a great event, but Papa already looked tired. "We don't have to do it this year. Everyone would understand."

"It's important to the people in this community." Papa knelt to polish the sleigh's runner, adding in a muffled voice, "It was important to your grandmother."

Jason blew out a sigh, picked up a rag and started cleaning the inside of the old sleigh.

They fed and watered the horses. As they started to pull out the harnesses, Jason noticed the old sleigh bells he and Kimmie had always fought over, each of them wanting to be the one to pin them to the front of the sleigh.

Carefully, eyes watering a little, he hooked the bells in place.

"You know," Papa said, "this place belongs to you and Kimmie. We set it up so I'm a life tenant, but it's already yours."

Jason nodded. He knew about the provisions allowed to family farmers, made to ensure later generations like Jason and Kimmie wouldn't have to pay heavy inheritance taxes.

"I'm working the farm okay now. But you'll need to think about the future. There's gonna come a time when I'm not able."

"I'm thinking on it." They'd had this conversation soon after Gran had died, so Jason wondered where his grandfather was going with it.

"I imagine Kimmie left her half to you."

Oh. That was why. He coughed away the sudden roughness in his throat. "Lawyer's going to call back tomorrow and go through her will."

"That's fine, then." Papa went to the barn door.

"Need a break and some coffee. You finish hitching and pull it up." He paused, then added, "If you remember how."

The dig wasn't lost on Jason. It had been years since he'd driven horses or, for that matter, helped with the farm.

It wasn't like he'd been eating bonbons or walking on the beach. But he'd definitely let his family down. He had to do better.

By the time he'd figured out the hitches and pulled the sleigh up to the front door of the old white house, Papa was on the porch with a huge armload of blankets. "They'll be right out," he said.

"Who?"

"Erica and the babies."

"Those babies can't come! They're little!"

Papa waved a dismissive hand. "We've always taken the little ones. Safer than a car."

"But it's cold!" Even though it wasn't frostbite weather, the twins weren't used to Pennsylvania winters. "They're from Arizona!"

"So were you, up until you started elementary school." Papa chuckled. "Why, your parents brought you to visit at Christmas when you were only three months old, and Kimmie was, what, five? You both loved the ride, and no harm done."

And they'd continued to visit the farm and ride in the sleigh every Christmas after they'd moved back to the Pittsburgh area. Even when their parents had declined to go to church, Gran and Papa had insisted on taking them. Christmases on the farm had been one of the best parts of his childhood.

Maybe Kimmie had held on to some of those memories, too.

He fought down his emotions. "I don't trust Erica. There's something going on with her."

Papa didn't answer, and when Jason looked up, he saw that Erica had come out onto the porch. Papa just lifted an eyebrow and went to help her get the twins into the sleigh.

Had she heard what he'd said? But what did it matter if she had; she already knew he thought she was hiding something.

"This is amazing!" She stared at the sleigh and horses, round-eyed. "It's like a movie! Only better. Look, Mikey, horses!" She pointed toward the big furry-footed draft horses, their breath steaming in the cold, crisp air.

"Uuusss," Mikey said.

Erica's gloved hand—at least Papa had found her gloves—flew to her mouth. "That's his second word! Wow!"

"What did he say?" It had sounded like nonsense to Jason.

"He said *horse*. Didn't you, you smart boy?" Erica danced the twins around until they both giggled and yelled.

Papa lifted one of the babies from her arms and held him out to Jason. "Hold this one, will you?"

"But I…" He didn't have a choice, so he took the baby, even though he knew less than nothing about them. In his police work, whenever there'd been a baby to handle, he'd foisted it off on other officers who already had kids.

He put the baby on his knee, and the baby—was

this Mikey?—gestured toward the horses and chortled. "Uuusss! Uuusss!"

Oh. Uuusss meant horse.

"I'll hold this one, and you climb in," Papa said to Erica. "Then I'll hand 'em to you one at a time, and you wrap 'em up in those blankets." Papa sounded like a pro at all of this, and given that he'd done it already for two generations, Jason guessed he was.

Once both twins were bundled, snug between Papa and Erica, Jason set the horses to trotting forward. The sun was up now, making millions of diamonds on the snow that stretched across the hills, far into the distance. He smelled pine, a sharp, resin-laden sweetness.

When he picked up the pace, the sleigh bells jingled.

"Real sleigh bells!" Erica said, and then, as they approached the white covered bridge, decorated with a simple wreath for Christmas, she gasped. "This is the most beautiful place I've ever seen."

Jason glanced back, unable to resist watching her fall in love with his home.

Papa was smiling for the first time since he'd learned of Kimmie's death. And as they crossed the bridge and trotted toward the church, converging with other horse-drawn sleighs, Jason felt a sense of rightness.

"Over here, Mr. S!" cried a couple of chest-high boys, and Jason pulled the sleigh over to their side of the temporary hitching post.

"I'll tie 'em up," Papa said, climbing out of the sleigh.

Mikey started babbling to Teddy, accompanied by gestures and much repetition of his new word, *uuusss*. Teddy tilted his head to one side and burst forth with his own stream of nonsense syllables, seeming to ask a question, batting Mikey on the arm. Mikey waved toward the horses and jabbered some more, as if he were explaining something important.

They were such personalities, even as little as they were. Jason couldn't help smiling as he watched them interact.

Once Papa had the reins set and the horses tied up, Jason jumped out of the sleigh and then turned to help Erica down. She handed him a twin. "Can you hold Mikey?"

He caught a whiff of baby powder and pulled the little one tight against his shoulder. Then he reached out to help Erica, and she took his hand to climb down, Teddy on her hip.

When he held her hand, something electric seemed to travel right to his heart. Involuntarily he squeezed and held on.

She drew in a sharp breath as she looked at him, some mixture of puzzlement and awareness in her eyes.

And then Teddy grabbed her hair and yanked, and Mikey struggled to get to her, and the connection was lost.

The next few minutes were a blur of greetings and "been too long" came from seemingly everyone in the congregation.

"Jason Stephanidis," said Mrs. Habler, a good-hearted pillar of the church whom he'd known since childhood. She'd held back until the other congregants had drifted toward the church, probably so she could probe for the latest news. "I didn't know you were in town."

He put an arm around her. "Good to see you, Mrs. Habler."

"And this must be your wife and boys. Isn't that sweet. Twins have always run in your family. You know, I don't think your mother ever got over losing her twin so young."

Mother had been a twin?

Erica cleared her throat. "We're actually just family friends, passing through. No relation to Jason."

The words sounded like she'd rehearsed them, not quite natural. And from Mrs. Habler's pursed lips and wrinkled brow, it looked like she felt the same.

What was Erica's secret?

And why hadn't he ever known his mother was a twin?

And wasn't it curious that, after all these years, there were twins in the farmhouse again?

When they returned to the farm, Erica's heart was both aching and full.

After dropping Jason, Erica and the twins in front of the farmhouse—along with the real Christmas tree they'd brought home—Papa insisted on taking the horses and sleigh to the barn himself, even though Erica saw the worried look on Jason's face.

"Is he going to be okay?" she asked as they hauled the twins' gear into the house in the midst of Mistletoe's excited barking.

Jason turned to watch his grandfather drive the sleigh into the barn. "He enjoyed the sleigh ride, but I think picking out a tree brought up too many memories. He'll spend a few hours in the barn, is my guess. That's his therapy."

"He's upset about Kimmie?"

"Yes. And on top of that, this is his first Christmas without my grandma."

Her face crinkled with sympathy. "How long were they married?"

"We had a fiftieth-anniversary party for them a couple of years ago," he said, thinking back. "So I think it was fifty-two years by the time she passed."

"Did Kimmie come?"

He barked out a disgusted-sounding laugh. "No."

Not wanting to get into any Kimmie-bashing, Erica changed the subject. "Could we do something to cheer him up?"

He looked thoughtful. "Gran always did a ton of decorating. I'd guess the stuff is up in the attic." He quirked his mouth. "I'm not very good at it. Neither is Papa. It's not a guy thing."

"Sexist," she scolded. "You don't need two X chromosomes to decorate."

"In this family you do. Will you… Would you mind helping me put up at least some of the decorations?" He sounded tentative, unsure of himself, and Erica could understand why. She wasn't sure if they had a truce or if he was still upset with her about the way she'd handled things with Kimmie.

But it was Christmastime, and an old man needed comfort. "Sure. I just need to put these guys down for a nap. Look at Mikey. He's about half-asleep already."

"I'll start bringing stuff down from the attic."

Erica carried the babies up the stairs, their large diaper bag slung across her shoulders. Man, she'd never realized how hard it was to single-parent twins.

Not that she'd give up a bit of it. They'd been so adorable wrapped up in their blankets in the sleigh, and everyone at church had made a fuss over them. One of the other mothers in the church, a woman named Sheila, had insisted on going to her truck and getting out a hand-me-down, Mikey-sized snowsuit right then and there. She'd promised to see if she could locate another spare one among her mom friends.

Erica saw, now, why Kimmie had sent her here. It was a beautiful community, aesthetically and heart-wise, perfect for raising kids.

She'd love to stay. If only she wasn't terrified of having them taken from her by the man downstairs.

Kimmie had seemed to feel a mix of love and regret and anger toward her brother. Now that she'd met him, Erica could understand it better.

A free spirit, Kimmie had often been irresponsible, unwilling to do things by the book or follow rules. It was part of why she'd smoked cigarettes and done drugs and gotten in trouble with the police.

Jason seemed to be the exact opposite: responsible, concerned about his grandfather, an officer of the law.

Erica wished with all her heart that she could just reveal the truth to Jason and Papa. She hated this secrecy.

But she would hate even more for Jason to take the twins away from her. This last thing she could do for Kimmie, she'd do.

And it wasn't one-sided. Kimmie had actually done Erica a favor, offered her a huge blessing.

Erica rarely dated, didn't really understand the give-and-take of relationships. Certainly, her mother hadn't modeled anything healthy in that regard. So it was no big surprise that Erica wasn't attractive to men. She didn't want to be. She dressed purposefully in utilitarian clothes and didn't wear makeup. She just didn't trust men, not with her childhood. And men didn't like her, at least not romantically.

So the incredible gift that Kimmie had given her that she could never have gotten for herself was a family.

She put the twins down in their portable playpen, settling them on opposite sides, knowing they'd end up tangled together by the end of the nap. Mikey was out immediately, but Teddy needed some back rubbing and quiet talk before he relaxed into sleep.

Pretty soon, they'd need toddler beds. They'd need a lot of things. Including insurance and winter clothing and early intervention services for their developmental delays.

And just how was she going to manage that, when she didn't have a job, a savings account or a real right to parent the twins?

Teddy kicked and fussed a little, seeming to sense her tension. So she pushed aside her anxiety and prayed for peace and for the twins to be okay and for Papa to receive comfort.

And for Kimmie's soul.

When she got toward the bottom of the stairs, she paused. Jason was lying on the floor, pouring water into a green-and-red tree stand. Somehow, he'd gotten the tree they'd quickly chosen into the house by himself and set it upright, and it emitted a pungent, earthy scent that was worlds better than the pine room freshener her mother had sometimes sprayed around at Christmastime.

Jason had changed out of church clothes. He wore faded jeans and a sage-green T-shirt that clung to his impressive chest and arms.

Weight lifting was a part of being a cop, she supposed. And obviously, he'd excelled at it.

Her face heating at the direction of her own thoughts, she came the rest of the way down the stairs. "It smells so good! I never had a live tree before."

"Never?" He looked at her as if she must have been raised in a third world country. "What were your Christmases like?" He eased back from the tree and started opening boxes of decorations.

"Nothing like a TV Christmas movie, but who has that, really? Sometimes Mom would get me a present, and sometimes a Secret Santa or church program would leave something on our doorstep."

Jason looked at her with curiosity and something that might have been compassion, and she didn't want that kind of attention. "What about you? Did you and Kimmie and your parents come here for the holidays?"

"My parents loved to travel." He dug through a box and pulled out a set of green, heart-shaped ornaments. "See? From Ireland. They usually went on an overseas trip or a cruise at Christmas, and every year they brought back ornaments. We have 'em from every continent."

"Wow. Pretty." But it didn't sound very warm and family oriented. "Didn't they ever take you and Kimmie with them?"

"Nope. Dumped us here. But that was fine with us." He waved an arm around the high-ceilinged, sunlit room. "Imagine it all decorated, with a whole heap of presents under the tree. Snowball fights and gingerbread cookies and sleigh rides. For a kid, it couldn't get much better."

"For a grown-up, too," she murmured without thinking.

He nodded. "I'm glad to be here. For Papa and for me, too."

"Where are your parents now?"

"Dad passed about five years ago, and Mom's living on the French Riviera with her new husband. We exchange Christmas cards." He sounded blasé about it. But Erica knew how much emotion and hurt a blasé tone could cover.

They spent a couple of hours decorating the tree, spreading garland along the mantel and stringing lights. By the time Erica heard a cry from upstairs, indicating that the twins were waking up, they'd created a practically perfect farm-style Christmas environment.

"Do you need help with the babies?" Jason asked.

She would love to have help, but she knew she shouldn't start getting used to it. "It's fine. I'll get them."

"I'm going to check on Papa, then."

Erica's back was aching by the time she'd changed the twins' diapers and brought them downstairs, one on each hip. But the couple of hours they'd spent decorating were worth it. When Jason opened the door and Papa came in, his face lit up, even as his hands went to his hips. He shook his head. "You didn't have to do this. I wasn't…" He looked away and Erica realized he was choking up. "I wasn't going to put anything up this year. But seeing as how we have children in the house again…" He broke off.

Erica carried the twins into the front room. "Let's see how they like all the lights," she said, and both men seemed glad to have another focus than the losses they were facing.

She sat on the couch and put Mikey on the floor, then Teddy. She waved her hand toward the tree. "Pretty!" she said, and then her own throat tightened, remembering the silver foil tree she'd put up in Kimmie's apartment. They'd taken a lot of photographs in front of it, Kimmie in her wheelchair holding the twins. Erica had promised to show the twins when they were older, so they'd know how much their mother had loved them.

The boys' brown eyes grew round as they surveyed the sparkling lights and ornaments.

"Priiiiiy," Mikey said, cocking his head to one side.

Erica had no time to get excited about Mikey learning another new word because Teddy started to scoot toward the tree, then rocked forward into an awkward crawl.

"Whoa, little man," Jason said, intercepting him before he could reach the shining ornaments.

"Better put the ornaments higher up and anchor the tree to the wall," Papa said. "It's what we used to do for you and your sister. You were a terrible one for pulling things off the tree. One year, you even managed to climb it!"

Jason picked up Teddy and plunked him back down on the floor beside Mikey, but not before Erica had seen the red spots on the baby's knees. "I need to get them some long pants," she fretted. "Sturdy ones, if he's going to be mobile."

"Can you afford it?" Jason asked.

Erica thought of the stash of money Kimmie had given her. She'd spent more than half of it on the cross-country drive; even being as frugal as possible in terms of motels and meals, diapers didn't come cheap. "I can afford some."

Questions lurked in his eyes, but he didn't give them voice.

Teddy rocked back and forth and got himself on hands and knees again, then crawled—backward— toward Mistletoe, who lay by the gas fire. Quickly, Jason positioned himself to block the baby if needed.

Mistletoe nuzzled Teddy, then gave his face a couple of licks.

Teddy laughed and waved his arms.

"Not very sanitary," Papa commented.

"Oh, well," Erica and Jason said at the same time.

From the kitchen came a buzzing sound and Erica realized it was her phone. She went in and grabbed it. An Arizona number. She walked back into the front room's doorway and clicked to accept the call.

"Hello," came an unfamiliar voice. "Erica Lindholm?"

"That's me."

"This is Ryan Finnigan. An old friend of Kimmie Stephanidis. Do you have a moment to talk?"

She looked at the twins. "Can you watch the boys?" she asked the two men.

Jason looked a little daunted, but Papa nodded and waved a hand. "Go ahead. We'll be fine."

She headed through the kitchen to the dining room. "I'm here."

"I'm not only an old friend, but I'm Miss Stephanidis's attorney," the man said.

"Kimmie had an attorney?" Kimmie had barely been organized enough to buy groceries.

"Not exactly. The medical personnel who brought her to the hospital, after her overdose, happened to find one of my business cards and gave me a call. I went to see her, and we made a will right there in the hospital. None too soon, I'm afraid."

She was glad to know that Kimmie had had a friend near and that she'd been under medical care, and said so.

"I did what I could. I was…rather fond of her, at one time." He cleared his throat. "She let me know her wishes, and I was able to carry those out. But as for her estate…she's left you her half of the Holly Creek Farm."

"What?" Erica's voice rose up into a squeak and she felt for the nearest chair and sat down.

"She's left you half the farm her family owns. It's a small, working farm in Western Pennsylvania. The other half belongs to her brother."

"Half of Holly Creek Farm? And it's, like, legal?"

"It certainly is."

She sat a moment, trying to digest this news.

"I'm sure it's a lot to take in," the lawyer said after a moment. "Do you have any questions for me, off the top of your head?"

"Did Kimmie…" She trailed off, peeked through the kitchen into the front room to make sure no one could hear. "Look, is this confidential?"

"Absolutely."

"Did she leave any instructions about her children?"

"Her *children*?"

"I take it that's a no." *Oh, Kimmie, why would you provide for them with the farm, but not grant me guardianship?*

"If Kimmie did have children…the most important thing would be that they're safe, in an acceptable home."

"Right. That's right." She didn't want to admit to anything, but if he'd been fond of Kimmie at one time, as he'd mentioned, he would obviously be concerned.

He cleared his throat. "Just speaking hypothetically, if Kimmie had children and died without leaving any written instructions, they would become wards of the state."

Erica's heart sank.

"Unless…is there a father in the picture?"

"No," she said through an impossibly dry mouth. Kimmie had told her that after abandoning her and the twins, the babies' father had gone to prison with a life sentence, some drug-related theft gone bad.

"If there's no evidence that someone like you—hypothetically—had permission to take her children, no birth certificates, nothing, then any concerned party could make a phone call to Children and Youth Services."

"And they'd take the children?" She could hear the breathy fear in her voice.

"They might."

"But…this is hypothetical. You wouldn't—"

"Purely hypothetical. I'm not calling anyone. Now, even if the state has legal custody, if you have physical custody—and the children in question are doing well in your care—then the courts might decide it's in the best interest of the children for you to retain physical custody."

"I see." *It's not enough.*

"None of this might come up for a while, not until medical attention is needed or the children start school."

Or early intervention. Erica's heart sank even as she berated herself for not thinking it all through. "If it did come up...would there be some kind of hearing?"

"Yes, and at that time, any relative who had questions or concerns could raise them." He paused. "It seems Kimmie had very few personal effects, but whatever there is will be sent to her family as soon as possible."

Her hands were so sweaty she could barely keep a grip on the cell phone. "Thank you. This has been very helpful."

"Oh, one more thing," the lawyer said. "You'll be wanting to know the executor of Kimmie's will."

"It's not you?"

"No. I'm happy to help, of course, but if there's a capable family member, I usually recommend that individual."

Erica had a sinking feeling she knew where this was going. "Who is it?"

"It's her brother. Jason Stephanidis."

3

The next morning, Jason padded down the stairs toward the warmth of coffee and the kitchen. Noticing a movement in the front room, he stopped to look in.

There was his grandfather, in his everyday flannel shirt and jeans, staring out the window while holding a ceramic angel they'd set on the mantel yesterday. As Jason watched, Papa set it down and moved over to a framed Christmas photo of Jason and Kimmie as young kids, visiting Santa. Papa looked at it, ran a finger over it, shook his head.

Jason's chest felt heavy, knowing there was precious little he could do to relieve his grandfather's suffering.

But whatever he could do, he would. He'd been a negligent grandson, but no more.

Mistletoe leaned against his leg and panted up at him.

He gave the dog a quick head rub and then walked into the room just as Papa set down the photograph he'd been studying and turned. His face lit up. "Just the man I want to see. Come get some coffee. Got an idea to run by you."

"Yeah?" Jason slung an arm around his grandfather's shoulders as they walked into the kitchen. He poured them both a fresh cup of coffee, black. "What've you got in mind?"

Papa pulled a chair up to the old wooden table and sat down. "Got someone coming over to do a little investigating about our guests."

"You, too?" Jason was relieved that he wasn't the only one who felt suspicious. In a corner of his mind, he'd worried that it was as Renea had said: he couldn't trust, couldn't be a family person. "I can't figure out why Kimmie left the farm to her. What were they to each other?" As executor of the estate, he needed to know.

The mere thought of there being an estate—of Kimmie being gone—racked his chest with a sudden ache so strong he had to sit down at the table to keep from falling apart.

"I'm thinking about those babies, for one thing," Papa said unexpectedly.

"What about them?"

"Something's not right about them, but I don't know what it is. So I've got Ruthie Delacroix coming over this morning. There's nobody knows as much about babies as Ruthie."

Jason remembered the woman, vaguely, from visits home; she'd always had a child on her hip at church, and he seemed to recall she ran a child care operation on the edge of town.

"And that's not all I'm wondering," Papa said darkly, "but first things first."

Jason grinned. Papa conniving and plotting was better than Papa grieving.

"I figure I have to take the lead on this, since you haven't shown a whole lot of sense about women. When you brought home that skinny thing—what was her name? Renea?—and said you were going to marry her, your grandmother had a fit."

Jason wasn't going to rise to that bait. And he wasn't going to think about Renea. He got up and started wiping down the already-clean counters.

No sooner had his grandfather headed upstairs to his bedroom than Jason heard the sound of babies babbling and laughing, matched by Erica's melodic, soothing voice. A moment later, she appeared, a baby in each arm.

Even without a trace of makeup, her fair skin seemed to glow. Her hair wasn't styled, but clipped back, with strands already escaping.

His heart rate picked up just looking at her.

As she nuzzled one of the baby's heads—was that Mikey or Teddy?—he was drawn into her force field. "Want me to hold one of them?"

And where did *that* come from? He never, but never, offered to hold a baby.

"Um…sure!" She nodded toward the wigglier baby. "Take Teddy. But keep a grip on him. He's a handful. I just need to get them some breakfast." As she spoke, she strapped Mikey into the old wooden high chair.

Jason sat down and held the baby on his knee, studying him, wondering what Papa saw that made him worry. But the kid looked healthy and lively to him as he waved his arms and banged the table, trying to get Erica's attention.

Which seemed perfectly sensible to Jason. Even in

old jeans and a loose blue sweater, Erica was a knock-out. Any male would want her attention.

Nostalgia pierced him. Erica moved around the room easily, already comfortable, starting to know where things were. It made him think of his grandfather sitting at this very table after a long day of farmwork, his grandmother bustling around fixing food, declining all offers of help in the kingdom that was her kitchen.

Papa was grieving the loss of his wife now, but his life had been immeasurably enriched by his family. In fact, it was impossible to think of Papa without thinking of all those who loved him. And when Jason and Kimmie had needed some extra parenting, Papa and Gran had opened their arms without a second thought. They'd been the making of Jason's childhood.

Unfortunately, Kimmie had seen more neglect before Papa and Gran had stepped in. She'd never quite recovered from their parents' lack of real love.

"Would you like some oatmeal?" Erica asked a few minutes later, already dishing up four bowls, two big and two small. "I'm sorry, I should've asked rather than assuming. The twins love oatmeal, and so do I, and it's about the most economical breakfast you can find."

"That would be great." He shifted Teddy on his knee. "Put his down here and I'll try to feed him. No guarantees, though."

"You don't have to do that."

"It's no problem. You had the care of them all night. At least you ought to get a minute to eat a bowl of oatmeal yourself."

"That would be a treat." She placed a small bowl beside his larger one and handed him a bib and a spoon. "Go to it."

Trying to get spoonfuls of oatmeal into a curious baby proved a challenge, and as Erica expertly scooped the cereal into Mikey's mouth, she laughed at Jason's attempts. How she managed two, as a single mom, he couldn't fathom.

"Hey now," he said when Teddy blew a raspberry that spattered oatmeal all over himself, the high chair and Jason. "Give me a break. I don't know what I'm doing here."

"Teddy! Behave yourself!" A smile tugged at Erica's face as she passed Jason a cloth. "When he spits like that, he's probably done. Just wipe his face and we'll let them crawl around a little."

Mistletoe had been weaving between their legs, licking up the bits of oatmeal and banana that hit the floor. Jason reached down to pat the dog at the same moment Erica did.

Their hands brushed—and Jason felt it to his core. "Nothing like a canine vacuum cleaner," he tried to joke. And kept his hand on the dog, hoping for another moment of contact with Erica.

"I know, right? We totally should have gotten them a dog back in Arizona."

And then her hand went still. When he looked up at her face, it had gone still, too.

"Who?" Jason asked. "You and their dad?"

"*I* should have gotten them a dog," she said, not looking at him. "I meant, *I* should have."

The detective in him stored away that remark as relevant. And it was a good reminder, he reflected as they both scarfed down the rest of their breakfast without more talk. He couldn't trust Erica, didn't know what she had been to Kimmie. Getting domestic with her would only cloud his judgment. More than likely, she'd been a bad influence, dragging Kimmie down.

Beyond that likelihood, he needed to remember that he was no good at family relationships. He was here, in part, to see if he could reset his values, and he'd vowed to himself that he wouldn't even try to start anything with a woman until he'd improved significantly in that regard. It wasn't fair to either him or the woman.

Just moments later, as Jason finished up the breakfast dishes, there was a pounding on the door. Mistletoe ran toward it, barking, as Papa came out of his room and trotted down the stairs to the entryway. Jason heard the door open and then his grandfather's hearty greeting.

Immediately, the noise level jumped up a notch. "Hey there, Andy! What's this I hear about babies in the place?"

An accompanying wail revealed that she'd brought at least one baby with her. Probably her grandson, whom she seemed to bring everywhere.

Jason walked into the front room, where Erica was sitting on the floor with the twins. "Ruth Delacroix," he said in answer to Erica's questioning expression. "She's a force of nature. Prepare yourself."

"Good morning, everyone!" Ruth cried as she came in, giving Jason a big hug and kiss around the baby she held on one hip. Then she spun toward Erica. "And you must be Erica. Andy was telling me about you, that you're here for a visit with some… Oh my, aren't they adorable!"

"Let's sit down," Papa suggested, "and Jason will bring us all out some coffee. Isn't that right?"

"Sure." Jason didn't mind playing host. He was glad to see his grandfather seeming a little peppier.

When he carried a tray with coffee cups, sugar and milk into the front room, the three babies were all on the floor, and Ruth and Erica were there with them. The pine scent from the Christmas tree was strong, and the sun sparkled bright through the windows, making the ornaments glisten. Papa had turned on the radio and Christmas music poured out.

"Mason! Stop that!" Ruth scrambled after her toddling grandbaby with more agility than Jason could muster up, most days, even though Ruth had to have thirty years on him. "He's a handful, ever since he started to walk."

Teddy, not to be outdone, started scooting toward the shiny tree, and Mikey observed with round eyes, legs straight out in front of him.

"Like I said," Ruth continued, "I'm down a kid, so I'd be glad to watch these little sweethearts anytime you need. A couple of my regular clients are off this week and kept their little ones at home."

"Thanks." Erica was dangling a toy in front of Mikey, who reached for it. "I'm not sure quite what I'll be doing, but knowing there's someone who could look after the twins for a few hours is wonderful. I really appreciate you thinking of it," she added to Papa Andy.

"No problem, sweetheart." Papa took a small ornament off the tree and held it out to Jason. "Remember this?"

"The lump!" Jason laughed at the misshapen clay

blob. "Haven't seen that in years. That's my master-piece, right?"

"You were pretty proud of it. Insisted on hanging it in a place of honor every Christmas, at least until you turned into an embarrassed teenager. And so here it is right now."

Jason smiled as Papa reminisced, egged on by Ruth and Erica. This was important, and Jason was starting to realize it was what he wanted for himself. Traditions and family, carried on from generation to generation. Just because his own parents hadn't done a good job of making a true home for him and Kimmie, that didn't mean he had to follow their patterns. He wanted to be more like Papa.

He had some work to do on himself first.

While he reflected, he'd been absently watching Erica—she was easy on the eyes, for sure—so he noticed when her expression got guarded and he tuned back into the conversation.

"What are they, seven, eight months?" Ruth was saying. "They're big boys."

"They're fifteen months," Erica said.

"Oh." Ruth frowned, and then her face cleared. "Well, Mason, here, he's real advanced. Started walking at ten months."

"They have some delays." Erica picked up Mikey and held him high, then down, high, then down, jumping him until he chortled.

Teddy did his strange little scoot crawl in their direction. Jason noticed then that Ruth's grandson was indeed a lot more mobile than the twins, a real pro at pushing himself to his feet and toddling around.

"Why are they delayed?" Ruth asked. "Problems at birth?"

"You might say that." Erica swooped Mikey down in front of his brother, and the two laughed.

Teddy pointed at the tree. "Da-da-da-DA-da-da," he said, leaning forward to look at Mikey.

"Da-da-da-da-da!" Mikey waved a hand as if to agree with what his twin brother had said.

Teddy burst out with a short laugh, and that made Mikey laugh, too.

"Now, isn't that cute. Twin talk." Ruth went off into a story about some twins she'd known who had communicated together in a mysterious language all through elementary school.

As the women got deeper into conversation about babies, Papa gestured Jason into the kitchen. He pulled a baggie from a box and started spooning baking soda into it.

"What are you doing?"

"You'll see." He tossed the baggie onto the counter and then pulled out a couple of syringes. He grabbed a spoon from the silverware drawer.

Jason stared. "Where'd you get that stuff and what are you doing with it?"

"From your narco kit, and it's just a little test. You'll see."

"But you can't… That's not—"

"Come on, hide in the pantry!" Papa shoved Jason toward the small room just off the kitchen. "Hey, Erica, where did you put those baby snack puffs?" he called into the front room.

There was a little murmuring between the two women as Papa hastily stepped into the pantry and edged around Jason. "Watch for anything suspicious," he ordered.

Helpless to stop the plan Papa had set into motion, Jason watched as Erica came into the kitchen, opened a cupboard and pulled out some kind of baby treats. Behind her, Mistletoe sat, held up a paw and cocked his head.

Erica laughed down at him. "It's not treats for you, silly. It's for the babies." She squatted, petted the dog and then stood and reached toward the jar of dog treats on the counter. "All right, beggar, I'll get you just one…"

She froze. Stared at the pseudo drug supplies. Looked around the kitchen.

Then she leaned back against the counter, hand pressed against her mouth, eyes closed.

She drew in a breath, let it out in a big sigh and picked up the baggie between two fingers as if it were going to jump up and bite her. "Papa Andy," she called. "Could you come in here a minute?"

Papa nudged his way around Jason and went into the kitchen.

"I found this." Erica held up the bag. "What's going on here?"

Papa frowned, turned back toward the pantry and spoke to Jason. "She knows what it is. That's a bad sign."

Jason sighed and came out into the kitchen. "Actually, most people know what that is. If she were using, she'd have hidden the stuff, not called you in to look at it."

Erica stared at Papa, then slowly turned to Jason.

There was an expression of betrayal on her face. "You guys were testing me?"

"Yes, ma'am," Papa said. "And if the expert here is right, you passed with flying colors."

"You thought I was a drug addict?" She looked from one to the other, then flung the bag onto the counter. "And so you set this up to test me, instead of asking me outright."

Jason waded in to defend his grandfather. "Papa just had to be sure. No addict would answer a question about being on drugs honestly, right?"

She rolled her eyes and crossed her arms, holding her elbows.

"And you know Kimmie well, obviously," he stumbled on. "She's struggled with addiction for years, as I'm sure you know, and it would make a lot of sense if you'd had a problem, too. But I've watched how addicts respond to drugs, and I can tell you're clean."

She straightened, her jaw set. "Yes, I am," she said, and stalked back into the front room.

Leaving Papa to look at Jason. "Guess that wasn't such a good idea," he said. He turned and followed Erica back into the front room.

And Jason just leaned back against the counter, disgusted with himself. He should have somehow stopped that from happening. Now they'd not only hurt her but lost her trust.

A few minutes later, Erica came back into the kitchen and glared at Jason, then at Papa, who'd followed after her. "I don't appreciate that you tried to trick me. That you thought I was an addict." From all the free therapists she'd seen in the course of living with her mother, she knew she ought to say next: when you mistrust me, I feel hurt.

She *did* feel hurt. But she didn't trust them any more than they trusted her, and especially not with her feelings.

What could you expect from men, anyway?

The thing was, Jason had been so nice to her and the twins. It had seemed like they were getting to know each other, that they might become friends. And Papa Andy... He'd seemed so warm, so welcoming.

In reality, they'd been conspiring against her, plotting.

"I'm sorry. It was a bad idea and we shouldn't have done it." Jason crossed his arms and looked at the floor.

"We trust you *now*, honey," Papa Andy said.

"Hey, what's going on out there?" Ruth's merry voice broke in. "I could use a hand here!"

The men turned toward the front room.

As Erica followed, years of feeling unworthy came back to her, an emotional tsunami she always tried to tamp down when it arose. But it refused to stay in its usual closed mental container.

She'd always been known as the addict's kid. Never any pretty clothes or new toys. Regular stints of homelessness, of trying to stay clean by way of public restroom sinks. The dread of Mom getting arrested, which meant another few months in a foster home.

Always moving somewhere unfamiliar, always the new girl in school. People didn't like her, didn't trust her, didn't want to be with her.

"Ma-ma." Mikey batted her ankle and reached up his arms.

Automatically she picked him up and cuddled him

close, and the sensation of a warm baby in her arms grounded her. She couldn't give in to that old, familiar sense of worthlessness.

But she also couldn't stay in an environment where she was being tricked and treated badly. That was toxic.

"Hey, Ruth," she said to the older woman, who was sitting on the couch beside Papa, trying to encourage Teddy to pull up and cruise along it. "You said you could babysit for me. How about giving me an hour right now?"

"You're going somewhere?"

"That's right. I can pay you your usual hourly rate, whatever's fair." Her cache of money was going down at an alarming rate, and she had to deal with that. But first things first.

"Why, sure, honey. I don't have anyplace I have to be until later in the afternoon."

"And if she has to go, I'll look after the little guys." Papa's voice was soft.

Erica spun toward Jason, who still stood in the doorway between the front room and the kitchen. "Could you show me the cabin?"

"What?"

She walked over to stand in front of him, out of earshot of the elders, feeling stiff as a robot. "The cabin on this property. Where Kimmie originally told me to go. I'd like to see about fixing that up."

"You don't want to do that, Erica. It's cold. It's a mess—"

"I can go alone if you don't want to take me." She turned toward Papa. "Could you give me directions to—"

"I'll take you!" Jason interrupted.

After she'd made sure Ruth had what she needed for the twins, after Jason had insisted on outfitting her in boots, gloves and a warm hat, she followed him outside.

He looked back as if he wanted to say something, but she glared at him and he faced ahead and beckoned for her to follow.

The walking was easy when they started out toward the barn. A trail was broken like a gully, with two-foot-deep snow on either side.

The brisk air stung her eyes and nose. Sunshine glinted on the surrounding snow, and trees extended lacy branches into the bright blue sky. Low chirps and chatters sounded from a row of evergreens, and as Jason turned from the path into fresh snow, a bright red cardinal landed on a fence post beside them, chirping a *too-eee, too-eee*.

Jason moved steadily and methodically in front of her, breaking trail. Despite his doing most of the work, she stumbled and struggled her way and was soon plenty warm, panting in the chilly air.

Impossible to maintain anger in God's beautiful world. Her emotions settled into a resigned awareness: something about her, probably an attitude or set of mannerisms she didn't even know she had, made people suspicious of her. If it hadn't changed by now, it wasn't going to. And if she was going to be alone, raising the babies, she needed to find a safe, healthy place for them to grow and thrive. And she needed to be away from painful encounters like what had happened this morning. She had to take care of herself so she could take care of the twins.

Her foot caught in an icy lump of snow and she stumbled and pitched forward on one knee. She caught herself with her hands, didn't sprawl full facedown, but snow pushed up the wrists of her jacket and sent its chill through her thin jeans.

"We're almost—" Jason turned, saw that she'd fallen and made his way back to her. "What happened? Here, give me your hand."

It would be silly to refuse. She grasped his glove-clad hand and he pulled her upright easily, brushing snow from her arms and then retrieving her hat.

"You okay? Anything hurt?"

"Fine," she said, her breath coming out fast.

"You're sure?" He was looking into her eyes. Very direct. Very intense.

She turned away and nodded. "I'm fine. Snow's soft."

"We're almost there," he said.

After a few more minutes slogging through the snow, Jason gestured ahead. "There it is, in all its glory."

Erica looked to see a weathered log cabin, small, with a steep, slanting roof and a front porch topped by a snow-covered wooden awning. One of the small front windows was boarded up, and the other needed to be, its glass clearly broken.

Behind the cabin and on one side, pine trees, their branches heavy with snow, gave the area a deep quiet and privacy.

"You still want to see inside? It's pretty run-down."

"Yeah," she said, breaking off into fresh snow to check out the sides of the cabin. It *was* run-down, but with work it could be cute.

For just a moment she flashed back on years of living in crowded, dirty cities. She'd always dreamed of a country getaway, a place that was safe, with privacy and no one to bother her. A place of her own—not just an apartment but a whole little house.

"Let me go in first." Jason tested the strength of the front porch boards before unlocking the door and going in.

Not much point locking it when someone had broken the windows out, but whatever.

"Come on in. It's just us and the chipmunks."

If he thought a few critters would scare her, he was sadly mistaken. She stepped over a broken stair and into the cabin's single room.

She'd feared it would be dark and gloomy, but it was bright, with side windows larger than those in front. A ladder led up to what must be a loft bedroom. The wood-plank walls looked sturdy, and a sink and stove lined one wall. No refrigerator, but that was easily obtained, and in the meantime, a gallon of milk would keep just fine in the snow.

A concrete floor showed through linoleum torn in one corner. That would have to be repaired, but for now, a thick rug would cover the ugliness. She walked to the back of the cabin and opened a door, discovering a storage area and bathroom.

She gave Jason a brisk nod. "It'll do. What would be the steps to getting the heat going? And I assume that once we turn on the water, the plumbing is okay?"

"Erica, you can't live like this. It's primitive and it's filthy." As if to punctuate his words, a small mouse raced across the floor, and he gestured toward it and looked at her.

"I grew up with an addict. I've lived in much dirtier places, with rats *and* scorpions." She tested the ladder, found it secure and started up to peek at the loft bedroom.

"Besides which, there's no heat per se—there's a wood-burning fireplace. Do you know anything at all about keeping that going so you and the kids won't freeze to death?"

"I'm a fast learner."

"You're not going to find someone to clean it during the holidays."

"I can clean it myself," she called down to him. The loft was even dirtier, if that was possible, littered with beer cans and newspapers and something that looked like a dead bird. Ugh.

Against one wall was a stained mattress that smelled bad even in the cold. Kids or hunters—or vagrants—must have taken refuge here.

For just a moment her courage failed as she relived dozens of dirty sleeping rooms she'd stayed in as a kid. Was she going backward in her life? Was filth and desolation her destiny?

She clenched her jaw. She was going to get rid of that mattress and clean this place to a shine. The twins wouldn't grow up as she had. She'd make sure the lock was sturdy and that the window got fixed. As a kid, she hadn't had a choice, but now she did. She would do better for her boys.

She climbed down the ladder. Now that she wasn't moving, she was getting cold, and she noticed Jason stamping his feet. Their breath made steam clouds in the cabin air, which she would've thought was cool if she'd been in a better mood.

"Look, Erica, I'm sorry. I was a jerk. I should have realized you weren't one to do drugs."

"I've never used in my life," she told him. "You don't make the same mistakes your parents made, though you might make different ones."

"You could be right about that." He rubbed his hands together. "But look, I'm sorry I was deceptive. That wasn't right."

His choice of words brought her to attention. Yes, Jason had been deceptive and it had made her angry. But his deception paled in comparison with the one she was trying to pull off, the fact that the twins were Kimmie's.

Certainly, her own deception was bigger. But she didn't know what he'd done to make Kimmie so mistrustful, only that he was rigid and judgmental, seeing everything in black-and-white. A perfectionist with a mean streak.

Not a person to raise kids.

Moreover, if Jason were sneaky and suspicious enough to attempt to trap her into revealing an addiction, he'd certainly be able to discover the truth about the twins, once his suspicions started to move in that direction.

And that couldn't happen, because he'd take the twins away. Kimmie hadn't wanted that. She'd wanted Erica to raise them.

Erica wanted that, too. They belonged to her and she loved them. In her heart, which was what mattered, she was their mother.

All the more reason to move out of Jason and Papa's house immediately.

"I can start cleaning the place tomorrow," she said, "and if you'll give me the information, I can make calls about the water and heat today. The twins and I can move in within a few days."

"You can't live here!" Jason lifted his hands, obviously exasperated. "How are you going to manage the twins when there's a ladder to get to the bedroom? Are you going to leave one up there while you carry the other down? There's no railing. It's dangerous."

"I can make it work," she said, feeling uneasy. He did have a point.

"And there's water, sure, but no washing machine or dryer." He shook his head. "It's the kind of place someone totally down-and-out would live in, not a mother and kids. In fact, no doubt we'd have some drug squatters here if Papa didn't keep such a close eye on it."

His objections were valid, but... "I'm sure we can figure out something."

"You run the risk of Children and Youth stepping in. These are bad conditions."

And you'd like nothing better. You'd probably call them on me yourself.

"Look, the property is half yours, once the will goes through probate. If it's because you're angry at me, I can stay out here and you stay in the house." He frowned. "I'd only ask that you let Papa stay in the house with you. He shouldn't be climbing the ladder."

"Of course!" She'd never kick an old man out of his home. "No, you and your grandfather need to stay at the big house. I'm the interloper. I'll move out here."

He shook his head. "No, Erica. Listen, I... I'm rotten at friends and family. Anyone will tell you. I apologize for treating you badly. It's nothing about you. It's me."

He looked forlorn and bitter all at the same time.

She steeled herself against the temptation to feel sorry for him.

"I really don't think you can get the place cleaned up yourself, but if you want to try, I'll help you."

Now, *that* would be a disaster. Working closely with the man who'd tricked her, but whom she still, to her chagrin, found attractive. The man she was starting to feel sorry for, at least a little. The man who looked so good in his lumberjack flannel and boots.

"I should get back to the twins," she said. And she needed to figure out whether living in the cabin was really viable. And most of all, she needed to figure out how to keep Jason and his grandfather at a distance—both so they didn't hurt her anymore, and so they didn't figure out the truth.

4

By the time they got back to the main house, clouds had covered over the midday sun. And Jason had a feeling that, once they went inside, any chance of a private conversation would be avoided or lost.

The need to know about his sister's last days and why she'd bequeathed half the farm to Erica overpowered his politeness. If he was going to be a jerk, he'd really be a jerk. "We need to find a time to talk about Kimmie."

"You don't quit, do you?" She skirted him to walk ahead in the snow.

All of a sudden she stopped, looking toward the house.

Since the skies had darkened, the front room was illuminated like a theater. Papa stood there alone, holding some small object in his hand. As they watched, he put it down and picked up something else.

"What's he doing?" she asked.

"Those are my grandmother's crèches," he said, and the lump in his own throat wouldn't let him say any more.

What would it be like to have a relationship as close as his grandparents' had been?

He opened the front door, and Mistletoe barked excitedly. Between the dog and the noise Jason made taking off his boots and helping Erica with her coat, he hoped Papa had the chance to pull himself together.

But when Papa came to the doorway of the front room, he had to clear his throat and blow his nose. "The twins are upstairs napping," he said, his voice a little rough. "Ruth fed 'em some lunch and put them down, and she says they're out like lights. She had to take off."

Erica touched Papa's arm. "I'm curious about your decorations," she said. "After I check on the twins, will you show them to me?"

Maybe it was cowardly, but Jason couldn't cope with looking through the family treasures and dredging up a bunch of memories. "I'll make lunch," he said.

In the kitchen, he soon had tomato soup heating and cheese sandwiches grilling in plenty of butter. Comfort food. Even if he wasn't good at sharing feelings with his grandfather, he was a decent short-order cook.

He started to check and see what everyone wanted to drink, but stopped on the threshold of the front room.

Papa was pointing to the star atop the tree, one of Gran's prize possessions, and pulling out his bandanna to wipe his eyes.

And rather than backing away, Erica put an arm around him. "Do you have any photos of her?"

Was she crazy? Or was she trying to butter Papa up, to get something out of him the way she'd gotten something out of Kimmie?

Papa nodded, his face lighting up. "Would you like to see our family albums?"

Jason beat a hasty retreat. If Erica could get outside of herself enough to comfort an old man to whom she owed nothing, then he was impressed. But was anyone really that nice? Most likely, she had some selfish motive. Most people did.

Once he had the plates on the table, he couldn't delay any longer. Still, when he walked into the front room to see Erica and Papa sitting on the couch side by side, the gray head and the red one bent over an old photo album, he had to swallow hard to get his voice into cheerful mode. "Lunch is ready," he said with only a little hitch.

Funny, the twins didn't have red hair. They must take after their father. Erica hadn't mentioned one word about the man, and from her reaction to being asked about Kimmie, she probably wouldn't welcome Jason opening the discussion.

As they ate their lunch, Erica kept the conversation going with questions about Gran, which led to talk of Jason's and Kimmie's childhoods.

"Our daughter was a bust as a mother," Papa admitted, his spoonful of tomato soup halfway to his mouth. "She had her reasons. I'm glad we could step in."

"I heard about that, some," Erica said. "Kimmie spent a lot of time talking about her mom."

She did? Jason got up, ostensibly to get some extra napkins, but really to cover his own surprise. How much had Kimmie told Erica? What else did she know? If Kimmie had aired their mother's dirty laundry, it spoke to Erica's ability to get close to people and find out their secrets.

Papa obviously didn't have the same suspicions. "I just wish…" he said, and then broke off.

"What do you wish?" Erica asked.

"I just wish it had worked out better for Kimmie." He put down his spoon and shook his head, staring off out the window.

Enough of taking Papa down their family's unhappy memory lane. It was time to learn something about Erica. "You said your mom had issues, too. Did you have grandparents to step into the gap for your mother?"

"Estranged," she said. "So Christmas can be sort of sad for me, too." She looked from Jason back to Papa. "Did you know there's a movement called Blue Christmas for people who are mourning at Christmastime?"

"What won't they think of next?" Papa waved a dismissive hand. "People are oversensitive these days."

"Or maybe more in touch with their feelings?" She softened her disagreement with a smile. "I think it's a good idea. Pretending you're having a Currier and Ives Christmas when you're not can make you even more depressed."

Papa chuckled. "Got your own opinions, do you?" He took a big bite of grilled cheese.

"Yes, and sometimes I'm even right."

As they talked on, Jason took note of the fact that Erica had neatly evaded his effort to probe into her background. He tucked that bit of knowledge away.

Against his will, though, he got caught up in Erica's description of the special church services they'd had back in Arizona for people who had a hard time dealing with the holidays. He wanted, in the worst way, to ask whether Kimmie had attended any such services. Had his sister been sad, missed the family during the holidays? Had she maintained the strong values she'd had as a younger woman, the faith they'd shared with Papa and Gran?

Guilt washed over him. Why had he let Kimmie become alienated from the rest of the family? Why hadn't he tried harder to find her and mend their differences?

He studied the woman talking with animation to Papa. No, she hadn't been Kimmie's drug friend. And yes, he was starting to care for her more and more.

But he still had questions. Okay, Erica had been lonely, had needed a surrogate sister in light of her own mother's absence. But what had Erica done for Kimmie in return that she'd gone so far as to leave her half the farm?

Later that afternoon, Erica got the twins strapped into their car seats and tried to back out of the space her little car had occupied since they'd arrived at Holly Creek Farm three days ago.

In the icy tracks, her wheels spun.

After a couple more attempts, she stopped and looked up "how to drive in snow" on her phone.

Go forward and back, get traction. She could do that. She put the car into Drive.

The wheels spun.

She clenched her jaw. She didn't even really want to attend the charitable clothing giveaway, but when she'd seen the flyer, she'd forced herself to copy the information in her planner, because the twins needed warm clothes. Now, to have this kind of obstacle getting there… She switched into Reverse and floored it.

The wheels made a loud spinning noise.

The car didn't move.

Teddy started to cry.

Why would anyone want to live in this snowy, obstinate state, when the blue skies and warm air and green palms of Arizona were just a few days' drive away?

A knock on her window made her jump. Jason. Great. She put the car into Park and lowered the window.

"Having problems?"

She clenched her jaw. "Obviously."

"Where are you headed?"

"I'm going to town," she said over Teddy's wails, "if I can get unstuck."

He squatted and studied her front tire, then stood. "Tires are almost bald," he said, "and this is a lightweight car. Why don't you let me drive you in my truck?"

"No!" The refusal was reflexive, automatic. Help usually came with strings. That, she'd learned at her mother's knee.

"I was planning to go in anyway. Give me five minutes to grab my things and pull the truck around."

"I don't need any help." Even though the evidence was blatantly to the contrary.

"My truck has a back seat. It's going to be a lot safer for the twins."

The one convincing argument. "Fine," she said, and then realized she sounded completely rude and ungrateful. "I mean, thank you. I would appreciate that."

Five minutes later, as they drove down a snowy, twisty, evergreen-lined road, she looked over at him. "Thank you for doing this. You're right. It wouldn't have been safe in my car."

Which meant she needed to get a new car, or new

tires at least. Add that to the lengthening shopping list in her head.

"No problem. Where are we headed?"

"The church." Heat rose in her face, but she forced herself to continue, staring straight ahead. "They're having a clothing giveaway."

"Oh." He steered around a sharp curve and then asked, "So money's a problem right now?"

"Yeah."

"What were you doing for work, prior to coming here?"

Her stomach tightened. Not because of the probing—he'd earned that right, driving her to town—but because of what he might find out.

She hated lying, always had. But she didn't want to put the detective in Jason on high alert, and she couldn't dodge the feeling that any talk of the past might do that. "I worked as an aide in a nursing home." Which was true. "And I was taking classes at the community college."

"Studying what?" If he'd sounded skeptical, she would have cut him off, but he actually sounded interested, like he believed her.

"Human Services. It could lead to Social Work or Early Childhood Education, if I went on for a bachelor's degree." She looked at him quickly. A few acquaintances had laughed about someone of her background going to college. If Jason did...

"Makes sense. What all had you taken?"

Relieved, she shrugged. "College Writing. Intro to Psychology. I was actually in a class called Introduction to Gerontology when...when Kimmie got sick." She clenched her teeth. *Stop talking.*

"No wonder you get along well with Papa."

Good, he was going to let the past—*her* past—go. "I like old people," she said. "Old people and kids." She opened her mouth to say that it was the people in the middle who caused most of the problems in the world, but she snapped it shut again. The less information she volunteered, the better.

"So you were out of a home and you went to stay with Kimmie?" he asked abruptly. "Did she take care of your kids while you worked?" An undertone of censure ran beneath his words.

"It wasn't like that." She crossed her arms over her chest. *Think, think.*

"What *was* it like?"

She had to give him some information, the bare bones at least, or he'd never leave her alone. "She was too sick to care for herself. I left my apartment empty to live with her and care for her." *And her babies.* Which of course, she couldn't say.

"If she was too sick to care for herself…how'd you manage the babies and the job and the schooling?"

She blew out a sigh. "My class was online, and I finished it." She was still proud of that accomplishment. "My job… I didn't have the time off, so…"

"So you lost it?"

"Yeah." She'd actually given notice and quit, but to someone like Jason, the difference wouldn't signify.

He was pulling into the church parking lot, and he didn't respond. She glanced over at him, expecting contempt, but instead he just looked thoughtful.

Inside, the church basement was crowded with people of all ages looking through tables full of clothing, toys and small gifts. Large signs explained the rules: one item from each table, as needed.

The stale smell of used clothes and unwashed people brought back memories. A girl of ten or eleven flipped through a rack of girls' clothing, her face tense.

Erica's gut twisted with sympathy.

She'd been that girl, desperate to find used clothes that didn't look used. Once, she remembered, she'd been excited to find a beautiful shirt with lace around the neckline and sleeves. She'd worn it to school, proudly, only to be found out by the rich girl who'd donated it.

She's poor. Look, she's wearing my old shirt.

She's poor.

She's poor.

"Let me hold one of the boys so you can see what you're doing." Jason held out his arms, and when Teddy reached for him, Erica let him go, swallowing hard.

She was reduced to charity, for now, but it wasn't what she wanted for the twins. She wasn't going to make a practice of this. She *would* get a job. Right here in this area, because thanks to Kimmie's bequest, she had a rent-free place to stay. She'd find a way to manage a job and child care.

Her kids were *not* coming to events like this once they were old enough to understand what it meant.

"Aw, are they twins?" A woman about Erica's age, but much better dressed, came over and ran a long, polished fingernail down Mikey's cheek, tickling his chin. "Such cute boys! Let me see if I can get permission for you to take two things from the tables."

"Thank you." Erica swallowed and started searching through the jeans and sweaters, trying not to wrinkle her nose at the stained ones, putting aside a couple that would be wearable, even cute, with a good washing.

The woman came back. "I'm really sorry, but rules are rules. You see, if we let one person take more than one thing—" she brushed back her hair and waved an arm around "—everyone would want to, and it wouldn't be fair, because—"

"It's fine," Erica interrupted. "Thank you, anyway."

Jason coughed and she looked over to see him lift an eyebrow and point to his own chest, clearly offering to claim the additional item as his own. She just shook her head a little, picked up the little pair of elastic-waist jeans she'd found for one or the other of the twins and moved on to the next table.

"Nothing like treating other adults like kids," he muttered.

"Yeah. Annoying, isn't it?" Of course, Jason wasn't accustomed to being spoken to in a patronizing way; he had a good job and had never been reduced to accepting handouts from anyone.

"What all do you need? I'll have a look around."

"Pretty much anything warm. They're fifteen months, but we could go as high as eighteen to twenty-four months, sizewise."

"There are more boys' clothes over here." Another well-dressed woman about Erica's age approached, this one with hollows under her eyes. She gestured Erica over. "Your babies are…" She swallowed hard. "They're really sweet." Her voice got rough on the last words, and she excused herself and walked rapidly out of the hall.

There was some story there. And it was a good reminder to Erica: just because someone was pretty and dressed in designer clothes, that didn't mean her life was easy.

Most of the people working were incredibly kind, and Erica ended up with a useful little stack of clothing that would help the boys manage winter for now. As she was trying to figure out whether she was done and could escape, there was a small commotion at a table behind her.

"Mommy! That girl has my Princess Promise game," the little girl behind the table said, pointing at a bedraggled mother and daughter.

"Oh! Oh, no, ma'am, that's my daughter's. These are the free toys." She indicated the much less shiny toys on the table.

"I'm sorry." The poor mother blushed as she handed the toy back and knelt to comfort her disappointed daughter.

"What'd she say, Chandie?" A scruffy-looking man with bloodshot eyes and the pinpoint pupils of an addict came to stand beside the woman and child. "She disrespecting you?"

"Nothing, it's fine." The young woman, Chandie, took the man's arm and steered him away, beckoning for her little girl to follow.

The little girl hurried after, looking frightened.

So there were drug problems even in the sweet little town of Holly Springs.

Erica made an internal vow. Once she got on her feet, she'd keep the twins miles away from anyplace people with those sorts of issues hung around.

She spent a few more minutes thanking the volunteers, then turned to locate Jason. She was done here.

And from the look of things, he hadn't found anything for Teddy. She wanted to leave.

They came together near the door. "Do you want to stay for dinner?" he asked. "I usually do. It's a holiday-type meal and it's open to everyone."

So that was the source of the mouthwatering smells, of turkey and pie.

"If you're staying, we'll stay, too," she said, squaring her shoulders. "If the twins fuss, though, I'll probably have to take them out to the truck."

"There's child care in the church nursery. In fact, Ruth usually takes charge of it, so she'll know what to do with the twins."

"That's good, then." She reminded herself to be grateful for the church dinner, and for the kind people who had put this event together, rather than being ashamed that she had to participate.

"Here, I'll take the stuff to the truck, and then I have to run out on a quick errand. By the time you get the twins settled, it'll be about time for the dinner. Do you want to shop a little for yourself?"

"Is something wrong with my clothes?" She narrowed her eyes, daring him to say it. Kimmie had always been on her to wear things that showed her figure rather than hiding it.

He backed away, palms up. "Nope. Nothing at all. I just thought most women like to shop."

"Nice of you to call it shopping." *Get that chip off your shoulder, girl. You're poor.* She forced a smile. "I really do appreciate your help. Take as long as you need. I'll see if Ruth needs help in the nursery, and if she doesn't, I'll meet you wherever those great smells are coming from."

On the way out, she saw Sheila, the woman who'd already given her the snowsuit for the twins, beckoning her over.

"Hey, I'm going to say something, and if it makes you mad, just tell me and I'll shut right up." She smiled at the babies. "They are so cute."

"I doubt you'll make me mad. Shoot."

"There's this green winter dress here. It's great quality and it's only been worn a couple of times." She flipped through the rack. "Look. Pretty, isn't it?"

And it was, absolutely gorgeous. A sheath dress with a lace overlay of the same shade over the shoulders and sleeves, and a row of gold grommets around the neckline.

"It's gorgeous," Erica agreed, fingering the fabric.

"I donated it, and it hurt me to do it, but—" she gestured down at herself "—these hips are never fitting into that dress again. You should take it."

"Oh, I couldn't."

"Why not?" Sheila held the dress to her. "It would fit you perfectly. And you'd rock it, with your red hair and being so tiny."

"Someone else could use it more. I never go out."

"It's not super fancy. You could wear it to a Christmas party, or a church service."

"That's true…" Temptation overcame her. She'd feel like a queen in that dress.

"It's been hanging here all evening and nobody wanted it." She tickled Mikey's chin, making him laugh. "Go on, take it. Otherwise it'll just stare at me from my closet and make me think about how much weight I've gained."

So, feeling a little foolish and a little excited, Erica let the woman wrap it up for her.

Once the twins were settled in the nursery with plenty of attention—no help needed, as Ruth had two other assistants—Erica went to the door and looked out into the parking lot. If Jason's truck were here, she'd find him, get his key and put the silly dress in the truck before going to dinner.

He was just pulling in, as it happened, so she went out to meet him. Cold wind whipped through the icy parking lot, and she was grateful for the coat she'd borrowed from the front closet back at the farmhouse.

Jason emerged from the truck, and when he saw her, he looked almost guilty.

"I got something for myself, like you suggested," she said, holding up the bag. "Can I just stick it in the truck?"

"Um, sure."

When she did, she saw that the floor of the back seat was full of bags that hadn't been there before. A red snowsuit peeked out of one, a big plastic tool set from another.

Slowly, she backed out of the truck and looked at him. "You…have friends with babies?"

"I hope you consider me a friend."

She stared at him, then at the bags, then at him again. "You did *not* just go out and buy a bunch of stuff for the twins."

"I actually did. But I kept the receipts. I got the sizes you said, but we can exchange them if anything doesn't fit or if it's not what you like."

"Why are you doing this?" Inside, emotions churned. She didn't deserve for someone like Jason to treat her well. She'd never had that. People like her didn't get treated well.

And beyond that, she was deceiving him, so she *really* didn't deserve his help.

Not to mention that taking such big gifts—charity, really—from anyone made her uncomfortable.

"You lost your job to take care of my sister, okay?" His voice was rough. "It's the least I can do."

"I didn't do that to get something." Which she could see now was exactly how it looked. Did people think she'd bribed Kimmie? *I'll care for you if you give me half the farm?*

"I can afford it," he went on. "I have a good job and a good salary." He frowned. "At least, I think I'll go back to it."

That distracted her. So he might not return to Philadelphia? Did that mean he might stay here?

"You're a good mom, you're doing your best, you love your kids." He said all those things flatly, as if they were facts, and the words buoyed her up. "We all need a hand sometimes. Kimmie did, and you gave it."

She opened her mouth to protest some more and then closed it. Looked up at the stars for guidance and didn't find any.

"Just accept someone doing something nice for you and your kids," he said, his voice persuasive now. He reached out to adjust her coat, pulling it higher on her neck against the cold wind. Then he cupped her chin in his work-roughened hand and looked into her eyes. For a breathless moment she thought he was going to kiss her.

And she thought she might let him.

But he pulled his hand away, his eyes dark and unreadable, and nodded toward the church. "Come on, we'd better get some of that good food while we can."

As they turned toward the church, she felt his hand at the small of her back, guiding her, gently caring for her.

It was appealing. Beguiling. Tempting.

And incredibly dangerous.

Because getting close to Jason—as her heart longed to do—meant betraying Kimmie's wishes for the twins.

5

Normally, Jason loved church dinners. He'd eat massive amounts of fried chicken, marshmallow fluff salad and green beans cooked to within an inch of their lives and still save room for a couple of pieces of pie.

Today, sitting across the long table from Erica, he wasn't even hungry.

This thing with Erica was getting weird. Intense. Dangerous.

He hadn't dated anyone since Renea, and for good reason; she'd pegged him correctly as bad at relationships. Before her, he'd dated a lot, but it had all been shallow. His heart hadn't been involved in the least.

But against his will, he was connecting with Erica, feeling strangely close to her. To the point where, when he'd seen her tension at the clothing giveaway, he'd wanted to ease it.

He'd *wanted* to pull her into his arms, but he knew better. So he'd done something to help her sons, instead.

He hadn't even minded, because he liked Mikey and Teddy, which was weird because he was *not* a baby kind of guy. He'd bought them a couple of matching outfits, flannel shirts and jeans, rugged country winter clothing they could wear as they crawled around the floor of the house.

That was the thing, though: he wanted them in the house, not out at the cabin.

He could blame his desire for them to stay on Papa, but the truth was he wanted them there for himself.

Wanted Erica there for himself.

"Eyes bigger than your stomach, young man?" Mrs. Habler, an apron tied around her waist, scolded as she looked at his still-full plate. "I made that three-bean salad, you know."

"And it's delicious," Erica said, giving Jason a chance to shove some into his mouth and nod.

Mrs. Habler turned to focus on Erica. "Still staying out at Holly Creek Farm, are you? Tongues have been wagging, I'm afraid."

"Erica was a friend of Kimmie's," Jason interjected. "Having her and her boys there is making Papa happy."

"Then that's reason enough, and I'll try to quell the gossip."

"Wait a minute, Mrs. Habler." Erica put a hand on the woman's arm. "You seem like you know a lot of what's going on in town. Do you happen to know of any job openings?"

Now, *that* was interesting. Suggested that Erica would stay around, as did her desire to fix up the cabin, actually.

The thought put way too much joy into his heart.

"I might know of a couple of things." Mrs. Habler pulled out a chair and sat down beside Erica. "I just heard Cam Cameron is looking for help at the hardware store. And there's going to be an opening at Tiny Tykes Day Care, since Taylor McPherson got put on bed rest today."

Erica's eyes widened. "I love kids. And maybe the twins…" Her cheeks flushed with obvious excitement. "Does anyone from the day care happen to be here tonight?"

"Ruth Delacroix is in the nursery, I believe. She's the owner."

"I know her!" Erica clapped her hands together. "Maybe that's what God has in mind for me. Thank you so much, Mrs. Habler!" She leaned over and gave the woman a one-armed hug.

"You're surely welcome." Mrs. Habler bustled over toward a small group of women clustered near the kitchen, clearly delighted to have put her interfering skills to work.

Erica looked to be brimming with excitement, but before they could discuss the possibility of her working at Tiny Tykes, Pastor Wayne stood to offer a message.

"Keep it short, Pastor!" one of the men cleaning off tables called, grinning.

"That's not in my skill set, George," the pastor called back to general laughter.

As he launched into a message welcoming guests and focusing on coming home to Christ if you'd been astray, Jason finished his plate of food, listening to the pastor's remarks with half an ear.

He hadn't felt the presence of God in some time, even though he dutifully attended church with Papa when he came home. He'd gotten angry at God for letting Kimmie go downhill so badly. Which was wrong, of course.

He hadn't done things right, faithwise. It looked like Kimmie hadn't, either. It occurred to him that he didn't know whether Kimmie had been right with the Lord or not when she'd died.

As for himself—was he right with the Lord? He'd certainly strayed far away.

Appropriately enough, the pastor was sharing the story of the prodigal son. As he started to wrap it up, Ruth Delacroix came into the fellowship hall and approached Erica. For a moment Erica looked excited, but as Ruth whispered to her, she looked increasingly concerned. As soon as the pastor finished, Erica followed Ruth out of the fellowship hall.

Jason debated with himself. He shouldn't follow after Erica, should he? For one thing, as Mrs. Habler had said, tongues were already wagging. For another, Erica could handle things herself and didn't need him interfering.

But the worry on her face…

Before he half knew what he was doing, he was out of his chair and headed out the same door where Erica had gone.

When he reached the nursery, the twins looked to be fine—a relief.

But Erica didn't.

She was sitting on the floor next to Lori Samuelson, the local pediatrician and an active member of the church, while Ruth dealt with the twins and two other toddlers and listened in.

It wasn't his business, and it wasn't right to eavesdrop. The twins were fine. But as he turned to leave, he caught Erica's concerned question: "So you think it's serious?"

"They're quite delayed for fifteen months. The earlier you get help for them, the more likely they'll catch up by the time they're in school."

He forced himself to walk away, but he couldn't force away the look on Erica's face nor the worried tone of her voice.

The twins were in some kind of trouble. And for better or worse, he cared. He wanted to help.

"Can I take you to lunch as a thank-you?" Erica asked Jason the next morning as they drove away from Ruth Delacroix's big Victorian home, half of which operated as the Tiny Tykes Day Care.

She felt like she was about to burst—with anxiety, with gladness, with worry and anticipation.

She'd basically gotten the job. She could start right after the Christmas week closure, provided her paperwork turned out fine. Best of all, the twins could come. They'd be together in the infants and toddlers' room, and Erica would be alternating between that room and the preschoolers' room. It would give the twins a lot of time with her, and some time without her, too, to get more accustomed to other people and to get a different kind of stimulation.

Their life here was shaping up—except for the secret she had to keep and the worry of getting the twins the help they needed. She had an idea about how to handle the early intervention issue, but she had to talk Jason into it very carefully.

"You don't have to buy me lunch," he said as he steered the truck through the snowy streets of downtown Holly Springs.

"I want to. What's the best lunch place in town?"

He grinned over at her and her heart just about stopped. "Well, if you insist… I do love a good burger at Mandelina's."

"Let's do it." It was just a thank-you, she assured herself. Nothing more.

In the corner diner, overwhelming stimulation confronted them. The combined aroma of grease and coffee. Bright Christmas streamers, multicolored lights and three Christmas trees. "Grandma Got Run Over by a Reindeer" blaring from corner speakers.

"The best place, huh?" she murmured as the hostess took them to the only empty booth.

"You'll see."

When the menus came, Jason plucked hers out of her hand. "I know what you're going to do. You're going to order a salad. It would be a mistake."

"How'd you read my mind?" She lifted an eyebrow.

"You're a light eater most of the time. But when in Rome…"

"Don't make assumptions. I might surprise you."

"Oh, really?" He held her gaze for a second too long.

The man was way too good at flirting. He was even tutoring her, a remedial student, in the art.

A chubby, twentysomething waiter appeared, pencil and pad in hand. "And what can I offer you fine people today?"

"I'll have a burger and fries, please," she said, earning a nod of approval from Jason.

"Same for me," he said, and gave her a gentle fist bump. "Only trick is, Erica, you have to save room for pie."

"You absolutely do, because it's coconut cream today," the waiter said as he took their menus. "It's to die for. I had two pieces for breakfast, which was a mistake, but one for dessert will make you the happiest you've been in weeks."

Hmm, she wanted Jason to be happy when she floated her idea. Should she wait until after dessert to suggest it? No, better do it now while he was smiling at her.

"I have a proposal for you." She leaned forward.

He smiled and lifted an eyebrow. "I'm flattered, but we barely know each other."

Her face heated. "Stop it! I'm serious." And then she plowed into an explanation of her idea.

His face grew more disbelieving as she spoke. Not a good sign. "So you want to sell me your half of the farm, but let you live on it?"

"In exchange for my fixing up the cabin, yes. If you need me to pay a small amount of rent, I could do that."

"But why would you do that, when you already own the place?"

She blew out a breath. This was the tricky part. "I need cash." Which was true. "It's been an expensive time, moving the boys across the country."

"And losing your job," he said, frowning. "But the farm will bring you a steady income. Surely that'll be a plus for you as the boys grow up."

She nodded and swallowed. "It would be. But I need the cash now."

"Why?"

The waiter appeared with their drinks. "Don't argue, be happy," he said. "Hey, Jason, did you hear about what's happening with Chuck and Jeannine Henderson?" And he launched into a dramatic breakup story that Jason appeared to want to avoid, but couldn't cut off.

Their conversation gave Erica a minute to think. She'd anticipated that Jason wouldn't warm to the idea immediately, so she couldn't let that discourage her. She'd been pondering and praying all night, and this was the solution she'd come up with—especially now that she'd gotten a job.

Staying in the area would be good for the twins. Staying near their relatives.

But she had to get them early intervention. And she couldn't get public assistance without a lot of paperwork, including birth certificates, which she didn't have.

She knew that someday she'd have to go through the appropriate channels to get the twins their birth certificates and other paperwork. Probably, she'd need to hire a lawyer, maybe that one who'd been a friend of Kimmie's.

But for the time being, lawyers' fees were out of reach.

And the boys needed early intervention, now, and on an ongoing basis. A onetime trip to some clinic wasn't going to be enough.

So she had to get private help, which would be no questions asked. The fact that it cost money was okay—as long as Jason would buy her half of the farm.

A busboy brought out plates, and their waiter waved a hand. "Thanks, Ger. Sorry I got to talking." He put steaming plates down in front of them, and the aroma of burgers and fries wafted up.

"Here you go, Jason and…what did you say your name is?"

"I'm Erica." She held out her hand.

"Pleased to meet you. I'm Henry, but you can call me Hank. And I need to get it in gear." He turned and headed off.

The burger was enormous, so Erica sawed it in half with her butter knife.

Jason picked up his whole burger. "There are two kinds of people in the world," he said, grinning. "The ones who are dainty with a hamburger and the ones like me." He took a big bite.

Good. Let him eat up and get into a good mood. In fact, this burger could put her in a good mood, too; it was delicious.

Hank returned to their table, coffeepot in hand. "How is everything? More coffee, Erica?"

She swallowed and held out her cup. "Yes, please."

She kept quiet during the rest of their lunch, letting Jason eat and thinking about what she needed to say or do to convince him. *Be strong, girl. It's for the twins.*

Jason finished his meal and Erica ate half of hers and asked Hank to wrap up the rest. After he brought Jason a piece of pie, she launched into her proposal again. "Will you at least think about making a deal with the farm? You wouldn't have to buy it all right away. We can do payments. Figure something out."

He held up a big bite of pie. "Sure you don't want to try it?"

"No, thanks. It's just that," she pushed on, "I need some of the money pretty soon, here."

He put down his fork. "For the twins?"

She bit her lip. The fewer details he knew, the better.

"Is the reason you're wanting to sell property so that you can pay for therapists and specialists?"

She looked away, trying to figure out how much to tell him.

"Look," he said, pushing the rest of his pie away, "I'd hate to see you sell. It's going to appreciate in value. You're thinking short-term."

"But they need help now," she protested, shredding a napkin with nervous fingers.

He put a hand over hers, stilling them. "There's a children's health insurance program for low income people. They should have good services. Pennsylvania usually does."

She pulled her hands away. "I don't want to get public insurance."

"I respect not wanting a handout, but programs for children's health are different. You've had a hard time here, and you have two little ones. That's exactly what those programs are for."

"I don't want it," she said. Let him think it was pride.

Around them, the noise of the diner went on: forks clattering, people talking, the bells jingling on the door as it opened and closed.

"Could their father help?" Jason asked.

"No."

"He should."

"He's in prison and he has no claim on them."

Jason looked startled, and for a moment, she could see him sifting through images in his mind, trying to figure her out. He'd thought she was a drug addict, but he seemed to have ruled that out now. However, having the father of her children imprisoned put her back in that same sketchy camp in his mind, she could tell.

What he didn't know, of course, was that the twins' imprisoned father was Kimmie's partner, not her own.

"I don't understand why you won't at least see a doctor and start the paperwork for CHIP. You could make a final decision later."

He was trying to be so reasonable, and it was killing her, because under normal circumstances he'd be right.

Oh, Kimmie, why'd you put me in this position? Why couldn't you have been up front with your family?

"Hey, Stephanidis." A man with a military haircut, about Jason's age and with similar muscles came over and shook Jason's hand, an encounter that ended in a slight test of strength. "How's the hard-line detective? Didn't expect to see you out of your mean streets. How's Philly going to stay safe without you?"

Jason introduced her but didn't try to draw her into the conversation, which was fine.

As the two men talked, Erica bit her lip and pondered. She'd prayed and she knew that God would be with her no matter what. And yes, Kimmie had been a flawed person, and maybe wrong about Jason, but he *would* be angry about the deception, right? Angry enough to take the twins.

And once he had them, he'd have no reason to keep her around.

A guy like Jason wouldn't *want* to keep someone like her around.

She loved the boys too much to let them go. Her desire to mother them grew every day.

As his friend left, Jason turned back to her, smiling. "Come on now, Erica. Won't you just try signing up for CHIP?"

"I'm not getting public insurance!"

"Don't you care about your kids?"

"It's because I care about them that I won't—"

"Hey, you two, I said no fighting." Hank was back with the check. "Look, I brought you kisses to make you feel all better." He put down the check with two foil-wrapped candies on top of it and spun away.

Erica reached for the check at the same time Jason did. She grabbed it, but his larger hand closed over hers. "Let me get this."

"I said I was taking you out to lunch."

"You need the money more than I do."

"I can afford a lunch!"

"Put the money into your fund to help the twins." Deftly, he got the check out of her hand, but she closed her hand on his.

His dark skin and large hand contrasted with her own small, pale one. But as far as calluses, she had as many as he did. She'd worked hard in her life, as had he.

"Let me have my dignity," she said quietly, and immediately he let the check go. Understanding and sympathy shone in his eyes.

"Thank you for lunch. I appreciate it and it was really good."

She could see that it cost him to let a woman pay, especially when Hank came over and took the money from her and lifted an eyebrow at Jason. But he didn't protest any more.

"Look," he said while they waited for change, "we need to talk more about the farm and what should be done with it. That's not a discussion to finish in an hour, over lunch."

"What do you say we talk about it while we're working on the cabin?" she suggested. Because she *had* to get out of that house.

"Possible," he said, nodding. "I have tomorrow afternoon free. Would that work for you?"

"As long as I can get Ruth to watch the twins again, yes."

"It's a date, then." His words were light. But she could tell that his suspicions about her had been raised again.

6

Jason pulled his truck in front of his friend Chuck's house, looked over at Erica and hoped this was all going to go okay.

They'd spent the afternoon working on the cabin, and *that* had been great. She'd opened up a little bit about Kimmie and their friendship, how they'd been in and out of touch, how Kimmie had been like a sister to Erica, albeit a flawed one.

It was what he'd done *after* working on the cabin that had him sweating a little. He was going to have to tell Erica about it tonight.

Instead, he told her the easier thing. "This could be a little awkward. They're both still living here."

As they headed up the sidewalk to Chuck's house, Erica touched his arm, stopping him. Almost stopping his heart. He was getting way too sensitive to casual contact with her.

"This is a nice house. I'm not going to be able to afford anything they have." Her voice was husky. Behind her, the sunset made her loose red curls glow like fire.

"I can afford it." As she started to protest, he lifted a hand. "It's an investment in the property."

"Does that mean you're buying it from me?" She raised her eyebrows.

He rang the doorbell. "I'm considering it."

Chuck opened the door, looking like he'd aged thirty years since they'd hung out together in high school. "Hey, come on in."

"This is Erica," Jason said once they were inside and taking off their coats. "She's going to move into the cabin on the property and she's looking for some furniture."

"Great—we could use the cash." Chuck ran a hand through his already-sticking-up hair and grabbed a roll of colored stickers. "Here, just put one of these on anything you want. Only not if it already has a sticker. I'm green and Jeannine's yellow. You can be orange."

Erica's eyes widened, and Jason felt his own gut twist a little. He'd never been this close to the sad details of a marital breakup before.

"Go on, walk through. She's out somewhere and I'm packing up the basement." Chuck sounded mechanical.

"If you're sure, man." Jason clapped his friend on the shoulder.

"*She's* sure." Chuck turned abruptly and strode out of the entryway.

When Jason and Erica walked into the front room, both of them stopped at the same moment.

The mantel was half decorated with evergreen garland and red bows, and a box containing more of the same sat on the hearth. A Scotch pine, unadorned, sent waves of Christmassy scent through the cozy room.

Erica looked over at him. "I don't feel right about this."

From the back of the house, a door opened. "Hey, I'm…" called a woman's voice, trailing off into dejection. Like she'd forgotten for a moment that happy greetings to her husband weren't part of her life anymore.

There was the sound of a heavy tread climbing the basement stairs. Chuck.

Erica's brow furrowed. "What should we do? Should we leave?"

"No, he was serious about wanting to sell stuff, and he said they both knew we were coming tonight. Come on. Maybe we should start upstairs." They headed toward the staircase, and if Jason put his hand on the small of Erica's back, he was just guiding her. Right?

"Were you ever married?" she asked as they climbed the stairs.

"Nope. Just engaged."

"What happened?"

He shrugged, nodding toward one of the smaller bedrooms, guiding her toward it with a light touch. "She regained her sanity and dumped me."

"You don't sound very upset."

"I'm not. Saved me from going through *this*." He waved an arm to indicate the whole house, the breakup of a marriage.

But Erica pressed a hand to her mouth as she looked around the room. "Oh, wow."

It was a nursery, perfectly decorated but empty of the clothes and sheets and paraphernalia that indicated a baby. There were no stickers on any of the furniture.

"Do they have a baby? Or…is she pregnant?"

He shook his head, opening the little blue dresser's drawers to confirm that they were empty. "This might be nice for the twins, huh?"

"Yes, it would, but..." She trailed off. "Are they sure they want to get rid of all this?"

"They did years of infertility treatments." He explained in the same matter-of-fact way Chuck had explained it to him. "She finally got pregnant, but about six weeks ago, she lost the baby. I guess...that and all the doctor's bills..." He shrugged.

"That is so awful." Erica's eyes got shiny as she ran a finger along the railing of the brand-new crib.

"Should I put a sticker on it?" His hand hovered over the dresser.

"Yeah. I guess. If it'll help them."

He really, really wanted to wipe that sadness off her face. He even felt a strange urge to do it by kissing her, but that would be a mistake. "What are you doing tomorrow?" he asked instead, to distract her.

She considered, then shrugged. "I don't know. The twins are getting bored. I'd like to find somewhere new to take them."

Footsteps sounded on the stairs. Light. A woman's.

Jason didn't know Chuck's wife very well, but he recognized her when she looked in the door. "Hey, Jeannine, good to—"

"Just don't." Her face crumpled and she spun and hurried away from the room.

"Oh, wow, that's the woman who looked so upset at the clothing giveaway. I've got to see if I can do anything for her." Erica went after Jeannine.

So obviously, Erica had had a better instinct about this than he did, or than Chuck did, either, for that matter. *Christmas, a miscarriage... Duh.* Not the time to participate in dismantling a home.

He heard a low murmur of voices from what looked like the master bedroom and headed downstairs to see what he could do for Chuck.

An hour later, he and Chuck were watching hockey when Jason heard the doorbell ring. It sounded like someone was singing outside. Maybe a lot of people.

Jason looked over at Chuck. The man was still staring at the TV, obviously trying to distance himself from what was happening in his life. "Want me to get that?"

"Sure." Chuck sat upright, elbows on knees, fists under his chin.

So Jason opened the door to a group of about ten carolers, adults and kids, singing one of his favorite Christmas carols: "O Little Town of Bethlehem." Behind them, in the light from a lamppost, he could see that snow had started to fall.

There was a sound on the stairs behind him, and he turned to see Jeannine descending, Erica right behind her. When she saw what was going on, Jeannine sat abruptly on a step about halfway down the stairs and started to cry. Or maybe she'd been crying all along.

Erica sat beside her and put an arm around her, murmuring quietly.

Chuck had come out to the entryway, too, and he stood listening as the carolers came to the last verse of the song: *Oh holy child of Bethlehem...cast out our sin and enter in...abide with us, our Lord Emmanuel.*

For sure, this household needed the Christ child to enter in. And Jason did, too. He was saved; he accepted

Jesus as his redeemer, but he didn't always let Christ in. Too busy trying to control things himself, fix the world by himself.

He waved a thank-you to the carolers and closed the door.

Chuck turned and took a couple of steps toward the staircase where the two women still sat. Erica got up and came quietly downstairs.

"She needs you," Jason said to Chuck.

"She doesn't want anything to do with me." Chuck's expression, looking up at his crying wife, was full of frustration and yearning.

Jason put a hand on his friend's shoulder. "You've got so much here, man. You should fight for it."

And then his eyes met Erica's, and they turned as one toward the door, grabbed their coats off the banister railing and walked out of the house.

"Wow," Erica said once they were outside. "Pretty emotional."

"Very." It was natural to take her arm on the icy walkway. "I don't know if you'll get that dresser or not."

"I hope not. I hope they work things out and get the chance to be parents."

"Me, too." He held the truck door open for her and helped her to climb in. And meanwhile, he hadn't gotten the chance to talk to her about what he needed to, and this was his last chance. Once they got home, it would be craziness, Papa and Ruth and the twins. A full house and a lively one, and he liked that, but it didn't allow time for quiet discussion.

Quiet persuasion.

For that, he knew exactly where he needed to take her.

* * *

Erica was so lost in thought, worrying about Chuck and Jeannine, that she didn't notice the direction the truck was going until it stopped. In the middle of a parking lot full of cars, apparently in the middle of a field.

"Where are we… Oh, wow!" She stared down at a wonderland of colored and white lights. "What is it?"

"It's the Mistletoe Display. Will you walk through with me?"

Her breath seemed to leave her chest. Why had he brought her here?

Against her will, her heart was warming to Jason, and maybe, just maybe, he was feeling similarly toward her. Why else would he have brought her to such a romantic place?

"We don't have to. If you'd rather get home to the twins—"

"No, no. I… I'd love to."

They walked down the path to a ticket shed, and he insisted on buying her ticket. "My idea, my treat."

Definitely date-like.

They strolled through winding paths, stopping to admire the light-made scenes scattered along the way. Here was portrayed a group of children carrying gifts; there, a family building a snowman. A brass ensemble played "Angels We Have Heard on High," and no sooner had those sounds faded than a quartet of singers in old-fashioned costumes sang "God Rest Ye Merry Gentlemen." Pastor Wayne was at a wooden stand selling hot chocolate and passing out invitations to the church's Christmas Eve service. Jason stopped, assured the pastor he'd be there and bought them both cups of hot chocolate, complete with peppermint-stick stirrers.

It was lovely and romantic, especially when Jason draped his scarf around her neck to keep her warmer.

"So, you're probably wondering why I brought you here," he said, sounding nervous.

"I wasn't, but…is there a special reason?" Her heart leaped to her throat. Was he going to make some kind of declaration? They weren't dating, although the things they'd been through together had made her feel closer to him than to anyone she'd dated. Not that there had been a whole lot of boyfriends in her life.

"There's something I want to tell you. Ask you." He led her to a bench beside a snowy lane, a little off from where most people were walking. "I… I'm going to Philadelphia tomorrow."

Her heart sank a little. She had grown accustomed to having Jason around, and she'd miss him if he left. But of course, they weren't really accountable to each other. "How long will you be gone?"

"Just a couple of days, three at the outside. I have to testify in the case that put me on leave."

"Okay." He'd told her a little bit about why he was on administrative leave, something to do with a corrupt partner. "Will this fix the problem?"

"It's a start." He took her hand. "You might be upset with me for what I did, but…how would you and the twins like to come with me?"

Erica's head spun. "Come *with* you? But…why?"

Her mind spun with possibilities. Was this a romantic proposition? Did he think she was easy and that, away from Papa's watchful eye, they could have a fling? But if that were the case, why bring the twins?

"I made an appointment with a specialist," he said, looking hard at her as if to see her reaction.

"What kind?" She wasn't following.

"A pediatrician who's, like, world renowned for helping delayed babies catch up."

Her jaw about dropped as emotions warred within her, chief among them an absurd sense of disappointment. He didn't want anything romantic, and this wasn't a date. "I *told* you I wanted to do this my own way. And I can't afford a famous specialist. You know that." She stood up.

"No, no, sit down." He tugged her hand, pulling her back down to the bench. "I just thought... I was talking about my visit to my buddy who has a child with Down syndrome, and he was telling me about everything they're doing for his daughter...you know, Philly has world-class hospitals and so I thought..."

"You thought you'd go over my head and get medical treatment for my boys?"

"You don't understand. It's so hard to get an appointment with her, but she had a cancellation. So... I went ahead and did it." He paused. "It's the day after tomorrow."

She stared at him as her head spun. Partly from his high-handedness and partly from fear. If a specialist wanted to look at the twins' medical records, she didn't have them.

"I wasn't planning to do this, Erica, but when it came up, I couldn't help but think of the twins. I care about the little guys. And about you."

"No." She was shaking her head before having even formulated a response. "Just...no. I don't want to visit some strange doctor, all the way over in Philadelphia, only to hear about treatments I can't afford in a place I can't get to—"

"My friend says lots of people come and consult with her and then do treatment in their own towns. And as for insurance…when I made the appointment, I explained that you didn't have coverage or the money to pay privately, and they sent some paperwork. The receptionist said it's not complicated at all, and that Dr. Chen works with a lot of…of low income patients. Don't you see, Erica? This way, you won't have to sell me the farm to get help for the boys. You can keep it for them."

She squeezed her eyes shut and tried to think as the hot chocolate curdled in her stomach.

He hadn't brought her here for a date. He'd brought her here to butter her up so he could find out the truth.

"No." She shook her head. "No. I'm not ready to take that step."

"You won't even do it for the twins?" His voice held a touch of censure.

He thought she was a bad mother.

She stared down at her denim-clad knees as waves of confusion and shame passed over her. She *was* a bad mother. Not fit for the wonderful gift Kimmie had given her.

Jason reached an arm around her shoulders, gave her a quick couple of pats and then pulled his arm away. "Look, I'm sorry to spring this on you, and I know you'd rather have time to think about it. You're a great mother. You want to take time and figure out what's best for your kids. You like to plan things out, and here I'm just throwing this at you."

You're a great mother. She looked over to see if he was mocking her, but his face was serious, earnest.

"For all kinds of reasons, I'd like for you to go. Mostly for the twins and the specialist, of course, but there's a Christmas party..." He trailed off.

"A Christmas party?" She couldn't keep up with the way his mind was working.

"For my department. It's at the home of my good friends, who have little kids, so you could bring the twins. We could even stay with them." He paused. "I'd really like for you to meet them."

She felt her forehead wrinkle. What was he saying?

That he wanted her to meet his friends because he was serious about her? Or that he wanted her to come to Philly for a fling?

He seemed to read her mind. "They have a huge farmhouse. You and the twins would have a big room and your own bathroom. I'd bunk down on the couch in the den."

Now she was thoroughly confused. "Do you... Why are you asking me to come? Besides just being kind about the twins?"

He dug at the snowy ground with the toe of his boot. "Look," he said, "I'm bad at this stuff. I'm bad at talking to people, working things out. I'm bad at, well, relationships, but... I'm trying to improve. Especially now that I have a reason to." He propped his elbows on his knees and rested his cheek on his hand, facing her. "I really like you, Erica."

Her heart pounded like a drum.

He was holding out a chance, however small, at everything she wanted: connection, someone to value her, a good family.

She couldn't have even a chance at that if she didn't take him up on what he'd offered, the trip to Philadelphia and the appointment with a specialist for the twins.

She looked up at the stars, sparkling in the cold air. *Should I go, Lord?*

The very question reminded her how much in the Christmas story depended on following a star, on faith.

Jason had overstepped by making the appointment, for sure. And figuring out how to manage that appointment without revealing Kimmie's secret was going to be a challenge.

Not to mention that any kind of a relationship with Jason was out of the question, as long as she was withholding the truth about the twins. How could she judge him for being a little pushy, when she herself was lying to him?

She glanced up at the stars again, took a couple of breaths and then met Jason's eyes. "Thank you for the offer and for what you're doing for the twins and me. We…we'll go."

His eyes lit and he pulled her into a spontaneous hug. A hug that went on a little longer than something friendly.

She pulled back a little and looked at him, her heart fluttering like a startled bird in a cage.

His eyes went dark with some unreadable emotion. He cupped her chin in his hand and studied her face.

"You are so beautiful," he said. And then he pressed his lips to hers.

All logic slipped away, replaced by almost-complete feeling and warmth and care. Almost complete, not fully, because something nagged at the edge of her melting consciousness: *this isn't going to work, because he doesn't know the truth about the twins.*

7

The small box was sitting on the table beside the door, where Papa always tossed the mail he didn't have time to sort.

Jason spotted it as he came whistling down the stairs. Something compelled him to take a closer look.

He could hear Erica talking to Papa in the kitchen. "No, no phone calls about the dog yet," Papa was saying.

"I think his foot is getting better," Erica replied. "Look, he chewed the bandage off again."

"It looks okay, but I don't think that fur is growing back. He'll always have a scar." There was the homey sound of dishes clinking and water running.

The box was addressed to him, in Renea's handwriting.

He should probably just leave it there, get on with loading up the car. They needed to head out so they could get to Brian and Carla's house and settle Erica and the twins before he hustled to meet with the lawyers.

But it would nag at him; he knew it. So he set his suitcase down and carried the little box upstairs.

In his room, with the door closed, he opened the

box up, feeling as if a viper might jump out. Renea had been furious about their breakup even though she'd instigated it, and the sight of her handwriting brought her angry feelings and words back to him. His sense of dread increased as he used a pocketknife to slit through the tape.

Inside was a small envelope and a wad of newspaper. Cowardly, he opened the wad first.

There was the engagement ring he'd bought her.

Okay, that wasn't a problem, really. He hadn't wanted it back, hadn't wanted the reminder of his failure, but he was getting past that now. Things were new and promising in his life, he reminded himself.

The thought of kissing Erica made him sit down on his bed and close his eyes, still clutching the ring and the note in his hands. She'd been hesitant but then so sweet and giving as he'd held her. And although he'd kept the kiss short and respectful, he had seen the emotion in her eyes and he knew it had been reflected in his own.

She didn't throw her kisses around and neither did he, these days. It meant something.

She was beginning to care for him, and that thought had filled him with way more happiness and joy than he'd had any right to expect.

He heard Erica trotting up the stairs, and then a minute later, something heavy bumping down. Erica must be dragging her suitcase down herself, and she shouldn't be; he should be helping her. He ripped open the note.

I've lost weight and they want to put me in the clinic again. Haven't been able to eat since we

broke up. Can you get this ring resized down?
Call me.

He looked at the ring, already the size of a child's
ring. The sight of it brought back the short two months
of his engagement.

How he'd looked up some formula of how much an
engagement ring should cost based on his salary and
saved up that amount. How he'd consulted with his
friends—clueless guys all—about what type of ring to
buy. How she'd said yes, and instead of feeling happy,
his heart had gone cold with the feeling of a cage door
slamming shut. And from then on, the whole relationship had gone downhill. She'd been discontented with
the ring and with how he expressed, or didn't express,
his feelings for her. He'd tried to whip himself up into
a proper type of enthusiasm for a groom-to-be, not
helped by a few of his friends who viewed their wives
as nags and marriage as a ball and chain. And others
of his friends, the more serious ones, who thought he'd
made the wrong choice of mate.

Most of all, there'd been the sinking realization that
being involved with a man brought out Renea's severe
eating disorder. Although she'd hidden it before their
engagement, she hadn't been able to hide it after. Her
parents had begged him to break it off with her so as
not to complicate her recovery. He'd tried, but she was
so fragile that it had never seemed like the right time.

When she'd gone into a rage one night and broken
up with him, he'd taken it as a blessing, especially
since his only feeling had been relief. And he'd held
fast against Renea's multiple attempts to get back to-

gether, each one ending in accusations that he had ruined her life.

He guessed the breakup had been fortunate. But had he changed any since then?

He didn't want to ruin anyone else's life the way he'd ruined Renea's. And obviously, he knew nothing about choosing a mate; he'd gone solely for beauty with Renea, and he'd almost made a huge mistake.

Ruined his fiancée's life.

Didn't save his sister.

He stood and looked out the window. Erica and Papa were loading things into the back of the truck, talking and laughing.

It would be wrong to go forward and try to get something started with Erica. Yes, she was beautiful, but Renea had been, too.

Why on earth had he kissed Erica? More of the same poor choices?

She's different, his heart cried as he trotted down the stairs double time, intent on setting right the wrong he'd committed. *She's a good person. Stable. Not hiding things.*

Papa must have gone inside, but Erica was there beside the truck, her breath making steam in the air in front of her beautiful face, a cap on her head unable to tame her red curls. Her cheeks were pink, and when she saw him, her eyes lit up.

"Hey." He sounded abrupt and he knew it, but that was what he needed to be. Short. Abrupt. Not paying attention to how pretty she was or to the concern starting to appear in her green eyes.

"Listen," he said quickly, "I shouldn't have kissed you last night. I want to apologize."

She frowned, tilted her head. Opened her mouth to say something, and then closed it again.

"I... I didn't mean to give you the wrong idea. I'm not... I'm not..." He trailed off, then forced himself to say it. "I'm really not up for dating or anything."

She waved her hand, her eyes shuttered. "It's fine. It was a romantic setting. Anyone could make a mistake like that." She turned to lift a bag of baby supplies into the truck. "Or... Did you still want us to come with you? Because we don't have to. Maybe it's best if we don't—"

"No, no. I want you to come. Gotta keep that appointment."

"Right, the appointment." Wrinkles appeared between her eyebrows and she frowned down at the ground. "But we could go another time. Get there another way. I don't want to impose—"

"No imposition," he said, trying to sound happy and hearty and like his heart wasn't aching. "I'd welcome the company and we're all set up."

She looked at him, confusion clouding her eyes.

"It's important for the twins. And that's what friends do for each other, right?"

She swallowed and bit her lip and looked away.

All the work he'd done to convince her to trust him, gone.

"I'm sorry," he said.

"I... Well, if you're sure you want us to come, I'll go get the twins."

"I'll help."

"No, it's okay. I'll bring them myself." And she turned and went back into the house.

Loser. He was such a loser. She'd been happy, excited about the trip, and then he'd come down with his hurtful announcement. Now she was sad. And this trip across the state was going to be extremely awkward.

I'm doing it for her. I don't want to ruin another woman's life.

Let alone the lives of a couple of sweet babies.

But the whole thing made his chest feel as heavy as if a three-hundred-pound barbell were resting on it.

Two hours later, Erica was just about to scream into the awkward silence when Jason spoke.

"You want to stop?" He indicated the road sign announcing a service plaza.

"Okay." Anything to get out of this truck. "I shouldn't let the boys sleep much longer or they'll never sleep tonight."

"Papa packed some lunch for us. Want to eat it now?"

"If that's all right with you, sure."

They were being painfully polite with each other. As if they hadn't gotten close over the past week and shared a kiss last night. A kiss she'd thought meant something.

Apparently not to Jason. Apparently he thought it was a big mistake, and that was fine. Just fine.

Say it often enough and you might even start to believe it.

She got Mikey out of his car seat, and when she turned, Jason was standing there, so she thrust the baby into his arms. Then she unlatched Teddy. The way he lifted his arms to her with a crooked smile made her heart melt. "Aren't you the happy little man?"

she cooed as she pulled him out and grabbed the diaper bag.

Mikey and Teddy were her priorities. She couldn't forget that, couldn't get too sad or upset. She had to take care of herself so she could take care of them. Like they'd said the one time she'd taken a plane ride: put your own mask on before assisting others.

She'd thought that Jason might be a positive part of her life, but if he was going to be negative and hurtful, then she didn't want anything to do with him. She flipped back her hair and followed him into the service plaza, determinedly not noticing how handsome he was and how easily he carried Mikey and the picnic container.

Once they'd put their bags down, Jason handed Mikey to her and then went to grab high chairs. Before she could ask it, he found disinfecting wipes and scrubbed the chairs down.

He was pretty good with babies, for being a novice.

"Aw, they look just like their daddy," a woman said as she carried her tray to a nearby table.

Jason gave her a half smile as he got out plastic containers of food, but Erica's heart pumped a little harder. *Did* the boys look like Jason? They were his nephews, but she'd never noticed a resemblance. Sometimes you didn't see things that were right in front of your eyes.

They each fed a twin. "You're getting pretty good at that," she said as Jason used a plastic spoon to scrape some food off Mikey's mouth. Then she froze. He didn't want to pursue a relationship, so did that mean she wasn't even supposed to talk to him?

But he smiled. "I'm a quick learner. And I think he's getting neater, isn't he?"

"Let's hope so."

Teddy wasn't hungry. He yelled and squirmed to get down, but Erica didn't like the look of the floor. She glanced around, trying to figure out what to do with him.

Jason seemed to read her mind. "I'll put my coat down and he can sit on it."

"But your coat will get filthy!"

He shrugged. "It'll wash." He spread it on the floor, and after a moment's hesitation, Erica put Teddy down on it.

Mikey, neglected, started to make some noise. "Mama!" he complained.

Jason looked over at her, grinning. "Now I see what people mean about traveling with kids." He lifted Mikey out of his chair and put him beside his brother, and Erica hurried to wipe both boys' faces.

"I couldn't do this without you. I'm really grateful."

"It's my pleasure." He met her eyes for a moment and then looked away.

But she needed to get the necessary words out now, all of them, while they were speaking to each other. "Mikey's getting more frustrated that he can't move around. And Teddy's fussing more, I think because he can't communicate. They really need the help, so… thanks for setting up this appointment and making me keep it." And please, God, let it not get them all in trouble.

"You're welcome. And, Erica…" He looked away and blew out a breath. "I'm sorry I was… This morning. I hurt your feelings."

Who *was* this man? He'd kissed her like he meant it, taken it back harshly like he meant *that*, acted as if he were the twins' loving father, and now he wanted to talk feelings?

"Look, there's something in my past. A broken engagement."

She blinked and nodded. So he'd been engaged and it had ended and that had somehow caused his seesawing behavior. "Okaaaayyy…"

"I didn't handle it well. The breakup."

"You mean you were upset about it, or you didn't do it right?" It seemed crucial to know whose idea the breakup had been.

"Mostly, I didn't do it right. I'm a perfectionist, hard on people. And I'm not good at talking to a…a girlfriend, I guess. Communicating."

"You're talking now," she said before she could think better of it. More than that, he was admitting to the problem that Kimmie had accused him of: being a perfectionist, being rigid. So maybe he was changing. Maybe he wasn't the hard-core, hard-line guy Kimmie had thought he was. Look how he'd analyzed his broken engagement, how he was trying to share his feelings.

And if this, the past relationship gone bad, was his big secret…

She needed to tell him the truth about the twins. Sooner rather than later. But how did you begin to say something like that? And would it be better to do it before or after the doctor's appointment?

If she told him and he got outraged at her and the twins, where would they be? She'd better wait.

"I'm talking now because I don't want you to feel hurt. I don't suspect you of sharing Kimmie's bad habits anymore. And… It was fantastic to kiss you, Erica.

I don't want to have any expectations out of it, or for you to, but I sure liked it."

He looked up and met her eyes, and she couldn't look away. Couldn't stop herself from saying, "I liked it, too."

In fact, she very badly wanted it to happen again. But Teddy crawled off the coat onto the dirty floor, and Mikey started to cry.

"We'd better get on the road. I've got to meet the lawyers at three, and we still have—" he checked his phone "—about two hours to Brian and Carla's place."

They rode in silence for a while, but it was friendlier, more relaxed. Jason found a radio station the twins seemed to like, and Erica even managed to doze off for a bit.

She sat up, refreshed, and looked around, and Jason glanced over at her. "Feel better?"

"A lot."

"I've been thinking," he said, "about Kimmie."

Her heart rate accelerated. "Yeah?"

"Did she talk about her family at all? About us?"

Erica considered how much to say. "She did a little."

"Was she angry at me? Did she see what I did as a betrayal?" The words seemed to burst out of him.

She blew out a breath. "It's water under the bridge."

"Yeah, but it's my bridge. I want to know."

"Why? So you can torture yourself some more, like you do with your ex-fiancée?"

He glanced over at her, looking startled. "Is that what I'm doing?"

"It seems like it. Blaming yourself for everything. Kimmie made her choices. She did what addicts do." *Like have kids and neglect them.*

"Wait a minute. You did Al-Anon, right?"

"Yeah, it was pretty much forced on me when I was a teenager. Why, does it show?"

"Uh-huh." He put on the truck's blinker. "And the other thing that shows is that you're good at being evasive."

She stared at him as sweat gathered on her neck and chest. "What's that supposed to mean?"

"I asked you about Kimmie, and all of a sudden we're talking about me. And this isn't the first time. Is there some reason you don't like talking about Kimmie or the past?"

Tell him. Tell him now.

Instead, she sidestepped the question. "I grew up having to keep a lot of secrets. It gets to be a habit." And it was one she should break. Look how Jason was trying to do better at communicating. "Kimmie talked about happy times when you guys were kids. She really seemed to love you."

He glanced over at her as if to see whether she was telling the truth. "Really?"

"Yes. And, Jason, she had good values in a lot of ways. It was just… Addiction is hard to break. Drugs nowadays are so strong…"

"Tell me about it." He shook his head slowly. "I remember when she was in high school, those chastity rings were the thing. She got one. Go figure." He looked over at her. "I don't suppose… I mean, she used to talk to me about how she wanted to wait for marriage."

Erica froze. Kimmie hadn't waited for marriage; not only that, but she'd had twins out of wedlock.

Twins who were sleeping peacefully in the back seat right now.

"Is that pretty important to you?" she asked.

"It's the ideal, and I hope..." He trailed off and looked over at her. "I'm sorry, Erica. I don't mean to judge. I haven't been perfect myself by any means."

Erica almost laughed and then restrained it. No need to give in to hysteria. Jason thought he'd offended her because of her supposed impurity, as an unmarried mom. Little did he know that she *wasn't* actually a mom. And that she'd barely dated, let alone gotten close enough to someone to conceive a child. Waiting for marriage hadn't been a challenge for her.

But there was a desperate hopefulness in Jason's eyes. She felt for him and she wanted to provide comfort, as best she could. "If you're asking whether there were a lot of men in her life, I don't think so. Times when I was around her, she was mostly on her own."

She was saved from expanding on that by the sound of a siren. She looked back, and red and blue lights flashed. Her heart raced and she felt guilty, like the police had somehow guessed she wasn't being completely honest.

Jason let out an exclamation and pulled over. "Wonder what's up. I wasn't speeding."

"Police make me nervous."

"You gotta remember I'm a cop myself. And in fact..." He was looking in his rearview mirror, and suddenly he laughed and opened the driver's-side door.

"Don't get out!" She couldn't keep the panic out of her voice. Bad things happened when you confronted cops. "Just sit still and keep your hands visible!"

"It's fine. Old friend. He's just busting my chops."

He jumped out of the truck and walked back to meet the uniformed police officer, and a moment later they were thumping each other on the back and laughing.

She couldn't take her eyes off him as he talked to his friend. That strong square jaw, dark with the beginnings of a beard. The messy-cut black hair that contrasted so sharply with his blue eyes. His athletic build, the confidence of his wide-legged stance.

Was she falling in love with him?

No sooner had she thought it than she shook her head and let her face sink onto one fist. No. Not that. She couldn't be in love.

Jason needed to hold on to a positive picture of his sister. It would help him heal.

But knowing Kimmie had had children out of wedlock would tarnish that image.

The web of lies kept getting trickier, more complex. Now, if she revealed the truth, she wouldn't just be breaking a promise to Kimmie. She wouldn't just be risking that Jason would take the twins away from her.

She'd be risking his own happiness, the image he was trying to create of a sister who'd been an addict but otherwise, had stuck to the values she was raised with.

Male laughter rang out, Jason's, and despite her racing worries, she couldn't help smiling.

When Jason was happy, she was happy. When he tried awkwardly to explain things and apologize, truly attempting to do better at communicating, her heart warmed toward him. When he unquestioningly helped with the twins, she felt safe, protected.

Yes, for sure. She was hooked. Falling, falling, fallen.

With the one person it would be a complete disaster to love.

* * *

After they'd arrived at Brian and Carla's house, escorted by his old friend Diego, Jason knew it wouldn't take long for someone to grill him. Sure enough, the moment he'd helped to carry the twins and the luggage to the guest suite, Brian was on his case, dragging him out to the garage, ostensibly to look at his new motorcycle. "Why didn't you tell us? She's a knockout."

"She's a friend. That's all."

Brian made a skeptical sound as he went to the refrigerator in the garage and pulled out a couple of sodas. "I saw the way you were looking at each other."

He shrugged. "I like her, sure. But you know better than anyone how I am with women."

"So you've made some dumb mistakes." Brian tossed him a soda. "You can't judge everyone by Renea."

He wasn't; he was adding Kimmie into the mix, and Gran if it came to that. He'd let them all down.

"How are you doing with Erica's twins?" Brian took a long swig of soda and then squatted down by his bike. "Check out these straight pipes. I never thought I'd go for them, but they're cool."

Jason snorted. "And that makes you think *you're* cool. I like the twins, if you can believe it. I even feed 'em and put 'em in their car seats."

"You?" Brian shook his head as he swung a leg over his bike and sat on it, despite the fact that, even with the garage door closed, it was freezing. "I'm itching to ride this thing, man."

"Might be time for a trip south."

"Can't. Carla's expecting again."

"This soon? You better slow yourself down, boy."

Brian grinned and spread his hands wide. "What can I say, man. I look at her, she gets pregnant."

"And then you brag about it while she does all the work." He clapped Brian on the back. "Seriously, man. Happy for you."

Brian got off the bike and gave it a regretful pat. "I'm getting over my shock that you like a woman with kids. But family's everything, and if she's willing to put up with a loser like you, you better grab her."

"Thanks, pal." But as they walked back into the house to a cacophony of babies rolling on the floor, guarded by Carla's two teen daughters, he was surprised to find himself actually considering his friend's advice. Family life was looking surprisingly good to him.

"I appreciate your girls taking care of Mikey and Teddy," Erica said to Carla as she unpacked a few things in the guest suite. "In fact, I appreciate your letting all of us stay with you. Are you sure we're not putting anyone out?"

"Absolutely sure." Carla lounged back on the bed and waved an arm toward the rest of the house. "This place is huge. And as for the girls, they're kind of fascinated by baby twins, since they're twins themselves."

"They're sweethearts." Erica pulled out the changing supplies and diapers she'd packed for the twins and stacked them on the dresser top. "Did they have delays?"

"Not like yours," Carla said. "I mean, they were a month premature, but they caught up by age one."

"You could notice the twins' delays just from those

few minutes?" Erica rubbed the back of her neck. "Are they really that obvious?"

Carla nodded. "I'm glad you're getting them checked out, and Dr. Chen is the best. Well, except for her bedside manner, from what I've heard."

"She's not nice?" Erica's heart sank. "How can a pediatrician have a poor bedside manner?"

"I know, right? It's not that she's not nice, it's just… I heard she's kind of awkward. But she's a genius researcher who knows everything babies need."

Maybe she'll be too preoccupied or oblivious to notice their lack of a medical history. Erica sat down on the room's other twin bed and looked around. "This is really nice."

Carla smiled. "I'm glad to have another adult woman around. Believe me, the fifteen-year-old girls can be a challenge, and other than that, it's just me and the baby when Brian's on duty." She patted her stomach. "And another on the way, so believe me, I grab every moment of girl talk I can get."

"You're expecting? Congratulations." Erica liked the openness of the woman already. It would be nice to be so relaxed and confident in your family life. Even though Erica was blessed, *so* blessed with the twins, she didn't anticipate ever being the kind of comfortable-in-her-own-skin wife and mother that Carla was.

"Maybe we can get the girls to make us tea." Carla leaned forward and listened at the door. "Nah. It's pretty loud out there. We should hide out in here for a few more minutes."

Erica stood, stretched and strolled around the room. "I like your samplers. Embroidery like that is getting to be a lost art." She leaned closer to read them. "Are they just for decoration or from your family?"

"Mine, my parents' and my grandparents'. And all of us are still around and still married."

Wow. What would it be like to come from that kind of legacy?

"So where's your family?" Carla asked, flopping back down on the bed.

Normally, that type of question made Erica self-conscious, but with Carla, she just felt a little sad. "I never knew my grandparents or my dad. My mom had a lot of issues." Then she broke off.

"Had? So you're alone in the world?"

"Pretty much. Except for the twins."

The sound of men's voices resounded through the house, contrasting with the girl and baby sounds. Jason came to the doorway and looked in. "This looks comfortable."

"It is. And it's Erica's. You get the couch, pal." Carla grinned at Jason with the familiarity that bespoke long friendship. She stood and slipped around Jason to exit the room. "I'm going to go manage the chaos."

"I'll be right out," Erica promised.

"Hey," Jason said to Erica, "we got a reminder call from the doctor. We're supposed to arrive fifteen minutes early and bring the babies' medical history."

Erica's stomach twisted with anxiety.

Tell him.

"Listen," he said, "I've got to run to that meeting with the lawyers. You okay here?"

She nodded. "Brian and Carla are really nice."

He walked a little into the room, hooked an arm around her neck and gave her a fast, hard kiss. Then he spun and left the room, and a moment later she heard the front door slam.

She put her hands to her lips, swallowed. This morning he'd apologized for kissing her, and now he'd kissed her again. She could smell his cologne on herself, just a trace of it.

She sank down onto the bed, needing just a moment before she went out to take care of the twins. Just a moment to think about and relish that kiss.

And a moment to try to calm her worries about tomorrow's appointment, the doctor with the poor bedside manner and the fact that she didn't have any medical history at all to show her.

Tomorrow would turn out okay. It was for the twins. She'd figure out an excuse. Wouldn't she?

8

As soon as Jason walked back into Brian and Carla's house, he noticed the smell of Christmas cookies and heard the sound of women's laughter.

The contrast with the hard-edged, seamy lawyer meeting he'd just come from couldn't have been greater. He loosened his tie.

He wanted to come home to this world.

Still, he had to remember that he wasn't ready. Screwing this up by acting too soon would be disaster. On some level, he knew that was what had happened with Renea; he'd been tired of the tomcatting life, had met Renea, thought she was something special, and had moved too fast. He couldn't make that mistake again.

Girded against his impulses, he walked into the kitchen.

"Where's Erica?" he asked immediately. So much for not focusing on her.

"We…we kind of made her go change," Carla said, laughing.

"Hey." Jason's protective instincts took over. "Don't be hard on her. She's new to how we all joke around."

"No, no, we were nice! It's just that…she didn't know this is an ugly sweater party. How could she?"

"And her sweater really was kind of ugly…" That was Lisa, Randall's wife. She had a good heart, but no filter. "But not ugly in the way it was supposed to be."

"Stop." Carla frowned at her. "I dug up one of my ugly sweaters for her and she's changing and getting the twins ready."

"So you really like her?" Lisa asked. "How'd you guys meet?"

He didn't want to contribute to the gossip train. "Long story. I gotta go get out of this monkey suit."

And on the way, as much as he'd intended not to do it, he found himself heading upstairs and knocking on the door of the guest suite.

When she called for him to come in, he had to stop and stare.

Normally, Erica wore loose, plain clothes. But now she was dressed in a snug-fitting sweater in a bright shade of pink with white fluffy fur on it. He supposed the sweater was a little silly, but it certainly wasn't ugly. She looked stunning, sitting on the floor with the twins while they played with a stack of blocks. He couldn't help but stare.

"What's wrong? I shouldn't have let them give me this sweater, should I?" She stood up and came over to him.

He reached out and took one of her hands. "You absolutely should have. You look gorgeous."

She looked down at herself. "It's a little tight. And it's supposed to be ugly, but…"

"Hey." He touched her chin so she had to look into his eyes. "You look really pretty, and it's not too tight. I say wear it. But…" He dropped his hand from her face because he was so extremely tempted to kiss her. And he'd decided he wasn't going to do that again. "You wear whatever's comfortable."

The hallway outside the guest suite was balcony style, with a direct view into the main family room, where the party would take place. Trying not to focus on Erica, Jason stepped outside and leaned over the balcony, looking down. Christmas lights twinkled on the tree, and a real fire glowed in the fireplace. Brian and Carla stood together, arm in arm, talking quietly.

Jason wanted what Brian had with a longing so intense that his chest hurt.

Erica came to stand beside him. Her wistful expression matched the way he felt.

"I hope they know what they've got," he said.

She nodded.

"Make you sad?"

"A little." She paused, watching as Brian tugged Carla into a hug and kiss. "But we have to remember that not everyone has it like that. For so many people, it's not like the commercials."

"Yeah. True."

"And," she added, putting an arm around his waist, "it's not what Christmas is really about."

The fact that she'd voluntarily touched him made him go still, every muscle controlled. He had to treat her like a bird that had landed on his arm, with gentleness, no sudden movements.

He turned to her and smiled, determinedly keeping his elbows propped on the balcony railing rather than letting them wrap around her as he wanted to do.

"You're right," he said. "Joseph and Mary weren't living the dream when Jesus was born."

"Exactly." She smiled up at him and then looked down at the cozy room below. "They're great, Carla and Brian. I like them."

There was a sound from the bedroom behind them, and they both turned back to see the babies. "I need to get them dressed for the party. Wish they had something cuter to wear."

She'd given him the perfect cue. "Hold that thought. I'll be right back."

When he returned to the guest suite, she was back on the floor with the twins, who were now stripped down to diapers. Teddy's scooting crawl was already a little more efficient, and Mikey seemed to be stage directing, waving his arms and babbling at his brother.

"Don't be mad," he said, holding out a bag to her. "I was walking from the car to the lawyer's office, and there was a kids' clothing store… I couldn't resist. Consider it my Christmas present to them."

She took the bag, looked at him with a wrinkled forehead and then opened it. He held his breath. Too silly? Not classy enough? He was opening his mouth to offer to return them when she let out a little squeal. "Oh, these are perfect!"

The joy on her face spread warmth through his whole body. He wanted to keep giving her joy, whatever the cost.

She laid the outfits on the floor beside each other. They were one-piecers with snaps on the bottom; he'd been with the twins enough now to know that was what you needed for the diaper set.

"Should Teddy be the elf and Mikey the Santa, or

the other way around?" She studied them and then looked up at him.

He sank to his knees beside her. "I was thinking Mikey's more the Santa type. Even though he doesn't move around much, he's kind of the boss. Teddy's like the sidekick who gets things done."

She turned and put her hand on his arm, and when he looked into her eyes, they were brimming with tears. "You already get that about them?"

"Hey." He reached out, and when a single tear rolled down, he brushed a thumb along her cheek. "I wanted this to make you happy."

She cleared her throat and nodded, her eyes never leaving his. "It does. You have no idea how much."

The sound of laughter from downstairs broke into their silence. "Come on, let's get them dressed."

As he dressed Teddy while Erica got the Santa suit on Mikey, something softened inside him. Not only did he care for Erica, but he was coming to care for her children, as well. He wanted with all his heart for Mikey to start crawling and walking and for Teddy to learn to talk. As he looked into Teddy's wide brown eyes, he felt like Teddy understood, because he offered a sweet smile before reaching out to grab for the button on Jason's shirt.

"Hey, quit that now." He batted Teddy's hand away and finished snapping the suit, then picked him up and stood him on his feet.

Teddy couldn't support himself or balance, but he was approximating a standing position, and when Erica looked up from putting on Mikey's hat, her eyes widened. "That's how he'll look when he's walking! Oh, Jason, I want so much for them to catch up."

"I want that, too." He sat Teddy down next to Mikey. "Listen, I need to run downstairs and see if I can borrow a sweater from Brian. But there's something I want to tell you."

He hadn't known he was going to say this until it came out of his mouth. He'd been thinking about how he'd given up his quest to find answers about Kimmie, but he hadn't lost track of the fact that he had some work and growing to do before he could hope to have a relationship.

The beautiful woman and adorable babies in front of him were making him want to speed up on that goal. Maybe he could learn it best by doing it. Strong, hot joy bloomed in his chest at the possibility that he and Erica might be able to build something together.

If there was any chance of that, he had to be honest. "I haven't always been the best... You know how we were talking about Kimmie's values? Well, mine haven't always been perfect."

"Whose have?" She watched him, her face accepting. "Are you worried about something tonight?"

"It's... There are some women." He hadn't been as bad as a lot of guys, but still, he didn't want Erica getting upset or hurt. "I dated quite a bit before I got engaged, and some of those women might be here."

"Trying to get you back?" she asked lightly, but there was concern underneath her light tone.

"No. But maybe not being the most... I mean, I wasn't..." He broke off and then started again. "What I'm trying to say, I guess, is that I care for you and I want to pursue something with you, if you're willing. But there's some baggage."

Her eyebrows rose a fraction of an inch. "That's not what you said this morning."

"I was fighting against what I felt inside," he admitted.

She looked at the floor and he thought he'd doomed himself with her. Then she started fussing with Mikey's outfit, adjusting his little white fur cuffs. "I…well, I have some baggage, too." She looked up at him. "Not the same kind, but it could hurt the chances that we could…"

He gripped her hand. "Whatever is in your past, I'm going to do my best to help you get over it and move on. And I hope you'll do the same for me."

She bit her lip and nodded, but this time, she didn't meet his eyes. She was shy. He had the sense that she was almost completely inexperienced with men.

He held out a hand and helped her to her feet, feeling the fragility of her slender fingers. She was vulnerable. Innocent.

He had to get this right. He couldn't ruin another woman's life, break another woman's heart. Especially when that woman was Erica.

As Erica walked down the stairs into the crowd of lively, laughing strangers, her stomach twisted with nerves. But she wanted to do this. Wanted to be a part of Jason's world. She tightened her grip on Teddy and Mikey and walked out into the party.

Immediately, she was surrounded by women, oohing and aahing over the boys and their outfits. Everyone wanted to hold them, and Teddy and Mikey, being budding showmen, smiled and laughed and agreeably let themselves be passed from person to person.

"Those outfits," a woman named Lisa said. "Where did you get them?"

Erica hesitated, not sure whether Jason would want to admit to having given the boys such a gift.

"Seriously, was it around here?" someone else asked. "Those are adorable."

"I think the bag said Children's Cloud Creations." She looked around for Jason, but he was nowhere to be seen. "Jason bought them."

"That place is expensive!" Lisa looked speculatively at Erica.

It was?

"Are you and Jason, like, together?" Lisa pressed.

Erica bit her lip and looked down, but that was bad because it made her notice that her borrowed sweater was a little more revealing than she would have liked it to be, especially now that the shield of the twins was gone. "I…uh… I don't really know."

Carla pushed between Lisa and Erica. "Don't mind her. She means well, but she's way too nosy."

"I didn't mean… Oh. I was overstepping, wasn't I?"

Carla nodded. "Yep. And you told me I should call you on it, so I am." She turned to Erica. "We're together all the time, the spouses, because our husbands work together. Well, and Delphine joins in, too, although she's the cop in the family." She nodded toward a tall, slender African American woman who was deep in conversation with Carla's husband, Brian, while a couple of toddlers played on the floor in front of them.

Carla and Lisa's ongoing conversation gave Erica a chance to regroup. She picked up Mikey and kept an eye on Teddy, who was scooting toward a bouncy toy.

She was overwhelmed with everything that was

happening, so much so that she felt like her mind was on overload.

Worry about the doctor's appointment tomorrow bounced against excitement that Jason actually seemed to like her. Her! The one with the druggie mother and church-bin clothes, the perpetual new girl and sometime foster kid, was the choice of a handsome, successful, kind man like Jason. The way he was with the twins brought tears to her eyes.

What would happen, though, when he found out that he was related to them?

Jason came inside with another man, carrying armloads of wood, which they stashed by the fireplace. Immediately, Jason looked around the room, and when he saw her, he headed her way.

All the people here and he chose to talk to her. Of course, he was kind and was acting as a host, but still, she felt special and cherished, truly honored.

Why had Kimmie been so adamant that Jason shouldn't have the twins, shouldn't even know them? Was it to maintain her own perfect image in her brother's mind, to continue thinking of herself as the big sister role model?

If that was Kimmie's reason, it was starting to seem a little bit selfish. Jason could offer so much to the twins. It was *they* who needed a role model, and Jason would be an amazing one.

A pretty, dark-haired woman stepped into Jason's path and put a hand on his arm. Erica couldn't hear the exchange, but she could read the body language. The woman was definitely interested in Jason.

He made a couple of quiet comments and nodded toward Erica. The woman turned and looked at her, cocked her head to the side and shrugged. Then she swooshed her arm as if to gesture Jason over toward Erica. He did as she bid, laughing, and behind him, the brunette pointed and nodded as if to provide an endorsement.

That was a little embarrassing, especially considering how many people had seen. But it felt good, too. If Jason was choosing her, maybe she *did* have something to offer, not just as a friend or helper, but as a woman.

Jason approached, and Erica hoped for a little time alone with him to catch her breath. But before he could get through the crowd, another couple came up to Erica. "Hi!" the woman greeted her, a toddler on her hip. "How old are your little guys?"

Erica steeled herself for the inevitable comparisons. "Fifteen months," she said, hugging Mikey a little closer.

"Hey, that's how old our princess is, too!" The woman nodded toward the little girl she was holding, all dressed up in a red-and-pink-striped dress and tights.

With the features of a Down syndrome baby.

"She's beautiful," Erica said. "Look, Mikey, this is…what's her name?"

"Miranda. And I'm Corrine. Miranda, say hi to Mikey." The woman lowered her voice. "I think… Jason talked to Ralph, here, about Dr. Chen. We consulted with her about Miranda."

"Thank you for the reference. I appreciate it." Which was true, mostly.

Jason finally arrived at their little cluster. "I see you've met. Hey, Miranda, sweetie!" He held out his arms for the baby.

Corrine and Ralph looked at each other. "You sure you want to hold her?"

Jason laughed self-consciously. "I'm known as the worst with babies," he said to Erica. To the couple he added, "I've had a little practice lately."

"He's great with the twins," Erica said, and finally the mother released little Miranda into Jason's arms.

The dad whistled. "Man, have you changed. Are you the reason for this?" he asked Erica.

She shrugged. "I guess I am," she said shyly.

Jason put an arm around her. "She's been very patient. And I've learned that you don't feed a baby in a white shirt."

Suddenly, the door to the party opened with a bang, letting cold wind blow in from outside. Beside her, Erica heard Jason draw in a breath and then mutter something. The party noise of chattering voices died down.

A woman stalked in, shaky on extremely high heels that she didn't need—she had to be six feet tall in her socks. Carla hurried to close the door behind the new visitor.

The woman looked around, obviously searching for someone. When her eyes lit on Jason, she stopped still. "There you are," she said in a husky voice. She slid off her fur coat and Erica couldn't help but gasp. In the light, the woman was starkly gorgeous, with sharp cheekbones, enormous dark eyes and blond hair down to the middle of her back. The dress she wore was red lace and fitted her like she was a model.

"Don't suppose anyone has a drink for a lady?" the woman said.

9

As he stared at the woman he'd once thought he loved, Jason's gut churned with the same feelings that had nearly driven him to despair two years ago.

Renea was beautiful and intelligent, but hopelessly, endlessly mired in alcoholism interconnected with an eating disorder. After knowing her parents, he could pretty well guess her problems stemmed from her childhood.

He'd tried, he'd failed, and they'd broken up. After getting the ring package from her earlier today, he'd sent her a brief text reiterating that it was over between them.

So what was she doing here now?

"Aw, look at the babies!" She teetered over toward the small circle of women and children by the fire. It looked like she was going to fall down until someone helped her into a chair.

Erica was there to see it all. And judging from the way she glanced over at him before focusing her attention on the twins, she could tell that Renea had been important to him.

"I'm gonna get married someday!" Renea gushed in a loud voice. "I'm going to get me one of these little buggers, too!" She reached down as if she were going to pick up Teddy.

Smoothly, Erica sank to her knees and swept the baby out of Renea's grasp. "You know, he just ate, and I'm afraid he'll spit up on your pretty dress. Is that a Christoson?"

"No!" Renea looked insulted. "It's DeBrady."

"My mistake." Erica smiled a little and cuddled Mikey.

The comparison between the two women was striking. Renea was the more classically gorgeous, for sure, and there'd been a time when that had been important to him. Plenty of men had envied him having someone like Renea on his arm.

But Erica, with her wise-beyond-her-years green eyes, her natural hair and her comfortable, kneeling position on the floor, one baby in her arms and the other attempting to crawl into her lap, looked like everything he'd ever wanted—even if he doubted whether he'd get it.

Seeing that Erica and the twins were safe and that the other women had engaged Renea in conversation, Jason took the coward's route and stepped onto the back porch. He took breaths of clear, cold air and tried to think.

Now that he was learning what love was, he knew he hadn't had it with Renea. But the question was, had he mended himself enough from the mistakes of the past that he could dare to pursue something with Erica?

You don't have a choice. You're already pursuing it.

But he could put on the brakes, stop it now before anyone got hurt.

He thought of how hurt Erica had looked when he'd told her their kiss wasn't real. *Too late.*

He looked up at the stars. Sometimes God seemed that far away, too cold and distant to help Jason with what seemed like a fairly impossible situation.

Even the thought brought back the minister's words from last Sunday's sermon: nothing is impossible with God.

He needed God's help to fix an impossible situation, to get to where he could manage to head a family like his friends did. Somewhere in the neglect from his careless parents, or maybe in his own horribly mistaken tough love for his sister, he'd gotten broken.

He hoped God could fix him. "Will You try?" he whispered to the stars. "I'm a sinner, but You took care of that. Help me do better."

There was a bang behind him and Brian came out onto the porch. "You okay?"

"Just getting a soda." Jason bent down to retrieve a can from the cooler full of ice. "Want one?"

"Sure. Um…you've got a situation in there, huh?"

"Renea?" Jason shook his head. "For real."

"She's all over Kameer." Brian laughed a little. "And she's really lit."

Jason looked past Brian into the living room. He couldn't see Renea—nor Erica, which was probably for the best—but he saw three of his friends, all guys, talking and laughing as they looked in the direction of Renea's shrill voice.

She wasn't his responsibility, but then again… "I'll

be back in just a minute," he said to Brian and went out into the backyard.

A minute later, he had Renea's mother on the phone. "No, I'm not coming to get her," the woman said. "She's made her bed and she can lie in it."

"Can I talk to Monty?"

"He's washed his hands of her, as well. And he's away on business, anyway." There was a pause. "She's a lost cause. We've given up on her for the sake of our own sanity."

When he didn't answer, the phone clicked off.

A lost cause. Jason pocketed his phone and shook his head. Despite all the tough cases he'd seen on the streets of Philadelphia, he didn't believe in those.

When he walked back inside, a couple more guys had joined the crowd watching Renea. Most of the women seemed to be in the kitchen, or in the play-room with the kids. He could hear their talk, mingled with the sound of kids playing. He hoped Erica was there with the other women, enjoying herself.

He looked over at Renea and saw that a strap of her dress had fallen down. She was leaning on the much-shorter Kameer, who looked like he didn't know what had hit him.

Jason could identify. He used to feel that way about Renea, himself. And Kameer was young, a new officer on the force.

Jason crossed the room and approached the couple. "Hey, Renea. It's time to get out of here."

"I found somebody else," she said, slurring her words. "He's a *very* nice man."

"Yes, and maybe you can get to know him better another time. Right now, it's time to go home."

"You don't get to have a say over me."

"The lady's right," Kameer said, getting a little in Jason's face. "It's her choice."

Jason stared down the younger man. "Sometimes a lady isn't in any condition to make a choice. And at that point, a gentleman steps away from the game."

"You just don't want anyone else to have me. You ruined my life, made a mess of me." Renea's words were loud in the room that had suddenly gone quiet. "Or maybe it's just that you want me back?" She teetered a couple of steps to Jason and draped herself over him.

She felt like deadweight.

"Let's get you home." He looked at Kameer. "Get her coat, would you?"

Kameer gave an indignant snort, looked again at Jason's face and headed to the front closet.

Renea leaned over and vomited into a wastebasket with an alcoholic's quick, practiced move, still clinging to Jason's arm for balance. Then she stepped away from him and opened the door.

Some of the women had come back out—it looked like their husbands had summoned them, probably because they didn't want to deal with a sick woman themselves.

Erica was among them.

He shot her a quick, apologetic glance. This sort of display was just what she wouldn't want, and between Renea hanging on him and talking trash about him, he couldn't blame Erica if she decided to back off.

All the same, he couldn't leave Renea to freeze to death alone. Even though he hadn't invited her, she was here because of him.

He grabbed her coat and shrugged into his own.

"You need some help, man?" Brian asked.

"No, I've got it. Sorry for the disruption," he called back into the party crowd. "Carry on."

"Come back after you get her home."

"Sure. I'll be back."

He looked at Erica when he said that, wanting her to know that, despite this scene, he wasn't abandoning her. But she was talking to another of the women with some intensity. He could just imagine their topic.

He headed out, caught Renea and draped her coat around her. He was trying to talk her into getting into his truck when the house door opened again.

Erica emerged and walked down toward the two of them, her hands in her jacket pockets. "Do you want me to go with you?" she asked him. "I know how..." She gave a shrug. "I know how to deal with someone who's impaired."

"Who you calling impaired?" Renea slurred, but without much energy.

"But the twins..." Jason said.

"Carla's going to put them to bed, or try to. It's fine." She frowned. "Unless you don't want me here. If you'd rather handle it alone..."

"So *you're* his new squeeze." Renea patted Erica on the head. "You've gone down in the world, Jason."

Erica looked up at the woman, at least a foot taller than she was. "Yep, I'm a pipsqueak," she said. "Want to get in the car? I'm freezing."

"I don't have anywhere to go." Renea looked at Jason. "My mom told me if I went out, I couldn't come back. Can we go to your place?"

"It's sublet," he said.

"You living with her now?"

"Nope." He took Renea's arm and urged her into the truck, with a manhandling move he knew from years on the narc squad. Not rough, but not particularly gentle, either.

He could smell Renea's trademark scent of alcohol covered by perfume and breath mints. And he was still a little stunned by Erica's matter-of-fact willingness to help.

After Renea was in, Erica climbed in after her.

"You're sure about this? It might not be pretty."

She gave him a little smile. "I know. I'm fine."

He jogged around to the driver's side and started the truck. They hadn't driven two blocks before Renea made a sound like she was going to be sick. Jason skidded to a stop and she leaned over Erica, who simply opened the passenger door and scooted Renea's upper body a little bit farther out of the truck, pulling back her hair and holding her head while she vomited into the street.

When Renea was done, Jason held out a bandanna and Erica wiped off Renea's face.

And then Renea settled down with her head in Erica's lap and went to sleep.

Jason reached out and touched Erica's face. "You're made of steel, you know that?"

She shook her head, looking down. "I'm really not. Where are you headed with her? Does she live with anyone?"

"Her mom won't take her in." Even as he said it, his gut twisted tight. He couldn't judge Renea's mom, because he'd basically done the same to his sister. Oh, he'd offered Kimmie a place to stay, but he'd set strict rules on it and refused to send her money, only an airline ticket.

She'd never come home.

"Does she have a purse?"

Jason indicated the sparkling thing he'd found with her coat.

Erica opened it and riffled through. "Let's see, there's—"

"You're going through her purse?"

She shrugged. "What else are we going to do? She kind of gave up her right to privacy when she threw up on me." She pulled a couple of cards out of Renea's small bag, and a crisp hundred-dollar bill. "The way I see it," she said, "we can either take her to this Welcome Home shelter for women, or we can check her into some safe hotel, or we can call this woman, her AA sponsor."

Jason nodded, stopping the truck at a red light. "You're good. And I'd say…" He plucked the shelter's card out of Erica's hand.

"The Welcome Home shelter. Me, too." She nodded decisively. "Because even in a safe hotel, she could get taken advantage of. And sponsors aren't supposed to take the people they sponsor into their homes."

"How do you know so much about addicts? Is it all from your mom? Or Al-Anon?" He turned the truck in the direction of the Welcome Home shelter.

She didn't answer.

He glanced over at her. "Kimmie?"

She hesitated, then nodded. "Mom, Kimmie…that's part of it. I also volunteered some after Mom died. And, well…" She shrugged and spread her hands. "I just… That's the people I grew up with. You get accustomed to finding ways to help." Before he could say more, she said, "Your turn to answer. How'd you get involved with Renea?"

As if hearing her name, Renea shifted restlessly, and Jason slowed. But then she sighed and settled back into sleep, her face childlike.

"She got caught up in a sting, but she was never convicted. We liked each other, so after a while, I gave her a call." Like an idiot.

Erica nodded but didn't speak.

"I guess I like to help people," he said. "Or maybe I was on a power trip. That's what Kimmie always said."

"Maybe you were trying to replace Kimmie in your life," Erica suggested quietly.

He frowned. "I don't think so, but…" He pulled into the shelter's parking lot.

"It's a Christian place?" She was looking at the blinking cross on the side of the building.

"Big-time."

"That's the only thing that'll help her. You feel okay about leaving her here?"

"She'll be as safe as she can be."

"Then go ahead on in and do whatever paperwork you need to. I'll wait here with her. Better to wait and wake her up when we have a place she can crash."

He shook his head, amazed at Erica's generosity and kindness. "If you're sure."

"It's no problem."

He nodded and got out of the truck. "You know all my dirt," he said, "but you still can tolerate me?"

A strange expression crossed her face. "Of course."

He walked into the shelter quickly, smiling.

* * *

The next morning, when her quiet phone alarm went off, Erica hit Snooze and buried her head under her pillow.

They were going to see the specialist today, and she didn't know if she could face it.

She was excited, of course she was. Maybe the famous doctor would have ideas of what Mikey and Teddy needed, some particular combination of physical therapy and nutrition that could move them along toward where they should be developmentally.

Being with the other women and children last night had just confirmed how far behind they were. She needed to get them help, the sooner, the better.

But she'd be walking through the doors of the prestigious research hospital with zero paperwork on these babies and a police detective at her side. That combination could mean disaster.

Upping the ante was the fact that she truly cared about Jason. He'd been nothing but kind to his drunken ex last night. And after they'd gotten Renea into the shelter, he'd had tender words for Erica as they'd driven back to Brian and Carla's house.

She hugged her pillow, happy butterflies dancing in her stomach, thinking of the tender moments they'd shared after coming back into the quiet house and checking on the twins.

He thinks I'm an amazing woman. Who had ever said such a thing about her, unless it was someone wanting to get something out of her?

But Jason hadn't had anything on his mind except helping her find towels for a shower and a snack because she hadn't managed to eat anything at the party.

He was truly a good and kind man. And the way he looked at her gave her the insane hope that maybe, just maybe, they could have a future together.

Except you couldn't build a future on a lie.

More than ever, she wondered why Kimmie had painted Jason in such negative colors, why she'd refused to let him, or her mother or grandparents, know about Mikey and Teddy.

Had Kimmie kept the secret to cover her own sins? Though she'd put on a party face for much of the time Erica had known her, the contrast between her and the rest of her family made Erica suspect that Kimmie had carried a deep sense of shame inside herself.

Teddy stirred, then rolled over in the crib. His round eyes met hers and he smiled, and Erica's heart gave a painful little twist. How was it possible to love a tiny little being so much? To want his good more than her own?

She reached a hand in for Teddy to play with and sank to her knees beside the crib. She couldn't control what happened today, and she knew she'd probably done some things wrong. But it hadn't been for bad intent.

I put it into Your hands, Father, she whispered. *If it's Your will, let this doctor help the boys. And let me raise them or at least help to raise them.*

Praying for something to work out with Jason was just way too much to ask, so she didn't. She just remained there, focused on her Lord and Savior, trying to rest in Him, until the clock and the babies forced her to stand up and face the day.

10

Jason pulled the truck into the Early Development Center's parking lot and looked over at Erica. "Ready?"

"This place is huge!"

"That's the university hospital over there," he said, waving a hand toward the big block of buildings to the left. "The Center is just this part, here." But he could see why she was impressed, or maybe intimidated. The two-story brick building looked brand-new and everything, from the signage to the landscaping, spelled *tasteful* and *exclusive* and *expensive*. His big, late-model truck was probably the cheapest vehicle in the lot. "This is the kind of facility you get when you're the best in the country. Dr. Chen has published lots of books and articles and done all kinds of studies. It was a good thing we had strings to pull and that she had a cancellation."

"Yes, and I appreciate what you've done. Really." She put a hand on his arm, squeezed and let go. Despite her tension, she was still appreciative. That was Erica.

He came around to her side of the truck, where she was leaning into the back seat to get Mikey out. As had become routine for them now, she handed him to Jason and climbed in to free Teddy.

He noticed the fine sheen of sweat on her upper lip as she emerged from the back seat with Teddy, and he extended a hand to help her down. Teddy dropped a toy, and when she bent to get it, the diaper bag on her shoulder spilled out half its contents.

"Oh, man," she said, "I'm a walking disaster today."

"Slow down." He squatted to pick up a diaper, a container of wipes and a plastic key chain toy and handed them to her. "I'm sure this parking lot is cleaner than some people's tabletops."

The day was cloudy, but the temperature was above freezing and the piles of snow were starting to melt, making the streets sloppy. Here, though, the parking lot was clear and dry.

"You know," she said as they carried the boys inside, "I'm still not sure this is such a good idea. I won't be able to come back here to get them any treatment."

"Dr. Chen does consultations for people from all over," he reminded her, wondering why she still seemed resistant. "She can refer you to local practitioners and therapists."

"And I don't have any of their medical records."

He held the door for her. "Why not?"

She hesitated. "They're back in Arizona." She didn't look at him, intent on studying the wall listing of offices. "It was a spur-of-the-moment decision to move. I have some stuff in storage. Oh, there's Dr. Chen. I guess we go to office 140."

"Did something happen in Arizona that made you decide to move?" She never talked about the twins' father, except to mention that he was in prison and had no claim on the twins. But a breakup would explain why her decision to move had been sudden, and also why she was so skittish with men. At least, with him.

Although her skittishness seemed to be fading, which was very, very nice.

Still, his detective instincts were aroused, just a little, by the way she avoided answering his questions. But then Mikey dropped his pacifier and started to cry, and Teddy let out a few sympathy wails, and it didn't seem to be the moment to probe.

Inside, the waiting room was plush and quiet. Despite the small box of toys and the shelf of children's books, it didn't look much like a pediatrician's office. One other couple was waiting, and a mother had a sleeping baby in a carrier. Diplomas and awards lined the walls.

When they approached the receptionist, she greeted them cordially and smiled at the twins. "You must be Erica Lindholm. With Mikey and Teddy?"

"That's right," Erica said.

"I'll just need your insurance card."

Erica bit her lip. "We're paying privately. Do I need to prepay?" She fumbled in her purse.

"It'll be taken care of." Jason slid the woman a credit card. "I'll handle whatever needs to be paid for today, and you can send the bill to the address I'm going to write down for you, if you have a piece of paper."

The receptionist lifted an eyebrow as she handed him a notepad and pen. "Here you go."

"Jason!" Erica hissed. "What are you doing?"

He finished writing down the address, handed the woman his credit card and turned to her. "Don't worry about it. The officers in my precinct always pick a Christmas charity for children, and this year…"

"We're your Christmas charity?" she interrupted. "Are you serious?"

She walked over to a seating area near the toys and sat, putting Teddy down to crawl.

Jason finished his transaction and brought Mikey over. "I thought you might be happy. Did I do something wrong?" Even as he said it, he knew where she was coming from; independent as she was, she wouldn't necessarily be thrilled at accepting the gift.

"I don't feel right about accepting charity. I mean, I'm going to own half that farm. I won't need that kind of help, and it should go to someone who does."

"You need it now, and the guys were looking for an opportunity." He touched her hand. "Accept it in the spirit it's given. It'll help the babies."

She looked down at Mikey, then Teddy, and then she nodded. "You're right. Thank you."

"Mrs. Lindholm?" a nurse called at the door.

Erica stood, hoisted Mikey and the diaper bag, and squared her shoulders. When she didn't turn to get Teddy, Jason took it as an invitation to join the appointment. He picked up Teddy and followed her in.

"Let's weigh and measure them right here." The nurse was a broad-faced, no-nonsense-looking person in scrubs. "They're fifteen months? Were they preemies?"

"Only by three weeks."

The nurse made a notation and then passed a tape measure around Teddy's head, then measured him from heel to the top of his head. "Just a few questions before you see the doctor. Let's talk food. Breastfed, bottle fed?" She looked inquiringly at Erica.

"Ummmm…breast?"

Odd that her answer sounded like a question.

"How long?"

"Just a couple of months."

"Okay. And when did they start on solids?"

Erica opened her mouth and then closed it again.

The nurse turned from the computer to face her. "I asked about solid food. Is there a problem?"

Erica closed her eyes for just a moment. Then she opened them. "Look," she said, "there's a whole period of their lives that I don't know much about."

Jason tilted his head, wondering if he'd heard that right.

The nurse's lips flattened. "And why's that?"

Erica sat up straight and gave the nurse a level stare. "I'd rather hold the rest of my discussion for the doctor."

"But our protocol is for me to—"

"Can the doctor see me even if I don't answer all of your questions?"

"Ye-es…"

Jason felt like his world was spinning off somewhere he didn't understand. He'd never seen gentle Erica act quite like this.

Well, actually, he had. When she was defending her kids.

"Then I'd rather save the rest of the interview for the doctor herself." Erica didn't look his way.

Something was *definitely* going on here.

The nurse looked at him as if to say, can't you control your wife? But he didn't rise to the bait. If he admitted he wasn't any relation to Erica and the kids, he'd probably be sent out into the waiting room. And despite her huffy attitude, he had the feeling Erica needed support.

"Fine." The nurse stood. "Follow me." She stormed down the hall and flung open the door of an exam room. "The doctor will be in shortly." She slammed Erica's folder into the plastic holder beside the door and stomped off.

Erica went into the exam room and he followed behind, Teddy in his arms. "So what was that about, how there's a period you don't know about? Did you just not like her attitude, or…" He didn't want to contemplate the other alternative. That she didn't remember because she'd been in some way out of it, in trouble personally or with the law.

He'd known people with big blackouts in their pasts, but drugs or alcohol were usually involved.

She'd set Mikey down on the carpeted floor, and now she lifted Teddy from his arms. "Jason."

There was a funny tone to her voice. "Yeah?"

"I'd like to speak to the doctor alone."

"Of course, I can leave after—"

"No, I mean now." She lifted her chin. "I don't want you here."

The words shocked him. He'd thought they were getting closer, thought that she liked and needed him. He wanted to hear what the doctor said about Mikey and Teddy.

And why would she—

"So could you leave?"

She was standing there with her shoulders squared, facing him, but she wasn't meeting his eyes.

"You want me to leave."

"Yes, please." She glanced up then, and he saw that her eyes were a little shiny. "If you don't want to wait around for me, it's okay. I can call for a ride. A taxi or something."

"Car seats?" He shook his head, backing out of the room. "No. I'll be outside." He turned and spun out of the room.

He walked right through the waiting room and outside. *Goodbye, softhearted nice guy. Welcome back, Detective Stephanidis.*

In the windy parking lot, he pulled out his phone and scrolled through his contacts. "Hey, Brian," he said a moment later. "Could you do a little bit of investigating for me?"

An hour later, Erica sat in the examining room with the two babies cuddled on her lap. "I realize that you might have to report me," she said to the white-coat-clad doctor in front of her, "but I hope you won't."

Dr. Chen tapped a pencil on the table. "There's such a thing as doctor-patient confidentiality, and I believe in it. On the other hand, I'm *required* to report any situation where a child is at risk."

Erica nodded, dismayed. She was making one move at a time here. She'd only thought of kicking Jason out of the pediatrician's office this morning. If he wasn't there, she'd realized, she would be able to be completely honest with the pediatrician.

And she had been. She'd spilled the entire story: what she knew of Kimmie's pregnancy, of the early months with the twins, of their father and of Kimmie's relapse.

And she'd explained all the things she *didn't* know.

Dr. Chen had listened and watched the twins on the floor. She'd asked questions, held out toys for them to grasp, listened to their babble. Her forehead wrinkled with focus, her questions for Erica pointed. Erica didn't find her awkward at all, as Carla had said; she was just very, very intense.

Finally, after about twenty minutes of observation, Dr. Chen had nodded briskly. "Teddy's just about to crawl, and that mobility will help his mind develop," she'd said. "But he'll come along faster with some physical therapy. Speech, too. Mikey…" She'd studied Mikey's feet again, bent his legs at the knees, rotated his ankles. "He may just go directly to walking. His muscle tone is pretty good."

"I'm so relieved that you think they'll be okay," Erica said. "Look, I know there are probably a million ways I could have done better with the twins. Maybe I should have stayed with Kimmie, let them be taken into foster care. I just…" She shook her head. "I've *been* in foster care, and I know how wrong it can go. I know how siblings can be separated. And Kimmie didn't want that for them. So… I did what she told me to. I brought them here."

"Do you think she was trying to get them back together with her family?"

Erica shook her head. "For whatever reason, she didn't want her brother to find out. She thought he was hostile, judgmental. And… I realize now, she was ashamed of having them out of wedlock, and she didn't want him to know. He idealized her, you see."

"Why did you bring the twins here," Dr. Chen asked, "knowing you might be reported?"

Erica shrugged, her arms still around the boys. "Once they were able to get me the appointment and I thought about it and prayed about it, I knew I had to do what was right for the twins." She met the woman's steady brown eyes. "I know you're the best, and I want the best for them. They need to get started on early intervention, like you said. If I didn't tell a specialist—tell you—everything I knew about their past, they could suffer for it."

The doctor held her gaze, then nodded. "From what I see at this moment, the twins are loved and well cared for."

Erica's breath went out in a sigh of relief.

Dr. Chen held up a hand. "However, if you decide not to get them the help they need, now that you know more about it, I would consider that to be neglect." She leaned forward. "You're going to have to come clean about all of this, you know. Their need for medical attention will be ongoing. Nothing in medicine is inexpensive." She glanced at the chart. "Even without seeing test results and writing it up, I know they'll need therapy. Speech and physical, at a minimum. That's not cheap."

Erica nodded. "I know, and I mean to go through their mother's things and contact the hospital where they were born, do a little digging. I need to… I need to let their other relatives know about them."

"Is the man who accompanied you one of those other relatives? Or is he just a boyfriend?"

"He's a relative."

"The courts might leave them with you, even once your lack of formal guardianship comes out. Unless there's another relative claiming them. Just keep doing what you're doing and after the holidays, when you can get all the testing done and I can analyze it, we'll figure out a program of treatment."

As they exited the turnpike and headed toward Holly Creek Farm, Erica breathed a sigh of relief that this hard day was almost over.

It had been an uncomfortable ride home. Jason had rushed them back to the house after the doctor's appointment with literally not a word, his face set and angry. Then he'd headed off to testify while she got the twins ready to go home.

He hadn't spoken except for short, efficient communications since they'd gotten in the car.

He'd taken off his overcoat but was still in his dark suit, white shirt and thin tie, and he looked so handsome he took her breath away.

And she'd ruined any chance of being with him.

The moon made a path on the snowy fields and stars sparkled above. A clear, cold night. As they rounded a corner on the country road, she couldn't help drawing in a breath. "This is where I went off the road, right?"

"Yep." He didn't volunteer more.

But emotions flooded Erica. She'd been desperate then, worried about Kimmie, not knowing where she'd land with the twins, not knowing if she could manage them.

Now she was half owner of a farm and she'd started to become part of a community. Sad, because she'd lost Kimmie, but stable.

A big part of why was Jason.

They were almost home. There wasn't time for a full discussion and she recognized her own cowardliness in that. But she had to say something. "Look, Jason, I'm sorry."

He didn't speak, didn't look over. Just steered the truck.

She looked back and saw that the twins were still sound asleep. "I'm sorry about shutting you out. You've been nothing but kind to us and... I'm sorry I had to do that."

He was silent a moment more, and then he glanced over. "I'm trying to be an adult about this, but I don't understand."

"I just... There are some things about the twins' early months that are private."

"You said you didn't remember. Was that true?"

She thought. Should she just tell him now? But no, they were only a few minutes away from home and Papa would be there, and the twins would wake up...

"Is it their father? You've never really talked about him and I've respected your privacy, but did he do something to you or them? Because that can be prosecuted. He should have to pay. Let alone pay child support, but to cause a blank out of months or to cause delays..."

"No, it's not that."

He fell silent. A waiting silence.

She couldn't form the words.

"I thought we were building something together!" He hit the steering wheel and stepped down on the gas.

She cringed. "Be careful! The twins!"

Immediately, he let up on the gas. "Sorry. I'm angry and upset, but that's no way to act."

He was going to be *really* angry when he found out the truth. "I'll talk to you about it tonight," she said. "There *is* something you need to know about their background, and I... I promise, I'll tell you."

She was promising herself, too.

Jason pulled into the parking place at the rail fence in front of the farm.

The house was dark.

Jason frowned. "Wonder if Papa had something to do. He didn't mention it."

He turned off the truck, opened the door. She opened hers, too.

And looked at him. "Wouldn't the dog..."

"I have a bad feeling. Let me go in first," he said.

Protective to the core, and why should that surprise her?

He went inside, and from the way his hand moved under his suit jacket, she knew he carried a gun. But she also knew he was safe. She trusted him with that gun. She watched as he disappeared inside. He flipped on lights, and she saw him moving from room to room.

Papa must have gone somewhere. They were being overcautious. Surely that was all it was.

Still, she felt lonely and vulnerable, just her and the twins in the cold truck. She slipped out and into the back seat between their car seats. Cramped, but she wanted to be there when they woke up.

Father God, she prayed, *help me to tell Jason the truth.* And then she prayed what she hadn't dared to this morning. *And if it be Your will, let me be with him, Lord. I love him. Keep him safe.*

He wasn't coming back out. Her prayers got more fervent. *Keep him safe.*

The twins were stirring.

She loved them so much.

Jason didn't emerge. Should she go to him?

She opened the door, torn as to what to do.

Then, suddenly, she heard an explosive sound, not from the house but from somewhere off beyond the barn.

A gunshot.

11

The sound of the gunshot crashed into Jason's consciousness. He ran out of the house, and Erica met him beside the truck.

Papa. If Papa were hurt…

"It came from the barn area, maybe beyond," he told her. "I'm going out. Take the twins inside and lock the doors."

"Should I call the police?"

"Call and tell them we heard a shot and Papa's missing. He could be out in the barn, and the shot could be hunters, but…"

"I'll do it. And my phone's on." She gave him a fierce, fast hug, but she didn't offer to go along. She needed to stay with the babies and he needed to move. Fast.

He saw lights in the barn and walked toward it on the path worn through the snow, now icy. When he glanced back, he saw Erica framed in the doorway of the house, waving to let him know they were safely inside.

His breath froze in his nose and his mouth. Was

Papa out here somewhere, in the cold, freezing? Why had he left Papa alone?

Of course Papa didn't want protection or babysitting, but maybe he needed it.

His phone pinged and he glanced at it. Brian from Philly. He turned it off.

When he got to the barn, the door stood open and the lights were on. "Papa? Hey, Papa."

There was no answer, and disappointment pushed in. He checked out the whole place, though. Maybe Papa had fallen or even fainted.

But the barn was empty.

Back outside, he noticed there were tracks leading away from the barn. Human and animal. Why would Papa have gone that way? Unless…it was the direction of the cabin, but why…

Another shot rang out, close this time.

He gripped his own weapon tighter and sent up a prayer. *If You let Papa be all right, I'll stay here with him. I'll take care of him.* You weren't supposed to bargain with God, Jason knew that, but he was desperate.

He moved forward. Heard a faint sound. Then barking that sounded like… Mistletoe?

He ran toward the sound, and a moment later an excited snow-covered dog leaped up at him, bounced off and turned toward the woods, looking back over his shoulder, his tongue lolling out.

"Where's Papa, Mistletoe?"

Mistletoe gave one short bark and trotted toward a small stand of bushes. Jason followed.

There was a rustle and a grunt. Then: "About time you got here."

Jason had never been so glad to hear Papa's crotchety voice in his life. He rushed forward, nearly slipping on icy ground, and sank to his knees beside his grandfather. "What happened? Did you break a bone? Where does it hurt?"

"It doesn't hurt, but I'm cold. I can't seem to get myself up."

Mistletoe romped in a circle around them, kicking up snow and barking.

"Hit an icy patch and my legs went out from under me." Papa propped himself on an elbow and grimaced. "Every time I try to stand up I fall back down. And that's not good at my age, so I figured I'd call for help this way." He patted his rifle. "Might scare out the squatters in the cabin, too."

"You came out here alone because you thought there were squatters in the cabin? You could've been killed!"

"You're not going to be in town forever. I have to be independent." Papa was breathing heavily as he got himself into a sitting position. "Except that crazy dog wouldn't leave me alone. Curled up right beside me. Kept me warm for close to an hour." He rubbed Mistletoe's head. "Didn't like me shooting off the gun, though."

Jason ran a hand over the dog. "Steak bones for you tonight, buddy." Then he braced himself and lifted Papa's not-insubstantial weight, getting a shoulder under him, almost falling himself. "We'll talk more once you're inside and warm." He clicked on Erica's name and dictated a text. "Papa's fine but cold. Turn up heat."

And then, as he and Papa made their way toward the house, he sent up a prayer to God. *Thank You. I'll keep my promise.*

* * *

Erica couldn't stop looking at Papa's dear, tired face. She fussed over him, bandaged a scrape on his hand and brought stacks of blankets downstairs. The front room was toasty, and they soon had Papa ensconced by the fire.

"Tell us what happened." Erica sat down at Papa's feet.

"All of it," Jason added.

Papa pulled up the blanket Erica had put over his legs, settled back in his chair and smiled from Erica to Jason, almost as if he were enjoying the attention. "I missed you two and those babies," he said. "Aside from Ruth Delacroix calling to check on me, I didn't speak to a soul while you were gone. Got to feeling blue, and the cure for that is work, so I went out to do some extra chores in the barn."

"Papa!" Jason sounded exasperated. "You could've let it go until I got home."

"I told you, son, I was feeling blue. So I was out there mending that broken board on the front stall, and I thought I heard noises. When I went outside, I saw a light bobbing up and down out toward the cabin."

Erica glanced at Jason, who was studying his grandfather, and wondered if they were both thinking the same thing. Had he really seen something, or was his mind wandering? Papa seemed sharper than she was, most days, but he was definitely old.

"A light like...a lantern? Headlights?" She adjusted Papa's blankets again.

"I couldn't tell. So," he said righteously, "I got my shotgun and headed down there."

Jason let his head sink into his hand. "Papa. What

were you going to do if you found a crowd of drug squatters out there?"

"Why do you think I brought the shotgun? And the dog?"

Jason shook his head. "You should have just called the police."

"I'm a farmer. Independent. We don't call the police unless we really need 'em." He looked suddenly concerned. "Did you call them when you didn't find me here?"

"Of course I did," Erica said.

Papa made a disgusted sound.

"We were worried! Anyway, I didn't tell them to come right out. I just wanted to have them on alert. I called them back as soon as Jason let me know you were okay."

Papa sat up. "I'll never live this down. They'll be busting my chops at the diner for weeks."

"Those guys!" Jason snorted. "If anything, they'll be impressed."

"Wait, so you headed toward the cabin," Erica said. "Then what happened? You didn't see anybody suspicious, did you?"

Papa gestured toward his leg. "What happened next is that my bad knee went out. I fell and I couldn't get up."

The image of Papa struggling alone in the dark and cold twisted Erica's heart. "You could have frozen to death! Papa Andy, promise me you won't go out without one of us anymore."

Papa Andy looked at her as if she'd lost her mind. "I'm not making a promise like that, young lady. I'm fine ninety-five percent of the time. It's just, that path to the cabin turned into an ice rink, what with the thawing and freezing. I couldn't get a grip on anything."

Jason shook his head and added another log to the fire.

"I didn't want to break a bone," Papa said matter-of-factly, "so I shot off my gun. Figured somebody would hear me."

"That was smart... I guess," Erica said. "Where I grew up, shooting off a gun was an invitation for someone else to open fire on you, but you country folks are different."

"It would have been smarter to call someone on your cell phone. You took a couple years off my life!" Jason actually still looked shaken.

Papa looked at the phone on the end table with obvious irritation. "That cell phone is a nuisance. Keeps going off, and by the time I find it and answer, there's no one there."

"I don't care if you don't like it." Jason glared at his grandfather. "I don't want you anywhere without a phone in your pocket from now on."

"One little mishap," Papa grumbled, "and every young person thinks they can tell you what to do. I have more knowledge in my little finger than you—"

"Would you like some more tea?" Erica said to interrupt their argument.

"Tell you what I'd like," Papa said, "is to take a look at those babies, and then get in bed. I know it's early, but lying out there in the cold took a lot out of me. I'm just going to listen to the radio and stay warm."

And that way, he wouldn't get into more of an argument with Jason. Men. When they felt emotional, they fought.

After they'd taken Papa upstairs to peek at the babies, they got him settled in his bed, propped up with pillows, TV remote in hand.

"One more thing," he said as Jason and Erica were leaving. "I want you to check the cabin."

"Papa…"

"I saw lights," he insisted. "I'd check it out myself, but I've had enough for one night."

"I don't think it's anything," Jason said. "Just moonlight or an animal."

"If that's the case," Papa said, "then why was that path worn to an icy gully instead of just snowed over?"

Erica and Jason looked at each other. "Good point," Erica said, suddenly uneasy.

Jason's phone went off for the second time that evening. He looked at the lock screen and shoved it back in his pocket. "You stay with the twins," he told Erica, "and I'll go look over the cabin."

"I'll keep an eye on the twins," Papa said, sounding irritable. "I'm good for something at least. She should go with you. Not to confront anyone, mind you, but to call for help if needed."

Erica looked at Jason. "He's right." And she wanted to help. Wanted to build a closer bond with Jason before she told him the difficult truth about the twins.

Jason turned to Papa. "I'll only consider you staying here if you have that cell phone out and on. If anything goes wrong, with you or the twins, you call me and then the police."

Mistletoe jumped onto Papa's bed, seeming to smirk at Jason and Erica.

"You're not supposed to be there, boy, but we'll let it slide tonight," Jason said, thumping the dog's side.

"You and Papa watch out for each other, okay, Mistletoe?" Erica massaged the dog's large head and then punched her own number into Papa's phone. Quickly, she enlarged the text, just as she'd used to do for the seniors where she'd worked. "See? One click. I made myself and Jason your favorites."

"You *are* my favorites," Papa said gruffly. "Thank you for getting an old man out of a tight spot."

Erica felt tears rising to her eyes. She was growing so fond of Papa, almost like he was her own grandfather.

Out in the hall, Jason turned to her. "You've done nursing work, right? Do you think he's really okay?"

"He's fine. Probably needs a little time to himself to regroup." She turned toward the twins' room. "I just want to check on them once more, and then we can go out together."

"As long as you agree to stay well back, out of any trouble we might find."

She held up her hands. "I'm not aiming to be a hero."

In the twins' room, she listened to their even breathing. Then she leaned over the crib railing and touched a kiss to each beloved forehead. "We're going to get you the help you need, little ones," she whispered. "I promise I'll take care of you."

Outside, the sky had cleared, leaving a mass of bright stars. Heaven seemed close enough to touch.

She followed Jason, and when he got to the icy section where Papa had fallen, he broke new trail so they wouldn't have to walk on the same precarious path Papa had.

The aroma of wood smoke grew stronger. "Do you

smell that?" she asked. "Is it coming from the main house or the cabin?"

"I think maybe Papa was right," he said. "Look."

Sure enough, in the direction of the cabin she saw lights. Jason turned slightly and held out a hand. "Stay back."

"Okay." Her heart pounded, hard and rapid as a drumbeat.

He crept forward, his body naturally graceful, practiced in the moves of surveillance and detection. He approached the window cautiously and peeked in.

Then he stepped back, rubbed the window with the sleeve of his jacket and cupped his hands to his face as if making sure of what he saw. Why wasn't he being more careful to avoid getting caught?

Then he turned in her direction. "We need an ambulance!" he yelled. "Somebody just had a baby!"

Jason experienced the next ten minutes as a crazy blur. Erica, staggering through the deep snow toward him as she shouted into the phone. Himself, giving the dispatcher exact directions, and then pounding on the cabin door. A pale-faced young husband answering, acting protective—and then, when he realized Jason and Erica wanted to help, looking relieved.

Inside the cabin, on a sleeping bag with a blanket over her, was an exhausted-looking, smiling woman and a squalling newborn.

Jason was afraid to even approach the damp, fragile little being. He'd gotten confident with babies of the twins' sturdy size, but not this tiny thing. Erica, though, waded right in. "Is she…he…okay?" She knelt beside the blanket-covered woman, who was propped on one elbow, wrapping the baby in a towel that at least looked clean. "Here, let me help you. Oh, he's precious!"

"We didn't cut the cord yet." The man stood beside Jason, sounding shaky and worried. "I was afraid... none of this is sanitary." He waved an arm around the cabin.

"How'd you even know what to do?" Jason nodded at the mother and child. "I mean...the baby looks fine."

"Truth?" the young man said. "YouTube videos. My phone's running out of juice and it's super old, but I got enough to know how to help her, and what to do right after the baby was born."

Jason was impressed to see, now, that the area in front of the fireplace had been scrubbed clean. An old cast-iron pot sat beside the blazing fire, and a bucket of snow was nearby. "You melted snow for water."

"We found some dishes here. I didn't expect the baby to be born so soon. We don't even have a name yet." He rubbed his hand through his hair. "This is our hometown, and I thought we'd find someone to take us in, but everyone's busy at Christmas."

Erica glanced up from her position beside the mother and child. "We want to help, right, Jason? Although I think a hospital is the first place for you. All three of you."

"Absolutely." The young man sat down on a large cut log as if it were a stool. "Man, look at this. I'm shaking." He held out his hands to illustrate.

"You did a good job," Jason told him.

"He did," the young woman said.

"And so did you." Erica smoothed the young woman's hair back and found a backpack to tuck under her head as a pillow. "You made an amazing baby." Her voice was soft.

Jason's phone buzzed. Brian, again. When would his friend get the message that Jason was way too busy for a chat?

"Come down here?" The woman was looking at her husband, and he immediately got down on the floor beside her, slipping an arm underneath her neck and touching the baby's hand. "I love you, babe. And I love him, too."

Erica found another sleeping bag in their stack of gear and put it over the two of them, leaving the baby free. Then she scooted back, stood and looked at Jason. "Can the ambulance even get back here?"

"It's four-wheel drive. They'll be fine."

"Then let's give them privacy." She walked over to the cabin's kitchen area and leaned against the counter, and Jason came to lean beside her.

"Is it okay that they didn't cut the cord, do you think?" Jason was still processing the fact that a kid under twenty had just helped his equally young girl-friend have a baby.

"Smart, I would guess. The paramedics will know what to do."

"Where'd you have the twins?"

"What?" She looked at him blankly.

"The twins. Did you have them at a regular hospital, or at a birthing center or something?"

She hesitated. "They were born in a regular hospital."

There was something odd, off, about the way she said it. "Does this bring back memories?"

She shook her head. "These guys seem loving and

happy, even though they're basically homeless. It's so sweet."

Their disagreement of earlier that day, the fact that she'd kept him out of the doctor's office, seemed trivial in the face of what this young couple had just experienced and of the scare about Papa Andy. He put an arm around Erica's shoulders, and after a moment, she cuddled in, slipping her own arm around his waist.

It wasn't romantic, not this time. It was comfort, a desire for human closeness, and she seemed to feel it to the exact same degree that he did. As the couple lay together, bonding with their baby, so he and Erica, two people alone in the world, bonded, as well. It was a Christmas moment.

Soon enough, though, the ambulance pulled up, right to the cabin's back door, and all the tranquility was lost. The paramedics asked questions of the mother and father, did tests on the baby and loaded them all into an ambulance in a matter of minutes. Jason and Erica gave their names and numbers, and the ambulance pulled out.

And then they were gone, and it was just Erica and Jason at the cabin. They made short work of putting out the fire and locking up.

"You know," she said, "you were right about something."

"You're kidding," he joked.

She swatted his arm. "I can admit when I'm wrong. And I was wrong to think I could have lived here with the twins. It would never have worked. It's too primitive."

"You're welcome," he said. "Just ask me anytime you need advice."

"You're impossible," she said, and then yawned hugely. "We'd better get back to Papa Andy and the twins. I'm beat."

Jason felt the same, only with a bit of an edge of adrenaline still hanging on. He wanted to hold her in the worst way, but he also knew they had differences to resolve. And they were both exhausted. "Let's head back."

Halfway down the new broken path, his phone buzzed yet again. He looked at it and rolled his eyes. What did Brian want? Impatient, he clicked into the phone call. "I'm kinda busy here, and it's late. What's up?"

"I have some news," Brian said, his voice stiff, guarded. "About that matter you asked me to investigate."

Erica. Kimmie. Arizona. "Oh, man, it's been crazy here. I forgot all about that."

Erica glanced back at him, questioning. He waved her ahead. "I've got to take this," he said to her. "Go get warm. I'll be right there."

She nodded and headed toward the house. Jason walked slowly behind. "What's up?" he asked Brian.

"You're going to want to be sitting down to hear this," Brian said.

12

Jason stood outside the house and listened to Brian's incomprehensible words. Surely his friend had gotten it wrong. "You didn't find this out for sure, right? It's just a theory."

"It's true." Brian's voice was flat. "Those twins are your nephews. Your sister was their mother."

"But why—" He broke off. "What could Erica…"

"Can't say. She trying to get something out of you? Money? Land?"

He thought of the will, how Kimmie had left Erica half the farm. But his head was spinning too much to understand.

While he and Brian had been talking, Erica had gone into the house. Now lights came on in the front room, and he watched as she moved around there, picking up a cup from the coffee table, adjusting an ornament, bending down to pat Mistletoe.

From where he stood, it was like watching a Christmas movie. The perfect setting, the beautiful woman. A happy home.

And it was all a lie. "Was she married?"

"What do you mean?"

His hand was sweating on the phone. "Kimmie. Was she married to the father of the twins?"

"No." There was a dim sound of papers rustling. "She didn't name a father on the birth certificates, but my contact out there did a little digging, looked up her past addresses and other public records. Apparently she was cohabitating with a man around the time they must have been conceived, but he went to prison before the babies were born."

Cohabitating with a man.

People did that all the time. Who was he to judge?

All the same, the image he'd always carried of his sister—beautiful, laughing, pure—seemed to shatter into a million jagged fragments.

"You still there?" Brian asked. "Listen, I wouldn't worry about the father having any claim on those kids."

"Yeah. Thanks, man. I'll… We'll talk."

"One more thing," Brian said. "When I spoke with Kimmie's landlord—piece of work, that guy—he said there was a box of your sister's personal effects that was sent to your grandfather's address. Should have arrived by now."

Maybe it had, and Erica had hidden it. Suddenly, he wouldn't put anything past her.

"I guess there could be a note, some kind of explanation."

He closed his eyes for just a second, then opened them again. "Yeah. Thanks, buddy." He clicked off the phone.

And then he just stood still and looked up at the starry sky. The twins were Kimmie's. His, now. He'd been getting to know them, coming to care for them, never even realizing—

The front door opened. "Jason? Everything okay?"

Erica was framed in the doorway. The soft light behind her made her skin and hair glow.

A little bit like Kimmie had always glowed in his mind.

In truth, Erica, like Kimmie, had lost her luster, if she'd ever even had it.

He strode up the front steps and brushed past her into the entryway. Sitting down on the bench, he took off his snowy boots and tossed them into the pile of shoes by the door. They made a satisfying crash.

"Shh! The twins!"

He looked at her, and it was like she was a different person from the woman he'd been getting close to. "Yeah," he said. "We should talk about the twins."

Her eyes widened. "What was the phone call about?"

"Let's take this discussion into the front room." He watched her face. "We wouldn't want to wake up Kimmie's babies."

Her hand flew to her mouth and her eyes went impossibly wide. "You know."

Until that moment, in a corner of his mind, he'd thought Brian might have gotten it wrong. Or that maybe, Erica hadn't known the babies were Kimmie's. Which didn't make any sense, but was easier to believe than that sweet, gentle Erica—the woman he'd fallen in love with—had been lying since the moment they'd met.

"Jason…"

He jerked his head sideways toward the front room. "In here."

She walked in ahead of him, shoulders slumping, and perched on the edge of the couch. He sat in the chair that was kitty-corner. Mistletoe lifted his head from his bed in front of the fire and whined softly.

They both stared at the floor.

Finally, she spoke. "Jason, I've been wanting to tell you about the twins practically since the first day I knew you. It's just… It's been complicated."

Understanding dawned. "That's why you didn't want me in the doctor's office."

"Yes. I knew I had to tell the doctor the whole truth, and—"

"You owed more honesty to the doctor than to me?" He knew dimly that his remark wasn't fair, but he couldn't make himself stifle it.

"It was for the twins." She leaned forward, elbows on knees. "The doctor needed to know everything so she could give them the best help possible."

A log crackled and fell in the fireplace. Mistletoe stood, turned in a circle and flopped back down with a sigh.

"All this time," he said. "Knowing it, being what I thought was close, and you didn't see fit to tell me those boys are my own *nephews*?" His voice was too loud, but he couldn't seem to control it. "What does that say about you?"

"I… Jason, I'm so sorry. I wanted to tell you."

He pressed his lips together so he wouldn't say the immediate, awful things he wanted to say.

She'd lied to him. That was one thing to focus on.

The fact that the twins were his sister's, were his blood—that was too big to take in right now.

His body felt like it was going to explode. He

jumped up and paced the room, picking things up and putting things down. "Why'd you do it, Erica? What are you trying to get out of me and Papa?"

"Nothing. I don't want anything from you."

"Why, because you already got everything you need from Kimmie? What was that will about? Blackmail? Did you steal the twins from her?"

"No! I—"

"Because I'll prosecute. If you in any way made my sister's last days harder, if you…" He nearly choked as all the possibilities whirled in his thoughts. "If you caused her death, taking away her kids and stressing her out—"

"No, no!" She held up a hand, looking up at him, her eyes filling with tears. "Jason, it wasn't like that at all."

"Child abduction," he recited, his voice flat because he'd said it so many times before, though never in such a personal context. "Wrongfully removing a child by persuasion, fraud, open force or violence. I don't doubt that you'll see prison time over this."

"She gave them to me." Erica's face was white. "She asked me to take them, because she couldn't care for them herself anymore, and she didn't want them to go into foster care."

"You expect me to believe that? Why would they have been put into foster care when they had a perfectly loving family back here and a mother there?"

"Because…" She stopped, shook her head, looked away.

"Can't think of an answer, can you?"

She hesitated, then met his eyes. "I don't know if you want to know the answer."

He clenched his fists. "I want to know. Not that I'll believe one thing you say."

"She was using," Erica said quietly, "and the police were coming."

Jason pounded a fist into his hand as bitterness spread through his chest. "With her babies there, she was using?" All this time he'd been trying to maintain an image of Kimmie, and it had been false. For that matter, the same was true of Erica.

He shook his head. "So she asked you to bring them to me and Papa, and instead you—"

"No." Erica shook her head. "You have to understand, it was all hectic and hurried. She thought I could live in the cabin until I got on my feet. It was all she had to offer me for...for raising her children. But, Jason, I love them like they're my own and I want what's best for them. I'm not trying to pull something over on you. I did this—I've been taking care of them since leaving Arizona and even before—because I cared for Kimmie and I've come to love her boys." Her voice choked up on the last words.

"You can do better than that. You're a great liar."

"She didn't want you to have them." She was staring at the carpet, her voice low.

He wasn't sure he'd heard her right. "What did you say?"

She looked up at him. "Kimmie didn't want you to have the twins. She asked me to raise them and not to let you know."

Jason grabbed a plastic snow globe he'd loved since childhood and threw it against the wall.

Erica flinched as it shattered, water and little plastic pieces flying everywhere. Her shoulders hunched in, like he was going to hit her.

"That can't be true. Kimmie would have trusted me before someone like you. A liar with nothing. No connection to the family, no experience, no resources..."

She was looking at him now, her face set and serious, except that tears were running down her cheeks.

"Kimmie was smart," he continued, trying to work it out in his mind. "She knew the babies would need help—"

"They need help now," she said, standing up.

"What?"

"I heard one of them crying. Coughing. Something." She hurried toward the stairs.

He followed her. "You're faking this to get away from me. But I'm watching you. I'm not letting you take the babies again—"

"Or maybe you woke them up, throwing things like a little boy because you're mad at your sister." The words, tossed over her shoulder, cut into him.

Still, he followed her into the room she shared with them. Her nightgown hung on the bedpost, slippers at the foot of the bed. Her Bible and a little devotional book on the bedside table.

He swallowed the bile that rose in his throat and approached the crib.

The twins lay in striped Christmas pajamas, Mikey with his head toward one end of the crib, Teddy with his head toward the other. Their legs were intertwined, and as he watched, Mikey tossed back and forth, coughed and let out a fussy little cry.

They were Kimmie's babies. His nephews.

Jason's throat tightened.

Erica's breathing sounded choked and she brushed the backs of her hands over her cheeks. The flowery smell of her hair rose to his nose.

He ignored the tiny shred of sympathy and caring that pushed at him. He'd been about to fall for this liar.

He always picked the wrong person—as witness Renea and now Erica. He had a knack for it, choosing those who were already on the way to some kind of emotional ruin, and then nudging that train along to full speed.

Mikey fussed some more, kicking his legs restlessly, and Erica picked him up carefully, trying not to disturb Teddy. She jostled Mikey gently in her arms. "You've picked up a cold, haven't you?" she said in a quiet, bouncy voice. "Let's wipe your nose, huh?" She carried him over and got a tissue from a box on the dresser, wiped the baby's nose. Then she grabbed another tissue and blotted her own eyes.

Teddy thrashed in the crib as if looking for his twin and then let out a wail.

Before he could think about it, Jason had Teddy in his arms. He gently bounced him, stroking his soft hair.

This was his nephew. His blood.

The babies Kimmie had borne and hadn't told him about.

"Did she try to get in touch with me?" The question burst out of him. "Or Mom, or Gran and Papa?"

Erica shook her head. "She didn't want any of you to know."

"But the safety of her own children, their health!"

Teddy started to cry again and Jason swayed with him. Erica had found a little medicine bottle and a dropper and was filling it, blocking Mikey from rolling off the bed with her body. "Here you go, sweetie, this'll help your cold," she said, propping Mikey up and popping the syringe into his mouth.

Mikey turned his head away and spit out some of the bright red medicine. "There, but some got inside, huh?" she crooned, using another tissue to wipe Mikey's chin. "There, that'll help you feel better and sleep. Rock with Mama."

"You're not their mother."

She drew in a little gasp and her eyes flashed up to Jason's, and then she looked back down at Mikey again and rocked, back and forth.

"So when the nurse asked you if they were breast-fed…"

She shook her head, still rocking the baby. "I don't know. Kimmie said she was able to stay clean while she was pregnant and for a while after. I'd assume she at least tried."

"You weren't around her then?" His hunger for more information made him keep talking to the woman who'd betrayed his sister and lied to him.

She shook her head. "I wish I had been. I wish it so much. But that was when my mom was having so much trouble and I could barely… Anyway, I lost touch with Kimmie."

"Lost touch until when?"

"Until she called me two months ago and told me she was dying and she needed help."

He bit down the pain those words roused in him. "Why wouldn't she call us? Why would she call a young woman, a stranger with who-knows-what intentions…"

"We were friends, Jason, and I didn't judge her."

His mouth had been open to ask more questions, to vent more feelings, but her words made him stop. *Would* he have judged Kimmie, had he known what had happened in her life?

"Hey, what's going on in here?" Papa pushed through the half-open door, clad in flannel pajamas with a plaid robe tied on over them.

"I'm sorry we woke you up," Erica said.

He waved a hand. "Old folks don't sleep well. Are the babies sick?"

She glanced over at Jason. "I think they picked up a cold or something. They were at the doctor's and around other kids so much, it's inevitable."

"Why don't you tell him what else has come out tonight," Jason said to Erica.

She narrowed her eyes at him. "Is this the right time?"

"No," he said, "that would've been when you met us for the first time. But you didn't choose the right time, did you?"

She sighed. "No, I didn't."

"What's going on between you two?" Papa Andy sat down on the bed beside Erica.

"I... Papa, I'm really sorry," she said, "but there's a secret I've been keeping since I came to Pennsylvania. Jason just found out about it, and he's angry. Understandably. You'll probably be angry, too."

"Oh, now," Papa said, patting her back, "what could a sweet young woman like you do that would make an old man angry?"

She swallowed hard. "I... You know how Kimmie and I were friends, right?"

Papa nodded, tickling Mikey's foot.

"Well, one reason she and I spent a lot of time together, toward the end, was that…" She trailed off and looked at Jason.

"What she's trying to say, Papa, is that the babies aren't hers. They're Kimmie's."

Papa's mouth opened in an O. He stared from Erica to Mikey to Teddy.

Erica thrust the baby into his arms and fled from the room.

Erica ran down the steps and into the front room, gasping with sobs.

Why, oh why, hadn't she told them on her own terms rather than letting the truth be discovered? And what would happen now?

Would the twins be taken from her? Was her dream of motherhood already at an end?

"I'm sorry, Kimmie," she whispered. She picked up a photograph of Jason and Kimmie as kids with Santa. It was one of Papa's favorites, and she often saw him looking at it.

What had gone so wrong in this family that huge, painful secrets were needed?

She saw a tiny plastic Christmas tree on the floor in a little puddle of water. The nearby shards of plastic looked sharp.

She walked into the kitchen and got paper towels, feeling stiff in every part of her body, exhausted, old. She came back into the room and started cleaning up the mess.

Jason had been so furious. Of course he had. No one liked being lied to, and this was the lie to end all lies, a lie of major proportions.

She inhaled the piney scent of the Christmas tree as she searched out all the little pieces of a broken Christmas scene. For a moment she thought about saving them. Maybe the snow globe could be put back together.

She studied the bits in her hand. *No. Hopeless.*

She carried the pieces to the trash can and threw them in. Upstairs, she could hear Jason's and Papa's low voices, but no sound of crying babies. The boys had probably gone back to sleep. They were exhausted from their big day.

Loss, a huge hole in her chest, opened with such an ache that she sat down on the couch and hunched over, clutching her elbows.

She was a horrible person, not deserving of a family.

That little moment in the cabin, when Jason had put his arm around her like she was his longtime wife, when she'd cuddled into him, was the last time she'd have the opportunity to touch him.

And they'd take the babies from her—she was sure of it. Why wouldn't they? Papa and Jason were kind, loving men who could raise Mikey and Teddy to adulthood. If Kimmie had stayed in touch with her family, she would have known that, and Erica would never have even been in the picture.

Her heart felt broken into three distinct pieces. Four, actually: one for Mikey, one for Teddy, one for Papa and one for Jason.

The fun, happy moments they'd spent together played through her mind. How they'd decorated the tree, how Teddy had scooted toward it. The capable way Papa held a baby on his lap like he was born to it. The sleigh ride to church, bells jingling, the twins laughing.

There wasn't going to be any more of that for her.

Unbidden, a memory from childhood spread into her mind. She'd rushed home from school to the motel where they'd been living, excited to have a Christmas gift for her mother. A clay dish, fired in the school kiln. Now, as an adult, she knew it had been a lopsided, ugly thing. And indeed, her mother had laughed when she'd seen it, given Erica a quick pat on the head and gone back to partying with her friends.

Erica got up, walked over to the Christmas tree and looked at the little lump ornament Jason and Papa had laughed about. In a family like theirs, children's humble efforts at art were treasured and kept.

She'd always longed to be in such a family. And she'd had a brief moment there. But now that time was over.

Heavy footsteps sounded on the stairs. Jason came to the doorway and looked in at her, his expression a perfect storm of hurt and anger and mistrust.

He spun away. A moment later, the front door slammed.

It's over. She sank to her knees and pressed her hands to her mouth. *Help me, Lord.*

13

The next morning, at dawn, Jason was awakened by a rhythmic scraping sound. He looked around and blinked at the interior of his truck and the pink-and-gold glowing world outside. What was he doing here? And why was he so cold, despite the down coat stretched over him and his big boots and warm socks?

He turned on the car and cranked up the heat. Slowly, the night before came back to him. The revelation about the twins. The fighting with Erica. Storming out.

He'd driven aimlessly and then realized it wasn't so aimless; he was headed to the suburban Pittsburgh home where his family had lived during his elementary school years, after they'd moved back from Arizona. He'd sat in his truck in front of their old house, thinking about his sister, until he'd fallen asleep.

Now, as the defroster cleared the windows, he looked out to see that the Michaelson place next door was decorated with the same blue icicle lights and big blue-lit deer that the older couple had always argued about: he'd loved them, and she'd thought they were tacky.

As a kid, Jason had found the blue lights to be much cooler than his family's plain old white lights, and he'd loved the way the blue deer had raised and lowered their heads. He remembered the year that Kimmie had taken him over to pretend-feed the deer with burned, broken-up Christmas cookies they'd made. He'd been young, first or second grade. Probably, he realized now, she'd thought of the scheme to make him feel better after their cookies had turned out inedible.

Years later, she'd covered for him, taking the blame herself, when he and his friends had dragged one of the deer over to their bonfire and accidentally burned part of its back leg. He squinted through the dim morning light. Sure enough, one of the deer had a hind leg half the length of the other three.

How had he and Kimmie gotten so far apart that she'd died alone, not even telling him she'd borne two sons? That she didn't want him, the little brother who'd idolized her, to get to know her children?

Tap-tap-tap. He lowered his driver's-side window to see a bundled-up woman, white hair peeking out from beneath a stocking cap. "You're going to freeze out here, sir. What's your business in this neighborhood?"

The voice was familiar, if a little raspier than when he'd last heard it. "Mrs. Michaelson? I'm Jason Stephanidis. I used to live next door."

The old woman cocked her head to one side and studied Jason. "You're the little kid who once decorated my front bushes with those tinsel icicles?"

Another memory Jason had forgotten about until just now. "The very same," he said, turning off the truck, climbing out and shaking her hand. "I'm sorry about that. I'd guess you were picking those things up out of your yard for weeks."

Mrs. Michaelson chuckled, leaning on her snow shovel. "That we were, but we didn't mind. We always enjoyed the kids in the neighborhood, since we didn't have any of our own."

"I see you're still putting up the blue lights," Jason said, gesturing to the Michelsons' house.

"Sure do, every year, and sometimes I leave 'em on all night. The mister has been gone these past eight years, but it doesn't seem like Christmas otherwise."

So Mr. Michaelson had passed away. And Mrs. Michaelson, although she looked spry enough, had to be well up into her eighties. She'd seemed ancient even when Jason was a kid.

"Can I help you shovel your driveway?"

"No need. I just do the walkways, and they're done. I don't drive anymore." She sighed and gestured at her thick glasses. "Vision problems. I turned in my license before they could take it away from me."

"Sensible decision." He looked around the neighborhood. "I have good memories of living here."

"You look like you could use a cup of coffee," she said. "If you'd like to come in, I could fix you some breakfast, as well."

There was the tiniest undertone of eagerness in the old woman's voice. "I would appreciate that," he said, and followed Mrs. Michaelson inside.

After breakfast and promises to stay in touch, Jason drove back to the farm. He felt ashamed of having left Papa alone to deal with Erica and the twins, but when he arrived, Erica's car was gone and the house was quiet. He had a moment of panic. "Papa?"

"Up here," his grandfather called.

Papa was putting on a Christmas sweater-vest that had to be as old as Jason was, his hair wet from a recent shower, his face freshly shaved.

"Where are Erica and the twins?"

"She took 'em to the Santa Claus breakfast at the church."

After the bomb that had exploded here last night, she'd gone to a Santa Claus breakfast? "You let her go? What if she abducts them?"

Papa waved a hand. "If she were going to abduct them, she'd have done it already. She'd never have come here at all." He leaned closer to the mirror to straighten his bow tie. "She said she'd promised to help with the breakfast, and she didn't want to let Mrs. Habler and the ladies' crew down."

"Oh." Jason stepped next door to her room. The bed was neatly made, but all her and the twins things were still there. A weight seemed to lift off his chest, even though he *thought* he wanted her to leave, to get out of their lives.

"Where are you going?" he asked his grandfather.

"Christmas Eve ham delivery," Papa explained. "Remember? The Men's Group has been doing it since I don't know when."

Jason did remember, how Papa went to a Christmas Eve luncheon with other men, out at some restaurant, and then did a surprise ham delivery to some of the poorer members of the congregation.

He didn't want to ask, but the words burst out of him. "How was Erica?"

Papa shook his head, pressing his lips together. "We didn't talk much. She was broken up, though. Red eyes. Kept apologizing." He eyed Jason. "I don't know what to think or do about this whole situation, except to make sure those babies are cared for and loved."

"What's she going to do?"

Papa picked up a comb and ran it through his hair. "I doubt if she's gotten that far in her thinking."

"I just can't understand what she did. Kimmie, either."

"Some things don't make a whole lot of logical sense." Papa put on his dress shoes and checked himself in the mirror again. "Tell you what you need to do, though. Get a shower. Get yourself cleaned up. You'll feel better."

Jason gave Papa a half smile he didn't feel inside. "Sure. Will do."

As he left Papa's bedroom, he heard a car approach and a door slam. His heart leaped. He hurried to his bedroom window to look out.

It was only Papa's ride.

Jason didn't want to see Erica, anyway.

After he'd showered and put on clean clothes, he didn't know what to do with himself. Erica and the twins hadn't come back yet, not that he was waiting for them. Once again, he got into his truck.

As he started to turn out of the farm's long driveway, a brown delivery truck appeared and stopped in front of the drive, brakes squeaking. When Jason saw that the driver was a high school acquaintance, he waved.

"Got a package for you and your grandfather," Elmer called, hopping down and carrying a two-foot square box to the truck's window. "Want me to throw it in the back of your truck, or should I take it up to the house?"

"Throw it in the back. Thanks."

"Merry Christmas!" Elmer waved and the brown truck chugged off.

Jason stopped at the hospital to check on the young couple who'd given birth in the cabin. He found them in good health, just waiting for the doctor to release them. He admired their new son and envied the loving smiles on their faces. Exhibit A that you didn't need material things to be happy.

Since it seemed they had no idea where they'd go once they left the hospital, Jason found the hospital's social worker and made an anonymous donation for a month's rent for them.

But it didn't make him feel a bit better.

Aimless, he drove around and finally ended up at the mall two towns over, thinking to pick up a little something more for Papa. He wandered until he found a bookstore and picked up a copy of Papa's favorite author's new hardcover spy novel. The thought of Papa's reaction—"I could have gotten this at the library for free"—gave Jason a minute's pleasure. Secretly, Papa would be glad he didn't have to join the long waiting list to get the book.

He looked at his watch and realized he'd killed only half an hour. Package in hand, Jason sat down on a bench.

Repetitive Christmas music played, audible over the sounds of people's voices, some irritable but most happy and excited. People crowded through the mall and into the stores, and he heard snippets of conversation.

From a man in a wheelchair, talking to the young nurse pushing him: "Figures my disability check would be late this month. But I know, I know, I should stop complaining and be grateful I can still get something for the grandkids."

From one frazzled-looking young mom to another: "Did you see the Dino Dasher is finally on sale?"

From a pretty teenage girl: "If I get Aunt Helen an extra large, she'll be insulted, but if I get her anything smaller it won't fit."

Families. None of them having perfect Christmases, but the holiday spirit shone through the complaints and the crowding.

The smell of candied nuts tickled his nose, and he looked around, spotting the source in a kiosk in the middle of the mall. His mother had always loved those nuts. He should call her.

He turned away from the crowds and covered one ear and put in the call, but there was no answer. Either she was out or maybe all the circuits were overloaded, it being Christmastime. Did wireless circuits get overloaded?

He strolled over to the kiosk and bought a paper cone of candied nuts, then wandered through the mall, nibbling them.

"There's the most handsome detective in Holly Springs." The voice behind him was merry and loud, and he turned to see Ruth, as always with a baby in her arms. "Doing some last-minute shopping, are ya?"

He held up his bag. "You, too?"

"Sure am. Do you know the Glenns from church?" She introduced him to a bedraggled-looking man who didn't smell any too good and his much younger, stressed-out-looking wife. Then she held up the baby for him to see. "And this is little Maria. We're out doing some shopping for her. Gotta make her Christmas bright!"

"Nice to meet you," he said, and watched the small group head into a baby store. He could guess who'd be footing the bill there. Ruth was widowed, and she wasn't wealthy herself, but she had a generous heart. She must have taken it upon herself to play Santa for the Glenn family.

On his way out to his truck he spotted Chuck and Jeannine, walking arm in arm through the parking lot. He was happy they were back together, but he didn't want to intrude on their holiday.

But Chuck called out a greeting. "Jason! Come hear our good news!"

Standing in the cold parking lot, they explained that they'd decided to keep all the baby furniture because they were planning to adopt.

"I finally figured out it doesn't matter how kids come into a family," Chuck said. "I was on some kind of male ego trip, wanting my descendants to be my own blood."

"But he finally realized that was ridiculous." Jeannine squeezed her husband's arm. "What's important is how much love is there."

How much love is there. Jason wasn't feeling any excess of love, himself. He had Papa, of course, but even Papa had plans today, long-standing friends in the community. Everyone in Holly Springs, single or married, seemed to be rooted and connected. Everyone except him.

Maybe he ought to think about staying here, settling down. The pace of life, the way people cared for each other, was starting to appeal to him. Maybe, like Papa and Ruth, he could build a life here even though he was single.

He drove by the Mistletoe Display and, on impulse, turned in. Twilight was gathering, and he figured he might see a cheerful crowd. He didn't feel like being alone.

But as he drove up to the gates and parked in an almost-empty lot, the display's lights clicked off. A worker came out and hung a sign. "Sorry, buddy, we're closing down."

"No problem. Merry Christmas." Jason waited until the guy had gone back in to lock up the office and then read the sign. "Closing early so our workers can spend Christmas Eve and Day with their families."

Jason wandered along the fence, looking into the now-dark display. In the rapidly deepening twilight, he spotted the bench where he and Erica had shared their first kiss.

The emotions from that evening washed over him, and this time, he didn't even try to push them away.

He'd cared so much for Erica. He could admit it to himself now: he'd fallen in love with her.

But in the end, she'd betrayed him. Just like Kimmie had, and Renea, and even his own mother.

A nagging, honest voice inside his head said: Who's the common element here?

I know. It's me! I make bad choices!

Honesty compelled him to push further. Was it really just about choices?

Renea had been his own bad choice. But he hadn't chosen his mother or Kimmie. They'd been his family, and while his mother had definitely been the one to distance herself from her children, he'd followed up on that by judging Kimmie, pushing her away.

It was a decision he regretted, and would regret his whole life.

Erica had come into his life as a result of that decision; in all probability, she'd have never been involved with Kimmie if he had taken the proper responsibility for his sister.

Or maybe not; Kimmie had been her own person, and she might have still chosen to run away.

God works all things to good.

Even bad things, like Kimmie's death, God had worked to good by bringing him, Erica and the twins together.

Except that, last night, he'd judged Erica harshly, yelled at her, pushed her away. Just like he'd done with Kimmie.

But she lied to me! He banged back into his truck and drove too fast to the diner. That empty feeling inside him was hunger. He hadn't eaten anything since Mrs. Michaelson's breakfast and a few of those candied nuts.

He had a moment's fear that the diner would be closed, too, but it was brightly lit. When he pushed the door open, bells jingled and steamy warmth hit him, along with the homey scent of turkey and stuffing.

He'd have Christmas Eve dinner here and then go to church services. He'd done holidays alone plenty of times, back in Philly. And there were other solo diners here, too.

Hank came out to take his order, dressed in a Christmas apron atop his black slacks and shirt. "Where's your friend?" he asked.

"What friend? I have a lot of 'em." Which wasn't true, at least not here.

Hank lifted his hands like stop signs and took a step back. "Whoa, I meant the cute redhead. But I *didn't* mean to touch a nerve. What can I get for you? Coffee first?"

Just to prove he wasn't pathetic, Jason ordered the full Christmas Eve platter—turkey, stuffing, potatoes and vegetables. "Give me pie, too."

But when the food came, he could barely stuff down a quarter of it.

He sat back and waited for the check and thought about the day. Thoughts about Kimmie, and then about Erica, edged their way into his mind and wouldn't leave.

He'd gotten so rigid lately, judged people harshly. Partly it came with the police work, but he knew himself well enough to understand that he was trying to keep control.

He'd condemned Kimmie harshly when he'd learned she was using. He'd gotten all strict and judgmental, and that had pushed her away.

Would he do the same to Erica?

But how could he forgive what she'd done to him and Papa?

He gave Hank a credit card for the check, leaving an oversize tip as befitted the occasion and the fact that Hank had to work on Christmas Eve.

And then he ended up at church, even though he was an hour early for services.

It was where he probably should have been all along.

* * *

Erica carried the twins upstairs, her muscles aching, her mind and heart calling for rest. She'd stayed out all day on purpose, and it looked like her plan had worked; Jason's truck wasn't here. She wouldn't have to see him, to say goodbye.

Saying goodbye to Papa and the twins would be hard enough.

She set Mikey down on the floor and placed a basket of colorful blocks in front of him. Then she fastened Teddy in the bouncy swing she'd found at the thrift store a few days ago, and right away, he began to babble and jump. His legs were getting stronger by the day.

"Ma-ma, Ma-ma," he chortled, waving his arms.

She did a double take. *Teddy* had said a word. He'd called her Mama.

It was the first time. She knelt in front of him, laughing and crying at the same time. "Oh, honey, I'm not your mama. But what a big boy you are for saying it."

"You *are* his mama, or the closest thing he's got to one." Papa Andy stood in the doorway.

She looked up at the old man who'd become so dear to her, and her heart twisted in her chest. "I guess I am. But that's all going to change now."

"Does it have to?"

She sat back and wrapped her arms around her upraised knees. "Jason's going to report me to the local police. He said last night that I'd probably do jail time." Which was terrifying, but even worse was the prospect of losing the twins forever.

"What a man says when he's angry and what's true can be two different things."

Papa hadn't heard the icy determination in Jason's

voice. "I hope you're right about the jail time, but no one will disagree that he has more right to raise the twins. Along with you. You're their closest relatives, whereas I..." She was a nobody.

"Something you need to know about Jason. He's always seen things in black-and-white. I think he's growing out of that, but..."

"I don't." Erica hugged her knees tighter. "He sees me as evil now. I'm on his bad list, and I don't think there's any chance of a change."

"Huh." Papa gestured toward Mikey. "That one might walk before he crawls. You'd best keep an eye on him."

Erica turned to see Mikey next to Mistletoe, both little hands buried in the dog's fur. He was trying to pull himself up to his feet, and it had to hurt poor Mistletoe, but the dog didn't seem to mind. In fact, he tugged to the side a little as if he were trying to help Mikey to stand.

Erica pulled in a breath, her hand going to her heart. Was it possible to die of love?

"They grow fast," Papa said, and paused. "Mind if I come in a minute?"

She gestured toward the rocking chair in the corner of the bedroom. "I'm going to start packing, but I'd love some company."

"Where are you headed?"

She shook her head. "For the moment, to town. I lined up a room at the Evergreen Hotel." She sat down on the edge of the bed, facing Papa. "I'll say goodbye as soon as I've packed. I'll leave..." She stopped, swallowed hard. "If you can handle them, I'll leave the twins here tonight."

Papa leaned forward, elbows on knees. "You're a pretty strong woman."

"How do you figure?" So she wouldn't have to focus solely on her misery, she knelt to pull her suitcase out from under the bed and opened it.

Inside were all her shorts and T-shirts. Arizona clothes. It seemed like a lifetime ago that they'd been what she put on every day she wasn't working.

Maybe she'd end up going back there, get away from the cold. But the thought didn't give her the least iota of happiness.

Restraining a sigh, she opened her drawerful of cold-weather clothes and started refolding them and placing them, carefully, on top of the summer things. If she focused, maybe she wouldn't cry in front of Papa.

Mistletoe trotted over, toenails clicking on the wood floor, and nudged his shaggy head under her hand, whining faintly. Automatically, she tugged the dog against her leg, rubbing his back.

"It took a strong woman to care for your friend, sick with cancer. And then you drove her kids across the country, which couldn't have been easy. You got them early intervention. You've made yourself a place in a brand-new community, even though you've got barely two nickels to rub together."

"I had your help with that," she said. "Thanks to you, I've had a place to stay and food to eat." Honesty compelled her to add, "And it's thanks to Jason that I got in to see the developmental specialist. I could never have done that on my own."

Papa ignored her remarks. "It just surprises me, that's all."

"What surprises you?"

"That you'd give up so easily."

She stared at him. "Give up? What do you…"

"You love those boys, don't you?" In the midst of his wrinkled face, blue eyes shone out, bold and challenging.

"Like they were my own." As if to illustrate, Mikey held out his arms, and she scooped him up and hugged him fiercely.

"And I suspect you have some feelings for my grandson, as well."

Erica set Mikey down in the crib and went back to folding clothes, avoiding Papa's eyes. "You see too much."

"I see what's there. And I see what's there on his side, too. He's a hard one, that Jason, but you've helped him to soften up. You and the twins. That's worth something."

"Thank you, I…" She didn't know what to say, how to respond, but she stumbled to put some words together. "I hope there was something good he got from knowing me. It's been…" Her throat was too tight to go on. She took a sweater out of the suitcase and refolded it, blinking away tears.

"You also did something that hurt him. Hurt me, too, but—"

"I'm so sorry, Papa." She dropped the sweater and hurried across the room to kneel at his side. "You've been so good to me. It was unforgivable of me to deceive you."

He took her hand in his own hard, leathery one. "I'm also old enough to know that nobody's perfect and everybody makes mistakes. Yours wasn't for a bad cause." He tipped her chin up to look at him as her tears spilled over. "Seems to me our Kimmie put you in a mighty confusing dilemma. You tried to do the right thing for her and for the twins. How can we fault you for that?"

She swallowed and wiped at the tears rolling down her cheeks. "Thank you, Papa Andy. That means a lot to me."

"You mean a lot to me, sweetheart. You and these boys have helped me more than you know." He squeezed her hand. "Now, why don't you go find yourself a corner and do a little praying? I'll watch the twins."

"But I need to pack—"

"You in too big of a hurry to listen to God?" He lifted a bushy eyebrow, his sharp eyes pinning her.

"I… No. Thank you. I'd appreciate a few minutes." She grabbed her Bible from her nightstand and hurried downstairs to sit beside the Christmas tree and the nativity scene.

Half an hour later, she knew what she needed to do. Something terrifying, something unlikely to work, something against her whole shy nature.

And she needed to get started right away.

14

"I'd love to stay and talk more, but I have a sermon to preach." Pastor Wayne pounded Jason on the shoulder. "I think between you and the Lord, you can figure out what to do. You're welcome to my office, if you need a place to think."

"Thanks." Jason watched the pastor gather his Bible and leave, confident, ready for his next challenge.

That was how Jason had used to feel about his detective work, too. Now he wasn't sure of anything.

He needed to stay in Holly Springs with Papa. And he needed to take care of his sister's children.

But the big question was Erica.

Could he forgive her? Could she forgive him?

The church bells rang, announcing that services would start soon. Jason closed his eyes and slumped forward, elbows on knees, his forehead on his folded hands.

Ten minutes later, he still wasn't certain what to do, but he'd gained a measure of peace. The Lord didn't leave His sheep without a shepherd.

He stood and looked out the window into the twilight-darkened parking lot. People were starting to arrive for services.

And it hit him like a missile.

The box the postman had delivered.

Brian had mentioned that a box of Kimmie's belongings should be on its way.

Was it possible…?

He strode out of the pastor's office and into the parking lot, almost running to his truck. He grabbed the box from the back and brought it up into the cab, turning on the vehicle for warmth, clicking on the interior light.

He studied the package. An Arizona return address.

Hands shaking, he used his pocketknife to slit the tape and opened the flaps. Inside, there was a stack of envelopes held together with a rubber band and about four or five newspaper-wrapped items.

He set the letters aside and was opening the first packet when there was a knock on the window.

He lowered it.

Outside was Darien, the father from the couple who had given birth in the cabin. "Dude, mind if I get in for a minute?"

Yes. "No. Come around." He clicked open the locks and moved the box from the passenger seat to the middle.

"I got a ride here," Darien told him. "Hoping I'd see you. Thanks for setting us up with rent, man!"

Jason nodded. "Glad to do it. How're Caylene and the baby?"

"They're great. We're gonna live in a carriage house that belongs to one of my aunts. Now that we can pay rent, the relatives are being a little nicer."

"Good." Jason's eyes strayed to the box on the gear area between them.

"What's that?"

He picked up the packet he'd been opening, too curious to wait for Darien to leave. "Stuff from my sister." He cleared his throat. "She passed away recently."

"Sorry, man."

Inside the packet, metal clanked together. He got it open. "Gran's cookie cutters." He cocked his head to one side. "Wonder why she kept these."

"Must've been important to her."

"Yeah." Jason thought back. "At Christmas, as soon as us kids got there, Gran and Kimmie would always bake a bunch of cookies." He remembered it like yesterday, them laughing and talking, bringing out the final results for him and Papa to rave over and eat. Under Gran's watchful eye, the cookies had always turned out well. Good memories.

"What're these?" Darien was holding the stack of envelopes. "They all have your name on them, man." He held them out to Jason.

"I don't…" Jason shook his head. "I don't think I can deal with these right now."

Darien flipped through and whistled. "Some of these look pretty beat-up. But this top one here looks new. Maybe it's recent." He handed it to Jason.

Jason couldn't deal with it, but he couldn't resist it, either. He opened it up and read the first line:

I'm sorry I'm not what you think I am, but please don't hold it against my sons.

His throat tightened and he couldn't speak. He kept reading and learned that the reason Kimmie had relapsed into drugs was her terminal diagnosis. And that she'd strayed away from her faith, but with Erica's help, she'd read her Bible and discussed Jesus and prayed in the last days.

Erica is really a special woman. If you're reading this, give her a chance.

Words of wisdom from beyond the grave.

At first, I wanted Erica to keep the twins away
from you. But now, I keep remembering the good
times. I love you, Jason, and I know you love me.
I hope you'll give that love to my sons.

Jason's chest hurt. He closed his eyes.

"Check this out." Darien nudged him, reached into the box and pulled out a plastic sleeve with official-looking papers inside.

Darien pointed to the top document, visible through the plastic. "That's a keepsake birth certificate," he said. "Just got one of those for our boy today. See the footprint? And then you order the official one online."

"What's the Post-it say?" Jason heard the hoarse-ness in his own voice.

"For Erica Lindholm." Darien held the packet closer to the dome light. "Looks like there's medical records in here, too."

So Kimmie *had* meant for Erica to have the babies.

Jason didn't trust his voice, but he pulled the one remaining packet from the box, hard and flat. With trembling hands, he opened it.

Inside was an old picture frame he recognized as one Papa had made, years back, from barn siding. The photo in the frame was of the twins. He studied it, trying to figure out what looked familiar.

It was their clothes. They were just a little out-of-date.

They were Jason's own baby clothes. He'd seen them in photographs. In fact, Teddy's outfit was the one in the Santa picture back at the house.

How had Kimmie managed to keep those clothes for all these years, for all her moves through the gutter?

A whole wave of memories came back to him then. How Kimmie had loved dolls, had collected them when she got too old to actually play with them. How she'd showed him outfits that had belonged to him as a baby, outfits she'd saved from the trash or donation bin.

She'd told him how she'd played with him like a doll when he was a baby, and though Jason had no memory of it, he suspected that a good portion of the mother love he'd gotten had come from Kimmie rather than their mother.

And she'd kept his baby clothes, put them on her own sons.

He stared up at the ceiling of the truck to keep the tears in his eyes from falling.

"What's up with the picture?"

Jason drew in a deep breath. Let it out slowly, and then repeated the process. Cleared his throat. "My sister helped raise me and I guess she kept my baby clothes. She put them on her twins for this picture."

"Wow, heavy."

It *was* heavy, but Jason felt like a huge weight was lifting off his shoulders.

Kimmie had kept these things. She'd loved him and had remembered Gran and Papa warmly. She'd wanted

Erica to have the twins, and she'd wanted Jason to give Erica a chance.

Kimmie hadn't been perfect. And that was okay.

Erica wasn't perfect. Also okay.

And that meant Jason didn't have to be perfect, either.

A strange warmth came over him. He looked out at the parking lot, where more and more people were heading into the church, to celebrate the birth of the Christ child.

He grabbed Darien's hand and pumped it. "Thanks."

"Anytime, dude. I gotta get back to Caylene and the baby. You hang in there, hear? Let me know if there's anything I can do for you."

After Darien left, Jason put the precious items back into the box and set it on the seat behind him. Then he dropped his head into his hands. *I'll do what You tell me, Lord. Not my will but Thine.* He left the truck and walked into the church foyer.

As soon as he got inside, he saw Erica. Her back was to him, and she wore a green dress that hugged her slender silhouette and showed off her clouds of red hair. She had Mikey on her hip, and Papa walked beside her, holding a squirming Teddy.

His impulse was to go to them, but he was trying to follow God, not his impulses. So he leaned against the church wall and just watched and thought.

He loved her—he knew that. His feelings for any woman in his past paled in comparison.

But love was tricky and messy and people didn't live up to his standards. More important, he himself didn't live up to his own standards. The question was, did he want to hold back and judge, or did he want to wade in? And if he made the latter choice, was he healed enough to do it right this time?

She turned and looked over and saw him. He saw her mouth drop open a little, her posture tighten. Then she lifted her chin and held out her arms, low, palms facing him. As if she were offering him an embrace.

In front of all these people. He felt a wave of love for her that she would try.

But people surged around her, between them. Partly, of course, because the twins were so adorable. Partly because Papa was such a popular figure.

And partly because Erica was so incredibly appealing that all the males between fifteen and fifty were drawn to her like bees to a colorful flower.

Organ music rose up from the sanctuary, the signal for people to stop milling around and come in to worship. There was a general movement toward the sanctuary.

Jason had lost sight of Erica, but he was going to find her, no matter what.

Erica followed Papa into what was apparently his usual front-and-center seat in church. She probably would've chosen a seat in back, given that she had two wiggly babies to contend with, but she treasured that Papa had forgiven her, had wanted to come to church together.

When she'd seen Jason across the foyer, leaning against the wall, her heart had swelled with love for him.

Had she made a fool of herself, reaching out to him in that obvious way? He hadn't jumped into her arms, that was for sure.

On the other hand, maybe her gesture hadn't been clear enough. Maybe she should have run across the room to him and begged forgiveness. There would have been no ambiguity in that gesture, but it was totally against her nature.

People stood for the opening hymn, and she and Papa each scooped up a twin and joined their voices in "It Came Upon a Midnight Clear." The dimly lit sanctuary, smelling of fresh pine and spruce, the advent wreath at the front of the church, the greenery and red bows decorating the pews and railings—all of it brought her calm. Not joy, not yet, but calm.

It was a time of new life, new birth. She wanted so badly for that new life to be right here, raising the twins with their great-grandfather and their uncle.

And her prayers this afternoon had reminded her that she was forgiven, ultimately forgiven by God. That she had value and was worthy simply in Him, regardless of her own significant mistakes.

Feeling like she deserved love and good treatment and a chance—that would take a little more time. God had a lot of work to do in her, but she was starting on the path.

When it was time to share the peace, Papa tapped her shoulder and gestured toward a gray-haired man in a wheelchair, alone in the back of the church. "Need to go sit with Tommy. He's a Vietnam vet and this is his first time at church in years. He shouldn't be alone."

"Of course."

She cuddled the twins, one on either side of her, giving Mikey a board book to look at and Teddy a couple of colorful blocks. Surprisingly, they played quietly while the Bible passages and carols continued on.

They were so dear to her. How could she possibly say goodbye to them?

And what was in store for her afterward? A prison of loneliness? A real prison?

"Fear not, for behold, I bring you good news of great joy that will be for all the people."

Fear not. Erica repeated it to herself, over and over.

They were half an hour into the service when Teddy got restless. He slid down from the pew and tried to scoot along it, which was awesome—he'd walk soon—but he kept falling, and the effort to pull himself up again, the frustration of it, made him cry. Mikey, as was his way, babbled instructions, which got progressively louder.

Erica scooped Teddy up and put him on the seat beside her, but he wasn't having it. He cried harder.

Erica was starting to gather her things to leave when someone behind her picked Teddy up. She expected more crying, but instead he quieted down immediately.

She turned partway around.

It was Jason. "I'll hold him," he said, and his slight smile made her heart soar.

That hadn't been an "I hate you" smile.

With only Mikey to contend with, she was able to keep him entertained and even to listen and sing a little more. But she was hyperaware of the man behind her, singing in his deep bass voice, whispering to Teddy.

The lights dimmed for the candlelight part of the service, and as "Silent Night" echoed out from the choir and organ, Erica's heart filled to the brim.

Christ had been born for all of them. In this fallen world, how badly they all needed Him, and He had come.

God had seen fit to send His son to save sinners like her.

The candles were lit, person to person. She was struggling to keep hold of Mikey and sidle to the nearest person when Jason came around from his pew to hers. He lit her candle and met her eyes. "I'm sorry," he whispered.

"I'm sorry, too," she said.

And then she turned away to light her neighbor's candle and the twins babbled and everyone sang. But she was still unsure about the man next to her. What could it mean, his kindness, in contrast to the outrage he'd shown her yesterday?

Soon enough, the lights came back on. Joyous music rang out and people greeted each other, stopped to chat. Children shouted and ran with the excitement of staying up late and presents to come.

Ruth and Papa Andy approached as the crowd thinned out. Without a word, each took a twin, and they headed toward the reception in the foyer of the church.

That left Erica and Jason alone together, side by side.

His arm was draped along the back of the pew, behind her but not touching. "I've been thinking—"

"So have I, and, Jason, I'm so sorry."

He opened his mouth to speak again and she held up a hand. "Let me say this. I was wrong to pretend the twins were mine. Especially as you and I got closer. It was deceptive and that's a horrible thing to do. I was trying to do the right thing, but that's no excuse. I just… I really care for you, Jason, and I apologize for the wrong I did to you."

He looked at the floor, then met her eyes. "Thank you for that."

And then there was no sound but the organ music and a little distant chatter as people left the sanctuary.

Was that all? Erica wondered. Now that she'd apologized, were they done?

And then he took her hand and held it. "I've made a lot of mistakes in my life. One of them was saying some pretty harsh things to you, things that came out of my sadness about Kimmie and my anger at myself, more than being about you." He shook his head, looking away, then looked back at her. "I can be judgmental. A perfectionist. I've been like that all my life, but I'm trying to improve. I was hurt by what you did, but I shouldn't have said those things to you." He paused, cleared his throat. "To the woman I love."

"To the woman you…" Erica's heart pounded so quickly she couldn't catch her breath. "You *love* me?"

He nodded and smiled, touching her cheek. "Is that so hard to believe?"

She laughed a little as tears rose to her eyes. Jason wasn't angry anymore. He wasn't expecting her to be perfect.

He *loved* her.

A lifetime of feeling inadequate seemed to rise up in her like a wave, and then crash and dissipate. "Yes, it's hard to believe," she whispered. "You might have to tell me more than once."

"Then you'll…" He broke off. "We should be practical."

"Practical?" She lifted her eyebrows and clutched his hand. She'd never had an experience like this and didn't know how it was supposed to go. But *practical*?

"I want to stay in Holly Springs, at Holly Creek

Farm. Papa needs me, and I… I owe it to him to be here, like he was here for me and Kimmie."

"Of course," she said, hardly breathing.

"I can find work here. Probably police work, but there's so much to do on the farm, as well. I need to figure all that out."

She nodded. Inside, she was thinking, *He wants career counseling? Really?*

"Look, I'm making a mess of this because I don't know… How do you feel about me, Erica? Would you want to…"

She closed her eyes for a moment. *You have value. And you're strong.* "My dream would be to stay here, too, and to raise the twins with you."

There. She'd said it and it was out on the table.

"Like, coparenting?" He shook his head. "No. Erica, that's not going to be enough for me. I know it might take you a while to have the feelings, but I'd like to try to move toward a true, permanent partnership. Toward…" He swallowed. "Toward marriage."

"You want to *marry* me?"

"Kimmie knew what she was doing when she left us each half of the farm, I think," he stumbled on.

Was that true? Would Kimmie have left her part of the farm because she was *matchmaking*? Erica's head spun and her heart pounded. Jason loved her. He wanted to marry her.

"I know it's soon and we haven't known each other long, but—"

"But sometimes you just know," she interrupted, her eyes pinned on his face. "I love you, Jason. And my answer is yes. Yes, let's move toward marriage but I… I'm pretty sure that my answer is yes, forever."

He pulled her into his strong arms, and Erica knew she had found the home and the family—and the Christmas—she'd always dreamed of.

Epilogue

Twelve months later

Erica tucked the blanket tighter around Teddy and Mikey, nestled in back of the old sleigh.

"Ready everyone?" Up front, Papa made a clicking sound with his tongue, and the horses started to move.

"Ready as we'll ever be." Jason held Mistletoe by the collar and reached across the twins to squeeze Erica's shoulder.

As they approached the covered bridge, white with a simple Christmas wreath, Erica couldn't help but remember the first time she'd ridden in the sleigh, one year ago. Her life had undergone a radical change she never could have envisioned, and she was loving it.

Sunlight caught her wedding ring, making it sparkle like fire.

Papa cleared his throat. "Thought I'd stop and pick up Ruth," he said over his shoulder.

Erica looked at Jason, raising her eyebrows.

He leaned over. "Maybe Papa has some news to share, too," he whispered.

As they approached Ruth's house, Mistletoe spotted a rabbit and started barking, straining to escape Jason's strong grip.

"No, Miss-toe!" Mikey scolded.

"No, Miss-toe," Teddy echoed.

"Are you sure it's okay to bring the dog along?" Erica asked as Papa jumped spryly out of the sleigh and strode up the sidewalk to Ruth's front door, sporting its Tiny Tykes sign—a spot very familiar to Erica, since she'd spent a lot of time working there in the past year.

"Mrs. Habler wants to try him out as a camel in the pageant, and Hank promised to watch him during the service. He and his friend are running the hot chocolate and cider stand for Sleigh Bell Sunday." Jason shrugged. "Could be a disaster, but they insisted."

Ruth came out, dressed all in red, and Papa helped her into the front of the sleigh.

She twisted around to see the twins, laughing at them and pinching their rosy cheeks.

"Roof, Roof!" they said in rapturous voices, their adoration obvious.

"And don't you both look handsome in your new snowsuits," she said. "New boots, too!"

"Boots," Teddy agreed, holding a leg out.

Ruth looked over at Erica. "Honey, do you think you can sub for a few hours tomorrow? I know you want part-time, but—"

"Of course, no problem. You know I love the center." Erica gave Jason and the boys a mock-stern glare. "Just as long as these three let me study for my test tonight. You're not on duty, are you?" she asked Jason.

"No more evenings, remember? That was my condition for the promotion." Jason was enjoying small-town police work, but he was clear about making time for family. "And it's hard for me to let you study, but I'll do my best."

Erica blushed. "Leave your hat on, Teddy," she ordered as the sleigh drove on.

"No!" He looked up at her to see what she thought of his opinion.

"Told you he'd started his terrible twos," Ruth sang out from the front seat. "He's late, but you're not going to escape them."

"I know." But she relished every stage the twins went through. And now she could look forward to sharing every future stage with Jason. She snuggled down under the blanket, Teddy on her lap now, Jason at her side with Mikey on his lap, the dog at her feet. Papa and Ruth in the front seat.

Glorious stuff, for a girl who'd never had a real family.

At the church, they tied up and the twins were immediately off, shouting and running in the snow under Ruth's watchful eye. Papa started to follow them, but Jason put a hand on his grandfather's arm. "Papa," he said, "we have some news."

Papa stood still and looked from Jason to Erica. "Is it what I think it is?"

Jason nodded. "A little girl."

Papa folded them into his arms. "I was already happy, but you two young people just made me even happier."

Erica pulled back so she could look up at both of them. "I've been thinking about names," she said. "If it's okay with the two of you... I'd like to call her Kimmie."

It was just as well the church bells rang at that moment, because none of them could speak. They just stood, holding on to each other as the twins came back to grab legs and Mistletoe barked to be let out of the sleigh.

Full circle. Erica lifted her face to heaven with a prayer of gratitude and joy. And it seemed to her that her old friend Kimmie, all sins forgotten, must be smiling down at the entire family.

* * * * *

We hope you enjoyed reading

Next Time...Forever

by #1 *New York Times* bestselling author
SHERRYL WOODS

and

Secret Christmas Twins

by LEE TOBIN McCLAIN

Both were originally Harlequin® series stories!

From passionate, suspenseful and dramatic
love stories to inspirational or historical,
Harlequin offers different lines to
satisfy every romance reader.

New books in each line
are available every month.

BACHALO1119

SPECIAL EXCERPT FROM

Love Inspired®

Christmastime brings a single mom and her baby back home, but reconnecting with her high school sweetheart, now a wounded veteran, puts her darkest secret at risk.

Read on for a sneak preview of
The Secret Christmas Child *by Lee Tobin McClain, the first book in her new Rescue Haven miniseries.*

He reached out a hand, meaning to shake hers, but she grasped his and held it. Looked into his eyes. "Reese, I'm sorry about what happened before."

He narrowed his eyes and frowned at her. "You mean...after I went into the service?"

She nodded and swallowed hard. "Something happened, and I couldn't...I couldn't keep the promise I made."

That something being another guy, Izzy's father. He drew in a breath. Was he going to hold on to his grudge, or his hurt feelings, about what had happened?

Looking into her eyes, he breathed out the last of his anger. Like Corbin had said, everyone was a sinner. "It's understood."

"Thank you," she said simply. She held his gaze for another moment and then looked down and away.

She was still holding on to his hand, and slowly, he twisted and opened his hand until their palms were flat together. Pressed between them as close as he'd like to be pressed to Gabby.

The only light in the room came from the kitchen and

the dying fire. Outside the windows, snow had started to fall, blanketing the little house in solitude.

This night with her family had been one of the best he'd had in a long time. Made him realize how much he missed having a family.

Gabby's hand against his felt small and delicate, but he knew better. He slipped his own hand to the side and captured hers, tracing his thumb along the calluses.

He heard her breath hitch and looked quickly at her face.

Her eyes were wide, her lips parted and moist.

Without looking away, acting on impulse, he slowly lifted her hand to his lips and kissed each fingertip.

Her breath hitched and came faster, and his sense of himself as a man, a man who could have an effect on a woman, swelled, almost making him giddy.

This was Gabby, and the truth burst inside him: he'd never gotten over her, never stopped wishing they could be together, that they could make that family they'd dreamed of as kids. That was why he'd gotten so angry when she'd strayed: because the dream she'd shattered had been so big, so bright and shining.

In the back of his mind, a voice of caution scolded and warned. She'd gone out with his cousin. She'd had a child with another man. What had been so major in his emotional life hadn't been so big in hers.

He shouldn't trust her. And he definitely shouldn't kiss her. But when had he ever done what he should?

Don't miss
The Secret Christmas Child *by Lee Tobin McClain,*
available December 2019 wherever
Love Inspired® books and ebooks are sold.

Save **$1.00**

on the purchase of ANY Harlequin Love Inspired® or Love Inspired® Suspense book.

Available wherever books are sold, including most bookstores, supermarkets, drugstores and discount stores.

Save **$1.00**

on the purchase of any Harlequin Love Inspired® or Love Inspired® Suspense book.

Coupon valid until March 31, 2020.
Redeemable at participating outlets in the U.S. and Canada only.
Not redeemable at Barnes & Noble stores. Limit one coupon per customer.

52616541

5 65373 00076 2   (8100)0 12441

® and ™ are trademarks owned and used by the trademark owner and/or its licensee.

BACCOUP46999

Looking for inspiration in tales
of hope, faith and heartfelt romance?

Check out **Love Inspired**® and
Love Inspired® **Suspense** books!

New books available every month!

LIGENRE2018R2

SPECIAL EXCERPT FROM

HQN™

Surprise fatherhood, Southern charm and a heartwarming family Christmas—read on for a sneak peek at Low Country Christmas, *the conclusion to Lee Tobin McClain's Safe Haven series!*

Cash remembered coming out to Ma Dixie's place at Christmas time growing up. The contrast with his own foster family's home had been extreme. There, six themed Christmas trees were spread throughout the house, decorated perfectly by the commercial operation that brought them out each year and took them away after the holidays. That same company had wrapped garlands around the staircase and strung lights outside the house.

It had all been grand. He remembered being shocked and impressed his first year with the family, because it had been so different from the humble holidays back in Alabama. But he hadn't been allowed to invite his brothers over; too much noise and mess, his foster mother had always said. If he wanted to see them, he had to find a ride out to Ma Dixie's, which he had done frequently.

Here, Christmas really felt like Christmas.

He opened another box of ornaments, pulled out an angel made of hard plastic and handed it to Holly to place on the tree.

"Is this your tree topper, Ma?" Holly asked, holding it up.

"Yes, it is. I usually have Pudge put it up, but...could you do it, Cash, honey?"

He did, easily reaching the top of the small tree. "Is Pudge okay?" he asked Ma. "Is that why the place isn't decorated yet? He's too sick to help?"

Ma arranged the last figures in the Nativity scene and sank down onto the couch. "That's part of it. Mostly, it's me feeling blue. I'm not used to Christmas with no kids around."

Holly tilted her head to one side. "Did you have a lot of kids?"

"Dozens," Ma said with a wide smile. "That's the beauty of being a foster parent."

"Oh," Holly said as she sank down onto an ottoman beside Ma. "Do you…not foster anymore?"

Ma sighed. "I really can't with Pudge having all these doctor appointments. I guess maybe we're getting too old for it." She looked wistfully at the tree. "I just, you know, always enjoyed having the little ones around."

Holly looked thoughtful. "Is that why you wanted to take care of Penny? Not to help me out, but to have a little one around?"

"That's part of it," Ma said, "but don't you worry about it. I understand being picky where your child is concerned."

"It's not pickiness," Holly said. "If I were being picky, who better than an experienced foster parent like you?" She reached out and rubbed Ma's arm back and forth, two or three times, an affectionate gesture that made Ma smile.

Cash came over and sat at Holly's side, leaning against the ottoman. His heart, like that of the Grinch in the movie playing muted on the television, seemed to be expanding.

He'd taken plenty of women to high-end Christmas parties and fancy restaurants. But sitting here in Ma Dixie's house, talking with her about holidays and kids and family problems, decorating the tree with her, felt different. Like coming home.

Like coming home, with Holly beside him.

He put that feeling together with the questions his brother and Pudge had been asking. He was getting the horrifying notion that he might be falling in love with Holly. But he wasn't the falling-in-love type, or the settling-down type. And Holly wasn't the type for a short, superficial fling.

So what exactly was he going to do with all these feelings?

Don't miss Lee Tobin McClain's
Low Country Christmas,
available October 2019 from HQN Books!